Terroristic Signs

by

Karl Boyd

International Standard Book Number 13: 978-1-60452-095-8
International Standard Book Number 10: 1-60452-095-7
Library of Congress Control Number: 2014943087

BluewaterPress LLC
52 Tuscan Way Ste 202-309
Saint Augustine Florida 32092

http://bluewaterpress.com

This book may be purchased online at -
http://www.bluewaterpress.com/signs

Printed in the United States of America

Terroristic Signs

CHAPTER 1

As Katie Adkins and her two companions sit in the front seat of her badly-dented, no-longer-white 1999 Volvo, her mind races. Katie is twenty-one-years-old, a student in her junior year at Southern Colorado University, (SCOU), and more frightened than any other time in her young life.

The information she possesses is so vital and earth-shattering, Katie knows she can't report the contents over a landline or send the same using e-mail. She must deliver the threat and proof to the FBI. For the hundredth time since beginning this desperate last-ditch effort, she asks silently, *Will the FBI believe me, or think I am a nut? How can I convince them the threat of a terrorist attack on the President and hundreds of thousands of Americans is real?*

* * *

When Katie first learned of the horrific plot and told her co-workers at the research laboratory, they shared a laugh at her expense. Even in this day and age of mayhem and murder, no one wanted to believe her, especially when she revealed the source of her discovery.

In a way, she couldn't blame them, but why wouldn't just one listen and offer to help? No, they were too worried about protecting their cushy jobs and not looking like fools. So Katie is taking this seemingly frantic action of her own initiative, knowing when she is vindicated, they will laugh from the other side of their stupid mouths.

A fleeting smile comes to her lips. *To hell with them.*

While glancing at her two passengers for comfort and waiting for a break in traffic so she can turn left onto Mulberry Street, Katie nervously taps her short red fingernails on the steering wheel. To further ease her mind, she turns to her friends. "I have you as my witnesses."

Both turn her way and nod in agreement. For a few moments, Katie feels better. But a nagging doubt still makes her stomach churn. Silently, she prays, *Dear God, they have to believe us.*

Using one hand to shield her eyes from the rays of the rising sun, Katie edges her aging wreck closer to the oncoming stream of traffic. "Come on, someone give me a break."

Then her male passenger tugs at Katie's sleeve. When she glances his way, he indicates he is hungry. But Katie replies, "You will have to wait."

At the same time her other companion indicates she needs to use the bathroom. Again, this isn't the time or place, and Katie lets her know. Neither is truly upset, but both squirm in their seats, as youngsters are apt to do when they don't get their way.

While Katie is waiting, a large moving van pulls to the curb and partially blocks her view of traffic from the left. She shakes her head in disgust and mutters in frustration, "So far this day has been one damned irritating thing after another."

Then cautiously, she eases the old car down the driveway until she can see around the truck and measure oncoming traffic. Without asking first, the female passenger undoes her seat belt and pushes the window control button. The glass slides downward with a sound like a wiper blade swinging across a windshield on a rainy day.

Because the day is chilly, and fearing her passengers' safety, Katie wants to tell her companion to raise the window and buckle up. But just then, a Good Samaritan stops his white Cadillac a few feet behind a tan Oldsmobile van. This leaves Katie enough space to pull out and into the second lane, so she decides to wait to say anything until they are on the way.

If the woman driving the van will roll forward a few feet, Katie can pull into line behind. She looks left, sees a tanker truck approaching from a half-block away, misjudges the vehicle's speed, makes a quick decision and pulls out. The engine compartment of the old Volvo fits into the vacant space, but the driver's area is exposed to oncoming traffic.

Thankfully the line of vehicles moves on, but the driver of the minivan either doesn't notice or is preoccupied. Apprehensively, Katie glances in the direction of the fast-moving fuel truck and cries out in frustration and fear. "Come on lady, move it or park it."

She taps the horn to awaken the old gal. But the vehicle remains in place, as if pegged to the ground. There was no way Katie can know the female driver is unable to respond to her pleas.

* * *

The driver of the fully-loaded five-thousand-gallon-capacity fuel truck is Ted Branski, a young, brown-haired and black-eyed thirty-five-year-old father of two children; an eight-year-old named Liz, and David, five.

Ted is listening to and singing along with country music on the radio. When he sees Katie's vehicle pull out from the driveway, he begins to let up on the accelerator, but doesn't complete the maneuver. Ted never hears the shot that kills him, doesn't see the side window of his truck explode in a hail of shattered glass or feel the bullet enter his skull above his left ear and blow his head apart. One moment, Ted is alive; the next, he is stone-cold dead.

The driver of the van is a petite brunette named Nora Smith, a mother of three-year-old twin boys, Erin and Darren. Ten minutes ago Nora dropped them off at day school with no way to know she kissed her boys goodbye for the last time.

Five seconds prior to Ted's murder, Nora met the same fate. So in spite of Katie's urging, she can't move her van. As Katie watches in helpless horror, the gas truck roars down the street and smashes into her car. A piercing scream tears from Katie's throat, but is lost in the roar of a powerful explosion.

* * *

The dark night has been long and chilly for a paid assassin named Claude Werner. He shivers in his hiding place and shifts his six-foot frame around so the cold, damp, hard ground won't hurt as much. Claude's medium-long coal-black hair is wet from the morning dew. Although he is tired, his black eyes stand out like holes drilled in marble as he peers through a high-powered scope of a custom-made rifle.

This morning the sky is cloudless and sunny with the azure blue associated with late summer in Colorado. After the chill of the night, the heat from the orange orb blazing its way upward warms Claude's weary back. He is glad rain hasn't fallen. He hates to work when wet and miserable.

Claude's features are above average and his suntanned face is handsome, but his looks are not on a par with any well-known movie star or rock musician. If you passed Claude in a crowd, you would never remember him. And that is his desire – anonymity.

He has no idea who ordered the hit on his three intended victims, and doesn't care. The main objective is the money – five hundred thousand dollars for a clean contract.

This is Claude's last job, and he is anxious to see the deed completed. Ten years ago, when he became a hired gun, Claude set a goal of fifteen million dollars in the bank; then retirement. When he receives his payoff from this job, his aspirations will be met with an extra one hundred thousand in his account.

Claude hoped to kill and be on his way in a few minutes, but things haven't worked out the way he planned. Throughout the night, his targets remained hidden behind closed blinds in an apartment on the top floor of a building three hundred yards from any cover or concealment.

To enter the building, kill them there, and then attempt to make his escape is too risky. There are too many variables he can't control. The original plan called for him to first eliminate Katie's two companions, and then kill her. But so far he hasn't had a clear shot.

Claude knows Katie will soon depart, so decides to wait and take out the two passengers as they near the end of the driveway. Then he will complete the contract by killing Katie.

When her garage door slowly creaks upward, he shifts his weight, takes a deep breath to steady his nerves and achieves a good sight picture. As the Volvo eases out from the garage, the sun reflects off the windshield, temporarily blinding him. Before Claude can acquire his target again, a large moving van pulls to the curb, blocking his shot. This is something he didn't plan on. For a moment, Claude fears he might not complete his mission and curses in frustration.

Then, as he glances at the flow of traffic again, the chance comes to finish the job and make the outcome appear to be an accident. While the head of the driver of the van is a clear shot, the position of the truck driver relevant to Claude's lair is an awkward one. But Claude is an expert marksman, well paid for his expertise, so takes the chance. The results pay dividends far beyond his expectations.

Claude's first bullet strikes Nora in the forehead, killing her instantly. Her body first jerks backward, recoils forward and then slumps against the wheel.

Two seconds later he kills Ted with a head shot.

Eight seconds later the fuel truck crashes into the Volvo, crushing the old car against the front of the Cadillac. One and two seconds later, two separate bullets strike the cargo compartment of the truck. The volatile mixture explodes in a tremendous fireball.

From where Claude is hiding on a hill across the street, he actually feels heat. Calmly, he breaks down his weapon, packs the rifle into a custom-made container resembling a flower box, closes the lid, stands up and walks nonchalantly through small brush and weeds to a sidewalk meandering through the tree-shrouded park. In his haste, Claude never looks back to check his work. This is his first mistake.

* * *

If the fire department weren't located two blocks away, an entire city residential area might have gone up in flames. Even with fast response and yeomen work on their part, after the fire is extinguished, six victims are dead and twelve severely burned. The fire destroys three apartment buildings, seven cars and ten trucks, while injuring three firemen, none seriously.

Four hours later, with the fire extinguished, and a fleet of wreckers working feverishly to clear the road of burned vehicles, District Fire Chief Hiram Fletcher leans back and rests his sore, tired back against the fender of a fire truck, looks toward heaven and says, "The fact we don't have more dead is a miracle."

* * *

The sun slides behind a narrow white cloud on the far horizon and seems to wink as if to say goodnight. Silently, the rays fill the sky with a spectacular display of pink, orange, rose and grey tints spreading out like thin wispy ribbons. As far as Sergeant Joe Francone is concerned, this is the perfect ending to a miserable day.

A five foot and seven inch tall, worn-out cop, Joe is wearing a set of civilian clothes that look as if they came from a local Salvation Army recycling center. Although only thirty-nine, Joe appears much older. His long unkempt black hair needs a trim, and his large blue eyes often seem to be staring off into the distance at nothing in particular. Surprisingly, Joe misses nothing that happens around him.

He isn't overly handsome – one of those semi-rugged indoor types that struggle daily to maintain their weight. Women still like Joe, and he enjoys his share of romance when in the mood. But he hasn't felt love for some time. Little by little, day by day, the job and people he deals with have worn him down.

Overweight for his height, and twice warned about his appearance by his shift captain and immediate supervisor, Joe tries in a half-hearted way, but the pounds keep piling on. The only exercise he gets is bending over backward to please his boss, jumping to conclusions too soon, and lifting a cold one in the local hangout.

Since his wife, Shirley, left him three hard years ago, Joe drinks too much and eats at fast food restaurants whenever and wherever available. Something has to give, or he will soon be out of a job.

After climbing from his bruised and battered blue and white, Joe walks to a green metal door set into a grey concrete and red brick wall, where he stops and reaches into a pocket of his long brown coat. Knowing in advance what awaits inside, and having had enough to do with the stench of roasted flesh today, he stands outside the county medical examiner's room and pulls a jar of Vaseline from his coat pocket.

After twisting off the cap, Joe holds the top and jar in his left hand, while scooping a goodly portion with his right index finger and pushing the light-green grease into his nose. Since Joe possesses a large hooked beak, several scoops are required to fill both nostrils. Then he replaces the cap and returns the jar to his pocket.

From another, Joe takes a white handkerchief with an embroidered blue F on one corner and wipes his hands. To save time as he cleans his fingers, he leans his elbow against the doorbell button and pushes.

* * *

Inside the examination room at the rear of the building, Chief Forensic Scientist Sarah Gruber is examining a shattered skull with shards of charred skin still clinging to the bone. A few moments earlier, as Sarah removed the torn remains of the victim's brains and placed them into a chromed bowl, a crumpled and smashed bullet clunked against the side. In an automatic reflex action, she used a small pair of tweezers to lift the lump of metal and placed the battered chunk of lead into a thin manila evidence envelope.

Although small in stature, what Sarah lacks in height, she makes up in pure guts. No one else can or will do the things she does and smile at the same time. If Sarah is upset with you, her green eyes can dissect you like a scalpel, or grant you absolution when you deserve less. Those that know her well say Sarah has a heart as big as Wyoming. Those that don't think she is a heartless bitch who loves to cut up people.

At the sound of the doorbell, Sarah looks around the room where four forms; three large and one small are lying on cold metal tables with their remains half-exposed under stiff white sheets. Fluorescent lights overhead glare down on the bodies like floodlights on a hot burlesque stage. Burned skin shines like burnished copper.

At two tables, Sarah's assistants are attempting to identify what little remains. Another helper, Judy Eskew, is examining something red and bloody under a microscope. Judy is a former operating room nurse and Sarah's favorite co-worker. They first met when Judy was seriously injured in an automobile accident that killed her husband. Three days after the wreck, when Judy hobbled in on crutches to claim his body, and she and Sarah met, they both felt instant admiration for their shared determination. Shortly after her recuperation, Judy applied for a vacant position in the lab and was hired. As a result, they have remained co-workers and good friends for years.

* * *

Sarah asks, "Can you get that, Judy?"

"Sure," Judy says and limps briskly across the room to open the door. When she sees Joe wiping his greasy hands, she says, "Hello, Joe."

As Joe walks in, he replies, "Hi, Judy, I hear you have some crispy critters."

While leading him to where Sarah is standing with the skull still held in her hands, Judy says, "Joe, sometimes you are too gross for words."

Sarah smiles and says, "Welcome, Joe."

Joe glances down at the burned corpse. Then looks at Sarah, where she is standing as if on stage. With a smile, he says, "You look like a character straight out of Macbeth, that should be saying, 'Alas, poor you're Icky, I knew him well'. You know what I mean?" Without waiting for a reply, he asks, "What have you got for me this time, Doc? This place smells like a wiener roast gone haywire."

Sarah shakes her head, and her eyes flash in momentary anger, but she can't remain upset with her favorite cop. "Stop, Joe. Making sport of the dead isn't funny."

"Okay Doc, I apologize. What have you got?"

Sarah points to the stiff on her table and nods in the direction of the still smoldering body on an adjacent one. "This man and the woman over there weren't killed by the fire - they were shot."

"No way!" Joe exclaims. Excitement in his eyes replaces the boredom he has shown since first arriving. "Did you find the slugs?"

"Yes, we recovered both, but there isn't much left. They were head shots, and the bullets are crushed. Your crime lab experts will have to dig deeper to determine the caliber."

Joe looks around the room. "What about the other vics, Doc?"

Sarah points to another table. "The other woman died from the fire."

"What about the one on the last table?"

"That's what is really strange, Joe. That's not a person. It is either a monkey or chimp."

"No way?" Joe exclaims again.

Sarah laughs at Joe's limited vocabulary. "Yes, way, Joe. How does that grab you for suspense? You should write a novel."

* * *

Worn-out, hung-over and sleep-deprived, Officer "Fad" Dean, one of Sulfur Springs' finest ends his second fruitless attempt at sleep. Yesterday, Fad and his salt-and-pepper team member, Joe Francone worked the graveyard duty tour. Before they knew where the time went, their night of crime ran into the day shift. On top of that, just before their tour ended, they covered the big gas truck explosion and fire. Processing the scene took all day. Joe is presently talking to the medical examiner.

After twenty-four straight hours on the job, Fad is bushed. Joe knows his partner isn't going to be much help if he doesn't get some shuteye. He told Fad to take off and get some Zs, and that is what Fad is attempting to do.

Because Fad missed breakfast and lunch while working the grisly accident scene, he didn't go directly home. After smelling singed hair and roasted flesh for ten hours, eating something fried doesn't sound very appetizing. Even if he were hungry, he doubted he could keep the food down. Initially, Fad's intentions were honorable. He stopped off at O'Grady's Bar and plopped his six foot and three inch frame onto a stool for one drink to unwind after a horrible day.

To the surprise of no one, including Fad, with the bar a hangout for cops, there were several other officers and patrolmen there hefting a few as they talked trash or bitched about life in general.

Somewhere along the line, Fad lost count. His one Coors Light turned into four or six. On an empty stomach, they hit him harder than usual, so he was lucky to arrive home in his beat-up Chevy without having a DUI hung on his record. As a result, he is wired and wide-awake.

* * *

For an estimated four hours since 2400 hours yesterday or 0001 today, take your pick, Fad tossed, turned, rolled, kicked off the covers and pulled them back on as he fought bravely, cursed silently and failed miserably in his quest for forty winks.

Finally, Fad gives in, but sits on the edge of the bed with his eyes tightly shut, afraid to confirm his greatest fear. Although he knows his thoughts are irrational, Fad believes his mind is actually a complicated computer controlled by an ugly, green, four-eyed and three-armed Martian.

In Fad's mind, this alien monster works the graveyard shift on the red planet downloading useless informational updates onto Fad's hard drive. Behind the back of his immediate supervisor, this spaced-out, outer-space dweeb also plays violent video games.

The rationale behind Fad's strange belief is that after his first stint in the sack, which he knows had to be four hours in length, he was still unable to sleep. But, when peeking at the clock, he discovered the time was only 1 a.m. *How can that be?*

Slowly, Fad raises his ancient left arm, extends his nail-bitten index finger, and works carefully but diligently with the wrinkled digit as a broom to sweep away two pounds of sand from his left eye, deposited there by the fairy Sandman.

From past experience and few clues left behind, Fad knows the Sandman is a weirdo. The guy's strange M.O. of performing breaking and entering, (B & E's), every night throughout the city while carrying nothing but a gunnysack of sand and a tiny coal scoop tells Fad that. Add to this the Sandman's fetish for leaving sand in his victim's eyes instead of hauling away any loot, plus his love of anything gritty, and you have a real nutcase on your hands.

As far as Fad knows, the Sandman has never been busted and doesn't have a rap sheet. Over the years two sightings were reported, but both came from little old widows with a vivid imagination and a long time in-between having a man in their bed. Fad thinks their reports were wishful thinking on their part.

Let's face facts. If the Sandman possesses the power to cloud men's minds, and women's too, he would choose the homes of young, good-looking, well-built broads. After gaining entry, he would crawl into the beds of his victims, jump their bones and leave them with a smile on their face and a kiss on their eyelids instead of some lousy sand.

Fad turns his head toward the clock radio. His sore and bloodshot left eye peeks through a sand-encrusted slit and latches onto the glowing clock face. *It's only 1:30. The frigging Alien must be working overtime.*

Then, while running his hands through his thin, kinky black hair, Fad wonders what to do.

* * *

Fad isn't actually the black cop's name, but a nickname laid on him by a fellow officer of the law. Fad wishes now he had never told the idiot the story behind his nickname. He might as well have sent an e-mail to everyone in the department. Within fifteen minutes, Fad's entire shift and some others he doesn't know heard the tale. Since that day, he has been known as Fad.

His given name is actually composed of three first names; Frank, Albert and Dean. His unmarried and not-too-bright mother, Ruby Dean gave him the moniker. In one of her movie magazines Ruby misread an article proclaiming the latest FAD was using three first names to make a trendy name for a baby. She mistakenly thought this meant the three names must begin with F, A and D. In a drug-induced fog, she knew her baby would have a foot up on the competition. *After all, his last name already begins with a D.*

A child, seventh-grade graduate and eighth-grade flunkee, at the ripe old age of fifteen years, ten months and three days, Ruby realized she was pregnant. Throughout the ghetto, rumor said she could read fairly well and actually possessed a three-hundred-word vocabulary, some of which contained as many as three syllables, and a wide variety of colorful curses. If Ruby had to, she could even scrawl a few misspelled phrases.

Published through a poorly construed interpretation of the First Amendment, Ruby's prestigious reference library consisted of a twelve-inch high, equally divided pile of pure unadulterated trash.

The bottom section contained supermarket scandal sheets with headlines that glared from the racks and contained overly suggestive photographs. The middle area was sub-divided into vivid tell-all movie magazines and torrid romance novels. The last, but by no means least portion was a well-rounded collection of small black-and-white sex books.

Ruby believed every bold statement and overblown story in the scarlet tabloids. She also copied her favorite star and starlet's bizarre behavior and tacky dress codes to the letter, while hoping someday to meet her Prince Charming as the romance book heroines did. By the apparent heavy wear and tear to the small comics, she evidently studied them diligently.

When Ruby died of an apparent drug overdose three days before her twenty-first birthday, police canvassed the neighborhood for clues. Nosy neighbors reported Ruby faithfully practiced every sexual act and position contained within her little books with a wide variety of partners. But no one was ever connected to her premature death.

* * *

Fad's aching mind can stand no more reminiscing. He decides to take one last chance to catch some much-needed Zs. After crawling back under the covers, he raises his head skyward and says, "Time to take a break, my Martian friend."

* * *

On Mars, a third-level computer engineer, Allie N. Moon-star, focuses his fourth eye on the watch wrapped around the wrist of his third arm. "It's time to quit for the day." Allie grasps the mouse with the suction cups at the end of the fingers on his second arm, moves the cursor to the log-off icon and left-clicks. His computer screen blinks and goes dark as Fad finally drifts off to sleep.

CHAPTER 2

Eight days previously:

A s he rushes out the door and down the blacktopped parking lot to his car, Larry Holgram thinks, *I'm late.*

Larry is a Lab Technician, GS-8 pay grade, employed by the National Nuclear and Chemical Commission at the old Camp Shaffer Army Base, just outside Sulfur Springs, Colorado. Two hours ago Larry called his wife, Carol, to say that although he had to work late, he wouldn't miss the party. But time got away, and now his ass is in a sling.

A few steps from his vehicle, Larry stops, slaps his palm against his head and says, "Oh no, I forgot Claire's present." Since Larry has no voice box, he doesn't actually say the words aloud.

* * *

When he was eight-years-old, Larry and a friend named Billy were playing catch with a piece of pipe. So far they managed to catch the projectile with no problem, but then disaster struck.

As they both climbed a flight of stairs, and Larry was in the midst of a shout of joy, without warning Billy turned and threw the pipe at Larry's head. The missile struck Larry in his open mouth and ran down his throat like a buzz saw, tearing loose everything in its path, including Larry's voice box.

After several hours of surgery, when Larry awoke in a hospital bed, doctors told his parents he would never speak again. The diagnosis was a shock, but Larry is a gamer, so thanked God he was alive, learned sign language, never looked back in anger, and went on to earn a college degree as a chemical engineer.

Larry stands five feet and eight inches tall, and weighs in at one hundred and seventy pounds. His body is trim and muscular from exercise, and he always wears a smile. Although Larry is forced to use a computer or hand-written notes to communicate with his co-workers if they don't know sign language, he finds them easy to work with.

Ten years ago, Larry met a brown-haired, brown-eyed beauty named Carol. Within six months they married. A day shy of a year later their daughter, Claire was born. She makes his heart sing, and tonight is her eighth birthday party.

Earlier in the day Larry bought Claire a gift of a small computer game she wants, but in his haste to get away forgot the package. Turning back on his path, he hurries to his office located on the fourth floor, two doors away from one of the deadliest places on the face of the earth - the laboratory where they tested nerve gas in the seventies and eighties when the Cold War ran hot. Now the lab is used for a different purpose – to neutralize and burn the same volatile mixture. His is not a job for the squeamish, but Larry enjoys his work.

* * *

Although the guard named Grady O'Reilly knows Larry on sight, Grady takes time to double check Larry's identity and badge. Security was tight before 9-11, but now has been ratcheted up a notch. Larry doesn't mind at all. This is one place in the world where terrorists mustn't gain entrance.

After passing muster, Larry logs in, hurries to the elevator, rides up to the fourth floor and walks down the hall to his office. Claire's gift is located in the bottom left-hand drawer of his desk, so Larry doesn't bother to turn on the lights, but walks quickly to his station, opens the drawer, removes the box and sets the gift atop his desk.

As he pushes the drawer closed and turns to go, someone enters the office next door assigned to Felix Mendez. Two men whisper in hushed voices, but Larry hears every word, and their conversation causes his voiceless throat to constrict.

An unknown voice asks, "How much nerve gas have you stolen so far?"

"Thirty-two ounces," Felix says. "The process took months, but I couldn't siphon off more than a portion of an ounce at a time or it would be missed."

The stranger asks, "How many people will we kill with that much gas?"

"If delivered correctly, an ounce will wipe out a town of several thousand. But we are after more. At least two hundred thousand people will be in attendance at the Cotton Bowl. Plus, with any luck, we will also kill half the population of Dallas and Fort Worth."

"The main target is the President," the stranger says. "Are you sure he will be there?"

"The President's alma mater is the University of Texas and he never misses a game, so what do you think?" Felix asks. Without waiting for a response, he answers his own question; "He will be there." Then he asks, "Can you replace the fire extinguishers on schedule? Changing out thirty-two will require some time."

The unknown man replies, "That won't be a problem. We have three months until the game, and one of our men works for the fire department. Let's collect the gas and get out of here before someone comes in."

"Don't worry, no one works at night," Felix says.

"Are you sure?"

Unseen, Felix shrugs. "They aren't supposed to, but you never know about these nerds. I hope they all go to the game. I won't miss them."

Larry can't believe anyone could be planning such a horrible scheme. But also knows he must get away before they discover he overheard their plans. As he moves toward the door, his arm brushes against the gift box, which falls to the floor with a thud.

"What was that?" The stranger asks.

Felix replies, "I don't know. Perhaps we aren't alone."

As quietly and quickly as possible, Larry opens his office door and runs out and down the hallway toward the elevator. Behind him, footsteps pound on the hard surface as Felix and his companion race after him.

Luck is with Larry. When he hits the down arrow, the door to the elevator opens immediately, beckoning him in like a warm mountain cabin on a cold winter day. Quickly, he punches the letter L for lobby and watches nervously as the doors slide shut, and the car drops four floors.

Larry runs past Grady and is out the door before the guard can say anything. Too late, Larry realizes he should have stopped and told Grady what happened. But then he wonders how a stranger gained entrance to the building at night. *Is Grady in on the plot?*

Since his car is too far away, and he knows pursuit will be swift, Larry turns right and runs toward the building next door housing the research and experimental laboratories of SCOU. Hurriedly, Larry punches in the entry code and slips inside. As the door closes, he catches a glimpse of two men running from the chemical laboratory. Silently, he prays they haven't seen him and moves down a hallway to the first doorway that opens into a large room filled with animal cages of all sizes and shapes.

Quickly, Larry runs to the first aisle and ducks down to hide behind a large enclosure. When he looks up, to his surprise one of the occupants says "Hello" in sign language. Although Larry thinks he is seeing things, he automatically returns the greeting. Then the chimp signs, "My name is Wilbur. What is yours?"

Larry is so amazed he doesn't answer immediately, so Wilbur asks again.

Then, like a magician turning a card to surprise his audience, a plan takes shape in Larry's mind. As he passes the information concerning the terrorists to his new friend, Larry's fingers and hands fly like sparrows after a handful of corn. Wilbur sets, watches, listens and shakes his head either in fear, disbelief or as a natural habit.

Although Larry wonders if Wilbur truly understands the message or what Larry means by his gestures, he thinks, *All you have to do is remember and repeat my words to someone.*

Then, from a corner of the cage, a female chimp appears by Wilbur's side. She grins widely and repeats Larry's message. When she finishes, she signs, "My name is Sadie."

Larry signs as fast as he can. "You are very smart, Sadie. Can you remember what I told you?" In unison, both Wilbur and Sadie reply positively.

Larry remembers the fire extinguishers and attempts to pass on that information. But before he can finish his message, the door to the room opens. Felix and a swarthy man enter and see him. Larry jumps up and runs, but his attempt at escape is easily foiled. Felix tackles him by the legs, and they fall to the floor. Felix pulls Larry to a seated position and cocks his fist as if he wants to take off Larry's head. "What did you hear?"

When Larry doesn't answer, the stranger moves quickly to Felix's side and slaps Larry across the face with the back of his hand, knocking him backward. As Felix pulls Larry to a seated position again, he suddenly recognizes his victim. "Wait a minute Mohammed. This is the dummy from the office next to mine. He can't talk."

"Using my name wasn't smart. Can he hear?"

"Yeah, and I bet he heard everything."

"That's too bad," Mohammed says. Without another word, he shoots Larry in the head behind his left ear. For an instant, while there is still life in his body, Larry's eyes seem to smile, but Mohammed doesn't notice.

The sound of the shot echoes from the walls, startling the chimps and monkeys, and they scream in fear. After grabbing nearby vines, Wilbur and Sadie swing high into a concrete tree to hide. Their screams join those of the other animals, and the lab sounds like a zoo gone wild. Over the noise, Felix shouts, "Damn, Mohammed, why did you do that?"

"He can't hear or talk now, can he? Quick, wrap his coat around his head to soak up the blood. Then grab his legs. We'll haul him out the back door and dump his body into the lake, where he won't be found for days."

Although shaken at the sudden turn of events, Felix does as told. As they carry the lifeless form of Larry from the building, the two murderers leave behind a small pool of blood and a trail of drops leading from the side of the cage to the rear door.

* * *

When Larry doesn't arrive in time for Claire's birthday party, Carol shakes her head in disgust and reaches for the phone. *Dedication to his job is one thing, but this is inexcusable.*

Larry doesn't answer, and the phone rings and rings, so Carol grows worried. By 10 p.m. she is frantic, but when she phones the local hospital, there is no report of an accident involving his car. Finally at midnight, Carol calls the police to file a missing person report. The officer taking her call, Sergeant Bert Collins is pleasant, but from the tone of his voice, Carol knows he thinks she is worried over nothing.

She replies to Bert's latest question; "No, Larry doesn't drink. And before you ask; no, we didn't have a fight. Today is our daughter's birthday. Larry dotes on her, and there is no way he would miss Claire's party unless something happened to him."

Bert tries to reassure her. "We'll do our best to locate him, but there isn't much more we can do than you have. I'll phone around to see if anyone in adjacent towns has information and get back to you."

As Carol's eyes mist over, she says, "Larry can't talk. He only communicates by sign language. If he is injured, no one can hear him."

"I'll pass that information along to the patrolmen," Bert promises.

"Thank you," Carol says, hangs up, breaks down and cries.

After completing the missing person form, Bert sends the paperwork up the line to the detective in charge of these types of reports. Then he makes the calls he promised, but discovers nothing to help. When Bert phones Carol to inform her there has been no progress, he can tell she has been crying.

CHAPTER 3

During her younger years, Katie Adkins was an introvert; very shy and unsure of herself. At five feet and four inches tall and chunky for her size, Katie is cute in a wholesome way, but not as beautiful as most women in the magazines she reads. Her coal-black hair is long and shiny, and her matching eyes are set into a face reminding viewers of Pocahontas. Katie displays a small waistline, but to her sorrow, not as tiny as she would have liked.

Too many tacos at lunchtime, she thinks and promises God she will give them up soon.

Although Katie knows her limitations, life still frightened her most days. Her fears continued until she entered college and discovered there is existence beyond the small town of Shiprock, New Mexico.

Throughout her high school days, Katie earned good grades and did her best to succeed. Her diligence paid off when she became the first full-blooded Navajo to be awarded a full four-year scholarship to SCOU. College is a whole new ballgame and she seems to thrive in this environment. And then, as a bonus there are Wilbur and Sadie, who make school fun as well as educational.

Since her grandmother is deaf, Katie learned sign language at an early age. When she spotted an advertisement in the school bulletin for volunteers to teach chimpanzees to sign, Katie couldn't believe her eyes. She is majoring in social science, hoping to work with animals to better their lives and those of humans. Now here is a chance to see her dreams come true.

After an interview the next day, Katie was hired as a volunteer instructor and discovered the school would actually pay her to teach the chimps. At the same time, she is working in the research laboratory of her dreams. That was when she first met Wilbur and Sadie, and it was instant mutual attraction. Katie loves working with the chimps, and spends nearly every free minute at the lab, teaching them, while learning their ways.

The only downer is the thought of the close proximity to the nerve gas laboratory next door. The thought of what a few drops of that toxic potion can do to a small town like Sulfur Springs is enough to make Katie's skin crawl. According to the scientists, because of safety features they installed, there is no chance gas can escape. Still, the thought of an accident that could kill everyone nearby in a few seconds continues to frighten her. Every night, Katie prays nothing will ever happen, but there are times when the threat causes bad dreams.

CHAPTER 4

Ramon Sanchez is a conscientious worker and loves his job as a janitor at the research laboratory on the outskirts of Sulfur Springs. The old Army base sets out in the wilds below some medium-sized mountains. The fort is mostly deserted now, but Ramon thinks the place is beautiful. To see lines of large oak trees marching down the main drive and wild flowers now running amok where once thousands of troops drilled and paraded always puts pride in his step.

He smiles as he walks up the stairs and opens a side door to the lab with his own personal key. Although Ramon knows the access code to the front door, the thought that he has a key to this entrance and is trusted with so much responsibility makes him feel special.

* * *

Ramon has a habit of always arriving several minutes before everyone, making sure the coffee is perking, and emptying the trash can in the break room. Usually he has a cup of coffee and a doughnut. Then, although he swept before he departed last night, Ramon sweeps the floor outside the monkey cage. Sometimes the chimps get frisky and scatter fruit peels.

Thin as a rail from the time of his youth, Ramon has a dark face and black eyes, and wears the mandatory moustache favored by most macho men of his heritage. As a naturalized U.S. citizen, Ramon fought in Vietnam and is proud of his military service. Due to a piece of shrapnel taken in his right calf during one unforgettable battle, he walks with a slight limp. Now, after having seen his share of blood and guts, Ramon never wants to leave the United States again.

During his tenure with the lab, Ramon has taken a special liking to the two chimps they are teaching to sign. Sadie is lovable and cute in her own way, with a grin as wide as the Bay Narrows Bridge, and has a full set of teeth that glisten when she smiles.

On the other hand, Wilbur is often contrary, mean as hell at times and has a wicked set of molars that could chew chrome from a bumper hitch. He always wants to be the leader, but Sadie stands up to him and makes him behave, which is more than Ramon can do. But the trio gets along well.

* * *

Today for some reason, Ramon's two favorite chimps are preoccupied or frightened. They pay no attention when he walks by and says, "Good morning, you two."

When he accidentally drops his broom, and the handle hits the floor with a noise like a gunshot, Wilbur and Sadie scream and run to the back of their cage, where they huddle together with their arms wrapped around each other. Raymond feels something is amiss. "What is wrong with you guys?"

When both chimps ignore him, he says, "Okay, if that's the way you want to act, I'll leave you alone."

As he moves behind the cage, Ramon isn't paying attention to where he steps. When his foot slips on something slick, he almost falls to his knees. Looking down, he sees a small pool of reddish-brown liquid and spots of the same fluid leading toward the back door. After serving as a medic in Vietnam, Ramon knows the sight of dried blood, but this puzzles him.

Those spots look like blood, but where would it come from. I hope none of the chimps hurt themselves. But if one did, how would blood get all the way out here?

This is a mystery, but Ramon is thorough in his work, and knows this is something out of the ordinary, to be reported to the person in charge. Leaving the liquid as is, he steps around the puddle and walks to the office of Doctor Wilson, where he knocks softly on the doorframe.

Doctor Mona Wilson looks up and smiles. "Yes, Ramon, what can I do for you?"

Mona Wilson is one sharp-looking lady with a pair of breasts most women would die for. She also has deep blue eyes, luxuriously-coiffured blonde hair, long shapely legs running all the way up to the delicious cleft between her hips, and a marvelously-curved body. More than half the male staff is in love with Mona or lusting after her in their dreams.

Ramon smiles shyly and says, "I found something that looks like blood by Wilbur and Sadie's cage. They're acting funny this morning. I hope they haven't hurt themselves."

Mona stands up and walks around her desk. "That is peculiar. Please show me what you found." Without saying another word, Ramon leads Mona around the cage and points at the small pool and spots. Mona bends down to look where he indicated. "I see what you mean. This does look like blood. Let me find some swabs to take a few samples."

She hurries to the rear of the laboratory and returns a few minutes later with her assistant, Jerry Grimes in tow. Jerry is carrying several glass beakers in a small, chromed rack. He looks inquisitively at Ramon, but doesn't say anything.

First, Mona dons a pair of rubber gloves. Then Jerry hands a fistful of long thin wooden swabs to her. She kneels down and leans over to run six through the fluid, one at a time while treating both men to a fascinating view of more cleavage than they can handle. Then she places the swabs in individual beakers, and seems oblivious to their stares. She looks up at Jerry and says, "Run a blood test on two swabs and let me know if the results are animal or human."

Jerry puts his tongue back in his mouth and says, "Yes, Ma'am."

Mona inspects the spots again. "Refrigerate the others in case we have to report this to the police. They may want samples."

"Yes, Ma'am," Jerry repeats.

Then Mona orders, "Ramon, take masking tape from the storage locker and make a barrier so no one will walk here. No matter how inquisitive they may be, keep everyone away. I don't like the looks of this."

She turns toward Sadie and Wilbur's cage and signs the message, "Come here you two." Sadie runs to where Mona is standing and reaches through the bars to hold her hand. Wilbur remains aloof, so Mona signs, "Stubborn to the end, aren't you?"

The chimp turns his back on the proceedings, ignoring Mona as he climbs slowly up into a nearby tree. As Jerry walks off, he says, "That isn't like Wilbur. Something must have upset him."

"Sadie seems nervous too," Mona says. "Her pulse is higher than normal. I wonder what happened here last night. Neither appears to be hurt or bleeding. Let me know your findings as soon as possible, Jerry."

Mona turns to Ramon and pats his back. "Good job, Ramon." His face flushes with pride. Or did Ramon blush because of her touch?

* * *

An operator answers the phone. "Sulfur Springs Police, how may I help you?"

"This is Doctor Wilson at the University Research Laboratory. I need to report something suspicious that happened in our department last night. Is there a detective I might speak with?"

"Hold on, Ma'am and I will connect you with the detective bureau."

While the call is being transferred, Mona listens to Neil Diamond sing part of his hit, "Coming to America" and hums along with the tune. Thirty seconds later, Joe takes the call. "This is Sergeant Francone. How may I help you?"

After identifying herself, Mona says, "The janitor in our building discovered a small pool of blood on the laboratory floor and a trail of drops leading to the back door. I took samples and determined the blood is human. No one here has reported an injury, so where the blood came from is a mystery. In case something happened during our off-duty hours, I thought I should phone the police."

Joe likes this dame's voice and pictures her as something special. "Are you sure there isn't some other explanation?"

"No, we are sure the blood didn't come from any employee."

From her sexy voice, Joe continues to build an imaginary picture of this female doctor in his mind. "How long was the laboratory unoccupied?"

"The last person left at six p.m. yesterday. The janitor, Ramon Sanchez was first to arrive at six a.m. this morning. So the building was empty for twelve hours."

Joe grunts and says, "Don't let anyone touch the evidence and keep everyone away from the scene. It will require a few minutes to locate a forensic scientist, and then I'll come out to view the scene."

"I had Ramon tape off and guard the area," Mona says.

"Good work, Doctor. Let me have your address again."

"We are at seven fourteen General Sherman Drive on the old Army base, next to the chemical research laboratory."

Joe knows the place well. The thought of nerve gas often gives him nervous gas. "Oh yeah, I know where you are located. That's where they burn the nerve gas."

The nearness of the chemical lab also causes Mona anxiety. "Yes, I am sorry to say."

"Thank you Doctor Wilson, I'll see you in a few minutes."

After he hangs up, Joe stares at the phone and wonders, *Is Doctor Wilson as sexy as her voice?*

* * *

When Joe walks into Captain Hugo "Red" Hopper's office without knocking, Red is seated at his desk reading a report, with his feet resting on an open drawer. Red wears a nicely cut, two-piece blue suit, with a snow-white, crisply starched shirt, but his collar is open and a paisley tie pulled down. His plain face is highlighted by a large nose that seems to be permanently blushed a dark scarlet - hence the nickname "Red."

Red looks up and asks, "What's up, Joe?"

"I received a call from the research lab at the old Army base. A doctor claims there is blood on the floor they can't explain and wants someone to come out to take a look. I called Bill Favor in the forensic lab, and he will accompany me. The facility is next door to the lab where they burn nerve gas. I don't think this will amount to much, but as sensitive as the place is, we had better check things out."

Red puts his report down on the desk. "Yeah, you're right. Keep me advised. Let's hope someone cut themselves shaving."

Joe laughs and says, "This sounds like more blood than that, Red. The doctor said there is a trail of drops all the way to the rear door. If someone got whacked, they chose a bad place."

Red nods in agreement. "Do a good job."

* * *

Bert spends the morning with Carol Holgram at her home. Larry still hasn't been found or heard from, and Bert feels something bad happened to the young husband. Carol reiterates Larry is a devoted father, and no way would have missed Claire's birthday party. Through her tears, Carol tells Bert that Larry phoned yesterday at four p.m. to say he would work until six, but assured her that he would be on time for the party at seven.

Although Bert has his doubts, he says, "I'm sure Larry will be found soon."

Carol gives him Larry's work address. "Could you check his office?"

Bert hopes Larry's co-workers might shed some light on his disappearance, so says, "Sure."

* * *

When Bert pulls into a parking space outside the chemical lab, he is surprised to see Joe Francone's cruiser parked three spaces away. *What's Joe doing here?*

Bert flashes his badge at a rent-a-cop on duty, but that doesn't get him past the security post. The guard, Fred Wilkins by his nametag holds up his hand and asks for Bert's I.D. After taking Bert's badge and identification and checking them carefully, Fred asks, "What can we do for you Sergeant Collins?"

"I received a missing person report on one of your employees, Larry Holgram. I would like to speak with his co-workers to see if they know his whereabouts."

Fred points toward three green scraped and stained steel and plastic chairs that look like they have been there for a decade and hated every minute. "Have a seat over there, and I'll call Mister Holgram's supervisor."

"Thanks," Bert says, but doesn't mean it. He tries two of the offered seats. Both have uneven legs and wobble like a shopping cart with one wheel off the ground. The third is almost level, but displays a well-worn seat and bent back. This one looks the best he will find, so Bert sits on the edge and leans his arms on his legs. To any bystanders, he knows he looks like a tardy schoolchild waiting to explain why to the principal. *Millions of dollars spent for nerve gas, and not a few bucks to spare for some decent chairs. That's our government and my tax dollars at work.*

* * *

Next door, Joe is leaning back in a nice, soft cushioned recliner sipping a cup of coffee in Mona's office. Her workplace is spacious, outfitted with modernistic furniture, and has windows on two sides. The main attraction is an outstanding view of surrounding mountains and forested slopes, where snow-capped peaks beckon skiers to come try their luck.

Joe tips his cup to Mona and says, "You were right about the blood; it's human."

"What do you think happened?"

"I don't have a clue. How many people have access to this building?"

"Probably a hundred or more – we have twenty-three people on staff and fifty volunteers that work with the chimps, monkeys and other animals. Our front door is controlled by a four-digit access code, but I'm sure it is common knowledge among the students. Many come by to watch our training sessions."

Joe takes another sip. "Well, that narrows our search down to less than the number of citizens in Sulfur Springs."

He likes the way Mona's hair hangs over one eye. As she brushes back her mane, bright red fingernails glisten in the overhead light. Red is Joe's favorite color, but he stops checking her body. "I need a list of your staff, volunteers and anyone that might have the combination. Right now, all we have is a lot of blood but no body or indication of foul play. If things turn ugly, I'll need to speak with them."

Mona flashes a dazzling smile. "My assistant, Jerry Grimes will provide the information."

Joe attempts to pay attention, but at the same time thinks how Mona's teeth are perfect and shine like ivory. The tip of her tongue slips through, and she licks her upper lip in a sexy way that makes Joe daydream of jumping her bones. As if Mona can read his thoughts, her eyes twinkle.

I would give up doughnuts for a year to spend an hour in the sack with her, he thinks to himself. But knows he should return to business at hand, so says, "I'll let you get back to work and see what Bill has discovered."

They shake hands, and he thinks she holds his a moment too long. As they part, Mona's long nails trail across Joe's sweaty palm and her smile seems wicked. But then she changes to the standard smile she earlier gave to Bill.

Maybe I'm reading this broad wrong, but I hope not.

* * *

When he walks through the lab, Joe discovers Bill squatting on the floor taking pictures of various blood spots and splatters. Little numbered plastic triangles set beside each. Without looking up, Bill asks, "Can you smell cordite?"

Joe sniffs the air and inhales fumes saying a gun was fired here within the past twenty-four hours. He and Bill are blessed with big beaks and take a lot of ribbing from other cops. But they can smell gunshot residue when others can't, and ninety-nine times out of a hundred are right.

Joe nods and says, "Yeah I can. Last night, someone got shot here."

Bill points toward a man in his mid-forties, with brown, shoulder-length hair and wearing a white lab coat over tan slacks and a light-green polo shirt. "The assistant over there, Jerry Grimes said the animals were all shook up this morning. I don't doubt his statement. If you fired a gun in here, the resulting clamor would make anyone go bananas."

While chuckling softly at the pun, Joe looks around the room, taking note of two chimps in the cage nearest the scene. "Is there anything special about these chimps, Jerry?"

"Only the fact they are being taught to sign."

"Sign?" Joe asks. "You mean like deaf and dumb people?"

Jerry sounds like a nerdy professor. "People aren't deaf and dumb, Sergeant. They are only handicapped, and we're attempting to assist them. We think chimps will aid us by teaching children to communicate using sign language. The kids have fun talking to the chimps and learning at the same time."

"Okay, I stand corrected. That's a cute idea. No wonder students volunteer."

Jerry nods in the direction of a young girl that just entered the facility. "Here is one now. Sergeant Francone, meet Katie Adkins."

Joe looks up from his notes to see a young student in a light-green dress. Her plain face is dark and her hair thick and long, but she isn't black. *More like an Indian,* Joe observes.

Katie holds out her hand and says, "Pleased to meet you."

As they shake hands, Joe says, "Likewise."

She asks, "What's going on, Jerry?"

"Ramon discovered blood on the floor that we can't explain. It's nothing to worry about, Katie. Go ahead and work with your two friends. They're upset this morning. We need to calm them down."

Joe points toward the cage. "Maybe they saw something and will tell you."

Jerry shakes his head, and says, "I don't think so, but you might ask, Katie."

Katie says, "I'll see what I can do." She turns to Joe, smiles again and says, "It was nice to meet you, Sir."

"Likewise," Joe repeats. Then he asks, "Are you done here, Bill?"

"Yeah, I'll type the blood at the lab and do a DNA to determine if we can match anyone reported missing."

Joe nods to Ramon, who has been standing by the edge of the cage and listening to the group speak, but hasn't said a word. "If you wish to, you may clean up this mess now."

Ramon pushes a bucket from under a rail near the cage and wrings out a mop with his bare hands. For some reason, when Joe sees Ramon shake his head in disgust, he knows this isn't the first time Ramon wiped up blood. Unknowingly, at the same time, both hope this will be the last.

* * *

So far, Bert is getting nowhere fast in his investigation. But at least he is now seated in a more comfortable chair in the office of the director, Hershel Witte, who asks, "Would you like a cup of coffee?"

Hershel wears a three-piece blue suit, white shirt and black bow tie. A pair of wire-rimmed glasses covers his brown eyes. From his general appearance, Bert concludes Hershel is the half-bald bookish type, small-framed and short, probably not over five foot and five inches tall. His fingers are also short, and as he speaks, he has a nervous habit of clicking his pen.

Bert smiles, looks at Hershel's pen, and says, "No, I'm fine. Are you Larry Holgram's supervisor?"

"Yes, I am." Click. "I was surprised when he didn't show up this morning." Click. "Larry has been a pillar; always arrives on time, and when necessary stays late. It isn't like him not to call in." Click, click.

Bert tunes out the sound of the pen. "In the past year, how many times has Larry been late?"

"Only twice, and his tardiness was due to weather or an accident on the highway. Both times, Larry used his cell phone to keep me informed."

Bert is puzzled. "I thought you said Larry couldn't talk. How did he call in?"

Hershel points to his cell phone on the desk. "He text-messaged – that's how he carries on most conversations, that and instant messaging on the computer. Only a few dozen here know sign language, but one way or another, Larry always gets his message across."

Bert asks, "Has there been any rumor of hanky-panky with a co-worker?"

"Larry?" Hershel asks in return. "Hardly, he is a devoted family man."

"Is there any other reason he would just up and vanish?"

"None I can think of. Would you like to see his office?"

"Yeah," Bert says.

* * *

When Hershel pulls out a set of keys to open the door to Larry's office, first he tries the knob. "Why, the door is open."

Bert pushes past him. "Let me go in first."

Three feet from the desk, a gaily-wrapped package meant for Claire is lying on the floor. A lump comes to Bert's throat, and for a moment, his eyes water. He points toward the package. "We had better let the experts look at this. Apparently Larry departed in a rush. There is no way he would leave the present for Claire behind."

Hershel nods in agreement. "That is strange."

After taking a fast look around and seeing nothing out of the ordinary, Bert says, "Lock the door and keep everyone away until the crime scene unit arrives."

"Yes, Sir," Hershel says.

"Who has the offices to both sides of this one?" Bert asks.

"Felix Mendez has the one to the left. Harold Stockman is to the right."

"I need to speak with both, Mister Witte. Will you ask them to report to your office separately so I can question them?"

"Yes, Sir," Hershel repeats.

"How does one enter the facility after-hours?"

"They are checked in by the guard. An access card is required and each entry or exit is logged."

Bert nods as if lost in thought. "I need to see the log and talk to the guard on duty last night."

"Grady is off duty now, but I will telephone and ask him to come in."

"Is Grady the name of the guard?"

Hershel replies, "Yes, Grady O'Reilly. He is an Irishman down to his green socks."

Bert adds Grady's name to his notebook. "Have him stop by our office this afternoon before he goes to work and ask for me. That way, he will be fresh. Perhaps he may remember something to assist in the investigation."

* * *

Talks with Felix and Harold produce nothing to aid Bert. According to their statements, neither worked late last night. After leaving the building, they hadn't seen Larry again. The logbook authenticates their stories. Larry was the only person logged in after hours – just a few minutes after leaving for the day. *Larry must have forgotten something – the present. But what happened in those few minutes?*

When he is finished with their interviews, Bert returns to Hershel's office, where he asks, "Isn't everyone required to log out when they leave the building?"

"Yes, they are. Why do you ask?"

"I don't see a log notation indicating Larry checked out. According to you, that isn't like him."

"No it isn't. I'll ask Grady about the discrepancy."

Bert shakes his head either in frustration or to cancel that idea. "When I see Grady this afternoon, I'll ask. Thanks for your assistance, Mister Witte. The crime scene team will arrive shortly. If I discover anything new, I'll let you know. I hope Larry shows up alive and well, but this doesn't look good."

"I hope so too. Carol must be terrified."

"She's hanging in there," Bert says. "But she is worried."

CHAPTER 5

In a brisk chilly wind, Bert is standing beside his car in the parking lot waiting to see why Joe is on the Army base. While he was inside, the wind changed direction and is now blowing from the north. Overhead, thin clouds sail slowly by on their way to a warmer clime. Bert's hands are growing numb, and he is thinking of climbing into his squad car to turn on the engine and heater when Joe finally walks out the door of the research lab. Bert waves and calls out, "Hey, Joe, I thought that was your vehicle. What's up?"

Joe jerks his thumb over his shoulder to indicate the laboratory. "Nothing much, Bert, they found human blood on the floor inside, but no one seems to know why or how it got there. Why are you here?"

Bert smiles at the news. "This is a coincidence. I have a missing person next door in the nuke lab, a Mr. Larry Holgram. His name didn't come up in your investigation, did it?"

Joe checks his notes and says, "No, his name wasn't mentioned. How long has he been missing?"

"Last night Larry was a no-show for his daughter's birthday party. His wife called in to report him missing. I checked his office, and there is a package on the floor, probably a gift for the little girl. Apparently Larry departed in a hurry. His door was unlocked, and he didn't log out."

With a nod, Joe says, "Perhaps our cases are connected, Bert. Do you think his wife will allow a blood sample from the daughter so we can do a DNA match?"

"At this point in time, I believe Carol will do anything to help locate Larry. I'll phone and ask."

"Thanks, Bert; I'll see you at the office."

* * *

When Katie signs, "Good morning," to her two friends, only Sadie replies. Instead of displaying his usual toothy grin, Wilbur frowns and remains high in the fake tree. Katie waves to make sure Wilbur sees her. When he looks her way, she signs, "Feeling moody today?"

When she receives no reply, Katie turns to his mate. "Well Sadie, apparently we will have to work alone. Did anything happen last night?"

Without warning, Wilbur swings down from his perch to land in front of Katie. As his hands fly, she makes out, "Bad men, loud noise, frightened."

She is surprised. "What bad men?"

"Two," he replies, holds his hands over his ears and spins around in a circle with his head tilted back and teeth tight together while chattering to the roof in chimp language. Katie thinks, *Something has really upset him.*

Sadie tugs at Katie's sleeve. When Katie looks down, Sadie's fingers move almost too fast for her to follow, but she catches the words terror, gas and bad man. Then Sadie makes a motion with her fist like a gun and signs "loud bang."

Sadie and Wilbur may have seen someone shot last night. Either that or someone made a loud noise that frightened them. Jerry said there was blood on the floor. I don't like the sound of that.

Katie shakes her head in disbelief, but needs to know more. "Calm down. Speak slowly and tell me what you saw."

As Katie reads their signs, Sadie begins her story, and Wilbur mimics her actions.

* * *

On a crisp clear autumn day, Sally Wright is seated on her usual bench enjoying another beautiful morning. Although the sun is attempting to shine through a thin wispy layer of clouds, the weather remains cool, but Sally doesn't mind. She likes winter and can't wait for the first snow. Another thing Sally loves is her ducks. Well, they aren't really <u>her</u> ducks. They are wild and don't belong to anyone. But Sally enjoys watching them on the lake behind her house directly across from the old Army base.

"When they feed, all you see is duck butts," she tells her husband, Sam, who laughs appreciatively.

Each morning when the ducks are migrating south, Sally walks down to the edge of the lake, sits on her bench, throws corn to the birds and talks to them as they feed. The quiet, peaceful scene helps calm her inner spirit, and she feels as one with nature, especially on a cool autumn day when the sun is rising in the east and promising good things to come for the remainder of the day.

But today something is wrong. Sally's friends aren't in near the shore where they usually wait. The ducks are farther out, swimming in circles, chatting like magpies and seem excited. When Sally throws a few kernels of corn toward them, the birds refuse to come near to feed. She is puzzled and can't understand their behavior. *Since they won't come to me, I'll move closer.*

Sally stands and walks to the edge of a high bank, where she glances down to notice something large and brown bobbing in the water. At first, she thinks the litter is a roll of carpet discarded in the lake. Silently, she curses the litterbugs of her generation. But then she sees the object is a man's coat. As Sally watches in horror, with the action of small waves, a body rolls over, and the wrinkled, white face of a man with dead, dark-black irises stares at her.

Sally screams in fear, drops her bag and runs toward her home to phone the police. The noise frightens her ducks. They rise majestically from the water in a huge raft and fly in a ragged formation to a spot farther down the lake, where they settle uneasily to the surface.

From that day forward, they will never return to the spot near Sally's favorite bench. Neither will Sally. The event continues to haunt her dreams for years to come.

* * *

By lunchtime, Katie is worn from the long morning session with Sadie and Wilbur. Now she feels she must share their story with someone. Three hours of continually asking her friends to repeat the message were required before Katie has the entire story, and the meaning is too much for her to handle alone. She needs assistance to determine which law enforcement agency to contact. Across the room, Katie spots Mona's assistant, Jerry Grimes. *He will know what to do.*

She rushes to his side and says, "Jerry, you will never believe what Sadie and Wilbur told me."

As if he really isn't interested, Jerry asks sarcastically, "What did your two primates have to say this morning?"

"They said last night a man was shot here by two bad men that plan a terrorist attack on the United States."

Jerry laughs loudly. "Whoa, a terrorist attack predicted by two chimps. That story will make the six o'clock news for sure. Where did they dream up that scenario, or have you been reading science fiction to them?"

This isn't the reaction Katie expected. "No, they are sure. Why don't you ask them?"

"Not me," Jerry says. "Can you believe the bad publicity such a crazy story will bring to the lab? The government will probably cancel all our grants for the next ten years. You can't be serious."

"Jerry, they don't have any reason to make up a story. Can't you at least listen to Sadie and Wilbur to see what they have to say?"

Jerry continues to blow her off. "I told you; they concocted something they heard on TV. We allow the chimps to watch way too much garbage on the boob tube."

Katie remains persistent. "I believe them."

Jerry's voice grows harsher, and there is a frown on his face. "Well, you can keep your thoughts to yourself. You're just a part-time volunteer. The rest of us depend on this place for our livelihood. Don't make waves or you'll be sorry. Sadie and Wilbur are just chimps."

They are probably one hundred percent smarter than you, Jerry Grimes, Katie thinks, but she acts as if he put her down. "Okay, Jerry, if that's the way you feel."

As Jerry turns to walk away, he says, "Now you're making sense."

Katie knows there is no way in hell she will let this go. *There must be some way to get the story to someone that will believe me, or even if they don't, will investigate to determine if my story is true. But who?* Then the answer strikes her – *The FBI.* As she makes plans, her mind races, and she forgets about lunch.

* * *

Felix is worried. He didn't think Larry's disappearance would be noticed so soon. This morning when Bert questioned him, Felix knew he gave the correct answers. Grady ensured the log didn't reflect Felix's entry, so if the authorities check, Grady's actions will authenticate his story.

When he woke Grady to tell him about the cop, Grady said the director phoned earlier, asking him to report to Sergeant Collins this afternoon.

Felix was angry. "You weren't very smart to let us in without mentioning Larry was upstairs."

"I forgot. I'm sorry."

Grady didn't sound truly apologetic, so Felix's voice grew harsher. "Sorry won't cut the mustard, Grady. Get your act together and story straight. No one came into the lab except Larry, and before you could stop him, he ran out. No, you don't know why. Maybe he was in a hurry to get home for his daughter's birthday party. When Larry returned, he told you of the planned celebration. You got that?"

Still the braggart, Grady said, "Don't worry. I will handle the cops. The one that should concern you is Mohammed. He's too fast on the trigger. Why did he kill Larry in the lab? You could have taken him someplace where they wouldn't have found blood."

Felix retreated a little, but his voice was still hard. "I agree. Mohammed is too high strung, but is instrumental in getting the job done. In the future, I'll keep him under control."

"You had better," Grady said. "All we need now are more cops nosing around."

"Tell your story the way we discussed."

"I told you, I will handle this guy. Don't sweat it. Go back to work."

* * *

The cooler weather forced the brown-bag brigade inside, so when Felix walks in at noon, the cafeteria is packed. He is lucky to find a seat near three employees from the research lab. Although Felix usually hates to listen to their nerdy talk, today he is astounded when he hears Jerry tell his two companions, "You won't believe what Katie came up with this morning."

"What?" One asks.

"She says her chimps saw someone killed last night. The perpetrators are two terrorists planning an attack on the USA."

"Where does Katie get this stuff?" The first man asks.

With a smirk on his face, Jerry says, "She has a vivid imagination, I suppose. I told her the chimps watch too much CNN."

The older man shakes his head slightly. "Maybe next we will be invaded by Martians."

Continuing to smile and relish every moment of putting her down, Jerry says, "Katie said the chimps know all about this terrorist attack and she wanted to call the FBI. Can you imagine what the government would do if such lunacy were reported? Our grants would be history."

"I see what you mean," the younger man says.

Felix is amazed at his luck and choice of seats. The Gods of fate smiled on him today. *I'm surprised the dummy in the next office was smart enough to pass on his story to the two chimps. But I doubt anyone will believe this woman, Katie, whoever she is. To be sure, I must find and eliminate her, plus the chimps. But how will I accomplish such a feat? We can't have another killing connected to the nerve gas or the cops will get suspicious. Her death and the chimps' must appear to be an accident. I'll contact Mohammed. He will arrange something.*

CHAPTER 6

At Joe's request, and with Bert's blessing, Fad conducts the interview with Grady O'Reilly. "If Grady is connected to this in any way, it will piss him off to have a black man asking questions," Joe says. "Lately there are too many Irish guys ranting and raving about the IRA."

Fad nods in agreement. "Okay, if you say so, Joe. I'll ask Grady personal questions about his sex life. That always makes their hot Irish blood boil."

"That's the idea."

* * *

Fad saunters into the room as if he is some cool cat from a rap group looking for a new song to sing about the injustice of the system. He smiles and says, "Good afternoon, Mister O'Reilly."

Grady looks up from studying his fingernails, and asks, "Hi, are you Sergeant Collins?"

"No, Bert has been unavoidably detained."

Then Fad pulls a chair from under the table, puts his left foot on the seat, bends over and looks Grady in the eyes. His opponent is approximately six feet tall and has muscular arms. From general appearances, Grady has more in his head. Although Fad knows Grady works indoors, his face is darkly tanned. Fad continues to stare and says, "I understand you were on duty last night at the chemical lab. Is that correct?"

"Yeah I worked last night."

"Do you happen to remember Mister Holgram?"

"Yeah he was the guy that left and came back because he forgot his kid's birthday present."

"Did he seem depressed or unhappy?"

Grady picks at a scab on his wrist and looks bored. "No, he was in a hurry to get home. I guess that's why he ran out of the elevator and forgot to log out. If he was late for the party, his old lady would be pissed."

"There wasn't anyone chasing Mister Holgram?"

Grady's brown eyes blink, and Fad notices. Such a reaction is the sign of a lie about to be told. "No, Mister Holgram was the only one in the building at the time. No one else came in while I was on duty. The night was long and boring."

Fad changes the tone of his voice. "Do you know anything else about Mister Holgram? Did he run around on his wife with some chick at the lab?"

Grady shakes his long brown locks. "No, he was straight arrow. I don't think he even noticed the good-looking women here."

"You ever hook up with any?" Fad asks.

"No, why should I? I have a good woman at home."

Fad continues to stare Grady down. "You take any drugs, do a little coke, smoke some pot or drink in excess?"

"No, I don't, and you are pissing me off."

With an insincere smile, Fad displays an even set of sparkling white teeth through full dark lips and says, "Gee, I'm sorry."

"Yeah, I'll bet."

"You're a tough guy, 'eh?"

"I'm tough enough."

"You have connections within the Irish Republican Army?"

"No, I don't," Grady shouts.

"Are you sure? We can check through Interpol."

"I said no. How many times are ya gonna ask?"

"As many as are required to receive a straight answer," Fad replies. "I think you're hiding something, Grady – but what? Do you play around with college boys? You look the type."

Suddenly Grady stands up with his fist cocked, ready to fight, and cries out, "You son of a bitch!"

The next thing he knows, he is flat on his back and Fad is straddling his stomach with an elbow pushed down on Grady's throat until he can barely breathe. With an evil smirk, Fad says, "I take offense at your portrayal of my mother as a bitch." He continues to smile wickedly as if enjoying his work. "Try that again and I'll kick your ass all over this room."

Through a constricted windpipe, Grady chokes out, "Get off me."

"In due time. Now, where were we? Oh yeah, you were about to answer my question whether you played around with young school boys."

"I'm straight," Grady says, coughs, and spittle flies from his lips. "Let me up."

"You promise to be a good little boy?"

Grady's eyes blaze with raw hatred. "Yeah, get off me."

Fad jumps up and stands back to watch Grady slowly pull himself up off the floor and back onto the chair. He can tell the Irishman is steamed, but knows <u>he</u> has the upper hand. "So, you aren't gay, don't do drugs or chase teeny-boppers at the university. What do you do for fun?"

Grady continues to stare at Fad with loathing in his eyes, but doesn't reply.

Then Fad says, "Tell me again about last night."

"I told you; Mister Holgram left and came back a couple minutes later. He said he forgot a present for his daughter. I logged him in and he was upstairs maybe five minutes. Then the elevator came back down, and he ran out of the building and didn't stop to log out. I yelled after him, but he didn't hear. What else can I tell you?"

Fad frowns at his answer. "And no one else was in the building or came into the facility during the entire time you were on duty?"

Grady snarls, "Yeah that's what I said. How many times do I have to repeat the same story?"

"Until I'm satisfied you're telling the truth."

The young guard stares at Fad with unabashed fury in his eyes and lies, "I am." But his eyes blink a different story, and Fad knows. "Sit there and don't move until I return, Grady."

He walks out the door to where Joe has been watching the interview through a one-way glass. "So, what do you think, Joe?"

"I don't like Grady's looks, but that isn't enough to put him in the slammer. Grady's story is pretty pat – too much so. Something went down out there last night, and he isn't about to share the story with us. When Larry ran out, he was spooked. If he didn't fear for his life, he wouldn't have broken company policy."

"Yeah," Fad says. "After reading your report, I feel the same way. This asshole is lying like whale shit on the ocean floor, but I doubt we will get anything from him tonight. I'll cut him loose, and we'll see what falls out of the trees."

"Go ahead; we know where to find him. He can run, but can't hide."

Fad laughs and says, "That's the truth." He opens the door to the holding pen where Grady is still sitting and staring with hatred at Fad, as if he would like to kill. "You're free to go."

Grady stands and strides from the room so quickly that he doesn't hear Fad laugh again.

* * *

After four days, Katie decides on a viable plan to steal Sadie and Wilbur, and take them to the FBI. With the rebuke she received from Jerry still fresh in her mind, she knows she can't trust her co-workers or so-called friends to help.

When I'm vindicated, they will be the ones with egg on their faces. Screw them and their high-priced jobs. What's more important; their cushy positions or the fate of the United States? I believe Sadie and Wilbur. The FBI will too.

Early this morning, Katie phoned the FBI and spoke with Agent Kris Hefner and said she overheard two men planning a terrorist attack. "Are there any other witnesses?" He asked.

"Yes, I have two others that will verify my story." She didn't dare tell him they are chimpanzees. Katie knew he would think she was some kind of nutcase and blow her off.

"Is there somewhere we can meet and talk?" Kris asked.

"I would like to bring my witnesses to your office. They are both handicapped. You will need a person that knows sign language."

"I'll make arrangements for them," Kris said.

"When would you like to meet?" Katie asked. "I know where your office is located. What about 10 a.m. tomorrow?"

"Sure, that's no problem, Katie. I'll leave your name at the desk. Just ask for me, and the guard will phone."

"I'll see you tomorrow morning," Katie said and hung up before Kris asked for more information.

* * *

Since he was on the phone until late last night setting up a contract to get rid of the little Indian pest and her two primate friends; Mohammed is tired when he phones Felix early today. When Felix answers, Mohammed says, "I am worn out and not in the mood for any crap this morning, Felix, so listen closely. Our little problem with this Katie person will be solved shortly. Give me her address, and I will pass it on to our man, Mister Jones."

Felix knows when to reply with just the basics. He isn't going to argue with Mohammed. "Her name is Katie Adkins. She lives at 742 Mulberry Street, Apartment 4-C. The license number of her old white Volvo is 73B-64Z."

Mohammed asks, "When does she work at the lab?"

"She's only a volunteer there, and her hours are unpredictable, but she spent a lot of time there this week with her two friends."

"We also have to take care of the chimps," Mohammed says. "Perhaps our man can arrange for some fried monkeys with an accidental fire."

Although Mohammed can't see, Felix shakes his head. "That wouldn't be wise. If too many strange things happen, they will only reinforce her story and make the police suspicious. Our man should tail her and hope she tries to take the chimps to the FBI."

"Why would she do that?"

"Her co-workers think she is crazy and the chimps have watched too much TV. There is no way she will go to the local cops with such a story.

They would put her in a loony bin. But before calling her nuts, the FBI would check her story. I'm sure she knows."

"Okay, we'll do this your way, Felix. I'll have Mister Jones follow her and take them all out at the same time."

"Good luck," Felix says. "Keep me advised."

* * *

After first locating Katie, for the last two days Claude has maintained a constant surveillance of her movements. Each day she spent several hours at the research laboratory. During the lunch hour, she sat outside, eating in the warm sun and making notes in a journal.

While waiting for the perfect moment to complete his contract, Claude wonders, *Katie is a pretty girl. Why does someone want her dead? But that's not my call. Do the job, Claude and forget about the contract. This is the last one, and then, for the rest of my life I'm on easy street.*

* * *

Ten minutes ago, at 8:45 p.m. Claude was seated in his rental car on the opposite side of the street watching the laboratory and saw his quarry enter the building alone. When only one small light came on, he thought, *She is up to something. Perhaps tonight is when she will attempt to take the chimps somewhere.*

A few minutes later when the light went out, and Katie hurried out the door, Claude's suspicions were confirmed. She was holding hands with two chimpanzees and moving fast. He watched as she helped the chimps climb into the back seat, and her hands moved in a funny fashion. Claude had no way to know Katie was signing, telling them to stay out of sight. Then she threw a blanket over them, got into the car and drove off.

As Claude waited for a break in the traffic to make a U-turn, he thought, *She'll probably take them to her apartment.*

When the opportunity presented itself, Claude pulled out and successfully made the maneuver. But as he began to speed up, red and blue lights reflected in his rear-view mirror. *That was stupid – I turned right in front of a cop. I'll never catch her now. I hope she does head home. If she goes elsewhere, I'm in trouble.*

* * *

Thirty minutes later, after receiving a lecture by a local policeman about the accidents caused by people that do what Claude did, plus a warning ticket, he parks across the street from Katie's apartment.

As quietly as possible, Claude makes his way along the sidewalk until he can see the interior of her garage. Katie's old car is parked inside, and he is relieved. The lights are on in her apartment, but she has pulled down the window blinds. Claude knows there is no way he can get inside without causing a disturbance.

His contact warned about just such an occurrence. "If possible, make their deaths appear to be an accident. But no matter what, this woman and her two friends must be killed within the next week. Your fee depends on completing the contract within that time period."

"I will fulfill my end of the bargain," Claude said. "You be sure to pay my fee."

"Don't worry, Mister Jones," Mohammed said. "You will get what you have coming."

* * *

At 9:15 in the evening, Jerry arrives at the lab to check on three experimental vaccines and cultures he made of new bacteria in Petri dishes. He is anxious to see the results, so punches in the access code, enters the building and turns on the lights. The lab is very quiet, as most animals are asleep. Jerry is glad they won't be a distraction.

As he walks by the large cage where Wilbur and Sadie are housed, Jerry chuckles. Out of curiosity, he peers into the interior to see how the foretellers of terrorist attacks are doing. To his surprise, neither is visible. After checking high in the branches of the fake tree, he turns on the overhead lights, but still can't see either chimp.

Jerry walks around the cage, picks up a flashlight hanging on a wall and enters through a small door. But when he shines the light around the interior, the two fortunetellers are nowhere to be seen. He calls out, "Where are you guys?" Nothing moves and there is no answer. *That is strange. Where they can be? Maybe they got loose somehow.*

Jerry climbs out of the cage and searches the entire facility, but again, finds no sign of them. Then he thinks of Katie. *I'll bet she took them somewhere. Maybe she went to the police. All we need is bad publicity. I had better inform Doctor Wilson.*

* * *

At 10:15 Mona's cell phone chirps the refrain: "There will be a hot time in the old town tonight," a little faster than the composer intended. When choosing the ringtone, Mona thought the tune fit her life style, but lately the song has become annoying.

The hour is late and Mona is busy tutoring her latest protégé, Mark Anderson, a blond-haired, blue-eyed freshman with a marvelous body. She wonders who could be phoning at this late hour and wants to ignore the call. But at the fourth repetition, Mark interrupts their rhythm, looks up and asks, "Aren't you going to answer?"

Mona frowns to show she is upset. "I suppose I must. Excuse me."

She gets up awkwardly and moves to a nearby table, where the phone is lying. Then she picks up the instrument and flips up the top. "Who is this?"

From the tone of Mona's voice, Jerry knows his boss is upset with him for phoning so late, but says, "Hi Doctor Wilson. I hate to bother you, but two chimps are missing. I searched everywhere and can't find them."

Mona shakes her head at Jerry's incompetence. "Who are they?"

"Wilbur and Sadie - what should I do?"

As she attempts to solve Jerry's problem and return to Mark, Mona says, "Wilbur is good at finding places to hide and probably took Sadie with him. Wait until tomorrow morning, and I will help you look."

She is surprised when he says, "I have a suspicion Katie Adkins took them."

"Why would she do such a thing?"

"The other day Katie came up with a half-baked story that Sadie and Wilbur know about a terrorist attack. I blew her off, and Katie wasn't happy."

After a moment of thought, Mona says, "I don't think Katie would do anything so risky. Sadie and Wilbur are probably asleep somewhere and you can't find them. Go home and get some sleep, Jerry. It's late and you're tired. We'll locate them tomorrow."

She breathes a sigh of relief when Jerry says, "Okay Doctor, I'm sorry to have bothered you."

"Thanks, Jerry," Mona says and disconnects.

Then she looks down at Mark, lying prone on her bed and notes he is still erect. *That's what I like about first-year students. They are full of vim and vigor. Nothing prevents them from furthering their education.*

She straddles him again. "Now, where were we?"

* * *

The next morning at 8:00, Mona arrives to find Jerry waiting near the front door. Disheveled brown hair is hanging over his brow, and a black mark on his left cheek appears to be grease. Apparently he hasn't located the two missing chimps. But she asks anyway, "Hi Jerry, did you find Sadie and Wilbur?"

Brushing back his hair, he says, "No, and several workers helped search. They aren't in the facility. I'm sure Katie has them. She was adamant about believing their story."

"I can't believe Katie would do something so irresponsible. Let's conduct one more search. If we can't find them, I'll phone the police and tell them of your fears."

CHAPTER 7

Rain fell last night, and this morning the sky is overcast. Due to a serious three-car pileup on the Interstate, Fad is late to work. On his way into the building, he steps in a mud puddle, looks down at his soggy shoes and says, "This is the beginning of another lousy day."

* * *

As Fad walks into the squad room, the phone rings.

Now what? Can't I even have a cup of coffee before Mister Crime starts beating on me with a crooked stick? No one else is in the office. They are either on a coffee break or hiding out in the john. *Aw to hell with it, I have to get started somewhere.* He picks up the annoying instrument and snarls, "Yeah?"

"Hey Fad, what's happening?" Bert asks.

"Nothing important - what's up, Bert?"

"Is Joe around?"

"Nah Bert; the sign-out board says he's on a call about some guy shooting bottle rockets in a park. I told him to let the Fish and Wildlife guys take care of those kinds of calls, but you know him. Let someone mention shooting, and Joe is on a tear."

"Yeah I know, Fad. When Joe returns, tell him our missing person was found with a bullet in his head. We fished Larry Holgram from the lake this morning. He was murdered."

"That figures," Fad says. "We were hoping Larry would show up alive. This will be rough on his wife and their little girl."

"Yeah, I went out to tell Carol. She is broken up. When Claire learns of her father's death, she will be in shock."

Telling it like it is, Fad says, "There is a world of hurt out there."

"Oh, one other thing, Fad; let Joe know the blood in the research lab is Larry's. The results of the DNA came back just before we heard about him floating in the lake. Apparently Larry was killed in the building with the chimps. That's why they were so shook up."

Fad shakes his head in disgust. "Nothing surprises me anymore. Why did I become a cop?"

Bert laughs wickedly. "Supposedly to help your fellow man."

"Yeah, Bert, but who is going to help us?"

* * *

When Joe hears the news about Larry, he says, "So, the two cases are connected. Great, now I will have a chance to see the tall drink of water with fabulous boobs and legs that won't quit."

Fad shakes his head and laughs. "Is sex all you think about? What about Law and Order?"

"What a great TV show," Joe says.

"Ain't that the truth? I love the way the actors track down clues in no time at all. I wish the jerks would work with me on the graveyard shift to see how crime cases really go down."

Now it is Joe's time to shake his head. "Yeah, as if that would ever happen."

The phone rings and Fad picks up the instrument to hear, "Bert here, more bad news."

Again, Fad shakes his head. It is becoming a habit. "What else do we handle?"

Bert says, "The beautiful doc Joe is always talking of phoned in to report two chimps are missing. I don't know what this has to do with Larry or whatever went on out at the lab, but it's interesting. Plus, the missing chimps give Joe a chance to drool all over the doc."

Fad turns to his partner and hands him the phone. "The call is for you."

As Joe listens, a smile forms on his face. Fad knows Joe is thinking of the good-looking female doc, wondering if he can make time with her. Maybe things will work out, but Fad won't take odds on that happening.

"Okay, thanks, Bert," Joe says and hangs up. When Joe looks at him, Fad smiles knowingly. "It looks like another trip to the lab. Do you want me to come with you?"

"Nah, you would only cramp my style with the lady doctor."

"What style, Joe? Do you really think she will fall for an old fart like you?"

Joe raises his eyebrows in an unspoken question. "You never know, stranger things have happened."

"Yeah, maybe in Istanbul, but not here," Fad says. "Have fun. If you do plan to stay overnight, phone in sick."

As Joe leaves the room with a smile on his face, he says, "Don't wait up, Daddy." Still laughing, he walks out the door and climbs into his cruiser. While picturing Mona in his mind, he thinks, *It will be nice to see her again.* Lost in thought, he almost sideswipes another cruiser.

The other driver shouts, "You drunk or something?"

"Sorry," Joe yells in response and chuckles when the cop gives him a one-fingered salute.

* * *

At 9:00, on a dark moonless night in the shadows of a large warehouse south of town, Claude is awaiting his payoff. Meeting with his customers is against his principles, but this job turned out badly. Before parting with the remaining four hundred thousand dollars, his latest anonymous employer wants to meet to discuss the particulars and supposed repercussions.

Crickets chirping as they call for mates and the lapping of small waves against pilings are the only sounds, other than a bullfrog singing his lonely song and listening to an answer by another farther away.

A scent of dead fish lingers in the air and another more pungent aroma of fresh dog droppings is somewhere nearby. After checking the soles of his shoes and finding nothing, Claude is relieved. He wants his money and an end to his career as an assassin. In his mind, there are plans for retirement in Acapulco or wherever his fancy leads him.

Twin beams cut through the night as a dark brown Cadillac drives slowly through an open gate and swings toward a loading dock where Claude agreed to meet his client. Claude remains in the shadows, watching Felix Mendez slip from behind the wheel to stand alongside the car with the door open.

The interior light remains lit, and Claude notes Felix is alone. He waits for a few moments before stepping out and walking silently to where Felix is smoking a cigarette and idly blowing smoke rings into the stillness of the night air.

Claude approaches so quietly Felix is startled. He moves backward and reaches awkwardly under his jacket. As Claude levels his revolver so the red dot of the weapon's laser beam sight remains centered on Felix's chest, he says, "Keep your hands in sight, please."

"So you are Mister Jones. You appear more German than English. What went wrong with the contract?"

"You aren't the one I spoke with. Where is he, and who are you?"

"He was detained by other business," Felix says. "I'm his partner. Again, what happened?"

Claude shrugs. "In order to complete the job within the time frame you indicated, I made a few adjustments. I'm sorry about the collateral damage, but their deaths were necessary to make the hit appear an accident. Don't worry, I won't charge extra for the others."

Felix shrugs as if the additional victims were insignificant as dead flies. "I hope your actions won't draw attention to our final objective."

"I don't know your plans, so how could my actions affect you? I performed the job as requested. All the principal players are dead. Now I'll take my money."

Felix smiles crookedly and says, "Apparently you have the upper hand."

His smirk bothers Claude. "What's so funny?"

Suddenly, two shots break the silence. The first bullet strikes Claude on the right side of his chest, rocking him backward. The second hits just below his right shoulder, knocking him backward off the loading dock and into a deep water-filled drainage canal. As Claude flies outward and downward, his eyes remain focused on Felix's face. The last thing he sees before going underwater is that Felix's smirk has grown into a large grin.

Felix speaks into a microphone hidden under his shirt. "Good work, Mohammed." He walks slowly to the edge of the loading platform and watches for a sign of Mister Jones. Seeing none, he says, "If you didn't kill him outright, he'll drown." Mohammed laughs in his earpiece.

Meeting Felix here is Claude's second mistake. The first error Felix made was failing to ensure Claude's demise. Unknown to Felix, this definitely will not be his last.

* * *

Drizzle is still falling when Joe drives up to the research lab and parks in a handicapped space near the door. He figures his stomachache qualifies. *For supper last night, I ate too many tacos with Jalapenos. I'll probably fart fire later today,* he thinks to himself.

Joe skips his way through small puddles in an attempt to keep most water out of his shoes, but one has a hole in the sole. By the time he gets inside, his sock is soaked. He squishes his way to Mona's office and knocks politely on the doorframe. With a smile that makes Mona Lisa look like a five-dollar-a-night streetwalker, she says, "Come in, Detective Francone."

Joe attempts to look suave and sophisticated, but his actions come off like the stain of catsup on a new white shirt. "You can call me Joe. After all this time together, we must be friends."

Mona sees through his nonsense, but still thinks Joe is cute. "Okay, Joe. What can I do for you?"

He thinks, *I would like to tell you, but you might punch me out.*

"I came about your missing chimps. Are they the same ones I saw last time? Aren't they called Sadie and Willie?"

Automatically Mona corrects him. "Sadie and Wilbur; and yes, they are the same. Jerry believes Katie Adkins made off with them."

"Why would he think that?"

"Katie told Jerry what he thought was an unbelievable tale that Wilbur and Sadie knew something about a terrorist plot. Jerry doesn't think chimps have brains, but they do. I wish I had known of Katie's fears. Perhaps I could have helped her."

Joe asks, "Is there any way to know whether Katie has the chimps?"

"Only if they are with her. And we don't know where she is. Katie didn't come in this morning."

Joe retrieves his trusty notebook and pencil. "Give me Katie's address. Later, I'll drop by to see her." Before Mona can respond, Joe's beeper chirps. "Excuse me." Joe checks his beeper and reads a text message to phone in immediately. Then remembers his hated cell phone is in his desk drawer at the station. "May I borrow your phone, Mona?"

"Sure," she says and hands her cell to him.

When Red answers, Joe asks, "What's up, Red?"

"There was a big explosion on Mulberry Street. A tanker truck blew up. If we can't get the situation under control, the whole block may go up in flames. I want you to go over there and take charge of the investigation. We may have major casualties, dead and injured."

Joe feels a sour taste in his mouth, and his stomach acid begins to churn and burn at the thought of what he will soon face. "That's all we need. I'll get right over there. Where is Fad?"

"He's on his way," Red says. "Get going."

After flipping the phone shut, Joe stands up and lays the instrument on Mona's desk. "I'm sorry. We'll have to continue this another time. There is an emergency in town. Thanks for the phone."

With her eyes sparkling, Mona says, "You're welcome. I look forward to seeing you again."

"The feeling is mutual." *I hope she means what she said.*

* * *

Sadie is terrified, cold, hurt and alone in a world she doesn't understand. When the truck hit Katie's car, the impact threw her out the open window and she landed hard on the asphalt road. The terrible sound of an explosion came unexpectedly and the blast blew her across the pavement and into a group of nearby shrubs.

The sounds frightened Sadie so she lost control of her bladder. Then heat from the flames singed the hair on her back, and a few drops of liquid fire fell onto her right arm, blistering her tender skin. She looks for Wilbur but can't find him.

In the excitement, no one notices Sadie scamper away to a tall oak tree, where she scurries up the trunk and into the highest branches to remain there throughout the day, crying softly and licking her wounds. Off and on during the afternoon, sirens, noise from gas tanks exploding and flames from the inferno a few hundred yards away continue to startle and confuse Sadie. As day turns to dusk, she becomes groggy and falls asleep tucked into a fork where three branches meet.

A few hours later, in the darkness of night, Sadie awakens to pain and loneliness. She misses Wilbur and cries softly while scanning the underbrush for a sign of her mate. Finally, hunger overpowers fear, so she climbs down from her perch to search for food.

While making her way down back alleys and keeping to shadows, Sadie avoids contact with humans. Knowing stealth is her ally, she quietly removes lids from several trashcans and rummages through the contents until she uncovers edible remains of vegetables or fruit. Her arm continues to ache, and she licks the burns to ease the pain.

Three blocks into her search, Sadie finds the cornucopia of her dreams in the form of a large Dumpster behind a grocery store. With ease of a thief at night, she scampers into the dark space. After discovering a large and broken wooden box half-full of out-of-date apples, pears and bananas, she eats until she feels her stomach will burst. Then she falls into a fitful sleep.

* * *

As the sun climbs slowly into the sky, warmth penetrates Sadie's hiding spot. Unfamiliar with her surroundings, she awakens with a start. The burns are now swollen with fluid and ache like the fires of hell. After breakfasting on the remains of last night's meal, she glances around cautiously. Seeing no one or anything to frighten her, she climbs slowly from the Dumpster and makes her way to some bushes behind a nearby aging apartment building.

Inborn survival instincts tell Sadie to stay close by her food source. After burrowing into the interior of the brush, she makes a nest from dead vegetation. Then she falls asleep again, dreams of Wilbur and their comfortable cage, and whimpers softly as tears of pain and loneliness run down her cheeks.

* * *

Alice Grabowski is only eleven-years-old, but is more upset than ever before in her short life. One of Alice's seventh-grade classmates, Danny Shackley, is not only an ugly, fat-headed dork; he is what her father, Harold, would label a horse's ass. Alice's mother, Dorothy, says Danny must have a crush on Alice, because he continually teases her. But Alice thinks Danny is plain mean and pig-headed.

Up until today, Alice has managed to slough off his unwanted attention and mockery, but this afternoon after school was the final straw. Danny came up with a new idea and began calling her "Grab-ass-ky." Several friends of his took up the chant and made her cry.

Alice has never been so embarrassed. She runs all the way home, where she knows she will find sympathy from her mother. But Dorothy isn't there, so, while cursing the name of Danny Shackley under her breath, Alice walks out onto the back stoop to cry alone. She hates Danny so much her stomach hurts. *Just wait, I will come up with something to pay him back – but what?*

A solution is too much for her young brain to contemplate. Continuing to feel forlorn; Alice dries her eyes and sits with her knees drawn up under her arms. Resting her head on the soft platform they form, she looks out into the trash-littered backyard, while savoring a bite of an apple saved from lunch.

For years, Harold did his best to keep the backyard clean, but the grocery store down the alley doesn't care and lets their garbage blow wherever it wishes to go. As a result, most trash ends up in Harold's open backyard. *Maybe if we had a fence instead of those stupid bushes, I could play out here without worrying about rodents.*

Suddenly there is movement in the shrubs. Alice wonders if it is a rat. *I hate them because they carry all kinds of diseases.*

She thinks of jumping up and running inside, when a long hairy arm reaches out to grasp an old worn-out baseball that has lain there for ages. Alice can't believe her eyes. The first arm is followed by a second, and then a hairy body. A face with two sorrowful eyes looks up at Alice, and her heart does a flip. "It's a monkey!"

Afraid she might frighten her new guest, she asks softly, "Where did you come from?" Sadie tips her head to one side and studies Alice's face. Then finally making up her mind, drops the ball and signs, "My name is Sadie. What is yours?"

Alice stares at the monkey, wondering what it means by those hand signals. The motions remind her of sign language, something her teacher touched on during civics, but Alice isn't sure because she never took the time to learn. *Besides, where would a monkey learn to sign?*

Alice tosses the half-eaten morsel at the monkey. "Want a bite of my apple?"

Sadie jumps backward and retreats into the brush. A minute later, her hairy paw reaches out to grasp the fruit like a prized jewel. The arm and apple disappear, and Alice hears heavy teeth munch as Sadie bites into the juicy treat. When she has eaten, Sadie becomes brave enough to crawl from the vegetation. Sitting forlornly on her haunches, she looks at Alice with the biggest eyes she has ever seen and signs, "Where is Wilbur?"

Alice shakes her head. "I don't know what you are saying. What's wrong with your arm?" She reaches down slowly, touches Sadie's arm, and Sadie signs, "It hurts." So she won't spook her new friend, Alice gets up quietly. "Stay there. I'll be right back."

She goes inside to the bathroom, where she finds a big jar of green jelly her mother uses for sunburn or scrapes and cuts. After carrying it outside, Alice removes the lid, while Sadie watches every movement. Then, using her fingers, Alice beckons her new friend. "Come here, sweet thing. I won't hurt you."

By the tone of Alice's soothing voice, Sadie realizes in the midst of her sorrows, she has found a friend. Sadie holds out her sore arm, and Alice says, "Let me put some of this on your blisters. It won't hurt and will cool them. I can tell you are in pain. How did you get these burns?"

As the cool jelly eases her pain, Sadie smiles a toothy grin. Then, without warning jumps up onto the stoop beside Alice and holds her hand. Surprised and happy to have such a lively new friend, Alice thinks, *If old smart mouth Danny could see me now, he would be so jealous.*

After examining Sadie's hairy body, Alice says, "Why, your back is singed. I smell burned hair everywhere. I wonder if you were hurt in that terrible fire yesterday. The papers say several people were killed, which is so tragic."

Sadie signs, "Hide, three, two, fire, X."

Alice has no idea what the gestures mean, so leans out to pat Sadie's head. "Even with your burns, you are a pretty girl. What in the world shall I do with you?"

While displaying as many teeth as she can and leaning heavily on Alice's knee, Sadie puts her healthy arm around her new playmate to give her a hug. Alice admires her new pet, and knows she can't part with her. She is also aware what Dorothy and Harold will probably say about her plans.

"Well, I'm going to keep you," she says. "That's for sure. But we must hide you somewhere until I break the news to Mom and Dad. Come on; let's look where you have been living."

The two new best friends walk hand-in-hand to examine Sadie's lair, while Alice's mind races to determine a way to make her guest comfortable enough to stay put. She forgets Danny, and a smile lights Alice's face as she skips toward the alley with Sadie to find her hiding place.

CHAPTER 8

As Joe glances at the burned remains of the monkey/chimp on a table in the morgue, Sarah continues their conversation. "What's wrong with the fourth victim being a chimp?"

Joe shakes his head twice. "Nearly everything I touched this week has been connected with chimps. You wouldn't believe it."

Sarah is busy with her examination and wishes Joe would leave. "Whatever."

Joe points toward the adjacent tables. "Let's keep the news of the two gun-shot victims away from the press for a while, Doc. That might help us catch the perps. And, while we're talking of it, don't tell anyone about the chimp. The less these guys know of our business, the better we will be."

"Okay, Joe, if that's the way you want to play it."

Joe flips to a clean page in his notebook. "Do you have an I.D. on any of the victims?"

"Two of the six are still in hospital morgues," Sarah says. "I'll get their names later. I'm sure the Chaplain will notify their next of kin. The truck driver on table one was named Ted Branski. He had a wife and two young kids."

Joe jots down the info. "What about the women?"

"The driver of the Oldsmobile hasn't yet been identified. The other woman was a student at the University. We got her I.D. from motor vehicles when they traced her license plate. Her name is Katie Adkins."

Joe begins to write down the name and realization dawns. "Katie Adkins?" he asks in amazement. "I just met her a few days ago at the research lab while I was checking on a murder victim. She spoke to the chimps out there."

"Spoke to chimps?" Sarah asks. "How strange?"

"Not really, Doc. Katie used sign language to communicate. Man, something weird is going on at the lab. This is too much coincidence. The fried chimp must be one of two reported missing this morning. I was at the lab inquiring about them when I got the call concerning the explosion. Is there any way to tell if this is a boy or girl?"

"The usual," Sarah says. "He is a boy, or was. Now he's a roasted chimpanzee."

"Now who is making sport with the dead?" Joe asks and smiles.

"I apologize, Joe. Do you know his name?"

"Yeah, it's Wilbur. His mate is named Sadie. I wonder where she is."

Sarah shrugs in helplessness. "If Sadie is out there in the big city of Sulfur Springs, there is no way to tell. I think you have a major case on your hands, Joe. Who would want to kill two strangers to take out a student and two chimps? Somebody is really monkeying with your mind."

Joe smiles at Sarah's pun and walks slowly away. Over his shoulder, he says, "That's cute, Doc – real cute."

When he gets outside, Joe blows his nose hard to get rid of the Vaseline. Fresh air never smelled so good.

* * *

Bert is up to his hips in robbery cases and needs a break. Someone has stolen nearly every lawn ornament in town. So far, he counted sixty-eight separate reports. The burglary calls are coming in at the rate of four or five a night. *Someone must be about to open a new store soon. Why lawn ornaments? It beats me.*

The phone rings, and Bert hopes this call is anything but another burglary report. While picking up the instrument, he prays silently, *Please God, give me a break.* "Bert, this is Joe. Is there any chance you can walk up the hall for a sit down with Fad and me? We need to lay this thing out on the blackboard to see if we can make sense of what little we know."

Bert glances toward heaven to thank the Big Guy in the sky. "Sure, I'll be right down. Pour me a cup of that stuff you call coffee."

"Thanks," Joe says.

"No, Joe, thank you!"

* * *

Fifteen minutes later, Bert, Joe and Fad are gathered around a wooden conference table displaying so many cigarette burns, Joe wonders if they should rent a sander to make an even surface to write on. As Joe begins the discussion he says, "Okay, we're all on the same wavelength. Fad, you handle the chalk, and we'll go over the timeline to see what we have."

"No sweat, Joe."

Joe begins to read from his notes. "First, Monday night, Larry Holgram goes missing. A little after six p.m. he leaves his office. Then remembers his daughter's present and returns to the building. That much we know from logbook records and our reluctant witness, Mister O'Reilly. Larry was upstairs approximately five minutes. Then suddenly he runs from the elevator, out the exit and into the building next door. Is that how you see things, Bert?"

"Yeah, while Larry was in his office, he was spooked. Either he overheard or saw something that made him fear for his life, and ran."

Fad adds, "Supposedly no one else was in the building. If they weren't, who or what frightened Larry? I think Grady lied."

Joe nods in agreement. "So do I, but can't prove he did, so let's move on. How did Larry get into the building next door? Did he have the access code? Doctor Wilson says almost everyone on campus knows the combination."

"Which doesn't help," Bert says and chuckles sadly. "So, now our suspects are narrowed down to only several hundred students, research lab staff and workers at the chemical facility."

Joe taps his notebook again. "Okay, here's another strange coincidence. Larry couldn't speak. He conversed mostly by using sign language. That much we know. Now comes the really weird part – the monkeys could also sign."

"They aren't monkeys, Joe; they're chimps," Fad says.

"Okay, I stand corrected, chimps that sign. Mona said they taught them sign language, and the chimps are able to communicate. Then, four days after Larry gets whacked, we have Katie Adkins as a victim of a fire/ homicide and one of the chimps named Wilbur fried medium rare. Katie just happened to work with the chimps, knows sign language, and now they are missing, or at least one is. How weird is this?"

"Pretty far out," Bert says. "But things are beginning to make some sense. Katie had the chimps with her for a specific reason. That's how we wound up with Wilbur fried to a crisp."

"Yeah," Joe says. "Wilbur bought the farm, but where is Sadie,"

"I just picked up on the 'Mona'," Fad says. "Are you two getting pretty cozy, Joe?"

Joe feels a blush on his cheeks. "That slipped out, but yeah, we're getting along fine, which reminds me. When Red phoned, Mona had begun telling a far-out story of how Katie received a message from Wilbur and Sadie concerning a planned terrorist attack in the very near future. I have to hear more about that."

At Joe's statement, Bert looks up from his notes in surprise. "What do you mean by 'a terrorist attack'? Did Mona say where or when?"

"No, she didn't. We were interrupted by the explosion, and I had to leave."

Bert turns his attention to Fad. "Add those facts to the board as another piece of the puzzle."

The phone rings, and Fad answers the call. After listening for a moment, he asks, "Can you hold? I'll see if he is available."

Fad punches the hold button and turns to Joe. "Do you know an FBI agent named Hefner?"

Joe chuckles. "No, I don't. Is he Hugh's son?"

Fad laughs with him. "I don't think so, but he asked for you by name."

Joe picks up the phone and says, "Sergeant Francone here, Agent Hefner, how may I help you?"

Without preamble, Kris asks, "Did you know Katie Adkins?"

"Yes, I knew her. She worked at the SCOU research lab. Yesterday she was killed in an explosion."

"I know," Kris says. "Two days ago, Katie phoned to say she had two witnesses to verify her story of a planned terrorist attack on the United States, so we set an appointment for yesterday morning. When Katie didn't show, I thought she was some kook and the call was a prank.

"This morning I read the official police report of her death, and it didn't sound like an accident. Shooting and killing two people to set up a trap for her car was too coincidental."

Joe thinks, *This guy is smart and a man after my own heart. I don't buy Katie being there as a coincidence.* "I like the way you think, Kris. I don't believe her death was an accident either. Someone very clever set up this scenario."

Kris asks, "Did Katie say anything to you concerning this supposed attack?"

"No, she didn't. I heard about her fears the first time yesterday from her supervisor, Doctor Wilson, who was filling me in when I received the call about an explosion."

"We need to talk," Kris says. "What time would be convenient?"

"As we speak, two other officers and I are laying out the time line. Why don't you drop by and give us a hand?"

"I'm on my way."

"We're in room 303. I'll leave word with the desk sergeant to pass you up."

"Okay, Sergeant. I'll be there in fifteen minutes."

Before taking coffee break and waiting for Kris to arrive, Joe fills Bert and Fad in on what Agent Hefner added to the pot.

* * *

As everyone shakes hands and Joe introduces Kris to his fellow officers, he takes Kris' measure. He is impressed with the agent's manner and appearance. Kris is young, slim and trim, and probably twenty-seven or so, but looks a little older in a well-cut, dark brown suit, white shirt and tan tie. Kris has blond hair, blue eyes and a quick smile, and gets right down to business.

"Please call me Kris. As far as I'm concerned, this is your show. So far, no federal law has been broken; however, the FBI is always interested in any terrorist threat, imagined or real. Katie said she possessed vital information she couldn't trust by using e-mail or speak of over the phone. She also said there were two witnesses to verify her story. Do you know who they are?"

Joe smiles funny, and Kris notices. "Yeah, we do, Kris, but you're not going to believe me."

"Why?"

"The witnesses are chimpanzees, Kris."

"You have to be kidding me – chimps? Is that who or what Katie had to verify her story? She sounds more and more like a kook."

"No, Katie wasn't a nutcase," Joe says sadly. "She worked with these chimps, teaching them sign language. According to Katie's supervisor, the chimps used sign language to speak to humans and each other."

"Now I've heard everything," Kris says.

"Look at our board," Joe says, and brings Kris up to date on all they know. As he concludes his briefing, Joe says, "The only thing I can determine is that during the short time Larry was in the building, and before someone shot him, he passed on some sort of a message to Sadie and Wilbur."

Bert nods and says, "The chimps repeated the message to Katie, who told her boss' assistant, Jerry Grimes, but he blew her off. That made Katie angry, so she phoned you, Kris. Does all this make sense?"

"Sort of, but how did the perps that killed Larry hear about this in time to take out Katie and the chimp? And where is Sadie?"

"We don't know," Joe says. "We think Mister O'Reilly lied about no one else being in the building. There had to be someone Larry overheard or saw that frightened him enough to run."

Fad says, "We need to talk to Grady again. He will love having me in his face for a second time."

Joe thinks for a few seconds. "Maybe we should have you conduct the interview with Grady, Kris. He'll think you're a youngster attempting to make his bones, but maybe the title of FBI agent will sink in, and he'll let something slip."

Kris nods, but suggests, "First, let's talk to Doctor Wilson. I need to learn more of what Katie told Jerry Grimes. If there is actually some sort of a terrorist threat to the USA, we still don't know what, when or where it is planned."

Fad shakes his index finger at Joe. "Look out Joe, or Kris will horn in on your territory."

"How is that, Fad?" Kris asks.

"Joe has staked out the fair maiden, Mona for his own. Don't get between them, Kris, or you might get trampled like a young bull elk during mating season."

"I consider myself fairly warned. I'll stay out of your way, Joe."

Joe's face is red, but he doesn't care if they saw him blush. Mona is some kind of a hot woman, and he wants to stoke her fire. "You won't cramp my style, Kris. I'll give Mona a call and we can meet with her later today."

"Good enough, Joe."

As Fad heads for the door, he says, "I'll go by the medical examiner's office to see what else Sarah can tell us. You want to come with me, Bert?"

Bert shakes his head. "No, I have to talk to Carol Holgram. Besides, I hate the morgue. I can't stand watching someone cut up dead bodies."

"I don't blame you," Joe says. "Let's meet here at four and compare notes."

CHAPTER 9

Claude dreams he is on an ocean cruise and waves are rocking the ship. Then his head bobbed forward and his mouth filled with water. As his shoulder cries out in agony, he coughs and spits out the oily-tasting fluid. The pain brings Claude from a fog he has been in for the past fifteen minutes since being knocked into the water. Luck alone kept Claude from drowning.

When Claude first surfaced under the dock, his coat snagged a rusty nail sticking out from a creosoted piling. The shot to his chest knocked the wind from his lungs, and his breath came in gasps. He attempted to take in air as quietly as possible while listening to the man he met speak to someone. Claude heard the name Mohammed. Then agonizing pain hit him like a bull moose on a rampage in a glass factory, and he lost consciousness.

Now awake and semi-alert, Claude clings to his lifesaving pole with his good arm and checks his body for injuries. His chest hurts like hell, but he is glad he wore a flak jacket under his coat. It saved his life.

As he attempts to move his right arm, he experiences such pain he almost blacks out. Either his shoulder or arm is broken and useless now. In a fog of semi-consciousness, he remembers hearing Felix's remarks and laughter when he thought he had killed Claude. *You should have made sure. Payback is hell. Now to get out of the water before I pass out again.*

Reaching up with his left hand, he gently unhooks his coat from the nail. Then, moving very gingerly, Claude feels his way around the slimy post until he sees lights across the canal reflecting on the dark, dingy surface. Twenty long feet across open water is a ladder attached to a piling that leads upward to the loading platform. *Can I swim that far? I had better or I will die here in this cruddy canal.*

Gritting his teeth, Claude struggles painfully from his coat, lets the garment slip from his injured arm and drift away. After fumbling to loosen the straps, he slips out of his flak jacket and lets the vest and his shoes sink into the depths. Then, although he hates the thought, Claude decides his second gun strapped to his left leg just above the ankle must go.

If the one that shot him and/or the man he met were on the dock, they would have heard him by now. Other than the crickets, Claude doesn't hear a sound, so bets both assailants are long gone. The gun weighs too much to leave attached to his leg when he needs all the help he can muster and as little hindrance as possible to make his way to the ladder.

After unhooking the Velcro straps, he allows the holster and weapon to slip down into the filthy water. Then he lets go from his lifesaving pole, and using a one-handed dog paddle, makes his way across the stretch of water that seems as long as an Olympic swimming pool.

He swallows and spits out half the water in the canal before grasping the bottom rung of the ladder and hanging on. The pain in his chest has subsided some, so now he might be able to use his right arm to support his body.

The dock appears to be a long way upward, but Claude is determined to reach the landing. After hooking one leg over the bottom rung, he balances there awkwardly, reaches up to the third rung and pulls his aching body from the canal. Rivulets of oily water run from his clothes to drip downward and splash quietly into the water, where they make small concentric circles that spread slowly across the oily surface.

Claude grits his teeth against the pain he knows is coming. Then turns and puts the elbow of his injured arm through an opening. In one quick motion, he lets go with his good hand, lunges upward and grabs another rung. The pain makes him scream in agony, but he manages two more rungs. *Only six more to go.*

* * *

How he accomplished the feat, Claude never knows, but after fifteen minutes of painful determination, he pulls his weary body over the top of the ladder and lies panting for breath on the splintered wooden dock. Never in his life has he been so glad to be on solid ground.

He tears the right arm of his shirt, ripping the fabric along the seam, and checks his wound to discover the bullet was a through and through. After entering three inches below his collarbone as a small pencil-sized projectile, the bullet expanded and exited his back, leaving behind a jagged hole an inch and a half in diameter. As he watches, dark thick blood seeps from the wound and trickles slowly down his chest. *I need help soon or I will die from loss of blood. Get up, Claude. Start moving and don't stop.*

By pushing painfully with his good arm until getting his legs under his body, Claude finally stands erect. Then he moves slowly toward the alley where his car is parked. As his wet soggy socks slap against the wooden deck, the sound reminds him of a washerwoman pounding damp clothing against a rock. To no surprise, his car is missing, taken as a souvenir by either his contact or his assistant. Claude pauses for a moment to rest and think. *Enjoy your freedom while you are able. When I catch up to you, you are in for a big surprise.*

He manages to stagger a few feet farther, and then leans heavily against a wall of a warehouse to catch his breath. From out of the darkness, a woman's voice says, "You look like a drowned rat. What's wrong?"

The sound startles Claude, and he reaches for his gun, only to remember the weapon is gone, drowned in the canal as he should have. Holding his good hand above his eyes, Claude sees a dim form of a woman standing a few feet away in the shadows of a building. "I was shot."

As the unknown female rushes forward and reaches to support him, she asks, "Shot? Good God, who shot you?"

"Not a friend," Claude says.

His unknown savior points in the general direction of the entrance. "I didn't think so. Come on, my car is over there. I heard sounds like shots or fireworks and wondered who was here. I thought some college students might be shooting bottle rockets and was worried they would set the buildings afire."

"I'm glad you happened by," he says.

They take a few steps, and she says, "I'll get you to a hospital."

"No; not a medical facility – they will want to know who shot me, and I don't want to tell them."

"You want to take care of your assailant yourself, right, Mister Macho?"

"We'll see," he says. "Will you help me or not?"

She attempts to joke. "I'm a sucker for a man that was shot. Okay, if you say so, I'll attempt to fix your arm. That's a nasty hole."

"Thanks," he says and lets her lead him to the passenger's side of a dark-red Pontiac Firebird convertible, where she says, "Here we are. Let me get a blanket from the trunk to put on the seat and wrap around you. I would hate to ruin the upholstery with your blood. Besides, you need something to keep you warm."

Claude holds on to the door for support while she pops the trunk. Then he asks, "Do you have any whiskey for a weak, wounded man?"

After she returns with the blanket and spreads it on the seat and helps him sit down, she says, "I think I have some at home."

Then she pulls the wonderfully warm wrap around Claude's legs and upper body. "This should help until we can get some booze in you."

"Thanks again," he says and passes out.

* * *

The report of the tanker truck explosion and associated casualties remain big news for three days. It and other related articles are featured prominently on the front page of the local rag until a house fire kills six siblings. Then the newspaper promptly forgets about the victims of a four-day-old accident. The editor in chief, Louis Bernstein tells his staff, "Blood and guts sell newspapers. Start a fund for the victims of the house fire and run old news on a back page."

Since the story of the authorities discovering Larry in the lake is not considered worthy of front page importance, it is located on page 3. What is one more murder to the general public immune to such daily carnage?

* * *

Alice thinks she is too cool to read the newspaper. She gets her news from TV, what she hears in school and at the breakfast table, where for days her parents forced her to listen to a discussion of the terrible explosion. Alice can hardly sit still long enough to satisfy her mom and dad that she is aware of the latest news before jumping up from her chair and making a beeline for the backyard.

* * *

This morning, over the sound of the TV, Alice hears her mother say, "The news is so terrible." Knowing Dorothy expects a reply, she asks, "What?"

Dorothy shakes her head and sighs, "Those poor people killed in the explosion a few blocks away. Just think; the accident could have happened on our street and we would be homeless."

Harold looks up from the sports page for a moment. "Thank your lucky stars it didn't."

Since she believes she has fulfilled her daily news intake, Alice carries her cereal bowl, spoon and glass to the sink, rinses the same and slips out the back door. She runs swiftly down the worn path and looks under the bushes until she spots Sadie staring back. "There you are sweet thing. Come out and let me see your arm."

Sadie climbs from under the bushes and squats by Alice's side, where she obediently holds out her arm to allow Alice to inspect the burns. After the first two days, the blisters broke and drained. The grease Alice placed on Sadie's burns helped ease her pain until they scabbed over. "They look like they are healing," Alice says.

Sadie bobs her head up and down, as if she really understands. Then for the hundredth time, she signs, "Where is Wilbur?"

"I wish I knew what you're trying to say. If I didn't know better, I would think you can speak in sign language."

Sadie signs, "I am hungry." After seeing the same thing numerous times just before giving the monkey some fruit, Alice knows what her guest means. She hands Sadie the last apple from the pantry. "Here, I hope Mom buys more without asking what happened to the rest." Sadie grins and bites into the fruit.

* * *

From behind, Harold asks, "What is that, Alice?"

Alice stands and lets Sadie hide behind her legs. "She's a monkey, Dad."

Harold approached so quietly neither Alice nor Sadie heard him. Now he looks closely at Sadie. "No, I think that's a chimp. You will have to turn it in to the authorities. There is a story in the newspaper concerning two chimps missing from a research lab at the Army base. Supposedly there is a five-hundred-dollar reward for their return. If that's true, we can put the money in your college fund."

When her father makes up his mind, and where money is concerned, Alice already knows her question or any objections are useless; but still she asks, "Do I have to?"

"Yes Alice, the chimp isn't wild. Just because you found it, he or she doesn't belong to you. You know right from wrong. This animal can't live in the wilds of Colorado. It needs special treatment and food. Maybe it has a mate somewhere. How would you like to be lost and all alone?"

At her father's words, Alice is ashamed for not considering such a scenario. "I never thought of that, Dad. Okay, let's phone the police. Come on sweet thing."

"Is that what you named it?"

Alice smiles at Sadie. "I think she's a girl, and yes, that's the name I picked out. She really is sweet."

Harold pats Alice's head. "In addition to the money, maybe you will be able to visit her as an additional reward."

"That would be nice," Alice says and rolls her eyes back into their sockets without letting her father see.

* * *

After Joe parks his car, he and Kris walk to the research lab. The weather looks as if it will produce another chilly, cheerless, dismal day. A bank of dark grey clouds hangs forebodingly over far-off mountains, blocking the sun. Joe hunches over and pulls the collar of his old coat around his neck to keep out the cold wind.

When Jerry meets them at the door, he shakes their hands and leads them down the hall to Mona's office, where he says, "Doctor, Sergeant Francone and an FBI Agent are here to see you."

"Thanks, Jerry. Please show them in." As they step into her office, Mona says, "Hello, Joe. Who is your friend?"

"Doctor Wilson, this is Agent Kris Hefner from the FBI."

As Mona stands, she laughs. "Don't be so formal, Joe. Remember, we're old friends." Then she turns to her other guest. "Good afternoon, Agent Hefner. Please call me Mona. You are cute, but I suppose you're married."

"Guilty as charged, Mona. Please call me Kris. Thanks for the compliment, but I won't tell my wife what you said."

Jerry turns to go, and Joe calls after him, "Would you stick around for a few minutes, Jerry? We have some questions for you." At Joe's words, Jerry's smile turns to a frown, but he says, "Sure."

As Kris sits down in a chair near her desk, Mona takes Joe's arm and leads him to the same comfortable recliner as before, where she asks, "What brings you out here again, Joe?"

Joe notices how Kris looks her over from head to toe, with a long pause on her breastworks. *Kris might be married, but can still look. I knew he was my kind of guy.*

* * *

After Joe phoned to make this appointment, he stopped by his apartment. Instead of having lunch, he shaved again and put on his best blue suit, a clean white shirt and light-blue tie. He even went so far as to brush his worn, but still serviceable and comfortable, steel-tipped black shoes. The last time he was here, he looked like a bum. Today, Joe wants Mona to see the real him. *Whatever that might be,* he thinks.

* * *

After Joe is seated, he says, "Kris is the newest member of our team. We are interested in the story concerning the terrorists that Wilbur and Sadie told Katie. By the way, I am sorry to hear she was killed in the explosion on Mulberry Street."

"We're all saddened by Katie's death," Mona says. Joe knows she means what she said. Her eyes turn misty, and she dabs at them with a tissue. "Katie was a real asset. She loved Wilbur and Sadie."

"Yeah, I know," Joe says. "Were you aware the two chimps were with Katie when her vehicle was hit by the truck? We found Wilbur's body, but not Sadie's. Do you have any idea why they were with her?"

"No I don't. The night before the accident Jerry phoned about ten-thirty to report Sadie and Wilbur were missing. He thought Katie took them, but I thought they were probably frightened and hiding somewhere. I didn't know of Katie's story or I would have been more concerned. We will miss Wilbur, too. Is there any report on Sadie's whereabouts?"

Joe turns to Jerry. "No, but I would like to know why you blew off Katie's story concerning the terrorists, Jerry. Would you tell us why, in this day and age, you didn't consider her tale could possibly be true?"

Jerry becomes defensive. "How could I know Katie would be killed? I thought the chimps were putting her on. Maybe they saw something on TV to give them the idea. The smarter chimps watch CNN, and you know terrorists are the main theme of their news."

Kris interrupts to say, "Yes, but that doesn't excuse your behavior. Now Katie is dead, as is one of her witnesses, and the other is missing. If you had allowed her to act on her beliefs, maybe all three would be alive and we would know the entire story. Now, thanks to you, all that remains is a mystery and perhaps a real terrorist threat we know nothing about."

Jerry's face turns red, but he remains defiant. "I don't have to remain here to be insulted. I did what I thought was best for the lab and job security. I still don't believe Wilbur and Sadie knew anything. You will have to prove that to me."

"If we find Sadie, maybe we'll get lucky," Kris says. "But tell us everything Katie said, Jerry. Think it through and don't miss a word. Did she take notes, and if so, where are they?"

"Yeah, Katie made notes, but I don't know where they are - probably at her house, or she had them with her."

As Joe does the same, Kris takes his notebook from a pocket. "Okay, we'll look for her notes later. Tell us what she said."

"Katie said the chimps told her two men killed someone with a gun behind their cage. These guys were supposedly terrorists planning to attack the U.S.A. That's all she said - nothing more. Katie wanted to phone the police, but I told her what the chimps signed was nonsense. She finally agreed."

"Again, thanks to you, Katie took drastic action on her own," Joe says, and Kris nods in agreement. Then Joe continues the questioning. "Are you sure that is all Katie said?"

"Yeah, like I said, I didn't believe her story or want to hear more baloney. She asked me to speak with the chimps, and I refused. I'm sorry."

Mona looks at Jerry with contempt. "You should be."

"That's all, Jerry," Joe says. "You can go."

As Jerry slinks from the office like a guy that knows he is in trouble with his boss, Joe has the idea if Mona has anything to do with his job performance, Jerry won't have his cushy lab position much longer. At the same time, Kris' and Joe's thoughts are identical: *It couldn't happen to a nicer guy.*

After Jerry closes the door, Kris asks, "Did Katie say anything concerning this story to you, Mona?"

"No, I heard of her fears for the first time from Jerry the night he discovered Wilbur and Sadie missing. I wish Katie had spoken with me before taking them. I would have listened. I hope we aren't too late to hear Sadie's version of what happened. On the same subject, I phoned the newspaper, told them two chimpanzees were missing and offered a five-hundred-dollar reward each for their return."

"Maybe Sadie will be found," Joe says. "I wish you had checked with me before giving the story to the press. Now the perps will know Sadie is still alive. We have to find her before they do."

Joe gets up reluctantly. "I think we'll head back to the office. Thanks for your time, Mona. I hope to see you again soon."

Mona gives him another of her more-than-a-Mona-Lisa smiles. "Stop by anytime, Joe."

* * *

Claude finds he is dreaming again. In this fantasy, he is standing at the small, dark, smoky bar of the Zum Giesenend Restaurant in Osterath, Germany watching Frau Schmidt finish putting a frothy head on a large tankard of ale. In his mind, he relishes the delicious, liquorish taste of the schnapps he just drank, and longs for another.

* * *

Then, without warning, he comes violently awake as someone pours a fiery liquid down his throat. Claude chokes and coughs and lunges forward. His movements bring such pain to his shoulder he cries out in alarm, "What the hell?" From out of the darkness, a woman's voice says, "It's only the booze you asked for."

Claude looks down to discover he is still seated in her Pontiac with a blanket wrapped around his upper torso and legs. His sudden movement caused part of the cover to fall from his shoulders and bunch in the small of his back.

He turns his head slowly to the right, and for the first time is afforded a partial view of his savior. She is tall - approximately five feet and seven inches, and has a full head of long, red hair. For a fleeting moment a passing car's headlights are reflected in her eyes, and he notes she has deep-blue irises. The roofline of the car and darkness of the night partially obscure her face. But from past experiences, Claude knows with that hair and those eyes, she can't be ordinary. He attempts to smile through his pain. "Thanks again. I must have passed out."

"You're welcome. I couldn't carry you, so I went into the house and got you a double shot of whiskey. I hoped the liquor would bring you around so you could walk. Are you ready to try?"

"Let me finish the booze. It might help and sure can't hurt."

Claude takes the glass and drinks the remainder in one long satisfying gulp. Immediately, he feels warmth flowing throughout his body. "Two more of those and I'll let you operate with a dull knife."

Then pain turns his attempt at comedy into a frown. Although she chuckles, she also warns, "No more curb service. If you need additional liquor, you'll have to walk to the house. Take it easy and lean on me. You're still bleeding, but not much. After I sew and cover the wound, I think you will be okay."

"I hope you have ether or something to knock me out."

"I thought you were a big, macho man."

As Claude gets to his feet, he feels wobbly. "Not that macho. Okay, I'm ready. Let's give it a bloody good go."

CHAPTER 10

At 8:00 a.m., the phone on Joe's dresser rings, and he reaches out to grasp the instrument. His mind is still foggy from the drinks he and Fad poured down last night after work at O'Grady's, so he isn't functioning too well this morning. His mouth feels like half the Russian Army marched through during the night. From the foul taste left behind, Joe feels most stopped to take a dump. But he picks up the receiver and asks, "Yeah, what's up?"

Bert's voice sounds happy. "Bert here with good news, Buddy; Sadie has been found alive and well. Chalk one up for the good guys."

"Where is she, Bert?"

"A little girl named Alice Grabowski found her the day after the explosion. I guess Alice wanted to keep her, but her dad discovered her secret, saw the reward notice, and called it in. Alice and her folks live about four blocks from the crime scene, on Laurel Avenue – five twenty-six to be exact. I asked them to keep Sadie inside until you arrive. So far, the press hasn't got wind of the story."

"Thanks, Bert. I owe you one." After writing down the address and climbing out of bed, Joe's reflection in the mirror tells him more than he wants to know. *Hung over and hanging out. I have to go on a diet. What will Mona think?*

He laughs at his thoughts and smiles at his ugly, sorry-looking self in the mirror. For some reason, his reflection doesn't return the gesture. *I guess he's mad at me. Hell, I am too.*

Joe attempts to shave without an accident, but nicks his chin in two places and curses aloud. Then he searches for, but can't locate his little white styptic pencil. He finally gives in and puts small pieces of toilet paper on the cuts. "Today is going to be one of those days."

His blue suit lays rumpled on the floor. Apparently, he spilled beer on the left trouser leg, but they are better than his brown ones. Besides, as hung over as he is, Joe really doesn't give a damn concerning the way he looks. After brushing the suit coat, he pulls on a clean shirt and climbs into the wrinkled outfit. Leaving his tie behind, he heads out the door.

This morning is warm and small puffy white clouds dot an otherwise empty blue sky. High overhead, Joe sees two contrails from jets and wonders where they are headed. *I hope they're going somewhere with sandy beaches and topless girls serving tall cold drinks. I vote for anywhere but here, where they kill at the slightest provocation.*

He pauses at the corner Quick-Stop for Danish and a leaky cardboard container of coffee, two days old from the taste of it. Then he drives carefully over potholed streets while drinking the burned-tasting liquid. With his luck, a few drops fall onto his suit coat. The roll contains raisins, which Joe hates. They remind him of dead flies on a pile of manure. But rather than picking out the little fruit pieces and making a worse mess, he chokes them down.

Twelve minutes after leaving his apartment, Joe pulls up in front of a row of town homes at the address Bert gave him and looks down at his note pad. "Damn, I didn't get the unit number."

Without thinking of the consequences, he promises, *No more booze on work nights.* But as soon as the thought is planted in his mind, Joe knows the vow is a lie. Too much liquor ruined his marriage, and now is about the only thing that keeps him going when the job gets tough. Having to relax with the assistance of booze after a difficult day of working with bloody bodies or worse was something his ex-wife, Shirley never understood.

After climbing from the aging wreck the city politely calls a police cruiser, Joe brushes most crumbs from his suit jacket, carefully removes and discards the bloody toilet paper bits and walks to the main entrance where several mailboxes hang haphazardly from a wall. Two have no names or numbers, and he wonders, *How do they receive their mail unless the mailman is a mind reader?*

One of the other boxes, number 4, displays the name Grabowski, hand-written with a black marking pen in neat letters. Joe thinks kindly, *It must be Alice's work.* He turns to his left and makes his way to the entrance of number 4, where he knocks politely and waits for someone to answer.

A young girl of 9 or 10 opens the door until the chain catches and peers at him with suspicion in her brown eyes. "Are you a policeman?"

"Yeah, I am, Honey. My name is Joe. Are you Alice?"

"Let me see your badge and I. D.," she demands.

"Sure," Joe says, reaches into his back pocket and removes his identification folder and billfold with his shield attached to the inside. After taking the I.D. card from its holder, he hands it and the open wallet to Alice. *You've been watching too many episodes of Law and Order, haven't you, kiddo?*

Her thin arm reaches through the small space the chain allows and removes the items from his grasp. The door closes, but Joe notices the lock doesn't engage as she looks over the papers. Then she pulls on the door again and holds up Joe's picture to compare to the apparition standing on her doorstep. "You look a lot younger in this picture."

Thanks a lot, Joe thinks. "Yeah, I probably do. That was taken a few years ago, but it is really me."

Alice returns the items. "Okay, I believe you. I'm Alice Grabowski, the one that phoned. Are you here to pick up the chimpanzee?"

"Yeah, Alice, I am. Thanks for finding and taking such good care of Sadie. Was she hurt in the fire?"

Alice squeals in delight. "Is Sadie her name?" Without waiting for an answer, she says, "Yes, she was. Sadie had blisters on one arm and the hair on her back was singed."

From behind Alice, a man's voice says, "Open the door, Alice, and let the officer in." She pushes the door shut again, and the chain rattles. Then the door swings open wide, and Joe gets a good look at Alice wearing red flip-flops and a brown dress dotted with multicolored flowers.

Sadie is standing close by Alice's side. She waves, and Joe says, "Hi Sadie; how are you?"

Sadie signs, "Where is Wilbur?"

Alice says, "Sadie has been doing that all the time she has been here. I think she's asking about her mate."

"Could be," Joe says.

Harold holds out his hand. "I'm Harold Grabowski." As they shake hands, Joe says, "Pleased to meet you, Sir. Thanks for your call. We needed to locate Sadie in the worst way. I hope you will keep this to yourself for a few days. Sadie is an important witness to a crime, and I don't want anyone knowing we found her."

"Sure," Harold says. "Didn't the newspaper say something about a five-hundred-dollar reward?"

"Yeah, it did. Don't worry; I'll make sure Alice receives the money. As far as I am concerned, she is a real hero."

"Did you hear the policeman, Alice?" Harold asks. "Maybe they will put your picture in the paper." Alice rolls her eyes, and Joe winks at her, but Harold doesn't notice. "That will have to wait for a while," Joe says. "Are you ready to go, Sadie?"

Sadie looks up at Alice with sorrowful eyes and seems reluctant to let go of her hand. But finally, she does and grasps Joe's fingers with her paw. "Good girl," Joe says while showing Sadie his teeth. He asks, "How about a grin?" Sadie grins and her breath resembles fresh bananas.

Joe wonders what his breath smells like. *Probably Russian crap, Danish, dead flies, manure and stale coffee; what a great combination.*

As small tears run down her cheeks, Alice slides to her knees beside Sadie and hugs her tight. But in spite of her sadness, she attempts to smile. "I will miss you, Sadie. I love you."

Sadie signs "I love you." Harold is amazed. "Hey, I know what that means. The chimp just said she loves Alice in sign language. Can you believe it?"

Joe says, "Yeah I can. Sadie is a smart girl."

Harold stands there with his mouth hanging open like a Venus flytrap awaiting its next victim. Joe reaches down and pats Alice on the head, while winking at her again. Reluctantly, Alice lets go of Sadie. As Joe and Sadie walk toward his cruiser he says, "Thanks again, Alice."

Sadie blows Alice a kiss over her shoulder, and lurching back and forth like a drunken sailor on a three-day binge in San Diego, gallops alongside Joe.

* * *

In the converted kitchen of a three-room cabin 20 miles north of Sulfur Springs, Felix is seated at a work bench surveying his surroundings. The sun is hiding behind several dark clouds to the west, the evening is cool, and a scent of rain is in the air. A light wind blows through the window making the thin curtains flap slowly like sails of a pirate ship.

Why Felix is associating with terrorists and planning mass murder on a scale unheard of before is difficult to explain. He has a good job, and until a drunken Jewish driver killed them, also had a beautiful wife and family.

Perhaps that was the deciding factor for Felix's involvement. Since the day of the accident he has despised the Jewish faith. Such unwarranted hatred has warped Felix's mind, but he doesn't realize how truly mad he is. His burning desire is revenge, and the murder of thousands, perhaps hundreds of thousands doesn't enter his mind as being far beyond retribution.

In his madness, he knows all Jews are rich. Since only rich people are able to afford the high-priced tickets to the Cotton Bowl, accordingly everyone attending the game must be Jewish. Therefore; all attendees must die.

There are a very few times when Felix actually feels remorse. But then, thoughts of his lovely wife, Carmen, and their two small children, Roberto and Carlos, return, and his rage blocks any rational point of view.

While watching the curtains flap, Felix is frightened. This morning he read the report of the missing chimps and an offer of a sizable reward for their return. So far, the newspapers haven't reported them being killed in the fire. Felix wonders why.

Maybe I screwed up. Did Mister Jones do his job or miss them? I forgot to inquire about the chimps before Mohammed wasted him. That was stupid. If they are out there somewhere running loose, someone that knows sign language might recognize what they say. That's all we need.

The wind blows stronger and cooler, so Felix stands up, closes the window and pulls down a sweater from a nail, puts it on and continues to ponder. There also hasn't been a thing in the local rag about an unidentified man being discovered in the canal. *Did the fish take care of Mister Jones or is he still alive? I should have made sure.*

Felix read the story concerning Larry Holgram's murder on the third page. He was surprised Larry had surfaced so quickly, and smiles inwardly at his sick pun. But at the present time, Felix can't be bothered with such mundane things. Mohammed is on his case to have the nerve gas transferred into 32 of 36 fire extinguishers he purchased. The transfer will take some time. One little slip and Felix will be dead instead of their intended victims.

To hell with Mohammed; he isn't about to risk his life to be here when I prepare the bombs.

* * *

Over the past year, Felix manufactured a small laboratory in this tiny isolated cabin. Now he possesses all the equipment required to transfer nerve gas from the lab container and allow the liquid to flow, one ounce at a time, into each empty fire extinguisher. While purchasing the equipment piece by piece, one here and another there, from ten different stores in six cities, Felix always paid cash and used phony I.D.

Mohammed and his terrorist friends provided the unique detonators, primer cord and a small amount of C-4 plastic explosive to complete the devices. Each tiny remotely-controlled detonator is formed into a replica of the seal attached to every fire extinguisher. Just as the real item, the federal electrical inspection logo is imprinted on the face of each. The primer cord replaces waxed strings that run around the handle and through the seal.

With a single command, the remote control box setting at one end of Felix's workbench will detonate all bombs simultaneously. The detonator ignites the primer cord, which in turn sets off the C-4 and blows the container apart, thereby releasing the pressurized nerve gas into the stadium air. There are thirty-one entrances to the Cotton Bowl stands and reserved and box seats. The terrorists intend to place a bomb at each to cover the entire field.

"As the warm afternoon wind increases, the nerve gas should spread throughout the surrounding cities, killing thousands, perhaps hundreds of thousands," Mohammed said.

The location of the last bomb is in close proximity to the President's private front-row box located at the 50 yard line, so the leader of the free world and his party will have no chance to escape. The site is Felix's idea, and enthralled Mohammed. "No one will notice. Your plan is brilliant, Felix."

Felix glowed with pride. "I had the idea while watching re-runs of past Cotton Bowl games. The motorized stretcher used to carry injured players or for other emergencies is always there with a fire extinguisher attached at the rear. The stretcher sets near the middle of the sidelines, adjacent to the Presidential box. If the other devices don't kill him, this one will."

Even if the Feds are smart enough to discover the nerve gas came from the Sulfur Springs lab, Felix feels confident no one will be able to trace his movements or connect him to the attack. Before leaving, he will burn the cabin to destroy any residual evidence.

All these plans aren't worrying him. Plenty of time remains to prepare the bombs. Mohammed will have to wait until Felix solves another problem. The only weak link now is Grady. The police questioned him, and although Grady claims he can handle them, Felix has no further use of him. Now that the nerve gas has been removed from the lab, Grady's services are no longer required. "He will be one less link to me."

But how can he kill Grady and not leave a body to be discovered? Although he fervently supports the IRA, Grady is a good family man. If he cheated on his wife, perhaps Felix could set up a phony sex scene, making Grady appear to have been killed in an unfortunate accident while with a prostitute. But Felix doesn't think such a scenario would fly.

Mohammed wants to waste Grady as they did Mister Jones, but such action is too risky. Another murder even remotely connected with the chemical lab will surely make the Feds suspicious. *No, Grady's death has to be an accident, and if possible, his body shouldn't be found. And the solution to my problem has to happen soon.*

If the cops call Grady in and get rough, Felix doesn't know if he will keep his mouth shut. With two small kids, Grady would talk to save them. "Yeah, Grady has to go."

* * *

As Claude and his companion stagger into her home, he leans heavily on her shoulder, glances around the living room and notes a cozy domestic scene. The room contains a fireplace with a small log pile at one side, a green upholstered couch with wooden arms along the far wall and two comfortable-looking recliner chairs in a dark brown materiel setting a few feet away

Light shines from two matching sea-shell-filled glass lamps setting on small pine end tables. Several paintings of ships and the sea hang from two walls, and light-green drapes frame a wide window that overlooks the canal where Claude took a dive a few minutes ago.

They stop to rest, and her breath comes in short gasps. "Well, we got this far. I didn't think you were so heavy. Here, sit down in this chair. I can't hold you up much longer."

"Thanks again. What's your name? I can't continue saying, 'Hey you'."

"Carla – Carla Roberson. What is yours?"

He says, "Just call me Mister Macho," and her smile fades into a frown.

* * *

Claude takes time to study her from head to toe, while Carla stands still, watching his eyes take in every aspect of her body. Just as he thought, she is beautiful. While not gorgeous, she is more than pretty, with nicely-tanned skin from face to feet. Displaying an even coat of light-red polish to match her fingernails, her toenails peek out from brown leather sandals.

Carla's hands are not big, but larger than average, with long, slender manicured fingers. Her silky skin is smooth and tight at the base of her neck, so Claude estimates her age as somewhere in the late twenties. She has curves in the right places, shapely legs, wide thighs and nice breasts.

* * *

When his eyes return to Carla's face, she asks, "Have you seen enough?"

"Yeah, you are a well-put-together package, Carla. I mean that comment in a nice way. I'm not making a pass."

Her smile returns. "Thanks, but I'm not the one that needs to be looked at or after. That is you. We will get your wet clothes off and then patch you up. How do you feel?"

"Like I was in a hatchet fight without a hatchet. My shoulder burns, but the rest of my body feels like I am about to freeze."

Carla nods knowingly. "You're probably suffering from hypothermia. Here, let me take off those wet clothes. Don't be squeamish. I've seen men's bods before. You're nothing special."

In spite of his pain, Claude laughs. "Now you've hurt my pride. Go ahead. I'll help where I can."

Between them, they pull off his trousers without much difficulty or pain. The shirt is easy. Carla rips the remainder of the torn material from his back and good arm. Then she tears his bloody t-shirt from his body. "Just like Marlon Brando in 'A Streetcar Named Desire'," Claude says. If you don't mind, I'll keep my shorts on."

After she wraps a fresh, warm blanket around his legs and puts another over his left shoulder, Carla asks, "Why? Are you bashful?" Claude attempts to tuck the second wrap around him, but requires her assistance. "Thanks, that's better. I feel warmer already."

She hands him a jelly glass half-full of whiskey. "Here, have another stiff drink. You will require several before I am able to work on your shoulder. The good news is; your wound quit bleeding."

Claude pours half the liquor down his throat and coughs as the booze hits bottom. Within a few seconds warmth spreads throughout his body. He looks down at where the bullet entered his chest area just below the collarbone. He can't see the exit wound, but can feel the hole.

By using Carla's makeup mirror and another smaller one, he gets a good look at his injury. When he attempts to move his shoulder, although there is pain, there is no sound of a bone grating on another. When he flexes his fingers, Claude discovers they react to his mind's directions. With Carla's assistance, he finds he can swing his arm a couple inches each way, but his chest is sore and painful to the touch. Carla says, "You already have a large bruise there."

Claude can't tell her that he wore a flak jacket and was also shot in the chest. She already has enough on her plate. So, he lies. "I think that is a result of my hitting a piling as I fell into the canal. At first, I thought my shoulder or arm was broken. Now I know I was in shock. The bullet went straight through and didn't hit a bone."

After studying the two openings for a few moments, Carla says, "That's also my opinion."

When he finishes the drink, Carla pours him another. "So, while we wait for you to get plastered, do you want to tell me who shot you and why?"

"I can't tell you everything, Carla. Suffice to say the other fellow and I had a disagreement over money, and I was the loser. I believe the jerk thinks he killed me. In fact, I am counting on it."

"Oh good, then you will shoot 'the jerk', and if you don't kill him, someone else will patch him up, right? When does the feud end?"

Without thinking, Claude moves and grimaces at the sudden pain. "Hopefully when he is dead instead of me."

"Is killing him really necessary?" she asks. "Can't you just go to the police?"

"No, I can't. Please don't ask for more now. All I need is some assistance and time to recover. Then I'll get out of your hair and let you live the good life again."

Carla's lips change into a pout. "And I am supposed to smile and wave as you leave, and go back to work like nothing ever happened, right?"

Claude sighs at her stubbornness. "My story and life are too complicated now without getting you involved. Trust me; I don't want you hurt. Let us be ships that pass in the night."

"Drink your drink," Carla commands, and Claude sees fire in her eyes. "I'll get my sewing box. You know Mister Macho, I'm going to enjoy patching you up and watching you squirm with every stitch."

CHAPTER 11

After Joe opens the door to Mona's office, he calls out, "Here is Sadie," like he is Ed McMahon introducing Johnny Carson on the Tonight Show. His shout makes Sadie howl like a coyote seriously looking for a mate. She gallops into Mona's office on all fours and jumps up on the desk, where she scatters papers, pens and folders in all directions. The effect isn't exactly what Joe was aiming for, but does get Mona's attention.

"Hello, you two. God, I am glad to see you Sadie. Where have you been?" She takes Sadie's hand and helps her climb down from the desk.

Joe says, "I feel like Cinderella. Everyone gets noticed but me. Aren't you happy to see me, too?"

"Grow up, Joe," Mona says, but smiles, so he knows she is glad to see him, also. "Where did you find our little lost girl?"

"I didn't - an eleven-year-old named Alice found her the day after the fire. She kept Sadie hidden behind her house. Her father finally caught on when all the apples and bananas in the house disappeared. He had Alice phone us and I went out. By the way, Mister Grabowski is very interested in receiving the reward."

"I'll make sure Alice has a check," Mona says. "Give me her address, and I'll stop by to see her tomorrow."

Joe checks his notebook again. "526 Laurel Avenue, Apartment 4. You will love the kid. Alice is cute as apple pie a-la-mode and really broken up about having to part with Sadie."

"I'll make it up to her. Now, you little dickens, we'll put you back where you belong."

"Where is Wilbur?" Sadie signs.

"What do I tell her?" Mona asks. "She is asking about Wilbur."

Joe shakes his head to say he doesn't know. "Her day will probably be ruined if she learns Wilbur went to the big jungle in the sky. Maybe Wilbur is off visiting friends. Tell her any story to keep her happy. If she believes he will return soon, she won't be upset and forget what Larry told her."

"Your idea is cruel, but I agree," Mona says and signs, "Wilbur is on a trip to find a new home."

Sadie still looks forlorn, but instead of a frown, her grin returns and she asks, "For me?"

Mona lies and feels like hell. "Yes, for you and Wilbur."

Joe asks, "Is there some place we can hide Sadie until we debrief her?"

"No, not here. Don't you have any empty cells at the jail?"

At her response, Joe chuckles and asks, "A cell for a chimp?"

"You already have a lot of apes there," Mona says and grins. "What is one more?"

"You got me," Joe says and laughs. "Yeah, I suppose I can clear her hiding there with the boss. Red might not like the idea, but when I tell him why, he will understand. I should have thought of that possibility, but I was in a hurry to return Sadie and see you again. Oops, that slipped out."

As he blushes again, Mona says, "I'm flattered, Joe."

* * *

The day after Sadie returned to the lab, and Joe jailed her, Mona stops by the Grabowski home to speak with Alice. She discovers Alice looking sad as she sits alone on the back stoop with her legs dangling over the foundation, letting them swing back and forth.

Alice also has a handful of stones in her left hand, which she takes one at a time, aims at nothing in particular and throws them into the littered yard. The forlorn look on Alice's face breaks Mona's heart. She says, "Hi, Alice. I am Doctor Wilson from the research laboratory. Thanks for finding Sadie. We missed her."

Without looking up, Alice says, "Not as much as I do," and throws another pebble that hits a tin can with a loud ping and ricochets into the bushes where Sadie hid just yesterday.

"I know what you mean," Mona says. "May I sit down? I love to let my feet dangle and pretend I'm a princess."

"Sure, go ahead," Alice says. "Be my guest." Then she asks, "Are you a real doctor? Do you cut up monkeys, chimps or people?"

"No, I don't, Alice. I'm not that kind of doctor. The title in front of my name is an honorary thing that says I went to college and earned a fancy degree. There are many doctors of my kind in the world, but we don't cut up anybody or anything."

"That's good. I hate to think anyone would harm Sadie."

"We would never do that. Sadie is much too smart and valuable. She is as close to a human as she can be without actually being one. Do you understand?"

"You mean because Sadie can sign?"

"Exactly. We hope Sadie will help children learn sign language and make life fun at the same time. Would you like to learn to sign? That way you could speak with Sadie."

"Would you teach me?" Mona hugs Alice tight. "Yes I will. You are a very special young lady, Alice. Everyone at the lab is proud of you. We know you didn't want to part with Sadie, but knew what was best for her and did. That makes you wiser than many older people I know."

As joy replaces sorrow, Alice looks up and asks, "When can I begin? I would love to see Sadie again and be able to speak with her."

Mona smiles and asks, "Why don't you ask your father to bring you to the lab tomorrow morning at 10:00? I'll show you the animals and cages, and then we'll go visit Sadie. They have her in protective custody, and she will be glad to see you. By the way, I have your reward check. Your father says you have a college fund. Someday you may have a fancy doctor title in front of your name and work with animals the way I do."

As she hugs Mona in return, Alice exclaims, "Oh, I hope so."

* * *

Felix phones Grady and asks, "So, how did things go with the cops?"

To protect his macho image, Grady lies. "No problem. A big black buck called me everything but a white man and tried his best to intimidate me, but I was cool. I told the story just like you said. After an hour, they released me. The black sucker thought he was tough, but I showed him."

Since Felix knows Grady isn't as macho as he acts, he thinks, *I'll bet.* But he says, "That's good, but do you think the cops will want to speak with you again?" Grady continues his macho bravado. "I don't know, but if they do, they won't get a thing from me. They will have to find me first. On Saturday, I'm headed to Mexico for some deep-pit caving."

"Is that smart, Grady. Won't the police think you ran away?"

"Nah, this trip has been planned for months. I'm not about to cut out. I'll be back next week. If the cops want to question me again, I can beat them at their own game."

A plan begins to take shape in Felix's mind. "Are you going alone? I understand caves are dangerous." Unseen, Grady shakes his head. "A buddy of mine, Clete Palmer is going with me. We've explored two deep-pit caves in Mexico before, *El Sotano* and *Las Golondinas*, and have the right equipment and know what to do. Relax, we'll be okay."

"Your trip sounds exciting," Felix says. "Where are you headed this time?"

"A cavern called *Diablo's Hideout*. Not many people know about the place, because it's in the middle of nowhere. This cave is over four hundred feet deep. We should have a blast."

"Have fun, but be careful, Grady. Phone me when you return."

"Will do. Lighten up, Felix. I was cool." He doesn't mean it, but Felix says, "Yeah." After Grady hangs up, Felix listens to the buzz of the phone for a few moments as pieces of his plan begin to take shape. Then he puts down the instrument and makes some notes on a nearby scratch pad. A few minutes later, he says, "Yeah," again, but this time means it.

* * *

Since the last time he visited with Joe, Kris has been busier than a fire ant feeding his queen. After obtaining a search warrant for Katie's residence, he and four other agents descended the next day on her apartment. To Kris' bitter disappointment, they found no notes supporting a supposed terror attack. He didn't expect they would, as Katie probably would have had them with her when she left to meet him, and they burned in the fire.

In case they somehow survived, he drove to the police impoundment yard to check the burned shell of her crushed Volvo. The seats were nothing but charred and rusted springs with small pieces of burned upholstery clinging bravely here and there. Fire decimated the interior of the car and nothing salvageable remained. The vehicle smelled of burned flesh, and Kris was happy when his inspection ended. If paper notes existed before, now they were long gone.

The next morning when he meets Joe in the office, Kris says, "The only thing we found was a melted and twisted piece of plastic that looked like a briefcase handle." Joe nods and says, "I remember the scene vividly. The fire did a number on Katie, Wilbur and everything inside."

Kris says, "Yeah, gasoline will do that. Then he asks, "So where does this leave us?" Joe shrugs to display helplessness. "This afternoon, Mona will be here accompanied by Alice. She will ask Sadie to tell her story. Then we will follow any leads we develop from their conversation. If anyone can decipher what Larry told Sadie, Mona will. She worked with Sadie since the beginning of the program."

"That sounds good, Joe. Do you want me to stay?"

"Nah, there is no reason to waste your day here. As soon as we develop any leads, I'll phone, and we can study Sadie's story together." Kris smiles knowingly. "I think you want Mona all to your lonesome. Remember, when she walks in, you'll have to watch the other cops. They will froth at the mouth."

"Yeah, I know," Joe says. "But I can handle them. I guess you know I really like her." Kris chuckles and pats Joe's back. "When you blush so much, it's self-evident. I must admit she is a good-looking woman and has a chest that won't quit."

As he remembers an old joke, Joe smiles and asks, "Do you know why men can't make eye contact, Kris?"

"No; why not?"

"Because boobies don't have eyes."

* * *

When she sees her friend behind bars, Alice cries out, "Oh Sadie, they put you in jail." Mona shakes her head and says, "I told you that Joe had Sadie in protective custody. Sadie isn't a jailbird. She has been having a ball."

That is evident from the many banana peels and orange rinds surrounding Sadie, where she is seated atop a fold-down bed in her cell. Mona thinks, *Every cop in the building must be feeding her. I hope she doesn't get sick.*

"Hello," Sadie signs to Alice. "I am pleased to see you again."

"What did she say?" Alice asks.

"Sadie says, 'She is pleased to see you again'. Here, let me show you how to say 'Hello'." Mona makes the signs, and Alice copies them.

"How do I say 'I love you'?"

"Follow me," Mona says.

"I love you, too," Sadie replies, and Mona asks, "See how easy that was?"

"I want to learn everything," Alice says.

"I'll teach you all the signs, but not today. As your dad to bring you to the lab on weekends, and we will work together. Would you like that, Alice?"

"Can I help teach the monkeys and chimps?"

"Sure, as fast as you learn, you will take my place in a year."

"No, I won't. Look." Alice signs, "I love you" to Mona. Tears forms in her eyes as Mona says, "Thanks, Honey. I love you too."

Joe walks up to greet his two visitors. "It looks like you two are doing okay. I'm sorry I couldn't meet you, but I had to interview a witness to a robbery. I see Bert showed you where Sadie is. She is doing okay, isn't she?"

Mona laughs. "She has eaten far too many bananas. You'll be sorry when she has to go potty." Joe joins in the laughter. "I'll send one of our rookies down here to deal with that problem. I will also tell the guys to knock off the food. Ever since she arrived, Sadie has been a hit."

Bert adds, "Sadie is a lot more fun than most apes we have here."

"I told Joe she would be," Mona says.

Joe nods his head toward Alice. "We need to speak with Sadie about Larry." Mona catches his drift and turns to Alice. "I think we have taken up enough of Sadie's time for today, Alice. Let me take you home, and we will see her again soon."

"Okay," Alice says, as she reaches into the cell and wags her fingers. Sadie jumps down from her perch and runs to meet her. Alice says, "Be good. Remember I love you." She signs the message to Sadie, who grins and repeats it.

"This is how you say 'goodbye'," Mona says.

"Goodbye," Alice signs, gives Sadie another pat on the head and turns to take Mona's hand. Mona smiles at Joe. "I'll be back shortly." Joe's heart does a jump through a hoop. He knows he blushed again, and Bert saw his red face, but he doesn't care.

* * *

Kris isn't the only one that has been busy. Felix feels as if he has run the mile in three and a half minutes. His plan is taking shape, but took some doing.

* * *

After driving his pickup truck to a local sports shop, Felix rented a four-wheeled ATV and a ramp to load and unload the small vehicle. The dealer named Harry helped load the ATV and tie down the vehicle and ramp. Then he said, "Be careful out there. If you do foolish things, these things are dangerous. This four-wheeled model is more stable than a three-wheeler. Just don't attempt anything dumb like doing a wheelie, and you will be okay."

"Thanks for the help and warning. I'll see you next week."

At a local electronics store, Felix purchased a Ground Positioning System, (GPS), with a receiver and antenna, plus several other necessary items. At a nearby convenience store, he added a few packages of freeze-dried food that supposedly tasted fine without cooking. But in case the food wasn't as great as the labels proclaimed, when he reached the checkout, Felix picked up a handful of candy bars.

After loading everything aboard his pickup, Felix stopped and filled both gas and water cans at a service station. Then he drove home and parked and locked the vehicle inside his garage where it would be safe from thieves. In his neighborhood, if you leave a truck or car outside unattended for five minutes, nothing is sacred and everything is fair game. Then Felix went inside his small home and phoned for a taxi. When the cab arrived ten minutes later, he told the driver, "Take me to the Swifty rental place downtown."

"Sure Mac."

Forty-five minutes later, Felix returned at the wheel of a dark-blue Chevy Cavalier, parked the car in his driveway, locked the vehicle and went inside to eat lunch.

* * *

Later in the evening, as the sun was setting behind nearby mountains with an awesome display of brilliant colors, Felix emerged dressed in dark clothing, with a pair of binoculars in a grey leather case hanging from his neck on a leather strap. He climbed into the rental car and fired up the engine, drove across town to where Grady lived, and parked across the street at an angle a half-block away.

Using the binoculars, Felix watched Grady and his friend, Clete pack equipment into the bed of a double-cab, four-wheel-drive Dodge Ram. Grady's two kids ran around causing havoc, while Grady's wife attempted to keep them under control and away from the truck. When everything was packed, Grady and Clete roped a blue tarpaulin across the top, moved the truck closer to the house and went inside. Thirty minutes later Clete came out and climbed into a black Pontiac Firebird at the curb, tooted the horn twice and drove away.

Felix drove a few blocks until he came to a fast food place, where he stopped and went inside to eat dinner and read a local newspaper provided free. He lingered over a cup of hot coffee for an hour longer. At 9:30 Felix stood up, dumped the residue of his meal into a trashcan near the door and returned to his car. He drove slowly until he arrived where he parked previously, and continued to watch the house.

An hour after the lights went out in Grady's bedroom Felix checked the area for pedestrians and saw none. The neighborhood was quiet as chocolate mousse. In the distance, dogs barked occasionally, but none nearby, which was a blessing. Felix hates them.

At midnight, he exited his vehicle and walked across the street and down the sidewalk to Grady's truck. In his hand was the GPS and antenna strapped to a heavy-duty magnet. After crossing the lawn to the Ram, he knelt down and secured the unit under and behind the rear bumper where it wouldn't shake loose on uneven ground. When he pulled on the mechanism with one hand in an effort to extract it; he was unable to do so and thought, *Good enough.*

After returning to the rental car, he climbed in and reached for the receiver to check his work. When the small screen displayed the correct location, Felix smiled, started the engine and drove away.

CHAPTER 12

W hen Mona walks in the door Joe asks, "Are you ready to talk to Sadie?"

As she sits down for a moment, she says, "Yes, I hope she remembers whatever Larry told her. She's smart, but it's a shame we lost Wilbur. He was better at signs than she is."

Behind her, Joe sees four cops ogling Mona's legs and drooling at the mouth. *Kris was right about those yahoos.* Joe stands up and closes the door to eliminate their view, hoping they will disappear before Mona and he head downstairs to the cellblock where Sadie is holding court. He says, "Sadie is our only lead to Larry's murder and whatever happened at the chemical lab. Do you want a cup of coffee or something to drink before we leave?"

"No, Joe. I'm fine and ready when you are." As she stands, for a fleeting moment Joe is afforded a glimpse of black panties, his second favorite color after red. When Mona sees Joe's eyes on her legs, she smiles, and he blushes again.

They make their way through an unusually crowded hallway to the elevator, where three other cops are holding different reports, one of which is upside down. As they all climb aboard, Joe's fellow officers of the law don't pay much attention to their paperwork. Instead, they study their female companion. Joe stares at each and receives large smiles in return. He knows one patrolman named Hal Simmons, so asks, "Do things seem a little hectic on the floor today, Hal?"

With a straight face, Hal says, "Yeah, crime never takes a holiday." The other cops smile and nod knowingly. "You all headed to the basement?" Joe asks.

"Yeah," Hal says.

"That's strange - I thought Records was on the fifth floor." No one replies as the group rides down three floors. Mona keeps a smile on her face, obviously enjoying Joe's predicament and the cops' attention. When the door opens, Hal says, "After you, Miss." Mona steps out, and the cops attempt to blindside Joe, but he elbows his way through and grabs Mona's arm possessively. She looks down at his hand and smiles.

Joe blushes again and curses his fellow officers under his breath as they follow. When they approach the empty cellblock housing Sadie, he says, "No visitors beyond this point. Doctor Wilson and I are here to question a witness. We don't need you clowns hanging around to disturb us. Take off."

"Yes, Sergeant Francone," Hal says. As the trio turns and walks back toward the elevator, Joe sees one cop trip as he attempts to get a last look at Mona's legs. *I hope you fall on your ass.* Joe tightens his grip on Mona's elbow, and she doesn't pull away.

* * *

Two hundred feet down the shaft of Diablo's Hideout, Grady stops his descent and turns slowly to look upward, downward and at the sides of the cavern he and Clete plan to explore. The cave is huge and deep, lined with rugged broken rocks, crevices, outcrops and pinnacles. The pit is more fantastic than he thought it would be. He revels in the fact that for the entire weekend, the cavern is theirs alone to explore.

Above him, Clete is lying on his stomach at the edge, looking down into the abyss in an attempt to see Grady. The fierce sunlight above doesn't penetrate very deep into the cave, so he can barely make out the outline of his buddy against the black rock. Clete can't wait for his turn to ride the cable down into the depths to see the wonders of nature displayed as only she can. Apparently this cave is almost unknown and seldom explored. There isn't the usual litter and trash around the entrance.

* * *

After a long drive and hectic traffic in Nuevo Laredo, they arrived here late yesterday. Clete was glad they were driving Grady's four-wheel-drive vehicle. The last fifty miles of their journey was over rough, pot-holed gravel roads not meant for anything less sturdy than Grady's Dodge Ram. As soon as they found the cave, Clete and Grady set up the apparatus they had manufactured. The rig consists of a long twenty-foot arm resembling a crane, with a sprocket at the end allowing cable from Grady's truck to pass through.

The rig has two pieces of heavy-duty aluminum, both twelve feet long, interlocked for four feet at the center, with eight titanium bolts holding them together. One end is attached to the truck frame over the front bumper. Above that, the winch and pulley unit holds over seven hundred feet of study steel cable capable of hauling a ton of weight, more than enough for their needs.

After the arm was constructed, Grady eased the Ram to within four feet of the cavern edge and parked the vehicle there. Clete reminded him, "Leave the key in the ignition."

Everyone in the cave-crawler community knows the story of a guy that dropped the key to his vehicle out of his pocket on the way down into a deep pit cavern and then couldn't find it. When he and his companions had to walk thirty miles through the hot desert to the nearest civilization, they almost died of dehydration.

Although they know their combined weight won't cause the truck to stand on its nose, just in case, Grady and Clete loaded approximately three hundred pounds of rocks into the bed. Where safety is concerned, there is a right way and a wrong way. They always use the correct method.

As he displayed his latest acquisition, Grady said, "Look at this. I bought a remote control for the winch that has over a thousand feet of wire attached. As we descend, we will feed it out with the cable. The remote control lets us stop wherever we want and then continue downward. I can even have the winch rewind to move upward. We won't have any more quick one-way descents." Clete looked the unit over. "Hey, that's neat. I can't wait for my turn."

Grady jerked his thumb toward the setting sun. "Let's set up camp, eat a bite and get some shut-eye. I'm beat and want to be in good shape for tomorrow."

"I'm with you, buddy," Clete said. He grabbed the two-man tent from the bed of the truck, laid the canvas out on the ground and added, "Hand me the pegs and hammer."

* * *

Two thousand yards away, Felix is lying partially concealed behind a rock, watching his quarry.

* * *

With the GPS, he was able to follow Clete and Grady from a considerable distance. When they turned onto a rocky gravel road, Felix stopped his two-wheel-drive pickup and pulled into a grove of small trees. Watching Clete's and Grady's progress on his receiver, Felix saw them travel farther down the road. Then he unloaded the ATV, packed aboard what gear he thought he might need, hid the truck key under a nearby rock, started the ATV's engine and drove away.

The road is rough, but Felix knew he had all the time in the world, so drove slowly. A high-powered rifle is strapped across the handlebars, and under his left arm in a harness he carries a .38 caliber six-shot revolver. For the next hour, Felix pauses periodically to check the location of Grady and Clete. When they stop ten miles ahead, he thinks, *They must have reached their destination. Grady said the cave was out in the middle of nowhere, and he is right. I couldn't have asked for a better killing field.*

* * *

Although Felix's heritage is Mexican; and with the rifle and revolver hidden under his seat, he experienced no trouble while crossing the border. He had his passport and a Texas driver's license, which was all that was required at the crossing. When a border patrol agent asked about his citizenship, Felix displayed his driver's license and answered truthfully, "United States." Behind his truck, numerous assorted vehicles were waiting in line for blocks, so the harried agent waved Felix through without another thought or inspection. "Drive carefully."

* * *

Now Felix drives slowly so he won't kick up a dust trail. He doubts either prey will notice, but he hasn't lived this long without knowing not to take any unnecessary risks. When the receiver says he is within a mile of their location, he pulls the ATV into a small gully and unloads his supplies. Before leaving afoot, he takes the key with him and piles brush on the vehicle. Then he loads up and heads out at a trot.

When he arrives at his selected hiding spot, Felix sees Grady and Clete have completed their preliminary work prior to descending into the pit and are preparing a campsite. The sun is setting low on the horizon, and to his relief there is no indication of rain or clouds in the vicinity. After unrolling his sleeping bag, Felix lays it out and sits down to test the freeze-dried food.

The first package contains beans and rice, so Felix uses a small knife to cut through one corner and pours in water according to the instructions. After sitting and waiting fifteen minutes while the water is absorbed, he tries a bite, only to discover the food tastes like something a goat puked up. In anger, Felix tosses the foul concoction into the brush and grabs two candy bars instead. Then he washes the foul taste from his mouth, spits the water at the ground and devours the chocolate and nut combination.

I knew the stuff was going to be bad, but not that terrible. I wish I could have a fire, but that can wait until tomorrow.

Felix sets his wristwatch alarm for 0500 hours, lies down in his sleeping roll and covers his head with his cowboy hat. In ten minutes he is asleep like a wolf cub in the warm fuzzy curl of his mother's body.

* * *

"Hello, Sadie." Mona signs. "How are you today?"

"Good," Sadie signs. "Where is Wilbur?"

"Still looking for a home for you," Mona lies.

"Good," Sadie repeats and grins. Mona asks, "Do you remember Larry? He signed a message to you a few days ago."

"Yes, bad man hurt Larry. Make loud noise, hurt ears."

"Yes, that is him. Did Larry ask you to remember something?"

"Yes," Sadie signs.

"Can you tell me?" In reply, Sadie signs, "Bad man, fell X man is and Far East man,"

"Yes, I know they were bad men. What did Larry tell you?"

"Terror is, nervous gas; football game; kill president; thousands." Shocked by her reply, Mona asks, "Where?"

"Cotton; food bowl; fall," Sadie signs. "Wilbur knows, too."

"That is good, Sadie. What else?"

"Hide; three; two; fire; X," Sadie signs, then sets back and begins to pick something from her coat. "Is that all?" Mona asks.

"Yes; bad man; loud noise; Larry hurt; Wilbur and Sadie hide. Where is Wilbur? Sadie needs him." Mona turns to Joe, who has been writing furiously in his notebook as she translated Sadie's signs.

"I guess that's all, Joe. What do you think of her story?"

"I don't know, Mona. I don't like the part about 'kill the president and thousands'. That sounds like a terrorist plot. I wonder if she knows more." Mona shrugs in helplessness. "Let's ask Sadie to repeat the story again and then leave her alone. I can tell she misses Wilbur, and all these questions are upsetting her." Joe nods in agreement. "Okay, but slow down and let me compare my notes to what she says. When we have it all, we will phone Kris and then try to decipher her story."

* * *

Kris decides to speak with Grady again. First he studies Joe and Fad's notes and then phones Grady at home. When Grady's wife answers, Kris says, "Good morning, Mrs. O'Reilly, I'm Agent Hefner from the FBI. May I speak to your husband?"

"Grady isn't here. He left yesterday for a caving trip in Mexico."

"When will he return?"

"He and his buddy, Clete, said they would be back next week. Can I take a message?"

"Please have Grady call me at 555-7923, extension 45."

"I'll ask him to phone when he returns."

"Thanks," Kris says and disconnects. He turns to his partner, Ellis Crowder, and says, "I hope Grady didn't skip out on us." Ellis shakes his head. "I don't think Grady would run and leave his wife and kids here."

"I hope you're right," Kris says, but still isn't convinced.

* * *

When Clete hears a sound behind him, he turns his head to discover Felix standing there with a revolver pointed toward Clete's back. Slowly, without making any moves that the stranger might take as hostile, Clete stands and raises his hands. "Holy cow, man, I didn't know we were trespassing. Put down the gun." Felix keeps the revolver aimed at Clete's chest. "Is Grady at the end of the cable?"

"Yeah, he's about halfway down," Clete says, puzzled by this guy's sudden appearance. "How do you know Grady? Who are you? Man, put down the gun, you're scaring me."

"Thank you," Felix says, and shoots Clete in the chest. From the force of the bullet's impact, Clete reels backward, loses his balance and pitches backward off the cavern edge into empty space.

* * *

After clamping his remote control to the cable, Grady pulls a flashlight from his backpack to study the walls on the opposite side of the cavern. As the light shines into the darkness, the beam reflects from wings of thousands of bats hanging upside down along the walls. As they breathe, their motion resembles a grey tide beating against a distant shore.

Suddenly, Grady hears a loud pop. A moment later a pebble pings against his hard hat. As he turns to glance upward, Grady sees Clete's body falling toward him. In self-defense, he raises his arm, but one of Clete's legs hits his upper arm, knocking the flashlight from Grady's grasp. The impact also breaks his arm in two places so quickly he doesn't have time to scream.

Grady's eyes attempt to follow Clete's descent into the void, but his buddy disappears into the darkness in an instant. In anguish and pain, Grady cries out, "Oh my God!" His damaged arm is useless. In absolute terror, Grady grabs the remote control with his good hand and attempts to punch the up button with his thumb, but misses. Then, from above, Grady hears the roar of his truck engine. "What the hell is happening?"

Grady's second attempt at the control is successful. The cable begins to retract and pull him up, and he cries out, "Thank you, Lord!" As Grady moves swiftly upward for approximately fifty feet, he realizes whoever is at the wheel of the truck is helping pull up the cable by backing the vehicle. Suddenly the motor roars again, the cable slackens, and the bottom drops out of Grady's world.

Now, in absolute horror, Grady glances upward again to see his truck crashing over the side of the opening with the motor screaming like a creature from the ice age. As he drops like a stone toward the bottom of the pit, the heavy vehicle flies across the cave, hits the opposite wall with a thunderous sound and follows his downward plunge.

When his body hits an outcrop and his shoulder is crushed, Grady experiences a moment of tremendous pain. The impact also breaks half the bones in his body. A moment later, his head strikes a rock with such force his helmet splits in two, and Grady's neck snaps, killing him instantly.

Grady's torn, shattered body beats the truck to the bottom of the abyss by a few seconds, but his ordeal isn't over yet. Although he never feels a thing, the wreckage of the heavy vehicle lands atop Grady's body, spreading what is left of his lifeless shell over forty feet of cavern floor.

Fifty feet above Grady's remains, Clete's bloody body is skewered on a sharp pinnacle, spread-eagled upside down and backward. The knife-like rock entered Clete's upper back and now protrudes from his stomach, while his legs hang twisted in reverse over his head. Clete looks like a

Raggedy Andy someone discarded after too much use and abuse. His torn and steaming guts hang out obscenely, as blood and gore drip down the walls to join the smeared remnants of Grady in peaceful slumber.

As if insane creatures from Mars or Jupiter, thousands of bats beat their wings against the warm morning air to fly out of the cave. As they soar farther away from the source of their disturbance, their cries grow fainter. Soon the cave is as still as a bingo parlor where the players await the number of the next ball to be called.

At the edge of the gorge, Felix listens until the last pieces of the truck come to a noisy rest and silence returns. Then he reaches down to the campfire, takes a coffee pot from the coals, dumps cold coffee from a nearby cup and pours a fresh hot refill. After taking a sip, he exclaims, "Damn, that's good stuff. I wonder what Grady and Clete have to eat in that cooler. I am so hungry I could eat a jackass - hooves and all."

He turns toward the pit and thinks of his two victims while making a bad pun. "I don't think they're hungry. I just fed them a big piece of mountain goat."

CHAPTER 13

"I'll return in a few minutes," Carla says. "Go ahead, pour the whiskey down, or your pain won't get any better."

"Yes, Dear," Claude says. He is already feeling the booze. A few more swallows and he will be bombed. While she is away, he manages to get two more drinks under his belt.

When Carla returns, she is wearing a dark-red two-piece swimming suit. Claude can't believe his eyes. The skimpy apparel doesn't leave much to the imagination. A tiny halter strains against the amount of lovely flesh it is attempting valiantly to restrain, and the faint outline of her point of passion is pressed against the dark material of the bottom half. Carla is stunning, and Claude doesn't have to be half in the bag to recognize the fact.

"Okay," she says. "The first thing to do is get you under the shower. The canal did nothing to help your condition. As we speak, there is no way to tell what is attempting to get under your skin, and now they have two new openings to make things easier. Stand up."

"That makes sense," Claude says. She points downward. "And all modesty aside, those jockey briefs have to go."

"My love, I think you would do anything to get me out of my drawers." She shakes her head. "You are really something. Come on; stand up. I'll help you into the shower, hold you up and help you wash." Claude stands up slowly. "Anything you command, my love."

The booze must be working; the pain isn't as bad, he thinks to himself.

Carla helps him walk through her bedroom and into a large bathroom, where she commands, "Get in the shower," and Claude obeys. "Now for the shorts," she says, but as she reaches around Claude's legs to pull them down, her touch does something to him, and he becomes erect. "I'm sorry about that."

As Carla fights to get the shorts over his manhood, she exclaims, "I can't believe you. Gun-shot and half-drunk, you still have sex on your mind."

"That is a natural reaction when I'm naked in a shower with a woman as beautiful as you."

"Well, cool your ardor, Romeo. You won't get anywhere with this one." She turns on the shower, the cold water hits Claude's head, and he yells, "Damn!" Carla adjusts the control until the water warms. "It serves you right. Now stand still and let me wash you. Hang onto the towel bar and don't fall down."

"I won't," Claude says and lets her have her way with him. After the chill of the night, hot water coursing down his body feels wonderful. Carla scrubs him well, raising suds over his back and chest and paying special attention to his wounds, causing them to bleed again. Reddish water runs down Claude's legs and rolls in circles around his feet before exiting through the floor drain. She inspects her work and says, "Now that you are clean, your wounds should heal easily. As soon as I put antiseptic on the injuries, they will stop bleeding."

As she continues to wash his hips and legs, front and back, her touch feels marvelous. To her amazement, but not his, Claude's erection remains stiff and hard. Finally Carla hands him the soapy wash cloth and points to his penis. "Here, you can take care of that." She is still shaking her head in disbelief as she climbs from the shower and begins drying her hair with a large, fluffy white towel. Then she turns her back to him. "Stay where you are."

Claude is fascinated and watches silently as she undoes the halter and lets it drop to the floor. Next she reaches down and slips the bottom of her swimming suit from her shapely hips and legs. Carla reaches up to the back of the bathroom door and removes a large terrycloth robe, puts it on, ties the belt in place and looks up to see he has been watching her reflection in a mirror.

Claude has discovered Carla is a natural redhead, and with nipples as large as those, her breasts aren't implants. Carla's face flushes. "Did you get a good look?" Claude nods, and his head feels like it is made of iron.

"Now you," she says, as she pulls a clean towel from a small closet to her left and wipes the water from his body, beginning in back and working around to his front. As Carla towels his chest, she never takes her eyes from his. Claude steps from the shower, where she hands him the towel. "You can get your legs and other parts."

As she points toward old faithful again, Carla adds, "You really should do something about that."

"Don't I wish," he mumbles.

"You're a dirty old man," Carla says, but smiles and hands him a matching terrycloth robe. "Those who shower and dress together tend to stay together," Claude slurs.

"Boy, you really are smashed. Good, it's time to see if I should have passed 'Sewing One Oh One' in high school."

* * *

"Why white?" Claude asks.

"The thread doesn't have dye. You don't need anything to help the infection. You already stand a good chance of catching something terrible from the water you were rolling around in." After Carla threads the needle, which looks like a harpoon to Claude, she lays it aside on a small table between them. "You won't like this next procedure."

Claude motions toward the needle. "You mean your harpoon?"

"No, I mean the antiseptic, which will hurt."

"Shit," he says.

"No, that's what I am about to destroy. Don't be a big baby, Mister Macho. Show me how tough you cam be."

"If you say so, Dear." Carla poises the bottle over the worst wound - the one on his back. "You might want to hold onto something." Claude reaches across the table with his good hand and takes hold of her leg. She slaps his hand lightly. "Not that."

"You did say 'grab something'."

"God," Carla says, "I can't believe you." Then she pours the liquid from hell onto his wound. While gritting his teeth, Claude does his best to prevent uttering the words he feels like saying. But finally he gives in, and exclaims very slowly, "Son of a bitch!"

"Told ya," Carla says and laughs. Through clenched teeth, he says, "You are one heartless woman." She grins. "And a few minutes ago you called me your love. What changed your mind?"

Claude is in too much pain to reply. He shakes his head and moans under his breath. As she attacks the wound on his chest, Carla says, "Only one more to go."

"Damn!" He yells again. "That's all, my love," she says, teasing him. *Or, is she?* He wonders.

"Now we will get out my trusty Singer sewing machine and stitch you up." Claude continues to shake his head and curse under his breath, while Carla waves a piece of paper towel over his wounds to cool them. Finally, after five minutes of pure hell, they stop burning. He looks at the hole in front and sees the bleeding has stopped. *She was right,* He thinks.

"What are you, a nurse?"

"No, I'm a librarian and get to read a lot of books. You're lucky – I re-read my first-aid manual last week."

"Thanks," Claude says and means it. Carla looks into his eyes and knows it. "You're welcome. I think we will only sew up the worst of the wound in back. I won't attempt to knit the skin together. The hole is too big, and my sewing would cause more pain. The one in the front can be sewn together and won't leave a bad scar."

"You're the expert," he says. She hands him the needle/harpoon. "Here, hold this by the end."

"Am I supposed to do the sewing myself?"

"No, you idiot. I'm about to sterilize the point the only way I know." She lights a match and holds the flame under the point of the needle, which quickly turns black, and Claude's end gets hot in a hurry. "Okay, hand me the needle, but don't touch the point."

"Gladly."

After threading the needle, Carla says, "Well, here goes nothing," and sticks the needle/harpoon through the skin on his chest next to the wound. Surprisingly, it doesn't hurt that much, just a stick like he receives from a tetanus shot. Fascinated by her handiwork, Claude watches Carla continue to sew. When she finishes, she ties a knot in the thread and cuts off the residue with a small pair of fingernail clippers. "There, that didn't hurt much, did it?"

"No, you have a steady hand."

"Your back won't be as bad," she says. "I'll close a couple small skin tears and pack gauze into the hole to stop the bleeding and soak up any drainage. Hold still and I'll be done in a jiffy." The time taken to complete the job is longer than a jiffy, but again, the pain isn't bad. Carla snips off the last thread. "There, all done. How do you feel?"

"Pretty good for the shape I'm in." He pauses for a moment. "I just thought of something else. I need your assistance in one more matter." Jokingly, she asks, "You mean I haven't done enough? What now? You're not still thinking of sex are you?"

"No, my rental car," Claude says and doesn't know if she is disappointed. "The guy that shot me stole the vehicle. I need to report the theft, but can't in this condition, and I obviously can't walk into a police station to fill out a report."

"So, what do you want me to do?"

"Call the number on the receipt in my billfold," he says. "Tell them you are my secretary and I have been out of town. I parked the car at the airport for an extended trip. When I returned, the vehicle was gone. If they ask me to come in to fill out a report, say I am out of town again and won't return for a week. To square things, I will pay the rental until today, but since the car was stolen, the theft is a police matter."

She looks puzzled. "Won't the police want you to fill out a stolen vehicle report?"

"I hope they will find the car before seven days pass. I doubt my assailants kept it. They probably moved the vehicle away from the canal so as not to attract attention. If the cops discovered it abandoned there, they would search the canal. They don't want me found."

"Got everything figured out, haven't you?" she asks.

"No - not yet, I just don't want the police thinking I stole the damned thing."

"Now you're getting testy. Okay, I'll take care of your problem. How do you feel?"

"Thanks," Claude says, and his eyes feel like each lid weighs a ton. "I feel like someone shot me and threw me in a cruddy canal. I need some sleep." Carla smiles at his corny response and helps him to his feet. "Lean on me. You can have my bed. I'll sleep on the couch."

"That's very good of you," Claude whispers. "I would object, but am too damned tired. Thanks for everything."

"Shush, lie down and go to sleep." Claude starts to thank her again, but his eyes close and he is asleep in an instant. Carla stands over him, looks down at his still form and says, "You're not Mister Macho now, are you?" But Claude is beyond hearing.

* * *

Joe, Kris and Mona have been working for an hour attempting to decipher Larry's last words, what few there are. So far they have made as much progress as a snail attempting to haul an anvil across a railroad track. Joe stretches and asks, "So, what do you make of Larry's code?"

"Not a lot," Kris replies. "Was this all Sadie had to say or sign?"

"Yeah, Mona and I reviewed her response twice, and it was the same. I understand the part about killing the president and maybe thousands. At least that's my interpretation. Nothing else jumps out except for the two bad men and the fact the fire frightened Sadie, and she hid."

Suddenly the words begin to make sense to Mona. From across the table, she says, "I think the 'terror is' is supposed to mean terrorists."

"That's pretty good, Mona," Kris says. "How did you figure that?"

"Chimps have a pretty basic understanding of the English language. We make things easy by using words that could mean two different things or even three."

"Okay," Kris says. "I see your point. Look at the next two words. 'Nervous and gas' could mean nerve gas, couldn't they?" Joe claps his hands together in excitement. "Yeah, you're right. Now we're cooking. What else jumps out?"

"Well, 'football game' is pretty self-explanatory," Mona says. "But she could mean any type of ball game."

"Why would she?" Kris asks. "If Larry meant to say ball, he would have. He must have been very specific for Sadie to say football."

"Yeah," Joe says. "You're right again. Hey, look at the next line. Sadie said, 'cotton' and then 'food bowl'. I think Larry meant bowl, but Sadie substituted something she knew – her food bowl. Could he have meant the Cotton Bowl?"

"Which goes along with the next word, 'fall'," Mona says. "I think you're right."

"But, what does 'hide', 'three', 'two', 'fire' and 'X' have to do with the Cotton Bowl?" Joe asks.

"I'm not sure Larry signed those words," Mona says. "They may be in reference to the fire. Sadie might mean there were three in the car, two cars collided, the fire occurred, and Sadie hid."

Kris says. "What about you, Joe?"

"I don't know what they represent, but Sadie repeated them twice, exactly the same, which makes me believe Larry signed those words."

"Yes," Mona says. "But Sadie might have added the words herself because she was frightened and misses Wilbur so much."

"Well, I'll continue to work on a solution," Joe says.

"Me too," Kris adds.

"Let's look at the first line again," Joe suggests. "I know Sadie was fascinated by the two bad men. I suppose she doesn't know man from men, right Mona?"

"Right; that is a little too much to expect from a chimp. Remember what I said about using the same word for two meanings."

"Okay," Joe says. "So we have the bad men. I take it 'fell' must mean when Larry was shot. Why an X again?"

"I don't know," Kris says.

Mona adds, "I don't either."

Joe continues, "Then Sadie says 'is man and far east man'."

Kris says, "The first 'man' is probably a man, just what Sadie says; also possibly white. The 'far east man' could mean someone from Japan."

"What about an Arab?" Joe asks.

"They are from the middle east, Joe," Mona says.

"I know, but does Sadie?"

"Now I see your point," Mona replies and laughs. "Sadie may have the direction mixed or substituted far for middle. I wish Wilbur was here to get his version, but he isn't, so we have to make do with what Sadie provided."

"I go along with the Arab part," Kris says. "Right now they are our greatest enemies. Relations with the Japanese are good. I wish we had a name." Joe yawns and feels worn. "So do I, but, again, we don't. Here, Kris, take a copy of Sadie's story to study at your leisure. Let me know if anything falls out of your tree. For now we are stymied."

After Kris checks the calendar on his cell, he says, "The Cotton Bowl is still a ways off, which gives us time to touch base with operatives in the field to see if they've heard anything. I'll put the word out and shake some trees myself." Then he remembers Grady and the inability to question him again. "Oh, by the way, I forgot to tell you, Joe. Our buddy, Grady is down in Mexico."

Joe looks up from his notes in surprise. "You think he cut out?" Kris shakes his head. "No, Grady's wife said he and a buddy went down there to explore a cave, which is a hobby of Grady's. He is due to return next week, and I left word for him to phone. But in case I'm wrong, and he did run, I put Grady's name on Interpol's Watch List. I also notified our Mexican counterparts to be on the lookout for his John Doe."

"When you get Grady, shake his tree good," Joe says.

"I intend to."

* * *

Felix ditches the rifle and revolver in a cistern on a ranch outside Nuevo Laredo. Getting the weapons across the border from the USA was fairly easy. *Who wants to smuggle guns out from the states?* But taking the firearms across the US border is something else. If they are discovered in his truck, he will be in a world of hurt. The weapons can be easily replaced. The United States is a cornucopia of weapons for sale, anywhere and everywhere.

Felix makes his way across with ease, but the border guards give his truck a cursory search, so there is no doubt they would have found the rifle and pistol. If they hadn't, the dog that sniffed his vehicle would. The guards checked Felix's driving license, passport and renal contract for the ATV before allowing him to cross the international bridge. But his documents are in order, and Felix looks innocent enough, *doesn't he?*

He drives from the border straight through to Sulfur Springs, where he stops long enough to return the ATV and ramp. Then, pausing only for fuel and food, heads north to his hideaway in the mountains. Before anything else happens, he must complete the nerve gas transfer. Mohammed will want to know where he has been, so Felix reaches for his cell phone.

"Where have you been?" Mohammed asks, just as Felix knew he would.

"I've been tying up some loose ends. Grady won't be around to collect his portion of the money." Mohammed is quick on the uptake. "Will his body be found?"

"Hardly, Grady is four hundred feet underground, along with his truck."

"You will have to tell me how you accomplished that."

"Later," Felix says. "I'm going to the cabin to work on the product. Can you meet me there tomorrow afternoon at three? I want to test the detonators to see what they do to the containers before I load any cargo."

"Yeah, I'll be there. I want to see that myself. How long before the remaining containers will be ready?"

"A week or ten days at the soonest," Felix says. "What's your rush? The game is still weeks away."

"Lately too many things have gone wrong," Mohammed says. "What if they find Grady's body? That will lead them to his place of employment and you."

"The chances of that happening are very remote," Felix says and chuckles at his pun. "I hope so," Mohammed says. "I'll see you tomorrow."

* * *

Felicity Jameson is a gamer. Only twenty-seven-years-old, Felicity stands five feet and seven inches tall, and weighs one hundred and five pounds with or without a wet t-shirt. Her brown hair is closely cropped, and her breasts so small she is often mistaken for a young boy. But that doesn't bother Felicity. In her short life she has done everything imaginable and then some.

You name the feat and Felicity has been there and accomplished it. Scuba diving off the great barrier reef with sharks that could swallow her in one bite, sky diving over twenty different states and three countries in single and tandem chutes, hang gliding from the mountains of Switzerland, bungee-cord jumping from tall bridges, and BASE jumping from taller buildings and mountain cliffs to name a few.

But this is something new; hanging at the end of a slim steel tether and dropping down into Mother Earth at a cave called Diablo's Hideout or the Devil's Hole - take your pick. Felicity isn't actually frightened. To hear her tell the tale; nothing scares her, and all her friends will testify to that fact on her behalf.

After seeing a notice about the cavern in an obscure sports magazine, her cousin, Bill Dougherty had this stupid idea. Bill is a spelunker and loves to crawl around dark dismal caves. Felicity accompanied him once before and wasn't sure if she had claustrophobia, but once was enough. She toughed out the trip and never said anything, but whenever Bill mentioned spelunking again, Felicity was always busy.

But they sprang this on her without warning, and here she is; hooked to the end of a cable hanging from a long extension of the arm of an old wrecker. Felicity thinks she looks like a spider at the end of a silken thread, and after glancing down into the shadows of the dimly-lit shaft, feels about as insignificant.

The four; the wrecker owner, Jack, and Fred, a moron from Louisiana, plus Bill and Felicity crawled over fifty miles of bad gravel road leading to the cave. On the way Fred kept them entertained by swearing he knew Elvis was alive and well and living with a Creole woman in a rundown shack near Houma. When it comes to counting brains, Fred has about as many as a jackrabbit.

Felicity was sure the potholes in the terrible road would blow out every tire, and they would be forced to cancel the trip. Much to her surprise and disgust, they hadn't. So now is the time to show the boys she had a pair of balls, too.

"Hang in there cous," Bill shouts from the rim, "This ain't no big thing. Be thankful we gave you first chance. Not everyone gets to go caving." In reply, Felicity yells, "Thanks a lot." Then she hears his voice boom in her earphones. "We'll take things nice and slow – fifty feet at a time. Use your microphone to let us know when to lower you. Keep us advised of what you see, and use your flashlight to ensure you don't hit an outcropping."

Felicity gives Bill the finger. "If you are such an expert, why aren't you here hanging in space? Oh, what the hell, go ahead; lower me. The sooner I get there and back, the quicker you and your moron friends will do the same. Then we can head to town and a cold beer."

"Let her go, Jack," Bill yells, and Felicity drops so fast she is actually frightened, but forces back a silent scream. She will be damned if she gives the idiots the satisfaction of knowing they scared her. Then the cable stops just as quickly, jerking her upward again. She feels like she might regurgitate her breakfast, but manages to choke down the bile.

"You stupid son of a bitch!" she shouts into her mike. "What the hell was that? Take things slower, idiot."

"Sorry about that, cous," Bill says. "Old Jack don't know no moderation."

"He had better learn. Let me down another fifty." This time Felicity drops much slower and watches the sun disappear above as she moves into darkness so thick it feels like a cold, uncomfortable blanket. She turns on her flashlight and shines the beam onto the walls, where bats by the thousands are sleeping. She forgets about the open mike. "Damn, bats."

Her skin crawls with goose bumps. One thing she truly hates is these furry little balls of shit. The smell of their guano is rank. She gags as Bill laughs in her ears. "Yeah, there will be bats. I thought you knew."

After taking a minute to look down, making sure the fools aren't about to drop her onto some pointy rock and cut her legs, Felicity says, "Okay idiot – fifty more," and spirals downward again while checking her progress with the light. When something glistens on a ledge, she sees a chrome strip lying there. *That is strange. How did it get here?*

Then on another shelf Felicity sees glass fragments reflecting the glow from her flashlight. *That's weird.* She keys her mike again. "There is strange junk glowing down here, Bill."

"Someone always messes up nature," Bill says. "Damn the litter bugs anyway."

Felicity keeps her light moving. "Let me down another fifty." Now she sees more debris on several ledges; a piece of crumpled metal that looks like part of a truck fender and a chunk of chrome shaped like a bumper. "If I didn't know better, I would think someone junked a truck down here."

"Impossible," Bill says.

"Once more into the fray," Felicity says, drops fifty more feet and sees more debris and an abundance of broken glass, plus frayed and torn seat cover material. "There's more trash, Bill."

"Can we pull out the junk?"

"You would need a big wheelbarrow. They're difficult to come by out here in the desert."

"You're a real comic," he says. Felicity shines her light toward the bottom of the abyss and spots a large, shiny object. "There is something big gleaming down there. I bet it's a truck." Bill curses under his breath. "Stupid assholes that screw up a cave deserve to be shot on sight."

Felicity sounds more like a bidder at an auction than a cave explorer: "Another fifty." As she moves downward, Felicity rotates at the end of the tether, and something wet and icky brushes against her hair. *Great, damned bat crap in my hair.*

Turning her head, she sees Clete's legs hanging from the rock with his reddish-brown mass of flesh and guts suspended in air and time. At first, Felicity thinks Clete is a giant spider like one she saw in a movie as a child. Then the light shines on Clete's pulverized face, and she recognizes what it is. For the first time in her life she panics and screams, "Pull me up! Damn it, Bill, pull me up! Pull me up!"

"What the hell is going on?" he asks. Felicity screams louder. "You stupid son of a bitch; pull me up!" As Bill motions for Jack to raise the cable, he says, "Damn Jack, she flipped out. Pull her up before she shits her pants."

When they finally haul Felicity from the damnable pit, she continues to scream and curse for fifteen minutes before they calm her down enough to discover what she saw. Each time Bill comes close or attempts to speak with her, Felicity screams and lashes out at him. Never in his life has he seen eyes so wide, felt outright terror in a person, or heard his cousin use such foul language to describe his lineage. Bill stares down the dark foreboding shaft and asks, "What the hell is down there?"

In response, Felicity attempts to scratch his eyes out and screams louder. Jack shivers. "Who is brave enough to go down to see what's up?" No one volunteers. They will wait until Felicity tells them, which takes a long fifteen minutes.

* * *

"Well, let's see what you can do," Mohammed says. Felix and he are at the base of a mountain overlooking the valley beyond, twenty miles from his cabin hideaway. They have to be this far away so the signaling device won't set off the other detonators. All they are interested in are the four lying at the base of the mountain. The test is simple; if these fire extinguishers work, the others will.

* * *

Last night Felix worked until late into the night pressurizing four tanks to fifty pounds per square inch, enough to spray the contents into the air and spread the fluid quickly after the containers rupture. Then he installed detonators and primer cord. Even in the cool evening air, his hands shook and sweat ran down his arms to drip from his elbows. If he is this nervous working with no nerve gas present, what will he do with the real thing?

When he finally finished, he wiped perspiration from his forehead, stood back and admired his work. "They look just like the real thing." So he and Mohammed will be able to trace the distance the liquid traveled after detonation, Felix filled the fire extinguishers with water and dark-green dye. He knows this won't be a realistic test. *Nerve gas is much lighter and will travel farther. But I couldn't test the real thing. I do want to live to see another sunrise.*

* * *

"Let's move back a ways," Felix says. "I'm not sure how far shrapnel will fly. I would hate to kill either of us." Mohammed nods and appears a little frightened. "Yeah, at this date and time, that would be a shame." They move farther down the mountainside until Felix feels they will be safe. Then he glances around to ensure they are alone. After drawing in a deep breath, Felix says, "Fire in the hole," and pushes the red button on the electronic signaling device.

The four explosions come as one, making much more noise than Felix thought they would. The sound echoes from the surrounding mountains like cannons at a state funeral. Mohammed is startled and a little rattled. "Holy Allah - that was loud. I thought they would just pop." Felix shakes his head in wonder. "The C-4 is more powerful than I thought. I'll have to reduce the charge in the real thing."

"What difference will it make?" Mohammed asks. "Hell, leave it alone. The more noise - the more panic and people we will kill."

"You're right. The dust has settled. Let's see the results of our test."

* * *

What the hell was that? John Kawalski thinks, as an explosion startles and awakens him from a well-earned nap. John has been free-climbing this side of the mountain alone all morning and was worn by the time he reached the halfway point. But luck was with him, and he found a nice niche he could crawl into and rest. Fatigue and the high mountain air overwhelmed him, and John fell asleep, only to be rudely awakened.

After shaking his six foot frame loose from the interior of the crevice, John peers over the edge. Down below are two strange-looking dudes dressed for the street instead of the mountain, walking up a slight grade to a spot almost directly below his resting area, where a cloud of dust still lingers heavily in the air.

Farther below through an opening in the trees John sees a shiny brown Cadillac setting just off the park road. The fancy vehicle looks out of place here in the wilderness. *Must be some city dudes,* John whispers to himself and the mountain. *But who are they, and what are they doing with explosives in a national forest?*

No one answers his unspoken question, but that is no surprise. Old John talks to himself a lot since his ex-wife, Georgia left him two years ago. His friends have grown used to his mutterings. They look into John's brown eyes, see his clean-shaven face and flattop haircut, and know he decided on the sport of rock climbing in the hope that someday he will fall and end his misery. They wish John might forget Georgia and begin anew with one of several eligible widows living in his small community.

John watches quietly as the strangers arrive at the dust cloud area; where one reaches down to pick up something. The object is red and reflects sunlight like a gunshot. The first man hands his discovery to the second, and they both nod. Whatever they accomplished using the explosives seems to please them. As if he is in a train tunnel, John hears one say, "Look at the pattern of dispersal."

The wind picks up and he only hears part of the other's reply. The first man picks up two other red objects, and they nod again. Then one points toward the side of the mountain and down the hill in a circle, where John sees light green streaks on rocks and trees. *What the hell are they doing?*

As John shifts his weight to get a better view, he dislodges several pebbles. Hurriedly, he pulls his head out of sight, silently says, *Damn it,* and remains hidden.

* * *

As the sound of rocks falling, Mohammed jumps backward and slips to his knees. Felix asks, "What the hell was that?" Mohammed looks upward into the sun. "Some rocks fell from above." Neither sees any movement nor anything on the side of the nearly-straight-up wall, so Felix says, "It was probably a delayed reaction to the explosion. Have you seen enough, or do you want to stay until the mountain crumbles and kills us?"

"Let's return to your cabin. I hate the mountains. They are too unpredictable. Give me the desert anytime." Felix reaches down for more fragments. "Help me pick up what remains of the containers, and we'll get out of here."

* * *

High above their heads, John listens to a clink of metal on metal as the two strangers collect their hardware. Then they start walking down the mountain. He remains hidden for another thirty minutes until he hears the far-off sound of a car engine. Then John climbs down the mountain, not up.

CHAPTER 14

As Felix thought, it took ten long difficult and nerve-racking days and nights to complete the nerve gas transfer. At the end of that time, he is a mental and physical wreck. When he departed for Mexico, Felix had asked for and received two weeks leave from the lab. After this hairy part of the job took more time than expected, he phoned to extend his vacation. But now the transfer is finished. Thanks to his careful preparation and steady, no-nonsense approach, no nerve gas escaped. After each container was successfully filled, Felix was drenched in sweat, and his hands shook so badly he had to rest an hour or more to calm down.

While thinking of the consequences of his labor, sometimes Felix experiences second thoughts about this attack on America. Deep in his heart, hidden somewhere behind his hatred, Felix knows no one is to blame for his anger except the drunk driver that wiped his family from the face of the earth. Still, for a reason he can't fathom, Felix maintains a deep-seated hatred of the Jewish faith. The loathing is overpowering, driving him day and night.

The collateral damage the bombs will cause to every race and religion on the face of the earth doesn't enter into the equation. Without realizing, he reached the brink of madness, and instead of turning back, crossed over to the dark side. Now the only thing remaining is to load the phony fire extinguishers aboard Mohammed's panel truck. Then, when the Cotton Bowl rolls around, Felix will allow Mohammed and his cronies to complete the attack.

When the bombs explode, Felix will be in Jamaica on vacation. Perhaps afterward, he may be questioned, but there will be such an outcry for reprisal that the long arm of the law will forget small fry such as him.

Every day Mohammed phones to encourage him to finish, but at the same time harass him. "We need to get the job done," he repeats time after time. Felix is almost at the end of his mental rope. "I'll be damned if I will hurry the process. I'm exhausted. If I make a mistake, thousands of others and I will die, and they'll find the evidence. Have you thought of that possibility?" Mohammed knows he pushed Felix too far. "Okay, calm down. I understand. Do your best and let me know when I can move the cargo."

* * *

So, upon completion of the final container, Felix phoned, and Mohammed is on his way. The day is beautiful, with a bright blue sky, and small puffy clouds hanging high above. In the clear mountain air, the symbol of America; a bald eagle is drifting on the wind with his wings outstretched. Silently, Felix says, *He doesn't know, but in the fall, he is in for a big fall.*

He chuckles softly at his pun and lies back in a hammock to dream of his future. When he receives his five-million-dollar payoff, there are great plans for a condo in the Caribbean and perhaps another in South America, where he will disappear into the world of wealthy patrons and relish his vengeance. As Felix daydreams, he wonders; *Who was the person that coined the phrase, "Revenge is sweet?"*

* * *

Joe joined Bert in his office, and now the two are up to their hips in paperwork. Over the weekend the Lawn Ornament Bandits had a ball stealing so much stuff Joe wonders if they used a dump truck to transport all their loot. The amount reported stolen is amazing. *What will they do with all this junk?* The phone interrupts his thoughts. Bert seems inclined to ignore the call, so Joe leans over and picks up the handle. "Yeah, what is it?"

"Guess what, Joe," Kris says.

"I'm not in a game-playing mood, Kris. Today has been lousy, with too much crime and not enough cops." Kris chuckles in his ear. "Well then, you will be glad to know one of your boys won't be lying to you anymore."

"And who would that be?"

"Grady O'Reilly," Kris says and waits for Joe's response. "Grady?" Joe asks in disbelief. "Damn, I wanted to question him again. How did he buy the farm?" Kris keeps Joe in suspense. "You do remember when I told you that he headed south to Mexico to explore a cave?"

"Yeah, I do. Don't tell me Grady fell in and killed himself."

"According to the Mexican authorities, that is exactly what happened," Kris says. "They found what was left of Grady and his buddy, Clete Palmer, at the bottom of a four-hundred-foot deep pit, together with Grady's prized truck. Apparently someone goofed and the truck went in, taking both with it."

Joe says, "That was very convenient. Do you believe that scenario?" Kris laughs at Joe's serious reply. "Not really. We need someone down there to view the remains and see what they can discover that our Mexican friends didn't. I volunteered. Do you want to come with me, Joe?" Unseen, Joe shakes his head. "I'm tied up with paperwork, but what about Fad? I think he can bust loose for a short vacation south of the border."

"I would love to have him," Kris says. "I understand he speaks Spanish like a local."

"Yeah, Kris – Fad is a fountain of info, which will come in handy with the Mexican cops. They dig someone that speaks their lingo."

"I'm headed there in the morning by helicopter, Joe. Send Fad over this afternoon, and I'll provide the particulars. Okay?" Joe yawns and holds his hand over his mouth. "Sure, Kris; lately, Fad has been saying I work him like Simon Legree. He will be happy to get away from the whip for a while."

"Thanks, Joe."

"Don't make me regret my decision, Kris. Bring back something to tie Grady to Larry's death."

* * *

John finishes his downward path with ease. Now he is standing in the center of what was a powerful blast area, looking at a circular pattern of dispersal of a dark-green liquid among rocks and small trees. When he reaches to touch a few drops, his finger comes away wet. Taking his life into his own hands, he tastes the fluid only to discover it is nothing but water with green dye. Several circles are overlapping, so he knows more than one container exploded.

Why anyone would come all the way out here to set off something so powerful is puzzling. Doing so makes no sense.

As John lowered himself down the mountainside, the dust settled. Now he can see more than before. There are several pieces of red metal scattered about that must have been too small for the strangers to gather. Four or five chrome-plated pieces sparkle brightly in the sunlight. *I guess they figured the remnants would rust, or in time the sand would cover what was left behind. Wait a minute, what's that?*

Sunlight glints from a large piece of chrome that was blasted upward and outward and landed on a shelf about head high, fifty feet from the center of the explosion. What remains looks like part of a handle. For some reason, it is familiar. "I've seen this before, but, where?" Nothing comes to mind, so, while making a mental note, John puts the piece in his backpack, together with several tiny red shards of metal.

There is residue of writing on a couple. I'll take them with me and report this mystery to the park ranger. Setting off dynamite or whatever they used must be a Federal offense. Hell, without knowing, they could have hit me. Damn them anyway. I hate people that screw with Mother Nature.

While John is gathering his evidence, the sun slips further west, and dark clouds move into the vicinity. Now he is glad his climb was interrupted. If he was hanging from the cliff, and lightning started hitting the mountain, he might have fulfilled his supposed death wish. John shakes his head. "I have a mystery to solve now. Who wants to die before discovering what these jerks were doing?"

* * *

As he stands near the edge of Devil's Hole, Kris thinks aloud, "That's a good name for such a hellish place."

After taking a cautious look, Fad tries to stretch his back, which he thinks might be broken after a hairy ride down fifty miles of piss-poor road, to say the least. The ride shook Kris up too, but in a different manner. Before they departed he ate tacos for lunch. The huge bumps along the way drove whatever is irritating his stomach down into his lower bowel. Now Kris needs to find fast relief in the worst way.

When he discovers the Mexicans have a Porta-potty on site, Kris is happier than a hooker with five customers haggling over her wares. The outhouse is a foul, evil-smelling plastic shed with most blue liquid splashed onto the floor, sides, and especially the seat. But it is the best port the storm in his stomach has seen in many an hour.

Since Fad is no dummy, he stands upwind. When Kris joins him, they walk over to see where Grady and his buddy took their dive. Fad says, "Damn, that is a hole and a half."

"Yeah, are you sure you want to go down there?" After first shaking his head in response to Kris' question, Fad nods in resignation. "What I don't do for my country. Yeah, I suppose we must. The Federalies set this up for our benefit to show the great cooperation between our two countries. How can we refuse?"

"The cage looks stout enough," Kris says. As Fad climbs into the metal contraption and reaches down to assist his companion, he says, "Let's hope so." From within, hidden in darkness, Inspector Hector Gonzales startles both when he says in flawless English, "The trip down is not as bad as you would imagine."

Hector wears a spiffy tan uniform and a black hat with a spit-shined brim that would please any drill sergeant in the U.S. Army. "The pit is over four hundred feet deep, but we managed to pull out most wreckage. We found Mister Palmer speared on a rock formation, which wasn't a pretty sight."

"I bet," Fad says. "Where was our boy, Grady?" Without being seen, Hector grimaces. "We weren't aware Mister O'Reilly was there until we moved the truck. Then we discovered his remains smeared over forty feet of cavern floor. We used a shovel and sponge to retrieve most body parts. Our forensic scientists are attempting to put him together, but there are many missing pieces."

"Good God," Kris says, and Hector adds, "I agree."

"Amen," Fad says, before Hector continues his unsolicited briefing. "The truck was in gear - we know that much. The vehicle hit the far wall and bounced against several outcroppings on the way down. Pieces were found scattered throughout the cavern. The strange thing is; there was a long thin stick inside the cab. There are no trees or limbs nearby. Where it came from is a mystery."

Fad says, "Someone may have used the stick to push down the accelerator, put the truck in gear and jump out before the vehicle went over the edge. That has been done before in movies." Hector nods and says, "It is a possibility. We think Mister O'Reilly was hooked to the cable, and headed down into the cave when the truck went over. Mister Palmer wasn't wearing a harness like the one we discovered under the wreckage."

Kris asks, "How is his reconstruction proceeding?" Hector seems to shiver in the hot air. "There was more remaining of him than Mister O'Reilly. But as I said, he isn't a pretty sight. When we return to town, I'll take you to our morgue so you may view his remains."

Kris says, "I can hardly wait."

"Well, here we are," Hector says, as they arrive at the bottom of the pit. Fad is amazed. He hadn't felt their descent, but knew the day had grown darker, and now is lighter as they approach the bottom.

The police cooperation department has gone all out. A large diesel generator is setting on the ground and a bank of lights circle the cavern. The damaged outcroppings and scars made by the truck on its way down are clearly visible. A large pool of oily residue has formed near the middle of the cave.

Fad points to a long, slippery-looking, brownish-red streak running from the sloped side of the cave to the middle, and asks in amazement, "That's all that remains of Grady?"

"That and not much more," Hector replies. "We assumed the body was his, because the wreck is his truck. We hope what few teeth were found will allow us to match his dental records. Mister Palmer conveniently carried his driver's license in a pocket. Miracles do happen."

"We'll look around," Kris says. "But I don't think we will find a thing you didn't."

"Take your time, my friends," Hector says and smiles. "I get paid the same no matter where I am." His black eyes seem to glint in the light over a matching moustache as he walks over to join several other Mexican cops gathered in a group and chatting as they wait to be hauled from this foul pit.

"Let's not spend much time here," Fad says. "Damn, that must have been some fall."

"Yeah," Kris says. "I agree; rest in pieces, Grady."

"God, Kris, you're even worse than Joe,"

* * *

This morning when Mohammed arrives in his panel truck with a smile on his face and dream of this moment in his heart, thirty-two red fire extinguishers are lying in a neat row on a soft, cotton-filled mattress in the bedroom of Felix's cabin. Mohammed smiles at the sight. "So, you're done, 'eh?" Then his smile turns into an ugly sneer. Without waiting for an answer, he cries out, "Now the Americans will pay for their invasion of my homeland and many deaths of my people. Long live Saddam!"

After Mohammed's latest outburst, Felix shakes his head disgustedly. "Can't you resist the urge to spout ideological posturing bullshit for a few minutes? Let's load the cargo. I still must set the place afire to ensure no nerve gas escapes and we leave no evidence tying me to the attack."

"What's the matter, Felix? Are you getting cold feet at this point in time?" Felix appears angry with Mohammed's question. "Hell no; I want my money and a chance for revenge on the people that took my family from me. When they all die, I won't give a damn. I'll be living the good life in Jamaica, drinking rum and ginger ale."

Mohammed rubs his hands together as if he is a gold merchant watching his treasure ship come in, ignores Felix's anger and says, "Good, I can't afford to have you go soft. Let's load the bombs in my truck, and I will be on my way." Felix holds up his hands like a traffic cop at an accident scene. "Where is my money?" He demands to know.

Mohammed points toward a suitcase lying on the front-seat passenger's side of his truck. "Right there - do you trust me or want to count the cash before we load the merchandise?"

"No, I believe you. I'll help pack the containers and send you on your merry way. Then I'll take my reward and set the cabin afire. Make sure you are long gone so no one connects you or your vehicle with the fire. I'll be right behind you."

The next thirty minutes are spent carefully packing each fire extinguisher, one at a time into the special packing cases Mohammed brought with him. Both boxes contain sixteen soft foam rubber holes with four inches of thick padding around each. The fire extinguishers fit snugly inside without touching.

When they finish and have loaded the two containers onto his truck, Felix displays a small plastic case with an empty compartment where four batteries should be. As he hands it to Mohammed, he says, "Here is the signaling device, which holds four C-type household batteries like these."

After displaying the batteries to Mohammed, Felix turns and throws them into the interior of the cabin. Surprised, Mohammed asks, "Why did you do that?"

"Don't even think of putting the batteries in place until a minute before you detonate the bombs. That way you won't push the button by mistake and set off all of them in the back of your truck or wherever they are stored."

"That's very smart," Mohammed says and hands Felix a heavy container. "Here is your money." Felix opens the suitcase to discover neat stacks of one-hundred-dollar bills arranged across the entire interior, more money than he has ever seen in his life. With his back to Mohammed, he says, "Thanks, I'll count the money later."

"You're welcome," Mohammed says and shoots Felix twice in the back. The impact of the bullets drives Felix to his knees, where the case slips from his grasp. As he falls forward he gasps, "I should have known."

"Yeah, you should have," Mohammed says. "You tied up your loose ends with Grady. Now I took care of mine with you." As Felix turns his head to stare at his killer, his last thoughts are, *It's a good thing I planned for this eventuality. I will see you in hell, Mohammed.*

Although Mohammed knows he is speaking to a dead man, he says, "Thanks again." But to be certain, Mohammed sticks his right foot under the body, rolls Felix onto his back and shoots him in the forehead. After pausing for a moment to admire his handiwork and marksmanship, Mohammed reaches down to pick up the suitcase before it gets bloody and puts his burden on the floorboard of the passenger's side. Then he returns to where Felix is lying, grabs the body by the feet, drags him inside the cabin, drops the corpse there and walks to where Felix conveniently placed a five-gallon can of kerosene beside the doorway.

After pouring the flammable liquid throughout the interior of the cabin, Mohammed makes sure to thoroughly drench Felix's body. Then he stands back and throws a lit match into the cabin. With a loud "whoosh," fire erupts from the doorway and two windows. Flames lick at the furniture, and the curtains that waved so gallantly a few days ago catch fire and are consumed in seconds. Mohammed doesn't stay to savor his accomplishment. He climbs into his vehicle and quickly drives away.

* * *

After another long and bone-jarring ride over the same road but different bumps, rocks and potholes that threaten to swallow their Range Rover, Kris and Fad return to Nuevo Laredo for a quick dinner. This time, Kris avoids tacos, and they both opt for enchiladas. After two rum and Cokes, Kris' stomach feels much better.

Then Hector drives them to the morgue where Earnest Winslow, the forensic scientist they brought with them is waiting. Hector pulls his vehicle up to the curb and parks outside the lab, and then turns to his passengers. "If you don't mind, I'll stay with the car. I saw the remains earlier and just ate dinner."

Inside the foyer, standing by Earnest's side, is his Mexican counterpart, Jose Martinez, a tall, thin, dark-skinned doctor dressed in a white coat containing several blood spots on one sleeve. Apparently, he and Earnest were recently diving around in body parts, what few remain, of either Grady or Clete. Kris asks, "What did you find, Ernie?"

"Not much - there wasn't a lot to work with in the first place." Fad shakes his head in resignation. "Yeah, we heard. So, there are no clues, 'eh?" With a smile on his face, Earnest says, "I didn't say that. You asked what I found. Now ask Jose what he discovered." Knowing he and Fad have been caught in a grim reaper sick joke, Kris smiles and asks, "So, what did you find, Jose?"

Jose seems to enjoy Ernie's humor. He returns Kris' smile. "We were lucky Mister Palmer landed as he did. If he had hit right-side up, the pinnacle would have blown away his breastbone, and I never would have found this." Jose holds up a crushed piece of metal in a plastic bag, which all the lawmen know is a bullet. Fad asks, "He was shot?"

"You bet," Earnest says. "And whoever shot him sent the truck over the side to hide the evidence. The perp was plain stupid. He could have kicked or thrown Clete from the cavern edge and we would have written his death off as an unfortunate accident."

"Sometimes we get lucky," Fad says. "This looks like one of those times. Great work, Jose."

"Thank you. Here, you will want to take this with you." Jose hands Kris the plastic bag and adds, "Good luck. I hope you find the perpetrator." Fad shakes his head and says, "The gun is in a ditch or river. The killer wouldn't risk attempting to cross the border while armed."

"You're right, Fad," Kris says. "But now we can tie Grady to Larry's death and know there is something unexplained happening at the chemical lab. Katie, Larry and Wilbur didn't die in vain." Fad nods and says, "Yeah, but we have a long way to go to prevent whatever the terrorists have in mind. We had better head north of the border and go to work."

Kris appears deep in thought. "Yeah, you're right. Tell Hector we're ready to go. I'll phone and have the pilot fire up the bird. Thanks again, Jose, and you too, Ernie."

CHAPTER 15

Claude sleeps four hours and Carla snoops four minutes. While he rests, she searches through his clothes. Claude's trouser pockets hold the keys to a GM model car, a dollar and seventy-six cents in change and a wallet containing two thousand, five-hundred and sixty-seven soggy dollars. Inside the billfold is a damp German driver's license in the name of Claude Werner, a matching temporary driver's permit for the United States, a rental slip for the Chevy he is worried about, two credit cards from German banks in the same name, and nothing else.

Whoever Carla's guest is, he travels light, but has money. In her short lifetime, she has never had that much cold cash in her purse. Claude's ruined shirt holds absolutely nothing – zip, zero and nada. He wears a fairly expensive foreign-made watch with a leather band, most likely Swiss. No rings are on his fingers, and he doesn't appear to need glasses.

Carla removes the nearly dry rental receipt, calls the 1-800 Number and lies the way he asked. The rental agency buys her story, and she breathes a sigh of relief. The lady Carla speaks with is named Sharon. When they finish their transaction, Sharon says, "Please have Mister Werner call when he returns."

"Yes, Ma'am," Carla says sweetly. She hates to be called Ma'am. Using that term probably upsets Sharon, but Carla doesn't care. She is tired.

As Claude snores softly, she glances over at his still form, watching his chest rise and fall in rhythm with his breathing. The front of his robe has come undone, and Carla admires his muscular body from head to toe.

* * *

Although she is twenty-seven, Carla has never married. Over the years, she met her share of men and enjoyed sex, but never found the perfect partner. Now, she muses, *Maybe I never will.* But she continues to hope.

Why she is helping this complete stranger is beyond her comprehension. Such an act isn't like her. She is usually prim and proper and does the right thing. She should be on the phone speaking with the police, telling them she has a man in her bed with a gunshot wound. But for some reason she can't pick up the phone and make the call.

When Carla heard sounds like firecrackers, she drove to the warehouse area two blocks away. She thought she could handle any teenage kids that might be setting off fireworks. But when she saw Claude, *If that is really his name,* and he said he had been shot, she was intrigued, not wary. Now, apparently Carla is involved in this situation up to the top of her pantyhose.

* * *

She moves quietly to the bed and shakes Claude gently, until he awakens. "I'm sorry to disturb you, but you need some antibiotics. I have a few Cipro tablets with an out-of-date label, but it has always worked wonders for me. Let's try a couple. Here, take these. I'll hold the glass." Claude's eyes are heavy with sleep. "Thanks, I need to use the bathroom. Can you help me up?"

"Yeah, come on, you big baby." After Carla helps him to his feet, Claude stands there unsteadily until he gets his balance. She asks, "Can you get there alone, or do you want to lean on me?" He winks and says, "I'll try."

Claude shuffles off slowly, and she follows in case he needs assistance. But as he goes into the bathroom, he says, "You won't have to hold my hand or anything else." Carla catches the innuendo in his remark and replies, "You are weird." But she smiles to indicate she was not offended. Although the door is closed, she hears the sound of his urine hitting the bowl, which goes on for a minute or two before he finishes. Then the tap water runs as he washes his hands.

When Claude comes out, she says, "To help you heal faster and replace the fluids you lost, you should drink several large glasses of water." After emptying the glass she hands him, Claude says, "You're the doctor."

"No I'm just a librarian. It's back to bed and sleep for you. I must do the same. Don't be Mister Macho and do everything alone. Call if you need assistance. I put the Cipro and a glass of water on a bedside table. Take two each time you get up to use the bathroom, and drink another glass of water."

As Claude slips back under the covers, he grins. "Yes Dear. Thanks Carla. You have been wonderful."

"You're welcome, Claude."

"Been snooping, 'eh?"

"Yeah, but, we'll talk in the morning. Get some sleep. Good night."

"Sleep well yourself," he says. For some reason, although she is worn from the excitement of tonight, Carla requires a long time to fall asleep.

Then she dreams of Claude in a very sexy way. Now she realizes she is looking forward to the days ahead and knows she will awaken with a smile on her face.

* * *

The smoke draws John's attention to the cabin in the woods.

After his adventure high in the mountains twenty miles north, he spent several days traveling back roads searching for something to tie the two strangers to what he discovered. If he sees either man, John knows he will recognize him. He has made steady progress and eliminated most roads leading off the main highway, but until now hasn't been this far south.

John pulls up and parks thirty yards from the burning cabin and climbs out to note half the roof has caved in. There is no way to save anyone that hasn't gotten out by now. "Is anyone here?" he shouts twice, but receives no answer. Then John notices the brown Cadillac setting fifty feet from the conflagration. *That's the car I've been searching for. Where is the guy I saw on the mountainside? I hope he isn't inside the cabin.*

The left side of the vehicle is taking the brunt of the tremendous heat. Black smoke rises from the paint as it burns and curls off. "Whoever owns the car had better hope it doesn't explode." The words aren't out of his mouth for a moment, before it does just that. The force of the explosion knocks John from his feet. He smells singed hair and knows it is his. He crab-crawls back to his car, jumps inside and roars away backward from the two towering infernos.

John picks up his cell to call Parks and Wildlife to let them know about the fire, but he is too late – they are already on the scene. He watches two yellow tanker trucks and a red pickup pull into the driveway. The men on the tankers start hosing down the house and car, while the driver of the pickup walks over to John, looks at him inquisitively and asks, "Is that your place?"

"No; I was passing by and saw the smoke. I got here about a minute before the car blew up. When it did, I was almost blown away. Standing too close was stupid." The guy smiles and agrees. "Yeah, and your hair is singed too. Did you see anyone else around?"

"No, I called out a couple times, but no answer. If anyone was inside, they are history." The guy peers in John's window. "You can say that again. Haven't I seen you before?" He puts his hand through the opening. "My name is Wally."

"John Kawalski," John says and shakes Wally's hand. "Yeah I do a lot of free-climbing. We may have seen each other at the office when I signed for a permit." Wally nods and says, "Yeah, that's where I saw you."

He turns to check the progress of his companions. "It looks like they have the car under control, but the cabin will probably burn to the ground."

"I hope no one was inside," John says. Wally grins and makes a bad pun. "In an hour or two, we'll know if we have barbecue."

"You have a weird sense of humor," John says, but still smiles. As Wally ambles away, he says, "Before the license plate gets blown off by the hose, let me get the number."

* * *

Wally uses the license of the Cadillac to trace the identity of the badly-burned body discovered in the cabin as Felix Mendez. The postmaster serving that address also tells Wally who lives there. The difficult part is finding someone to notify. John and Wally drive into town to see what or who they can discover. According to Mister Mendez's neighbors in Sulfur Springs, after his wife and children were killed by a drunk driver, he became a recluse. When Wally hears this latest news he says, "Man, this guy had a rough life."

"Yeah," John says. "But if Mister Mendez was such a loner, who was the other guy accompanying him? Something doesn't add up." Wally shrugs and says, "There were several pieces of technical equipment in the cabin - mostly scientific gear; glass and metal beakers and a pressure tank that blew about halfway through the fire. We thought Mendez might have been cooking 'meth,' but the equipment wasn't of the right type. I'll ask the neighbors where he works and check there. His boss may know the whereabouts of his next of kin."

* * *

Claude has been recuperating for a week, and now is itching to discover what he can concerning the stranger he met at the canal and the guy he spoke with on the phone. They weren't the same. The caller was probably the guy that attempted to kill him. Of the two, he may have been the better shot, but Claude thinks, *He was good, but not thorough in his work. My turn will come soon. Then I will teach them a thing or two.*

Carla is fantastic. For the first two days she called in "sick" to work. Then Claude said, "Now that the initial shock is history, I will heal by myself. As every hour passes, I grow stronger. Within a few days of rest and recuperation, I should be back on my feet."

Carla presented her side of the argument. "Physical therapy is required to heal your arm and shoulder." But Claude shot down her idea. "You may assist at night and on weekends, but there is no reason to risk losing your job. I have been enough of a burden. Give me time to heal, and I will disappear from your life." Finally, Carla gave in. "Okay, but I would like to know more about you. You are from Germany, but where? And what do you do for a living?"

"I lived in a little town near Dusseldorf named Osterath," Claude said. Then he told the story he concocted in his mind. "I was a banker for several years. Then I began day trading and quit when I earned a million dollars. Now I am semi-retired and looking for a few new investments. That's what I was doing when I hooked up with a crook and was shot."

"And when you are healthy, you plan to find him somehow and do the same for him, right?"

"That was all 'Mister Macho' talk. Do I look like a killer?"

"No, but what is the description of a murderer? Wouldn't it be nice if we could tell one from his appearance?"

"Yes. Then maybe I wouldn't have done business with this guy."

"Do you know his name?" Carla asked. Claude shook his head. "I'm sure the one he used was phony. I should have done a better job of checking on him."

"I agree. I'm glad to hear you aren't out for revenge. That is a cold, bitter road."

"You're right," Claude said. "Let's talk about something lighter. What do we have for dinner?"

"I'll bring home a bucket from the Chicken Shack when I drive into town to buy your new clothes. The canal water did a number on your trousers. I threw out what remained of your shirt, T-shirt and shorts."

"Not my shorts," Claude exclaimed. "After you worked so hard to see me naked, I thought surely you would keep them as a trophy."

"Hardly," Carla said, but laughed anyway. "You have a one-track mind. Stop or I will turn you in."

"Okay, but you can't blame me for trying. You are a beautiful woman."

"Thanks, but I'm not in the mood."

"Later, perhaps?"

"Don't get your hopes up, Romeo. Take your antibiotic and lie down like a good little boy. Get some sleep while I'm away." As Carla walked toward the door, Claude smiled behind her back, "Yes, Dear."

* * *

Fred, the rent-a-cop on duty at the front entrance won't allow Wally or John to enter the main building. He points to the same miserable chairs Bert tested not many days before. "You'll have to wait over there until I call Mister Witte. He is Mister Mendez's supervisor."

After trying two seats apiece, Wally shrugs, and John sighs. They look at each other, give in, and remain standing with their arms folded until Mister Witte arrives to ask, "How may I help you?"

Not one to pull punches, Wally says, "I'm Wally Taylor, a State Park Ranger from Oak Creek Canyon. We believe one of your employees died in a fire yesterday. A cabin burned, and we found Mister Mendez's car parked outside. A man's body was discovered in the ruins."

Hershel appears shocked. "For the past two weeks, Felix has been on vacation. Four days ago, he phoned to extend his time because he was working on an important project. Are you sure the body is his?" Wally shrugs to show he doesn't really know, but then gives his rationale. "The body was severely burned. We must locate Mister Mendez's dentist to match the teeth with his dental records. But yeah, we're pretty certain the victim was he."

"Oh, my God," Hershel says. "This is our second tragic loss in less than a month. The man that worked next door to Felix, Larry Holgram, was murdered recently. Now we have this. What is next?" Without thinking, he moves to one of the wobbly chairs and sits down. "I must catch my breath. Have you notified the Sulfur Springs police?"

"No," Wally says. "First, we wanted to find Mister Mendez's next of kin and notify them."

Hershel turns to his other visitor. "And you are?"

"I'm John Kawalski. The other day, I saw Mister Mendez and another guy setting off explosives in the state forest. I was first on the scene of the fire, so came with Wally to see if I could help."

"That was decent of you," Hershel says. "But using explosives doesn't sound like the Felix I know. I believe you have the wrong man. To answer your question; as far as I know, Felix has no relatives living here. Not too long ago, his wife and children were killed by a drunk driver. Felix had a difficult time adjusting to life without them. At times he appeared bitter and inconsolable."

"I don't blame him," John says. "Mister Mendez had quite a bit of trouble on his plate in such a short period of time."

"I should phone the police," Hershel says. "They will want to know of this." Wally turns to leave. "I'll let you handle those details. Perhaps the cops can locate Mister Mendez's kin and inform them of his demise."

Hershel stands and shakes Wally's hand. "Thanks for letting me know. I'll take care of things from here." When Wally looks at John to ask if he is coming along, John says, "I would like to stick around and meet the police officer when he arrives."

"Will you be all right by yourself, John? I have to get back to work."

"Yeah, don't worry, Wally. I will rent a car. Thanks for bringing me with you. My mystery is getting deeper every minute."

CHAPTER 16

Mohammed arrives in Fort Worth to deliver the bombs and helps carry them into the rental storage space. He senses something is wrong when his controller named Hushan is angry. When Mohammed thinks rationally of what happened; he knows Hushan has a right to be. Killing Felix was stupid.

When Hushan is angry, his black eyes bore through the recipient of his anger like an electric drill, his moustache twitches as if he has a spasm in his lip, and his face turns red. Hushan is one of a chosen few to have met Usama Bin Laden in Saudi Arabia and kissed his hand. Now, as he looks in scorn at Mohammed, Hushan wonders why he ever recruited the idiot.

* * *

After Hushan's brother, Mustafa was sentenced to death for taking part in terrorist attacks against their sworn enemy; the United States, Al Qaeda operatives pursued Hushan as a potential leader of a sleeper cell. At the time they met with Hushan, Mustafa was languishing in prison. Hushan was anxious to avenge his brother, so eagerly joined their organization.

Over the past three years, Hushan discovered a number of individuals claiming they were anxious to avenge debts, real or imagined, against their own government. He was amazed, but at the same time their hatred of their own county was rewarding. Occasionally though, he made the mistake of recruiting a man only in the game for the killing. Now Mohammed has shown his true colors. Hushan must either raise hell with the idiot or get rid of him. Since Hushan knows he still needs the fool for a while, he chooses the former option; and unknowingly makes the biggest mistake of his life.

* * *

As he looks on knowingly and frowns, George, the guy employed as a fireman and the one to put the bombs in place stands by quietly out of the way of anything that might splatter.

Hushan asks, "Why did you have to eliminate Felix so soon, Mohammed? The plan was for him to die later, just before we settle the score for my brother and many others the Americans have killed in their invasion of our homeland. How can you be sure Felix didn't leave something behind to incriminate you or our organization? How could you have been so damned stupid?" In a lame defense, Mohammed says, "I am confident he didn't. Felix was a loner. I never saw him take notes."

"But you can't be positive, can you?" Hushan asks. "And Felix eliminated the guard that could have let you in to check his office. Between the two of you, I don't know which is a bigger idiot. But there is nothing you can do now. That avenue is closed. Pray to Allah that the fool didn't leave anything behind to reveal our well-laid plans."

"I can still get into Felix's apartment," Mohammed says. "If there is any evidence there, I will find it." Hushan stands on the balls of his feet and seems to tower over Mohammed as he says sternly, "Don't be seen." Hushan is tall, but when he does this little trick, he seems taller than Allah.

In his haste to make amends, Mohammed stutters a little, "I-I won't." Then he remembers and hands the detonating device to Hushan. "Here, this is the device to use when you set off the bombs. Felix warned not to install the batteries until just before you decide to detonate the explosives. Remember, all bombs are set on the same wavelength and will explode simultaneously. If you push the button by accident, you will kill yourself and those for miles around."

"Thanks for the warning," George says. "I'll remember."

Suddenly Hushan changes the subject. "Where is my money?"

"Still in the suitcase on the floorboard," Mohammed says. "The fool didn't look beyond the first layer. I placed one-hundred-dollar bills atop stacks of fives and tens. The lower rows are strips of paper." Hushan frowns and asks, "The four-hundred-thousand is all there?"

Thinking he is back in Hushan's favor, Mohammed smiles. "Yes, it is the same money I saved by getting rid of Mister Jones." Hushan is still not in a good mood. He frowns and orders, "Good, go outside and bring in the suitcase, George."

In another futile attempt to regain Hushan's good graces, Mohammed says, "Fine, I'll search Felix's house and let you know if I find anything." His ploy doesn't work. Hushan is still upset. "Then go, and keep me advised. Learn to control yourself, Mohammed, or your future will be very short indeed. There is no place in our organization for fools. May Allah go with you."

"And with you," Mohammed says as he walks quickly to his car, climbs in and drives away. His sweat-stained shirt soon grows cold from the air conditioner, so he shuts off the fan and rolls down a window. But the hot breeze does nothing to cool his feeling of trepidation.

Hushan watches him drive away and turns to George. "The idiot will be the death of us. He is a loose cannon and I don't trust him. The stakes are too high in this game we are about to play, but Mohammed doesn't realize how serious it is. Move the bombs to your garage."

"Sure," George says. As he bends over to pick up one of the heavy cases, a large black widow spider tattooed on his left bicep quivers in a web and seems to grow larger. For all his bluster, Hushan is deathly afraid of spiders. Despite his efforts, goose bumps rise on his arms and a chill runs down his spine. Hushan doesn't think George notices, but he does and smiles behind his leader's back.

* * *

Bert just finished logging all the Lawn Ornament Bandits' newest crimes. The list of stolen items is longer than any other he has ever seen. When the phone rings, he puts the paperwork aside, picks up the headset and gives the standard greeting.

"Sergeant Collins, this is Hershel Witte at the chemical laboratory. We spoke a few days ago concerning the strange death of Larry Holgram."

"Oh yeah, Mister Witte, I remember. How are things with you? Do you have any new information on Larry's disappearance and murder?"

"No, but another strange death occurred in our organization. Felix Mendez, who had the office next to Larry, was killed in a mysterious fire at his cabin in the state forest at Oak Creek Canyon."

"Felix Mendez?" Bert asks. "Wasn't he one of the men I spoke with?"

"Yes, he was."

"That's a strange coincidence," Bert says.

"Yes, I think so, too. A ranger named Wally Taylor and a man named John Kawalski drove down from Oak Creek Park in an attempt to notify Felix's next of kin. As far as I can tell, Felix didn't have any family in Sulfur Springs. After speaking to the two gentlemen, I thought I should let you know."

Bert adds the names to his notes. "Has anyone been in Felix's office?"

"No, Sir, Felix was on vacation for two weeks. Twelve days ago he phoned asking for an extension of two weeks. He said he was working on an important scientific project and needed the extra time to complete the experiment. Felix's death is a strange mystery. Mister Kawalski remained behind to talk with you about a strange occurrence he witnessed in the forest and thinks might be important."

Bert says, "I'll speak with the other officers that worked the case and we'll come out within the next hour or so. Will that be satisfactory?"

"Yes; Mister Kawalski says he doesn't mind waiting."

"Fine, we will see you shortly. Keep everyone away from Felix's office."

* * *

Over the intercom Bert asks, "Are you too busy to visit the chemical lab again, Joe? Hershel Witte phoned in to report another employee was killed in a suspicious fire up in Oak Creek Canyon Park."

"That is strange," Joe says. Bert laughs and says, "Yeah, the word strange came up about ten times in our conversation. Hershel has a guy from Bed Rock waiting to speak with us - a Mister John Kawalski who says he witnessed something strange." Bert pauses for a moment and chuckles softly. "Hell, there I go again, sounding like Hershel. Anyway, they are waiting for us at the lab. Do you think Kris or Fad will want to join us?"

Joe nods and says, "I'll send Fad for a search warrant for Mister Mendez's office. You did say Felix Mendez, didn't you? Why does his name sound familiar?"

"He was one of the guys I interviewed out there. Let me check my notes." Joe hears papers being shuffled and a drawer opens and closes. Then Bert comes back on the line. "Yeah, Mendez worked in the office next to Larry on the left-hand side. Said he didn't know a thing. Hadn't been to work that night and left earlier in the day. Not too friendly with Larry and doesn't know sign language. Very vague about the last time he saw Larry alive."

"Good notes," Joe says. "If Grady let him in for some reason, maybe Mendez is who Larry heard." Bert agrees, "Yeah, that makes sense. But who was Mendez speaking with? Remember, Grady said, 'No one came in'."

Joe snorts in disgust. "Yeah, and I would believe Grady if he swore on a pile of Playboys. He lied and we all knew. Look where he wound up; spread over half of Mexico. But to answer your question; yeah I want to tag along. I'll phone Kris and clue him in, and he can meet us there. Fad and I will be down your way as soon as I reach Kris."

"See you in ten minutes," Bert says.

* * *

Claude is restless. Today is a beautiful, clear, crisp late summer day. He just returned from a two-mile walk, but that isn't what he needs. Carla is at work again, and he misses her company. His chest is almost healed - both wounds are scabbed over and the pain is less each day.

Claude hates to think what kind of germs were floating around in that cruddy canal. He is lucky to have no infection. Carla and her Cipro are to thank for that small miracle. She called her doctor for a refill, so Claude is set with antibiotics for the next thirty days. Spending so much time with such a beautiful woman without feeling something for her is becoming difficult. Claude is afraid he is falling in love, and that won't do. "It is time to cut and run."

But that decision can wait for a little while longer. "I'll call my controller instead." He picks up his cell, dials a number from memory and hears the call switched through several computer centers until he receives a recording. "Leave your name and number, and I will return your call within a few minutes."

"This is Mister Jones. I must speak with you immediately. I'm at a secure location. My number is: 713-555-3241. Call immediately." After Claude disconnects, he holds the cell in his hand. Within thirty seconds, the phone rings. When Claude answers, his unidentified controller says, "You have two minutes."

"I had trouble with the payoff for the last contract. They attempted to kill me. I need to know who set up the hit on the Adkins girl."

"Impossible," his controller says.

"Not impossible." Claude replies forcefully. "I told you, he almost killed me. I need a name and address."

"I thought you were about to retire."

"Not until I settle the score. Won't you help me for old time's sake?" After a moment, his controller relents. "Mohammed Alta, Denver. Last name is spelled, A, L, T, A. That's all you get. Do you need assistance, equipment or supplies?"

"No, I prefer to work alone. I am set in the other categories. Thank you." His controller warns: "Remember, this is the end to our relationship. I don't know you and will not answer your calls. Your time is up." The line goes dead.

Denver, no wonder they could reach me so soon. I was there on vacation when the controller said he had a rush job. I wonder if Alta is listed in the phone book or does his business by cell phone. At least now I know who I am dealing with, but still have to find his partner.

* * *

As is his habit each day, Claude reads through the Sulfur Springs Herald Carla brought in from the front lawn, hoping to find a clue to his assailants. So far, he has had no luck, but today his fortune changes. He glances casually at the obits, and the face of Felix Mendez jumps out like a snake in the grass.

Damn, it's him – killed in a mysterious fire in his cabin at Oak Creek Canyon State Park. It looks like Mohammed got rid of his flunky, which is too bad. I have been looking forward to killing him nice and slow after I got every bit of info about his plans.

There is a postscript to the death notice informing readers to turn to page 4 for a story on the fire. Claude follows the instructions and reads a write-up three columns long. The material is interesting. He reads the article twice, noting the name of the man in charge of the investigation is Sergeant Joseph Francone.

After thinking for a few minutes, Claude finds the number he wants in a phonebook, picks up his cell, dials the number for the precinct, and asks for Sergeant Francone. The operator says, "I am sorry, but Sergeant Francone is out of town for the day. Can someone else assist you, Sir?"

"No, thank you," Claude says and lies. "Joe is an old friend. I was passing through town and wanted to say Hi."

"If you will leave your name, I will give your message to Sergeant Francone."

"That's all right, operator, I'll call later. Thank you."

"You're welcome," she says automatically, but the tone of her voice says she is miffed because Claude wouldn't identify himself. *Tough,* Claude thinks and disconnects.

* * *

The heat in the lab must be set at eighty. The weather outside is cool with a threat of rain in the air or perhaps an early snow storm, but this is ridiculous. As soon as they are inside, Bert and his companions begin shedding clothes the way a dry Christmas tree drops its needles after the holidays are over.

* * *

Fred had instructions to take them directly to Mister Witte, so there was no stupid chair sitting this morning. Bert glances at the waiting area and notices two new seats are available. The other sad, old ones are still setting there and looking like they would rather be in a dump.

They shake hands, and Bert introduces his fellow officers of the law. "Thanks for the call, Mister Witte. This is Sergeant Joe Francone from our office, and Agent Kris Hefner of the FBI. Both gentlemen have worked Larry's case. We would like to see Mister Mendez's office."

"My partner should be here shortly with a search warrant," Joe says. "We will wait until he arrives to make entry."

Hershel indicates a man seated on a brown leather chair near his desk. "This is John Kawalski. John came all the way from Bed Rock to speak with you. I'll leave you alone and let him tell his story. When your partner arrives, have my secretary notify me and I will accompany you to Felix's office."

Absentmindedly forgetting his offer to vacate his office, Hershel turns and sits down at his desk. The foursome of law officers and John realize Hershel has been rattled by recent events, so decide to wait for Fad in the hallway. When they are lined up like school children waiting to go to lunch, Kris says, "Felix Mendez, - that name has been running around in my head. Does it ring a bell with you, Joe?"

"Funny, I told Bert the same thing, Kris. No, I didn't know him. I would remember a name like that."

Kris turns to John. "Go ahead, Mister Kawalski, tell us your story."

"Hell, call me John. I'm a rock climber – like to go out and free-climb sheer cliffs alone. My friends often say I have a death wish. Maybe I did, but not now. I have a mystery to solve."

Joe wishes John would get to the point. "And that is?"

"A few days ago I was in the middle of a difficult climb. Half-way up an escarpment I was tired, so took a short nap in a crevice. An explosion woke me, so I peeked over the side to see this Mendez guy and another dark-skinned individual walk up to a cloud of dust to check what they had accomplished by setting off a device that must have been dynamite or C-4."

"How do you know that?" Kris asks.

"I worked with both in Vietnam. We knocked down trees with C-4 and det cord. The stuff would cut through a six foot diameter hardwood like a knife."

"Yeah," Bert says. "I heard about that." John nods and continues, "Anyway, I stuck around until they departed and climbed back down to see what they had done. Setting off explosive devices in a state park is illegal. Hell, they could have started a big forest fire."

"And what did you discover?" Joe asks.

"Several pieces of metal painted red, plus some chrome fragments. The biggest item was a curved handle I have seen somewhere before, but just can't place." Kris asks, "What did you do with the evidence?"

"I turned them in to the head ranger at the park, Ezra Parrish."

"Is that all?" Joe asks.

"No," John says. "There is more. I thought I would snoop around on my own – find these guys and read them the riot act for setting off explosives in the park. I rode up and down every gravel road near there searching for their car, but didn't get lucky until I saw the smoke from the fire in which this Mendez guy died.

"I was first on the scene. The cabin was already too far gone for anyone to get out alive. About fifty feet away, his Cadillac was on fire. Like a dummy I stood too close. The gas tank exploded and almost took me out. I had to get a crew cut because the flames burned off half the hair on my scalp." While John rubs his head to prove his point, Joe asks, "Where did you find Felix's body?"

"He was just inside the door on his back, well-done and charred on the outside. The local coroner came out, pronounced him, and took the body into the town of Bed Rock. They have Felix refrigerated, waiting for his next of kin to claim what remains."

"We need to get our forensic people up there," Kris says. "This is too much of a coincidence."

"Yeah," Joe says. "I'll bet we find a slug or two in Mister Mendez. Man, his name is driving me crazy. Why is that?" Bert shakes his head. "I don't know, but here is Fad."

* * *

"Go ahead, Hershel, unlock the door," Joe says. "Here is the warrant for your files in case anyone from the family wants to raise a stink."

"Thank you. If you don't mind, I will just wait in my office."

"That will be fine, Sir," Kris says. "We'll try to be as neat as possible."

* * *

"You first, Fad," Joe says. "Take shots of the entire office before we begin our search, so we can put the place back together before we depart."

"Sure," Fad says, opens the door, steps inside and begins taking a series of photos. After photographing the room from each side, he says, "I think that will do. Come in. Whoever this Mendez guy was, he was neat."

The office looks like an article from "Good Office Keeping Magazine," (*if there is one*). Since the door remained shut after Felix departed for vacation, there is a light sheen of dust on the desk. Other than that, his office is as meticulous as Bert's mother's place. Joe says, "Take each drawer separately. Let Fad document the contents with the camera. Then remove each item one at a time. Don't miss a thing."

* * *

Two hours later they are almost finished. Heat was their enemy until Fad climbed up on the desk and shut the vent. Bert thinks, *If he hadn't been able to stop the heat, by now we would be searching in our skivvies.*

All the drawers were checked and the file cabinet gone through like they were looking for Japanese codes from World War II, but nothing was found. Fad worked on the computer attempting to open Felix's files, and made his way into most, but not all. "The lab boys will have to break his entry code," he says.

Joe nods and asks, "Did you check under the desk drawers?"

"Yeah," Kris replies. "Twice - there are no envelopes or anything suspicious."

Bert decides to look through several books setting on a windowsill. Most are technical manuals, but one title gets his attention; a plain Jane book with a red cover titled: "Terrorists Are Among Us," which appears to be out of place. "Hey," Bert calls out. "Look at this,"

The others gather around, and Bert says, "Check out the title. The book doesn't seem to belong there. Everything else is technical crap only a chemical scientist could or would read."

"Yeah," Joe says. "Take a look inside. It's your find." Bert holds the book by its binder and gives it a shake. A small envelope falls to the floor, and Joe says, "Bingo. Don't use your bare fingers, Bert."

Bert asks, "Fad, do you have any gloves?"

"Yeah, four pair. Here Bert, try these on." After slipping his large hands into the gloves, Bert pulls until they slide onto his fingers. "They're kind of small, Fad." Fad grins and explains, "Your tax dollars well spent again."

Bert stoops down, picks up the envelope by one corner, and looks at Joe to ask, "Now what?" Joe indicates a letter opener on the desk top.

"Use the knife to slit the flap. Dump the contents out and spread them open on his desk. Try not to touch anything more than you need to."

"Roger," Bert says. When a sheet of paper falls out, he adds, "It looks like notes."

"Read them," Kris says and pulls his notebook from a coat pocket to jot down the contents. Joe beats him by two seconds, smiles over his pencil and says, "Never take notes in ink, Kris. You can't change them later."

"I'll remember that," Kris says and holds up his hand to display a fancy thin-lead pencil.

Bert reads the note: "Mohammed - possibly lives in Denver - terror attack on USA - Cotton Bowl. Nerve gas agent is to be used. Thirty-two containers disguised as fire extinguishers. Kill the President and as many Americans as possible."

Kris asks, "Is that all?"

"Hell, that's a lot!" Joe exclaims.

"Wait a minute," Kris says. "Felix Mendez – Sadie told us his name and we didn't know. Remember, 'Fell X Man is'. Damn, why couldn't we figure that out?"

"Because we didn't speak to Felix," Joe says. "Bert did, and the name Mendez never came up in on our brainstorming session, remember?" Kris nods, and his face is red as if he is blushing or upset with himself. "Yeah, I do. Hey, you were right about the Arab, Joe. Sadie must have substituted 'far' for 'middle'."

"Yeah," Joe says. "But we didn't know about this Mohammed guy then."

"Boy," Fad says. "We screwed up big time."

"Yeah," Joe repeats. "But Felix left the plan behind to trip up his co-conspirators in case they took him out. Now we know what to expect. We can find and nab the head guy and put him away for life, or get the death penalty. All we need to do is locate this Mohammed." With raised eyebrows, Fad looks at Joe inquisitively and says sarcastically, "Oh yeah, Joe, that will be easy. There can't be more than two or three million Muslims named after their spiritual leader."

Kris asks, "But even if you do catch him, what happens to the nerve gas? That is, if they do have it. How could they accomplish such a feat and not be detected?" Joe shakes his head in anger. "I don't know, but we need to speak with Hershel to discover what went on here. If they do have the gas, you are right. If we catch this Mohammed character and no one else, that won't ensure we retrieve the nerve agent. Damn, using phony fire extinguishers, that is some idea."

As Kris is looking over his notes, he is quiet for a few moments. Suddenly, he says, "Damn." At his outburst, the others look up in surprise, and Joe asks, "What is it, Kris?"

"We had the solution all the time. Look at Sadie's story. She said, 'Hide three two fire X'."

"I don't believe this," Joe says. "You're right again, but how would we have ever figured out the code?" Now it is Kris' time to shake his head. "Probably never, but Larry was pressed for time and did the best he could."

Bert says, "Too bad his attempt wasn't good enough. Carol will be happy to hear Larry died serving his country."

"You can't let her know," Kris says. "Look, the FBI is assuming jurisdiction of this case right now. Since you are already knowledgeable of the particulars, you will stay on as my assistants. I'll notify my boss, who will clear your working with us through your supervisor, and we will get all the assistance we require. Until then, we have to keep their plans hushed up."

"We need to know how much nerve gas is in each container. Talk to Hershel, Joe - see if any was missing, no matter how small over a long period of time. If so, you will have to let Hershel know what we think Felix and the others are planning, and swear him to secrecy." Fad nods in agreement. "You had better get up to Oak Creek Canyon State Park and Felix's cabin, Kris. He did something up there besides suck his thumb. Your forensic scientists need to be sharp."

Kris agrees. "See if you can talk Hershel into coming along, Joe. We need his expertise to determine what Felix was doing. Hershel will know if it is connected with nerve gas." Joe says, "I'll get him to go by putting the fear of God into his soul. If Hershel believes some nerve gas is missing, and Felix was responsible, he will break his ass getting there."

"I'll leave that to you, Joe," Kris says. "Fad, get on the computer. Try to get a line on this Mohammed. Bert will assist you. I'll drive up to Felix's cabin and secure the scene before someone walks off with any evidence." Joe offers some advice. "Before you leave, Kris, ask John about what he saw. He might be able to describe the equipment."

"Good idea, Joe. I'll see you and Hershel up there, post haste." Joe laughs and says, "I haven't heard that expression in years. Keep using big words, and I might learn English yet, Kris."

Kris grins. "Then you can impress Mona." Joe shakes his head again. "I haven't seen her for a while, and she is right next door. It's too bad I don't have time to check on our romance."

"Later, Joe," Kris says. "Get going."

"Yes, Sir; your Agentness," Joe says and bows. Kris misses the move. He is already out the door and down the hall.

CHAPTER 17

K ris shivers as he sits inside the medical examiner's office in Bed Rock waiting for an answer to his request. Outside the weather is chilly. Here it is colder than three-day-old snot blasted onto a snow bank by a boozer with a bad head cold. Silently, Kris asks, *Why do they keep the temperature so cold inside these places?* Then he answers his own question, *To prevent the spread of germs.* From the looks of things, the germs are winning.

Across the desk, the good Doctor Amos Witherspoon is seated with his face wrinkled into a frown, attempting to find a reason to deny Kris' request for an autopsy on Felix Mendez. The clothes on Amos' tall lanky frame are layered, so he doesn't seem to notice the cold. Amos is wearing an old, decrepit grey sweater with the elbows showing thin over a white jacket, which in turn is covering a two-piece set of dark-green scrubs. The legs are short, and Kris sees cotton long johns peeking out.

Doc Witherspoon's face displays four or five day's growth of beard and a bulbous nose that glistens like amber from the booze he consumes on a daily basis. (*Later, Kris will tell Joe, "The old geezer's nose was so round and red, you could have painted a three there to play pool, or let it alone and played snooker, take your pick."*)

A set of crooked tobacco-stained teeth with a few gaps here and there peer from the interior of Amos' thin mouth. When he speaks, his breath issues forth booze fumes he attempted in vain to hide with a large swig of mouthwash. Suddenly Amos hacks up a goober of phlegm, turns and spits into a soiled sink Kris would never want to use to wash his hands, let alone anything else.

After wiping his chin on the arm of his sweater Amos asks, "Who will pay for this, you young whipper snapper?" Obviously, his FBI credentials haven't impressed Amos, but Kris is persistent. "The Bureau, but if for some reason they don't, the city of Sulfur Springs will. Sergeant Francone will arrive later today to confirm payment for the procedure. Our forensic team will also be here in a few hours to assist you."

"Assist me like hell," Amos says angrily. "I have cut people up and down for years and don't need any help. If the yahoo taking my valuable cooler space..." Amos pauses and jerks his thumb over his shoulder to indicate the morgue behind him, and then continues without taking a breath, "was shot, I will know in a few minutes. Your guys will only be in the way and question my every move. Tell them to take a hike."

Kris says, "I would appreciate your allowing them to observe your procedures and gather any evidence."

"They can watch, and I will provide any slugs I find, but that's all," Amos says. "Now, I want your name, address and badge number. I've been stiffed by the government before."

Kris takes a business card from his billfold, enters the requested info on the back and hands it to Amos. *Finally, thank God and Greyhound. Now I can leave.* He stands to do just that and holds out his hand to shake, which the good doctor ignores like it is a carrier of Asian bird flu. "Thanks" Kris says, but of course doesn't mean it. He turns and walks out the door to where John is seated in comfort in the nice warm car.

When he discovered the rock climber planned to rent a vehicle for a one-way trip to Bed Rock, Kris told John he could ride home with him. Kris knows the rental would cost John an arm and a leg, something a human spider can't afford. Since Kris is headed there anyway, he would appreciate John's company and conversation.

* * *

After they have been on the road for a half-hour and exhausted about every subject known to man, (*John can talk and does*), John says, "If you have time after finishing your other chores, I want to take you up the mountain to where those two guys did their blasting." Kris nods, but keeps his attention on the road. "First, I have to stop by the morgue and arrange for an autopsy on Mister Mendez. Then we'll go to the cabin to secure the fire scene. I hope no one has been there to collect any souvenirs."

John shakes his head. "I don't think so. The cabin is a long way out in the woods. Not too many people know the road exists. Plus, there isn't a lot remaining that anyone in his right mind would want."

"Good," Kris says. "After Joe and Hershel arrive to check the place, I'll go with you, John. I want to see if the red metal pieces could be parts of a fire extinguisher."

"Damn!" John exclaims and slaps his forehead with his right palm. "A fire extinguisher – that's what the handle came from. I knew I had seen the thing before. Why would those two yahoos blow up fire extinguishers filled with green water?"

"What green water?" Kris asks. "You never mentioned that before."

"Hell, I forgot. Yeah, the fire extinguishers were filled with water and green dye that spread out over a fifty-foot radius and made interesting overlapping circular patterns on the rocks and grass."

"So, there was more than one," Kris says.

"You catch on quick," John says. "Yeah, that was my impression. I only heard one explosion, so they must have set them off simultaneously."

"Interesting," Kris says. "Now I can't wait to get there to see what you found."

* * *

Two hours later Kris and John are standing outside the ruins of a cabin now looking like blackened bones of a whale that beached itself here eons ago. A few minutes later, Joe and Hershel drive up in Joe's old, beat-up squad car. The vehicle resembles a reject from a junk yard, and is covered with a thick coat of dust. Apparently on the way here Joe didn't let any grass grow under his feet or on his ride. Now, if you spread grass seed on the hood, in three days you will have a portable lawn.

Kris and John haven't entered the ruins yet. They conducted their investigation from afar. The place is a charred shell, but if enough remains, perhaps Hershel will be able to determine what Felix was doing. If anything is missing, Kris blames the theft on pack rats or small ground squirrels. An overabundance of rodents is in the vicinity.

Although it rained two days ago, there are no fresh footprints in the mud or charcoal, so no one has been here since the firemen departed. As Joe and Hershel climb from the car; Joe stops and stares at the ruins. "There isn't much left, is there."

"Hopefully enough remains for you to inspect in detail, Hershel," Kris says. "Go ahead. If you need our assistance moving anything, shout."

"Thank you," Hershel says and walks gingerly through the remains of the entrance - a scarred and charred quarter panel of a burned door hanging forlornly from one blackened hinge like the tongue of a dog after a long run through a park.

They watch Hershel move slowly around the remains of a table. He picks up, examines and then discards several beakers and chromed, smoke-stained pieces of metal. Suddenly he stops and says, "Oh my."

"What?" Kris asks. Hershel points toward a section of roofing still halfway intact and only charred around the edges. "Will you please move this piece?" What Hershel is speaking of is covered with tarpaper and grey shingles and soaked by the rain, or perhaps still retaining water pumped onto the fire by local foundation savers. Whatever he wants to see is concealed beneath.

"Sure," Kris says. He turns to Joe and John, and asks, "Will you two give me a hand?" They move into the cabin and lift the heavier-than-it-looks rubble. Beneath is a four-legged contraption approximately three feet high, four feet long and three feet wide. Atop that is a badly-bent arrangement of bars that at one time contained thick glass, which has melted into clumps forming strange, obscure patterns.

One side pitched forward and remains almost undamaged. Two holes approximately eight inches wide are in the center, from which hang charred and melted remains of two long rubber tubes with gloves attached at the end. Three fingers remain on one glove. The other is beyond recognition.

"Damn!" Hershel exclaims. For such a mild-mannered man, the unexpected curse is out of place, so Kris asks, "What did you discover, and what was its use?" Hershel points toward a long, slender container with a hole in its side that resembles a tank used by welders. "Felix had an air-tight chamber attached to the ruptured pressure tank over there."

Hershel's explanation goes over Kris' head like lightning on a hot July evening. He looks at the others and sees they are as perplexed. "You care to explain that in layman's terms?"

"A larger unit similar to this is in our lab," Hershel says, "And used to transfer dangerous material from one container to another." Joe forgets John being present and asks, "Like nerve gas?"

"Yes, that's correct. I can't believe this. How did Felix fool us all?"

"Nerve gas!" John exclaims. "What are you talking about?"

Damn, Joe thinks, knowing he opened his mouth at the wrong time. Now the shit is about to splatter. All Joe can hope is that he doesn't catch the full brunt. He says, "That's what they burn in the chemical lab you visited, John. What you heard when I opened my big mouth is classified. I should have my ass kicked for letting you know, but now you do.

"So, you have two options: You can keep your mouth shut and forget I said anything, or you can spend the next few months in protective custody in the slammer in Sulfur Springs. I'm sorry, but what we're dealing with is so secret and sensitive no one else can know."

John raises his hands high. "Hell, you know I am trustworthy and will never tell a soul. Remember, I want to know why these guys were messing up <u>my</u> woods. I want to nail their asses to the wall as much as you; comprendere?"

"Okay, John," Kris says and shoots Joe an unforgiving look. Joe blushes and looks away. "I'm sorry Joe let his mouth run away with his brains. But now you know, and I doubt we could keep you quiet by the threat of jail time. Thanks to you, we know much more than when this investigation began. Stick around, but keep your mouth shut."

"I said I was sorry," Joe says.

"Okay, Joe. We all make mistakes."

Hershel interrupts their conversation. "If we may return to what I was discussing; that is a container from our lab lying over there." He points toward a scorched metal container like one you hook to a milkshake machine, with a rounded top and small opening at the apex. "That container held up to thirty-two ounces of fluid, but now is empty."

"Thirty-two, there's that magic number again," Kris says. "The same number of fire extinguishers contained in Sadie's message. Felix must have put an ounce in each."

"Sadie, who is she?" John asks. "And why thirty-two fire extinguishers?"

"Now who opened their mouth?" Joe asks. Kris looks as if he would like to kick his own ass, but manages to say, "That's what happens when civilians are present and we don't pay attention. I apologize for my remarks, Joe. Lawman or not, John, you are in this thing up to your hips, like it or not."

"That's okay by me," John says. "If I can help my country in any way, all you have to do is ask."

"You gentlemen will have to excuse me," Hershel says. "I need to sit down. You don't know how lucky we are Felix didn't slip and allow the nerve agent to enter the atmosphere and kill everyone for miles around."

Kris asks, "How many people could be killed by an ounce of nerve gas?"

"Thousands," Hershel says sadly. "If the wind is right, and the agent released in a heavily-populated area like New York, perhaps hundreds of thousands."

"Or Dallas/Fort Worth?" Kris asks. John is shocked. "Are those the targets?"

"I continue to open my mouth when I shouldn't," Kris says. "I suppose it's contagious. But yes, John, those are the targets for the bombs we think Felix manufactured here." Kris turns to Joe. "Joe, now that John knows most of the particulars of our investigation; you might as well fill him in on everything and see about having him deputized." Joe nods and says, "I'll take care of him."

Hershel walks to Joe's car and sits down in the front seat. His face is ashen, and he looks like he might throw up. "Are we finished here?" Kris takes pity on him. "Yeah, you told us enough, Hershel. The local police will provide security here until the forensic team arrives. They will gather everything and transport the evidence to Sulfur Springs. There isn't a chance anything dangerous was released into the air, is there?"

"No I don't believe so. Although Felix apparently completed the transfer and moved the final product elsewhere, the fire would have destroyed any remaining nerve gas. There was no evidence of fire extinguishers in the rubble."

Joe's voice reflects sadness and tiredness combined when he says, "Yeah, Felix moved them or got the fire extinguishers ready to go, and someone got rid of him and stole them. Man, these guys are ruthless. They kill without provocation and don't lose any sleep over their victims."

Kris agrees. "Their actions are typical of terrorists. No quarter is asked, and none given. We will need all the assistance we can get to find them before they use the nerve gas."

"Jesus," John says.

"Yeah," Kris says. "We could use <u>His</u> help, too."

Joe asks, "What's our next move, Kris?"

"John wants to take me to where he saw Felix and his partner detonating the explosive devices. Do you want to come with us, Joe?"

"Is the autopsy all set?"

"Yeah, the local doc reluctantly agreed. By now our forensic team should be in town to observe. Doc Witherspoon won't allow them to assist in the procedure."

"Then sure, I would like to tag along," Joe says. "Three pairs of eyes are better than two." He walks to where Hershel is seated. "I'll drop you at a hotel in town, Hershel. We should be finished by tonight. After the forensic team arrives, they will take over. In the morning, we'll head back to Sulfur Springs. Okay?"

"Yes Joe, that's fine. I still can't believe how Felix fooled us all. We wrote off a small amount of never gas missing from a series of canisters as a mistake in calculations when they were initially filled many years ago. Things back then were hectic and not as controlled as now. But that is no excuse. I am responsible for checking such details and let them slide by. If anyone is killed by these terrorists, I will never forgive myself."

John has listened to their conversations with an open mind. He is shocked to discover he is now involved in a horrific plot to kill thousands of his fellow Americans. He shakes his head in an attempt to make the horror go away. *My mystery is about to make me sick to my stomach.*

* * *

Claude's fantasy dream came true, and he can't believe his luck. He and Carla became lovers so casually the act seemed natural. But is he being fair to take advantage of her love with his lies, one after the other? *No, I haven't been,* Claude admits silently, but can't resist her temptation. Carla is like a tonic he needs to exist. One taste and he wants more.

* * *

Several days have passed since Claude was shot and met her. His wounds have healed sufficiently to begin a routine of physical therapy in the evenings after Carla comes home from work, and on weekends. At first, the exercises were pure hell, as he bent his arm and shoulder to the max, but with steady repetition, things improved. Now he only hurts for a short time, and when Claude really gets into them, the exercises become almost pleasurable.

Carla bought several outfits for him with his money. Claude never asked for an accounting. What he has is hers without asking. He knows he owes her more than money alone can repay. There is much more cash where the few thousand he has came from. *If only Carla knew how the money was earned. God, how can I explain <u>that</u> to her?*

So Claude lets the thought go to a hidden corner of his mind, to be dealt with at a later date. He remembers two days ago, when he was doing free weights.

* * *

Carla sneaked up behind, wrapped her arms around his chest and kissed the back of his sweaty neck. "Ugh; too salty."

Claude turned, and she met his mouth with hers. Her tongue searched for his in frantic haste, and he responded. They broke apart, and he pulled her around to sit on his lap. The movement hurt his shoulder, but Claude hid the pain well. "I have wanted to kiss you since we first met. Why the sudden change in attitude?"

"Hush, no questions," Carla said and curled into his arms as he kissed her deeply. They made love throughout the evening and into night. At first, she asked, "Does this hurt you?"

"No, but your love cured my heartache. I've thought of you every night and wanted to crawl into your bedroom to beg if I must. I think I have fallen in love with you." She blushed and said, "I feel the same way, but after all this time together, I'm afraid our feelings may be only lust. I hope it isn't, but if we discover otherwise, I will understand."

Claude held her at arm's length and looked deep into her eyes. "There is much you don't know about me. Some is ugly, and I can't speak of that. But I assure you the good outweighs the evil. I hope I can show you that side of me."

"You already have, Claude. As for the bad, it happened to me before, so I am no stranger to disappointment. If you feel like talking, I'm a good listener. If not, let's enjoy what we have together. If our romance ends, we both will know at the same time."

"You are a very perceptive woman."

"I suppose the librarian in me has been displayed. In my spare time, I read too many romance books. During the past few days, I have had some erotic dreams of you."

"Were any good as this?"

"No," she said. "You weren't really in my arms." For the remainder of the night, not much time was spent on conversation. If Claude died tomorrow, he would remember their first night together forever.

* * *

"Over here," John says. He is leading them on a steep climb from the parking lot, three-quarters of a mile away, and then, up to heaven, (*or so Joe thinks*). When they reach the top, he will be puffing like a locomotive requiring more steam. This high in the mountains, the temperature is cooler, but Joe is sweating like an Orangutan in heat.

Glancing at Kris, he sees beads of perspiration hanging on his brow, but Kris is breathing naturally. *Kris hasn't said a word and doesn't look winded. But then, he isn't overweight as I am. God, where is the top of this hill?*

At John's remark, Joe glances upward from where his face is dragging on the ground, about to be stepped on by his own feet, to discover they have finally reached the crest. Here, the landscape has leveled off and soil is sandy with medium to large rocks scattered about. Apparently the boulders fell from the mountain, landing where they chose to rest for eons before another ice age moves them on another endless journey.

Joe pauses for a moment to catch his breath and says, "Being a rock must be nice - everything is downhill. Then they rest for as long as God chooses."

John points upward and outward. "Rain fell since I was here last, so most dye has been washed away, but you can still see some faint traces."

The spots seem to ask to be joined together like a puzzle in a child's book at a restaurant. Kris walks to the steep cliff to look at a slight line of light-green dots. "I see what you mean. Where were the bombs detonated?"

John points to a small depression in the soil. "Right there - the hole was deeper, but the rain filled it in, too."

"Yeah," Joe says as he reaches down to pick two dime-sized pieces of red metal from the sandy soil. "The water also uncovered more fragments." The small remnants are hot to the touch, so Joe moves them from one palm to another to keep from being burned. "Damn!"

"The sun heats them," John says. "That happens here, where the air is lighter."

"Put them in your pocket, Joe," Kris suggests. Joe chuckles. "Yeah, and burn my private parts. No, thank you; I'll wait until they cool."

"Whatever," Kris says as he continues to study the dispersal patterns to determine how many containers were tested. He is sure more than one. "I believe they brought three or four fire extinguishers here to test. See how the green traces interlock and overlap? I estimate four. Does that leave thirty-two more remaining or just twenty-eight?"

John says, "I believe they come in a box of twelve, or thirty-six for three boxes - the math works out conveniently." Kris turns to his other companions, "See, I said John would earn his bread. Okay, so we still have thirty-two to locate." Turning back to John, he asks, "From the size of the depression you saw after they detonated the bombs, could you tell if they used dynamite or C-4?"

"I would say C-4. Dynamite is too unpredictable and requires more to do the job than they could reasonably hide on or in a fire extinguisher."

Joe nods in agreement. "I see your point, John. I know a little about plastic explosives. A small piece of C-4 goes a long way. I wonder how they set them off all at the same time."

Apparently John has already thought this through. "Your perps must have a signaling device set to one master frequency. They only have to push the control button once to have all the bombs detonate simultaneously."

"I believe we have seen everything there is," Joe says. He puts the cooled pieces of metal in his pants pocket and adds, "Let's head to town, find a place to down a few brews, and talk this over. We need to establish a viable plan."

Kris chuckles, "There you go again, Joe, using big words. The high altitude must allow your brain to breathe."

"Up yours," Joe says and starts walking down the hillside. From the way he rolls down the mountain, apparently Joe would make a good rock. But everyone knows he wouldn't lie around resting on his laurels the way they do.

CHAPTER 18

After breaking in through the back door of Felix's residence, for the past thirty minutes Mohammed has searched like a berserk bulldozer. Paper, books, technical documents and the contents of every drawer lay scattered on the floor. So far he found nothing and didn't think he would. But Hushan said to search, so search Mohammed is. He moves into the bedroom and tears the room apart, making more noise than he realizes.

The sounds travel across an alley to where Harriette Johnson is sitting on her rear stoop smoking a joint and rocking back and forth to music only she can hear. Harriette's short, kinky black hair done in cornrows swings to and fro in time with her movements. Then she hears noise from next door. *What's going on over there? It sounds like someone's tearing the little Mexican's place apart.*

She is no angel of mercy or Good Sam, but is protective of her neighbor's belongings. If someone can rob the Mex's crib and get away, hers may be next. Harriette has a good stash of hash on hand she doesn't want to see walk away. So she gets up, goes inside, dials 9-1-1, and leaves an anonymous message about a possible B and E at four seventeen Elm Street.

The operator asks for more info, but Harriette hangs up. *If they want to know more, they can come out and take a look.* If she is wrong, Harriette isn't about to have them hassle her, saying she made a false report. In her present semi-drugged state, Harriette forgets; when you phone the emergency number, the police know instantly where the call originated.

Hunkered down behind the back fence, she peeks through a crack to watch what will happen. The noises of mass destruction continue resounding throughout the house across the alley. *The cops better hurry or there won't be anything left.*

Harriette takes another hit that fogs her mind for a moment. She may have drifted off for a longer while, because when she looks again, a cop is walking up to the back door. She thinks, *Go get 'em, Lone Ranger.* Then the door seems to flake green paint, and the cop drops like he was pole-axed. Silently, Harriette asks, *What the hell? Damn, the perp shot the cop through the door. I didn't hear a sound, so he must have used a silencer. What a pair of balls.*

The door swings open, and Harriette ducks out of sight to ensure the killer won't see and waste her, too. When she gets enough courage to look again, the shooter is kneeling down by the cop, whose legs are twitching spasmodically like he is dancing the Mambo. To her surprise, he shouts "Help, police!"

His shout startles Harriette. *Why in hell is he calling for the cops? Damn, he just shot one. What is he; crazy?* She looks through the crack again to see a uniformed cop that must be the other one's partner run around the corner of the apartment building with gun drawn. The policeman looks down at the killer, who continues kneeling by the first cop's side like a guardian angel. Then the perp points down the alley to a car pulling away. "He shot your partner!"

The dumb cop buys the lie, takes his eyes from the murder scene and turns to look the way indicated. Harriette watches in horror as the killer pulls his gun from under his legs and pumps two shots into the second cop's back. A string of blood drops flies through the air like red raspberry Jell-O, and the cop drops like a stone.

The killer stands up and calmly shoots the first cop in the head. Then moves to the other cop and does the same. In her stoned condition, Harriette thought she said "No", in her mind. But she must have uttered the word aloud, because the killer glances her way.

Harriette catches a quick view of his profile before dropping to her knees and crab-crawling toward her back door. *Jesus, Joseph and Mary, don't let the fucker get me, and I will never touch another joint.*

She reaches the steps, but instead of going up them and into her house, she crawls under and hides behind the concrete risers. A moment later she hears the fence groan in protest as the killer leans on it. Her heart races and her breath comes in ragged gasps. She puts her hand over her mouth and holds her breath for what seems like an eternity, until she hears the fence groan again and footsteps running away down the alley.

Harriette stays where she is until ten minutes later, when she hears a scream of sirens. She figures, *Some other Good Sam called in the shooting.* In the future, Harriette will be damned if she will pay any attention to what goes on outside her yard. She forgets her oath to God, lights another joint, takes a deep hit, and waits for the cavalry to arrive.

* * *

Later in the evening, at almost 10:00, Joe's cell phone rings in his hotel room. *That figures, I settle back against the headboard with a cold one in my hand, and some idiot has to call.* He glares at the plastic monster with disdain. Joe hates cells with a passion and usually leaves his in a desk drawer. But he is out of touch without the phone here, so had to take the bastardly thing along.

Two hours ago, they finally received an autopsy report from Doc Amos, who discovered Felix had taken two .38 caliber slugs in the back and one in his head. Felix was dead before the fire turned him into ashes.

The phone chimes again like the bells of Big Ben, beckoning Joe to answer. "All right, you sucker, I heard you." He sets the brew down carefully on the dresser, picks up the noisemaker and flips the top open. "Yeah?"

"Joe, this is Bert." Instantly, Joe knows big trouble is in store, because in the background he hears Fad repeating "Son of a bitch!" over and over. "What's up Bert?"

"The shit hit the fan here, Joe. Two cops are down at Felix's house. Whoever popped them also shot them in the head to ensure they were dead."

"Damn!" Joe exclaims. "Who did it?"

"We don't know, but I think the shooter was this Mohammed character. We received an anonymous call from a junkie over on Watson Street. She lives behind Felix's place, heard whoever shot the cops tossing the place, and called it in. Fad sent two rookies from A Squad to check it out. Now he is blaming himself."

"Son of a bitch!" Joe says. He can't believe how casually these bastards waste someone. Two more are dead, and these were his fellow officers. *Damn this case anyway.*

Bert says, "Yeah, that's what we are dealing with here; some very smart and lucky sons of bitches. The neighbor claims the shooter popped the first cop through the back door. Then he kneeled down by his victim's side and shouted for the police. The cop's partner came on the run; the killer claimed someone else shot his partner and pointed to an innocent guy pulling out of a parking spot at the end of the alley. The rookie fell for his story, turned his back, and was wasted, too."

"Son of a bitch," Joe repeats. His heart is beating so quickly he feels he may pass out, so he turns and sits down on the bed to take a deep breath. "Is there any description of the perp?"

"She only saw his profile, Joe. Said he has a moustache, swarthy, dark complexion, and approximately six feet tall, maybe a little shorter. He wore dark clothes, nothing specific she remembers. When they discovered her under her back stairs, she was whacked out of her mind. She says the killer came after her when she cried out in alarm as he gave the cops the coup de grace."

Joe says, "It's a miracle she hid and got away, or we wouldn't know this much." He is calmer now, but would hate to see what his blood pressure might register on a pump. "Yeah," Bert says. "You had better return ASAP. Fad is broken up about this. I hope he doesn't go off the deep end and tie one on. This wasn't his fault."

"I'm on my way," Joe says, slam shut the phone, jumps up from the bed, throws open the door, and runs down the hall toward Kris' room.

* * *

As Mohammed drives toward Denver and his occasional home, he is running scared. Although he wore gloves so there wouldn't be any prints at Felix's place and knows there is no way to trace his gun because he never used the weapon before, Mohammed wonders how the police found him so quickly.

There is no way for him to know the master plan hasn't been compromised. All Mohammed knows is that somehow they found him, and he is more frightened than at any other time in his life. For a moment, he wonders, *What will Hushan say now? Hell, he will waste me as a liability. No, I won't contact him until I am sure of what happened.*

* * *

Mohammed is using the cover of a carpenter on a crew building Big Burger hamburger joints throughout the state of Colorado, with a home base located in Sulfur Springs. As a result, he moves to temporary housing periodically, but can also take vacation time when needed by the organization, which is a plus.

To avoid being seen, Mohammed takes all the back roads he knows, and makes good use of a map to discover ones he doesn't. He hasn't spent much time at the trailer since he signed the lease, but now it seems like an ideal place to hole up. Six months ago Mohammed found the dump and paid a full year's lease in advance, which pleased the pimply-faced landlord to no end. The main reason Mohammed needs the trailer is to provide a valid address for his driver's license and other documents.

He belongs to one of those so-called sleeper cells you hear so much of but never imagine you will discover hiding in your own back yard. Since Mohammed has no close friends, he stays with other members of the organization when necessary, but that doesn't happen often. No one asks questions. They keep their mouths shut and allow you to stay until time to move on.

No one in this game knows Mohammed's last name, which is one of the rules, and a good one for everyone concerned. Most members use phony first names, too. He tried for a while, but sometimes forgot to answer to his alias, and knew the time might come when he would slip up, so eventually reverted to his real moniker.

As far as Mohammed knows, there is no way to trace him to the trailer, so he feels safe by heading there. Although he keeps the bills paid by having them sent to a mailbox in Sulfur Springs, he doubts the heat will work after his long absence.

* * *

A few minutes after 9:00 p.m. Mohammed arrives safely, parks at the end of the trailer and pulls his weary frame from the car. He feels like he has been rode hard and put away wet, a saying he heard one night in a bar down in Amarillo, Texas. Mohammed likes the way the phrase sounds and believes naively it contains sexual connotations, although others don't perceive the corny saying that way.

He glances up and down the street, but doesn't see anyone in parked cars. *I'm probably worried about nothing. I thought someone cried out when I wasted the cops, but perhaps I was hearing things. I didn't see anyone in the yard across the alley. Besides, I doubt anyone got a good look. I wasn't there three minutes. Damn, Mohammed, calm down.*

When he gets inside, he finds the thermostat set at 50 degrees and the house not much warmer. After setting the thermostat to 76 degrees, Mohammed walks to the closet, grabs a coat, and puts it on while waiting to see if the furnace will function properly. When the heat actually comes on, he utters a sigh of relief, lies down on the bed to rest a while, and before long drifts off to sleep. For someone that killed as many times as he in the past few days, his slumber is peaceful.

CHAPTER 19

Wanthen Claude phones Sergeant Francone the next morning, Joe sounds tired, as if he hasn't slept for a day or two. "This is Sergeant Francone. How may I help you?" His voice cracks and Claude knows something is wrong. He hasn't watched TV or yet read the newspaper this morning, so knows nothing of two policemen being shot to death the previous afternoon.

"This is Mister Jones. I want to confess to a murder." Joe thinks he has another nutcase on his hands. "Listen my friend; two police officers were killed last night, so I am not in the mood to listen to your bull."

"I'm not lying," Claude says. "Does the name Katie Adkins ring a bell?"

"Damn!" Joe thinks, sucks in wind and snaps his fingers loudly. Fad glances his way, and Joe motions with his hand to trace the call. Then he asks, "Yes, how do you know her?" trying to stretch out the conversation, but his caller knows better. "Don't waste time tracing my call. I will be gone in a few seconds. Are you interested in speaking with me?"

"Yes, I am."

"Then give your cell phone number to me, and I will phone later. No tricks, Sergeant, or you will never hear from me again."

"Okay," Joe says. "The number is 731-555-7269. Got it?"

"Yeah, I will speak with you again very soon. I believe we can assist each other, especially if the name Mohammed means anything." When Joe hears Mohammed's name, he is surprised, but being a professional is quick on the uptake. "Mohammed? There are a million Muslims named Mohammed. Do you have a last name?"

He doesn't fool Claude, who heard Joe's quick intake of breath at the mention of Mohammed. "You mean you don't know his last name?"

There is silence from Joe's end, as he attempts to reply quickly with a response that makes sense, but his mind goes blank.

"I'll be damned - you don't, do you?" Claude asks.

"You son of a bitch!"

"No, I'm not, Sergeant, and I am not Mohammed. Stop thinking that way. I will speak with you later." The line goes dead, and Joe shouts in frustration, "Damn it anyway!" Everyone in the room turns his way, and Kris asks, "What's up?"

* * *

Last night, Kris followed Joe to Sulfur Springs in his rental car; at times both traveling in excess of ninety miles an hour. The siren on Joe's vehicle blared out a warning, and both vehicles were flashing their warning lights the entire trip. Then Kris phoned his supervisor, who approved his assuming command of the investigation and assigning Joe as his assistant, so both have been on duty nearly twenty-four hours.

"The guy that shot Katie phoned to say he wanted to confess. Then he mentioned the name Mohammed. Can you believe the balls he had?"

Kris is as surprised as Joe. "What did he say?"

"He wants to talk on my cell phone later in the evening. He must believe there is no way for a trace." Kris nods and agrees, "Not if he continues to move around. This guy is smart. Did he say anything else?"

"Not really, but when he mentioned Mohammed, his voice sounded as if he was pissed. Supposedly we may prove helpful to each other, whatever that means."

Fad comes running into the room. "Not enough time for a trace, Joe." Once again, Joe nods, but this time in anger and defeat. "Yeah, and he knew. Can you believe this?" Kris also shakes his head, but in frustration. "Although he is a murderer, you must hear him out, Joe. Any lead we receive on Mohammed's whereabouts is more than we have now."

"Yeah, I know," Joe says and lays his head atop his arms on his desk. "Damn, I am tired."

Fad asks, "Why don't you knock off, Joe? When you are beat, you're no good to us. The same applies to you, Kris. Head for the sack and get some rest. If this guy phones later, your minds need to be fresh."

Seemingly lost in thought, or just plain tuckered out, Kris nods. "You're right, Fad. Come on, Joe. Follow me to the rental place, and I'll return my car. Then we'll sack out at your apartment, and both be there when and if this guy phones. Did he give you a name?"

"Yeah, Mister Jones. Do you know how many there are?"

"Too many, and his is phony," Fad says. "Get the hell out of here, both of you."

* * *

Claude sits back on the couch and looks at the phone resting in his hand. *I'll be damned. They don't know his last name. I have a bargaining chip two miles wide and four deep.*

* * *

Two days later Claude's plans are complete. All that is required now is a car, cell phone, the equipment on his list and his guns. Then he will pay a visit to Mister Mohammed Alta. *It is payback time, you bastard. I told you it would be hell.* He turns to Carla, "I must borrow your car and may be away for a day or two, but will return ASAP. There is something important to do."

She is leaning over the sink doing dishes from supper, and asks, "What, chase down the guy that tried to kill you? I thought you were over that."

"I am," Claude lies. "I took your advice and phoned the police. They are interested in him for more than one reason, but I can't divulge why. It's a matter of national security." Carla turns, places her wet hands on hips and asks, "Are you for real? Do you expect me to believe that?"

"Yes, I do. I'm not lying. Did you read the article in the newspaper concerning the man killed in a cave accident?" While wiping back two strands of hair that have fallen over her eyes, Carla says, "Yes, but what does his death have to do with you?"

"What about the other man murdered and dumped into the lake?"

"Yes, I read the story, too. Where are you going with this?"

"One final question," Claude says. "Did you hear of the guy burned to death in his cabin in the state park?"

"Again, yes, I've read all those stories. What are you driving at?"

"They are all related to and work for the chemical laboratory."

"The police told you all of this? What are you, Claude, an undercover agent?"

"No, they only revealed a portion. I knew one of those involved; the one speaking with me when I was shot. He was also the victim of the fire, so I am no longer pursuing him. The cops require my assistance to identify the shooter, who is also a suspect in the killing of those two policemen. Now do you believe me?"

Finally Carla decodes to believe and trust him at the same time. "I don't believe you could falsify such a story. Okay, here are the keys to my car. I will ride with Sherry until you return. Will you be okay?"

"Yeah, I'm not in trouble, if that's what you mean. I also need to drive to Denver to complete several pending or overdue business transactions. I will phone each morning at six. Oh, I just remembered, I also must borrow your cell phone. Mine was lost in the water."

Carla hands her cell to him. "Phone tonight and tell me how you are."

"I will, don't worry," Claude says and kisses her eyelids. "You know I love you."

"Yeah, I do." She smiles wickedly and asks, "Do you have to leave this very minute?"

"No, I have time for a quickie."

"You dirty old man," she says, but takes his hand and leads him to her bedroom.

* * *

Despite Claude's apprehension, and for all Mohammed's secrecy, finding his address is easy. All that is required is a phone call to information. Mohammed's landlord listed his phone number when AT&T asked for the info. Mohammed isn't aware of that fact, as he never took time to check the telephone book. Even if he had, as far as he knows none of his acquaintances know his last name, so why worry? This will prove his undoing.

* * *

"Do you have a listing for Mohammed Alta?" Claude asks. "The last name is A-L-T-A, first name Mohammed."

"Hold one, please," the operator requests. Fifteen seconds later she says, "I have a listing for Mohammed Alta at 12335 Hill Avenue, Lot Number 5. His number is 555-2244."

"Yeah, that's him. Thanks operator."

"You're welcome, Sir. Thank you for using AT&T."

Claude lays the cell phone on the passenger's seat and continues driving toward Denver. He paused in Sulfur Springs long enough to retrieve replacement weapons from a locker-sized rental storage area, together with additional cash from an ATM. Having the feel of a gun pressing against his chest and another on his ankle is nice.

He turns into a parking lot of a combination merchandise/grocery store, parks, locks the car, walks inside, grabs a cart and walks to the hardware department. There, he spends a half hour finding all items on a long list of supplies. He completes his shopping and pauses for a moment in the fishing equipment aisle to acquire one very necessary item.

After double-checking his purchases, Claude notices a missing item, smiles wickedly and pushes his heavily-laden cart with a squeaky wheel across the store to the meat department, where he chooses a package of foot-long hotdogs. Then he squeaks his way to a checkout stand. The senior citizen on duty there asks, "Gonna do some home repairs, 'eh?"

"I have to clean up some loose ends," Claude answers and pays the bill in cash.

"Have fun," the clerk says.

"I intend to."

Claude's last stop is a store specializing in kinky sex apparel and associated trinkets involved with that type of sport where he buys four pairs of sturdy handcuffs with keys. The potbellied proprietor asks, "Are ya going to chain the old lady to the bed?"

"It wouldn't be the first time."

"Good for you," the guy says and leers openly. Claude shakes his head in disgust and walks out.

* * *

Cursing the day he recruited Mohammed as his right-hand man, Hushan throws the newspaper down onto his desk. *This idiot is leaving a trail of bodies and kills indiscriminately. Now he murdered two policemen. My God, what was he thinking? And he killed them outside Felix's home. Will the police make the connection? We may be doomed.*

He retrieves his cell phone from a pocket and dials the number for the Butler Avenue fire station. When an operator answers, Hushan asks for George Schroeder. While waiting for George to come on the line, he continues stewing in his own juices. *Mohammed must be stopped. I should have killed him when he delivered the bombs. He is of no further use to us now, and it's time for him to disappear.*

* * *

After Kris and Joe depart, Fad is almost sorry he told them to leave. They are now understaffed and hurting. Everyone is pulling more than their share of weight while working long hours attempting to discover any new leads or clues to their two hottest cases - the murders of two of their own, and the associated plot to kill thousands at the annual Cotton Bowl, which isn't far off.

Add to that, their continuing and distasteful efforts to resolve the tremendous backlog of burglaries attributed to the Lawn Ornament Bandits. For one reason or another, their rampage suddenly ceased, and thankfully, no new reports have been received for three days. When Fad glances around the room, he notices Bert isn't on duty; then remembers Bert hasn't been around the office the previous two days. *Where can the old fart be?*

As he turns to inquire of Red concerning Bert's absence, the phone rings. Fad grabs the receiver and answers in the prescribed manner. To his surprise, the caller is Bert. "Hey Bert, what's up, and where have you been?"

"Man, I have been more harried than a bloodhound on the trail of a chain gang escapee."

"Doing what?" Fad asks.

"You wouldn't believe me if I told you, Fad. Tell everyone there the drinks are on me at O'Grady's tonight at nine. I have something to celebrate and want everyone there present. Bring Kris along. He will enjoy what I have to say."

Fad acts amazed. "You're right; I don't believe you are buying a round of drinks. That is a first. What is the reason?"

"I'll let you know tonight."

"Okay, but I just sent Kris and Joe home. They received a call from a guy that says he knows Mohammed, so they are working the case. Everyone else will be there. We can use a break. Your Lawn Ornament Bandits have created such a tremendous amount of paperwork that we may have to go out and chop down our own trees to get the pulp."

* * *

Nine o'clock rolls around, and Bert is a no-show, but no one seems to mind. They are into booze and relaxing as only cops can or will. Finally, at nine-twenty, Bert makes his grand entry dressed in a formal uniform adorned with all his medals and ribbons. His black shoes are shined, and the bill of his cap reflects light like a billboard. An unauthorized large blue ribbon with a number one in the middle is attached to Bert's chest, and he is carrying a large cardboard box of whirly-gigs.

A sign attached to one side reads: "Three for ten dollars; guaranteed to scare the hell out of your moles. Get them while they are hot."

Fad points toward the blue ribbon and asks, "What did you win, Bert?"

"The jackpot – you do remember the Lawn Ornament Bandits? Thanks to yours truly and a sweet little lady named Grace driving a snazzy BMW, they are history."

"You caught them?" Red asks.

"Yeah, the dummies were decorating their own lawn and house with stolen items. Grace happened to drive by and noticed her two pet ceramic frogs on their lawn. Although the perps painted black rings around their eyes, Grace knew them on sight, phoned in, and I went out on the call.

"The frogs were hers all right; had her name etched on the bottom. We acquired a search warrant, and I have been hauling stuff from their house for the last three days. You won't believe the evidence room. It is packed to the ceiling."

"Congratulations," Red says. "What's with the whirly-gigs?"

"We had so many I thought I could sell them and donate the money to the Police Benevolent Fund."

Red moves to Bert's side and whispers in his ear, "You aren't serious, are you?"

"Time out," Bert yells above the noisy barroom. "I need a piss break." Then he continues in a hushed tone, "Come with me to the head, Red, you too, Fad. We need to talk."

Bert places his box atop the bar and leads his two companions into the men's room, where he turns to face them. "To answer your question, Red; hell no, I'm not serious. You know we can't sell evidence. That's against the law. We need the stuff to nail the Lawn Ornament Bandits asses to the wall. I purchased the whirly-gigs from my own pocket. The story of how I bagged the perps is true, but the rest is pure bullshit. I'm hoping to have some fun with the guys.

"They've worked their asses off attempting to catch this Mohammed or whoever wasted our two rookies. Fad, you, Joe and Kris are about out on your feet from working the terrorist threat. Now you and the others need to laugh a little before everyone returns to the same old grind. Play along with my nonsense and we'll have some fun. What could it hurt?"

Red laughs, and Fad joins in to say, "Good idea, Bert. We'll back your play. Come on Red; let's see what Bert has planned." They return to the bar, where several inebriated cops now are wearing whirly-gigs taped to their uniform caps. Bert shouts above the noise, "My evidence room is open for any and all bidders."

Red and Fad spread word of the gag among their closest friends. Going along with the joke, Fad asks, "Ya got any other good bargains, Bert?"

Bert turns his hat around and pulls a cigar from an inner pocket. After placing the unlit stogie into his mouth, he assumes a stance like a car salesman giving his best pitch. "Ya wanta buy a good used birdbath real cheap? It has hardly ever been swum in and features a fresh new coat of bird shit. We have twenty-seven of 'em. I will make ya a good deal."

"Nah," Fad says. "I'll wait until you grow desperate and the half-priced sale rolls around." Bert frowns and wipes his brow before continuing his spiel. "That's too bad, because for another five dollars I would have thrown in a couple Gnomes, or a full set of seven dwarfs."

A half-bombed Ernie asks, "How many of those do you have?"

"Thirty-six," Bert says. Ernie attempts to do the math in his liquor-fogged mind and fails, but doesn't realize. "That doesn't compute. Someone's missing. Poor Dopey and Sleepy, they are my favorites."

From the bar, where she is feeling no pain, almost like most of her customers, Sarah says, "The perps probably dropped some and broke 'em."

"I could use a big flower pot for my back patio," Red says.

Bert brags, "We hold our big truckload sale in two weeks. Don't miss it."

"You got any Snoopy stuff?" Sarah asks. "He's my favorite."

"Only two and they are collectors' items. I'm thinking E-bay, a bidding war, and big bucks."

Red asks, "How many cases did you clear, Bert?"

"One hundred and ninety-four - now you know the reason for the blue ribbon. I am number one."

"Let's give him an ovation," Fad says, and the entire bar gives Bert a one-fingered salute, telling him that he is number one in their notebooks. Bert ignores their signal. "Drinks are on me."

Fad shakes his head, and his mouth hangs agape in mock disbelief. "Now there is a first to go with your number one, Bert." Turning to the bartender, he adds, "Make mine a double, Clyde."

* * *

At one end of the bar, where he is standing and enjoying the nonsense, Red catches sight of a rookie patrol officer named Willie Clancy. Red has been searching for Clancy for some time. He shouts, "Clancy, come here."

Ignoring the fact that although they are in a cops' bar, rookies <u>do not</u> address their superior officers by their first names, Willie asks, "What's up, Red?"

"I had an interesting inquiry from the coroner concerning one of your reports. He wants to know what part of the body the "yet" is in."

"Hell, Red, I don't know. Am I a doctor?"

"No, but, you aren't much of a report writer either."

"What do you mean?"

Red pulls the report in question from a pocket and points to a sentence highlighted in yellow. "You wrote: 'Mrs. Bellows was shot by her husband, and the bullet is in her yet'. You should have used the word 'still'. The human body contains no 'yet'."

Willie sets his drink on the bar and reaches for the report. "Here, let me change it." He removes the paper from Red's hand, walks to the bar, and crosses through the word 'yet'" and changes the sentence as Red suggested. Then Willie hands the report to Red, who reads the change and says, "You stupid jerk. Now the report reads 'the bullet is in her still'. Was Mrs. Bellows a bootlegger? The sentence should read: 'the bullet was still in her body'."

"Gee, Red, I changed what you said."

"See me in the morning, Clancy. You <u>will</u> be scheduled to take a grammar class."

While shaking his head, Red turns to Bert, "Attempting to find brains in a rookie cop is like trying to catch fireworks with a butterfly net."

CHAPTER 20

A t 9:30 sharp, when Claude dials Joe's number, he is sailing along at seventy miles an hour on the outer loop around Denver. He doubts there is any way for the cops to trace his call, but keeps the conversation short and sweet after Joe answers on the first ring. "Is that you, Mister Jones?"

"Yeah, Joe - Listen closely. I have the last name of Mohammed and will trade for the latest info on what is amiss at the chemical lab. Deal or no deal?" Joe asks, "What do you mean?"

"Don't act stupid, Joe. I know of Felix, Larry and Katie, and their ties to the lab and chimps. Somehow I must make amends for Katie. I shouldn't have taken the job, but was greedy. I will hang up now. Think my proposition over; Mohammed's last name for the correct info. You have ten minutes to make up your mind. I will phone again then, and if you don't deal, you can find Mo after I am finished with him."

"Don't hang up!" Joe shouts, but is talking to a dead phone. In disgust, he says, "Damn!"

"No chance of a trace," Kris says. "He's on the move. What did he want, Joe?"

"Mister Jones wants to trade the last name of Mohammed for information on the lab. I have ten minutes to decide. If I don't deal, he won't call again. What do you want to do?"

Kris' squint wrinkles his brow until it looks as soft as the outside of a prune. "He has the upper hand. Go ahead, make a deal with the devil. If Mister Jones will give us Mohammed, we are making headway. Without him, we don't have a clue."

Joe grins momentarily, but then changes to a frown. "Don't I know it? Okay, let's trade. He seems to want to make amends for Katie. Maybe our hit man has a conscience after all."

"Let's hope so," Kris says.

* * *

Mohammed is tired of sitting on his ass in this little trailer, chain-smoking cigarettes and watching TV. Last night he slept like the dead. When he walked in, he didn't realize how tired he was, but now does. *I'm glad the cops weren't after me. As far gone as I was, they could have driven a tank in here, blown my ass away, and I never would have heard them.*

Today Mohammed is feeling good. From all indications and reports on TV, there are no leads in the double murder of two police officers in Sulfur Springs. His worries of yesterday were in vain. For a moment he thinks of phoning Hushan; but then remembers Hushan's last warning and decides no. Mohammed isn't sure the freak wouldn't waste him on general principles.

In case he is wrong, Mohammed remains in the trailer all day, still afraid to show his face. Occasionally he checks outside by peeking between the slats of window blinds to determine if anyone is watching his place or seems suspicious. So far, everything has been copasetic. He doubts there is anything to worry about, but playing safe is always best.

There aren't many streetlights in this part of town, and the cheap-ass landlord must have supplied forty-watt bulbs in the lamp over the outside doorway, which barely illuminates the stairs and doesn't reach far into the yard. Tonight is the dark of the moon, so Mohammed's property is as black as a coal miner's face at midnight, five hundred feet under Mother Earth.

* * *

At 11:00 p.m., after watching the late news, hunger is the deciding factor. For breakfast, Mohammed drank two cups of stale coffee and ate a power bar from an unopened, but out-of-date box. At noon, he consumed four, three-month-old candy bars and drank a coke. Small wonder he is starved.

One last time, Mohammed checks outside and sees nothing out of the ordinary, opens the door, walks out and stands on the stoop to look around as he stretches his weary back. Everything appears cool, so he walks to where his car is parked.

As Mohammed turns the corner, a piece of pipe swings from the darkness and strikes him in the middle of the forehead. He sees stars, and the force of the blow knocks him to his knees. Through a fog of near unconsciousness, Mohammed hears a somewhat familiar voice. "That was for Katie, you bastard." Then, whoever is there hits him in the back of the neck with the same pipe, and it is lights out. Mohammed never hears, "And that is for Larry Holgram."

* * *

With his knee pressed on Mohammed's back, Claude glances around to see if anyone overheard or witnessed his attack. The trailer park is dark and silent as a mosque before prayer time. No dogs bark and no one comes outside to check the noise. After slipping a pair of handcuffs on Mohammed's wrists, Claude ratchets them as tight as possible. He doesn't care if he cuts Mo's circulation – that is the least of Mo's worries now.

He stuffs a rag in Mo's mouth and wraps duct tape around his head until Mo looks like the "Mummy", and ensures Mo's nose passages are clear - he doesn't want him to croak, not quite yet. Then he uses more multipurpose tape to wrap together Mo's lower legs.

Leaving his victim on the sandy, grass-speckled driveway, Claude walks two blocks down the street to Carla's car, where he climbs in, drives quietly to the side of the trailer, parks, climbs out, and pops the trunk. The inside light comes on, so he hits the bare bulb with a knuckle of his right hand and glass shatters. His hand hurts, and he sees blood, so sucks on the cut and tastes warm, sickly-sweet fluid.

Then Claude drags Mo to the trunk, where he struggles to load his victim, torso first. Mo's shoulders finally clear the opening and his head strikes the bottom with a sound like a ripe watermelon being dropped into a cardboard box. After lifting Mo's legs, Claude bends them at the knees to ease the body into the trunk.

The space is tight, but Claude doesn't give a damn about the uncomfortable ride his prisoner will have. He eases the trunk lid down slowly until the lock engages, takes one more look around, picks up his pipe, throws it into the back seat, gets in, fires up the engine and backs onto the deserted street.

* * *

While Kris listens, Joe seals his deal with Mister Jones. As Joe tells a short version of what will happen if they don't capture the terrorists, Claude remains silent. "That's all," Joe says. "Now, what is Mohammed's last name, and where is he?"

"Alta," Claude says. "That's A-L-T-A. He lives at 12335 Hill Avenue, Lot 5 in Denver. But Mo isn't home right now."

"Damn you, we have a deal."

"We still do, Joe. I am about to do what you can't or would be too squeamish to accomplish. Hang near your phone. More info will be forthcoming. Thanks for your trust. Your story is safe with me." When Joe hears the buzz of a dead phone in his ear, he says, "You dirty bastard," then turns to Kris and adds, "I hope Mister Jones doesn't stiff us, Kris."

"I doubt so, Joe, but I'll check the name and address. If it's legit, we will take a SWAT team there." Joe shakes his head to quell that thought. "From what Mister Jones said, they won't be needed. My thoughts are that he has Mohammed and is lording it over us because he could capture him, while we couldn't. Cancel the cavalry charge. If anyone is watching, we will tip our hand. Our priority is the nerve gas. Now that we know his name, we can always capture Mohammed."

Kris nods as if lost in thought, "I agree, but will send one of our undercover agents to watch Mohammed's house. If someone shows, our guy will try to discover his name."

"He had better be good," Joe says, and Kris smiles knowingly. "He appears to be a wino on a binge and dresses the part. In that area of the city, he will blend in well."

* * *

While Mohammed slept, Claude was busy. Now the stage is set, and he slaps Mo awake. They are in a broken-down, deserted barn on an abandoned farm in the countryside east of Denver. The nearest neighbor or main highway is miles away, so screams won't be heard. Years ago, Claude hunted here and remembered the barn as a place where he and Mo could speak privately and not be disturbed.

* * *

After Mohammed regains consciousness, he moans and attempts to move his arms, which won't respond. He turns his head to discover he is staked out like a human sacrifice at some ancient ritual, naked and alone. His legs and arms are stretched to their limit, with wrists and ankles enclosed in handcuffs, which in turn are attached to plastic-covered, steel cables leading to four fence posts pounded into the dirt.

The area surrounding his body is illuminated by a four-cell flashlight with a large lens that is lying nearby on the frayed, green plastic seat of a bent and battered, chromed chair. When Mohammed attempts to move, he feels grit and pieces of straw under his back. The only range of motion he has is in the cheeks of his ass, and they don't do much except roll from side to side.

* * *

A figure of a man suddenly comes into his limited line of vision. The stranger reaches down and picks up the flashlight, turns and holds the light under his chin so Mohammed will see his face, and asks sarcastically, "Are you comfortable?" Now that the fog has lifted from his sore head and neck, Mohammed recognizes Claude as Mister Jones. *He's the hit man. I didn't kill him after all. What is he going to do?*

Fear clamps its heavy hands on Mohammed's heart, and he attempts to speak, but the rag in his mouth only allows a choking sound. Noting the terror in Mo's eyes, Claude grins evilly. "Probably not, but you look surprised to see me. If I were you, I would be very afraid. Are you?"

Mohammed attempts to maintain a game face and shakes his head as defiance shines in his eyes. However, a quiver in his hands silently reveals his bravado as an act, so Claude says, "You will be. I guarantee you will."

Claude reaches out and pulls on a short cord attached to a gasoline generator, which starts immediately, roars for a minute and then hums gently. A light bulb hanging from a rafter comes on overhead, illuminating a twenty-foot circle with Mohammed in the middle, staked out like the main course at a cannibal bakeoff.

Claude retrieves an electric nail gun from its resting place on the ground and plugs its cord into one of three remaining receptacles on the generator. "Have you ever used one of these, Mo? They pack a hell of a wallop. Let me demonstrate." Without waiting for an answer, Claude picks up a scrap piece of half-rotted two-by-four from the floor, holds it in his left hand and taps the nail gun against the board. Then Claude pushes the tip down on the board and presses the trigger.

The gun goes "pow," and the board flies from his hands. After laying the nail gun aside, Claude retrieves the wood and holds it near Mo's eyes so he can focus on the round brass nail countersunk deep into rotting wood. "Isn't that amazing, Mo? The nail went all the way in with just one quick motion. What do you say, Mo? Let's talk of the bombs. Where are they?"

Although he can't speak, when the question is asked, Mohammed's startled eyes betray him. With one swift move, Claude reaches down to rip the duct tape from Mo's face with a cruel flip of his wrist. Then he pulls the filthy rag from Mo's mouth. Mohammed turns his head, spits blood and phlegm onto the ground and chokes out his answer, "You will never find them."

Claude smirks with an evil smile and disagrees. "I believe you will change your mind, Mo, old buddy." Taking his time, Claude picks up a wider piece of plywood and places it under Mo's left hand. Then he spreads Mo's fingers wide, holding them flat against the board with his left hand while reaching for the nail gun with his right. As Mo watches, and fear fills his eyes, Claude moves the nail gun from one finger to another while singing a silly parody of a child's fairy tale. "This little piggy went to market and this little piggy took a walk..."

Before Mohammed realizes what will happen, Claude presses the nail gun to Mo's index finger and fires a one-inch nail through his fingernail and bone. The pain is instant. As he attempts in vain to pull his hand free, Mohammed's screams fill the barn. Claude holds Mo's hand tight, looks in Mo's eyes, and asks again, "Where are the bombs?"

Through clenched teeth, Mohammed says, "Go to hell." Claude shrugs and continues singing his ditty. "And this little piggy said, 'No, I won't talk'..." Then he fires another nail into the joint of Mo's thumb. Mohammed screams again, only this time louder and longer.

When he doesn't receive an answer, Claude continues to sing and ask the same question. But Mohammed hangs tough and won't divulge anything. During the next ten minutes, Claude works his way through the fingers on Mo's left hand, and then fires a single nail through a joint of Mo's big toe. Although sweat pours from Mohammed's face and head, and the pain is evident by the way his body twitches at the end of its tethers, he somehow manages to resist.

Between torture treatments, Mohammed's mind is racing. *I was prepared for death and reward of the promised virgins, but this is worse than death. When will my torture end?* His thoughts are interrupted when Claude grabs Mo by the hair and twists his head upward. "I can keep doing this all night or until you run out of digits, Mo. Let's see, what other place will hurt like hell? What about your elbow?" Claude shoots another nail into Mo's elbow joint.

Mohammed thinks his arm will fall off. He has never experienced such pain. His screams become almost constant. When Mohammed still resists, Claude moves the tool to Mo's shoulder. "This is for the bullet you put through mine." After Claude shoots a nail into the bone, he pauses for a moment to think and listen to Mo's screams. Then he smiles wickedly. "On second thought, there were two bullets. Here's another to even the score." Mohammed hears bone crunch, and the pain is unbearable. His whole body is on fire.

Claude smiles like a ghoul hungry for more blood. Almost in admiration he says, "Damn, you are one tough dude." Pausing again, he asks, "What is an Arab's favorite part of his body?" Looking deep into Mo's eyes, he answers his own question, "Oh yeah, your cock – let me show you something special I brought just for this purpose."

As Claude moves from view for a few moments, Mohammed continues to scream and moan between stabs of pain. Obviously, his tormentor is enjoying this torture routine, which will continue for some time.

When Claude returns, he is hiding something behind his back. Mohammed attempts to steel himself for whatever lies ahead, but pain is overcoming his will to resist. "I have a surprise for you," Claude says, pulls a fish-cleaning board from behind his back and asks, "Guess what I have in mind for this little jewel."

Mohammed screams, "No, you wouldn't!"

"Ya wanta bet, Mo? Let me give you a demo of what will happen if you don't talk." Claude reaches into his shirt pocket and removes a hotdog wiener wrapped in cellophane. "Does this look like something you know? It is bigger and longer than yours, Mo, but watch closely."

After placing the board on Mo's chest so he can witness the proceedings up close and personal, Claude peels away the plastic and clamps the wiener down at one tip. The meat splits open, and pinkish, sickly-looking fluid squishes out to run from the board onto Mo's bare chest.

Mohammed stares at the tool of the devil while Claude continues to smile evilly and pushes the nail gun down onto the wiener. In quick succession, he fires two nails. Pieces of meat fly through the air, but the majority remains speared to the board. Claude smiles knowingly at his prisoner. "One more time Mo; where are the bombs?"

Mohammed doesn't believe Mister Jones will actually carry through on his threat, so he remains defiant and spits out, "You will never know." Claude shakes his head at Mo's stupidity and dumps the ruined wiener on the floor. "Okay, you asked for this."

He reaches between Mo's legs and grabs Mo's limp penis with his left hand. With his right, Claude moves the fish-cleaning board between Mo's legs and lays Mo's flaccid manhood atop. After clamping Mo's tender foreskin to the board, Claude again retrieves his trusty mechanical friend.

His victim screams in fear and pain. Then Mohammed feels the cold steel tip touch his penis, and faints.

* * *

Two minutes later Claude slaps Mo awake again. Mohammed continues to moan in pain and humiliation as he checks between his legs. "Old Trustworthy" still remains intact, but pain from the clamp is excruciating.

"You fainted, Mo, and would have missed the fun and end of my game of Jeopardy. For the final time, where are the bombs? Talk or I will nail your prick so firmly to the board it will never come loose."

Mohammed has reached the end of his endurance. The pain from his wounds is excruciating, and he knows his body and mind can't tolerate the type of torture Mister Jones has in store. When looking into Claude's eyes, Mohammed knows his tormentor is serious, so he gives in to his emotions and shouts, "Allah may never forgive me, but I will tell you! They are in a storage area on the outskirts of Denver."

To emphasize his point, Claude taps the nail gun lightly against Mo's scrotum. "What's the name and unit number?" Cold shivers run up Mohammed's spine, and he feels faint. Between gasps of air to relieve his mind-numbing pain, he manages to reply in shortened sentences. "Store and Go. Unit number 10, 412 Oak Street. Key in my pocket."

"Who is your contact?"

"A man named Hushan. He lives in Fort Worth. That's all I know. We only used first names so no one could talk."

"Well, maybe not everyone," Claude laughs and temporarily removes the nail gun from between Mo's legs. Since now Mohammed believes his ordeal is over, the floodgates open, and he pours out his guts. For each positive answer received, Claude uses a pair of long-handled pliers to remove a nail from Mo's body. While Mohammed divulges the entire plan in detail, Claude listens closely to each statement, compares Mo's info to what Joe and his buddies have discovered, and realizes everything correlates.

As a bonus, Mo discloses names and addresses of three other men whose homes he used numerous times. Then Mo truly surprises Claude. Apparently he is smarter than the average terrorist. In a plea for mercy, and in exchange for his life, Mo offers a list of twenty other terrorists he compiled over the past two years, plus the cell phone number of his cell leader, Hushan. The other terrorists are either members of Hushan's sleeper cell, or those located in nearby states. "The list is in my billfold," Mohammed cries out. "Please don't kill me!"

"Thanks, Mo, old buddy. I will give your offer my utmost attention." He removes the wallet from Mo's trouser pocket, finds the piece of paper mentioned, reviews the contents, refolds the list and inserts it into his own billfold for future reference. Then, as Mo screams in pain, he removes yet another nail.

The last terrorist's name and address Mo surrenders is one working in the Fort Worth fire department and planning to switch fire extinguishers a week prior to the big game. "His name is George that's all I know. He is a stocky German that hates Jews, and is a big shot in the Aryan Brotherhood. He works for the fire department in Fort Worth, close to the Cotton Bowl. I don't know the station number."

"Is anything distinctive about George?"

"He thinks a tattoo of a spider in a web on his left arm is sexy."

As Claude pulls the last nail from Mo's index finger, sweat runs down Mo's face in rivulets, and he looks as if he might faint, again. Claude smiles at the relief displayed on Mo's face. "That worked out rather well, don't you think – the last bit of info and the final nail."

Through his pain, Mohammed actually says, "Thank you, thank you."

"You're welcome," Claude says, and without warning, fires a two-inch nail through Mo's penis, pinning his manhood firmly to the plywood. Mohammed screams in agony and passes out once more.

* * *

When Joe answers, Claude says, "Your boy is ready for delivery. The bombs are in a Store and Go storage area on the outskirts of Denver with an address of 412 Oak Street, Unit 10. Investigate a guy named George with a tattoo of a spider on his left arm in the fire department of Fort Worth, Texas.

"Mo's contact is named Hushan – H U S H A N. No last name or address except Fort Worth. That is all I have now. I'll phone later to tell you where to find Mo. I nailed him good. He may think of cutting out, but I don't believe he will go off half-cocked. He will be willing to talk. That I guarantee."

Joe asks, "Where are you?"

"Later, Dude," Claude says and disconnects.

"Son of a bitch," Joe says, but he is smiling.

"What's wrong?" Kris asks.

"Not a thing, Kris. Let me fill you in."

* * *

When Mohammed awakens, his hands and legs are free, and his foreskin is no longer attached to the cruel clamp. However, to his painful dismay, his penis is still nailed to the terrible board, now pegged to the ground by a steel stake driven through. No way in hell can he dislodge the nail without tearing his penis. *Oh most merciful Allah,* Mohammed prays and moves without thinking. In the middle of his prayer, he changes to a different God. *Oh, sweet Jesus; it hurts. Please make the pain go away.*

Mohammed's left shoulder, arm and hand are badly swollen and nearly unmovable. Every small twitch of his body pulls his penis against the horrible nail. His manhood is already swollen twice its normal shrunken size around the brass shaft, and a small trail of blood lies drying atop the board.

When Mohammed glances painfully to his right, he notices Claude standing a few feet away and watching his every move. Then a box cutter with a two inch blade comes into view lying near his right arm. Instinctively, he reaches out cautiously to grasp the tool, hoping to use it as a weapon. The movement causes extreme pain, and he cries out, not believing the agony caused by one nail.

Then Mohammed's eyes glance even farther right to where a handgun is just out of his reach. In his present condition, he knows he can't try for the weapon, so attempts to remain still as possible. His mind is racing. *What is going on?*

* * *

Claude casually observes his prisoner's movements. "Ah, you're back among the living. I see you discovered my present. How is your pecker, Mo? Sore, I'll bet."

Through teeth that won't unclench, no matter how hard he tries, Mohammed gasps out, "You bastard." Claude laughs cruelly. "You didn't believe I wouldn't repay you in spades for attempting to kill me, did you? This is how I see things, Mo. You have three options:

"One; you can attempt to remove your prick from the nail, but that is an awfully big head – the nail, not your dick. I'm afraid such action would do a number on your manhood, causing it to bleed severely. We're a long way out in the country, so you would have a hell of a time finding a doctor before bleeding to death.

"Number two; you can use the box cutter to cut free from the nail and retrieve the gun, which contains only one bullet. That way, you can do the honorable thing and put yourself out of your misery. But you still must do some serious surgery to your manhood. By the way, this idea is my favorite.

"Or, number three; you can remain still, hurt and bleed a little while waiting for the cops to arrive. I phoned a minute ago and told them where you are. Their arrival will take a while, but if you don't move around too much, and if the medics aren't too pissed at you for wasting those two cops, they may pull out the nail, and you will be free from pain.

"If they were me, I would bend the nail into a circle and leave it there to remind you of what a prick you truly are. I'm leaving now and hope to hear the sound of a shot before I am too far away, but it's your choice, Mo. Take care now, and <u>please</u> go off half-cocked."

Still laughing, Claude walks from the barn, where he pauses for a few moments to listen carefully. There is time to spare. He hasn't phoned Joe yet, but will when he reaches the highway. *Let the son of a bitch sweat a little more. Not Joe, but Mo.* He laughs again. All he hears in response is Mo screaming in Arabic. He knows Mo is cursing him, but he is too late. Claude is well aware of his own impending fate.

CHAPTER 21

As Claude walks in the door, Carla says, "So, you've returned safely. Did you nail your man?"

"No," Claude lies and almost laughs aloud at her unknowing pun. Then he hugs her to his chest and kisses the top of her head. "I've told you; the police will solve that problem."

Carla curls into his arms and returns his caresses. "I've missed you." She feels his heartbeat and the warmth from his body reassures her of his love. After all these years spent searching, his arms feel like home. "Umm, you feel good."

"Likewise," Claude says. "I thought of you every minute I was away. As proof of my love, I shopped in Denver to purchase a small token of my affection."

Carla looks into his eyes and asks, "What?"

Keeping her in suspense, he replies, "Someday I'll buy a larger and gaudier one to impress your friends."

"You can't mean a ring?"

"Why not; don't you want to make an honest man of me?"

"It's supposed to be the other way around," she says. "Show me."

Claude reaches into a pocket, extracts a small square blue box tied with a thin red ribbon, and hands her the present of her life. While tears run down her cheeks, Carla unties the bow and lets it slip to the floor. Then she pauses for a moment to stare into Claude's eyes once more before carefully opening the lid and peeking inside.

She hoped he would return tonight, so a fire is burning in the fireplace. Now, when reflecting the flames, the small stone shaped like a heart sparkles with red and yellow highlights. When Carla looks up again, Claude says, "I thought the ring would bring you joy. Don't cry."

"This is what women do when they are extremely happy." She reaches up to kiss him tenderly. "I have never seen anything so lovely, Claude. Thank you."

"Then I can consider myself engaged?" Carla slips the ring onto her finger and says, "Yes, you idiot." He points toward her hand. "I believe I was supposed to do that."

"Now I'm the idiot." After removing the ring, she hands his token of love to him. "Please do the honors." Claude does as asked, hugs her to his chest again and thinks of what he has just done.

* * *

While returning from Denver, he struggled with his inner feelings and the lifestyle he has led until this moment. Now he knows he is a fool for becoming a paid assassin and realizes the name says everything – he is an ass twice, in over his head.

Although Claude hopes the time spent with Mohammed is the culmination to his deadly career, he is aware much work remains to be accomplished in a short period of time. Now, perhaps the fate of thousands is in his hands and those of a few courageous police and FBI agents.

Fate is fickle, but sometimes gives one a chance to make amends for past transgressions. Perhaps this is Claude's opportunity to square things with the Big Guy in the sky. If He allows Claude's plans to succeed, Claude will spend the remainder of his life with Carla, raising kids instead of hell. The answer will be revealed by both, he and God – which is an unlikely alliance.

* * *

Carla breaks into his musings to ask, "What's wrong?"

"Nothing, I was just thinking how fortunate I was to be shot."

"How could that have been lucky?"

Claude smiles again and asks in return, "What chance is there I would visit your library to accidently meet you?"

"I don't know - probably none."

"Because I was wounded, I met you, which makes that day the luckiest of my life." She holds up the ring for him to see. "And today is my greatest."

* * *

In dim light, Mohammed remains as still as possible. Each unintended move is pure torture to his body, mind and soul as he awaits the law. *Come on. Come on,* his mind keeps saying. His teeth are clenched so tightly his jaw may be broken.

Despite Mohammed's efforts to prevent movement by his limbs, the cold ground causes shivers. Small stabs of raw pain shoot throughout his body, and tears run down his cheeks as he forgets and shakes his head from side to side, attempting to block the sight of his speared manhood from his mind. Silently, he swears, *God, the nail hurts, you son of a bitch, whoever you are.*

After Claude departed the scene, Mohammed digested his torturer's words and options. None are acceptable. He will be damned if he gives Mister Jones the satisfaction of hearing the gun discharge. While staring at the hand holding the box cutter, and then looking between his legs, he thinks, *No, I couldn't.*

Although the movement causes more pain, Mohammed throws away the knife. He is close to the brink of exhaustion with madness waiting only a step away. Then, from deep within his memory, he remembers a cohort saying, "Life sucks, but the alternative is unacceptable." The words calm him somewhat, but agonizing pain persists.

Thinking ahead, Mohammed knows the days and years of the future will be terrible. He will face prison time for sure, and hatred from his fellow inmates. Then, when Hushan and his men complete their horrific attack, perhaps death at their hands will be his final epitaph. But, he played this game and lost. Now his fate lies within the hands of Allah. Another involuntary muscle spasm occurs, and Mohammed screams in agony.

* * *

Over a speaker phone, Joe says, "You wouldn't believe the scene, Fad." After Mister Jones phoned the night before, he and Kris drove to Denver first thing in the morning. Today they are using an office at the rear of a Denver Police Station as their work area. Their plan is to stay in town as long as required to resolve the problems they face.

Kris says, "We received a call from Mister Jones, who gave us the location of Mohammed. We let the Denver cops know where to find him. When they arrived, they discovered him lying with his pecker nailed to a fish-cleaning board staked to the ground. He was in an old barn in the middle of a pool of light. We reviewed the pictures taken by the cops that look like something straight from 'the Omen.'"

"I'm sorry I missed it," Fad says. "I would have left him there."

Joe chuckles. "The cops claim Mohammed babbled like a baby. Whoever Mister Jones is, he did a number on our boy. Mohammed sang our song and kept talking after the EMS crew pulled out the nail."

Kris joins in the laughter. "When they learned this was the same guy that killed two cops, they were anything but gentle."

Fad asks, "Where is Mohammed, Joe? I have a few questions myself."

For a moment, Joe continues to laugh, but then his voice grows serious. "Mo's sorry manhood doesn't look very well, Fad. Currently, a doctor is checking his condition. Surgery may be next on his horizon. But for now, we are keeping him isolated. No one speaks to or with him."

"Why?" Fad asks. Unseen, Joe shakes his head. "The bombs weren't where he said."

"Damn!" Fad says. "I thought we could trust this Mister Jones." Although Fad doesn't see, Joe continues shaking his head. "I don't believe Mister Jones knows. When he phoned, he was upbeat and made several puns, such as: 'he nailed Mohammed good', and 'he wouldn't be going off half-cocked', and sounded like a man sure of his work. I also doubt Mohammed could have faked his answers - not with the pain he went through. If it had been me, I would have been singing opera.

"Mohammed doesn't realize someone moved the bombs. He was truly remorseful for spilling his guts before Mister Jones nailed his pecker onto the board. The leader of this moronic group probably saw a report on TV concerning the cops being killed and labeled Mohammed as a liability."

Kris adds his own observation. "Or they didn't trust Mohammed and moved the bombs without allowing him to know."

"So where does this leave us, Kris?" Fad asks.

"Second in line at a suicide pact with only one bullet remaining - we have only forty days to find the bombs. If we don't, there is a huge task awaiting us. Can you imagine the effort involved in cancelling that annual event and evacuating Dallas and Fort Worth?"

Joe shakes his head again, which is becoming a habit, again. "No, I can't, and hope Mister Jones will help prevent that from happening. You know, although I don't approve of his methods, you can't fault the results."

Kris nods his appreciation of Joe's comments. "Yeah, I agree - Mister Jones isn't us, and not constrained by modern society's rules, but does what he feels is necessary to achieve the most direct response to his questions. Then he only asks once before responding with dire consequences to any negativity. Just ask Mohammed."

Fad also agrees. "No matter how they might despise torture, if the average man or woman knew what Mister Jones accomplished with his style, they would cheer for our mysterious assassin turned vigilante, who understands terrorists don't answer to anyone for their actions, so why should he?"

Joe breaks in to say, "Mister Jones provided another lead confirmed by Mohammed. The guy named George working for the Fort Worth fire department is the only remaining viable resource. Everyone else is either dead or in custody except for him, the head honcho and whatever other idiots are his followers."

* * *

After stopping across the street from Mohammed's trailer, George parks his SUV under the umbrella of a large, live oak tree. George is a well-built, heavily-muscled young man with blond hair and blue eyes, very proud of his German heritage. If WWII had gone his way, the Germans would have won and be running the world.

The rag heads George deals with aren't the chosen race, but are the ones continuing the war against impure America. With George's assistance, and providing they are victorious, perhaps he will join them in world cleansing and eradicate his share of infidels. *(Illogically, (and who ever said he was an intellectual?), George hasn't yet considered the fact <u>he</u> is one.)* As far as he is concerned, too many Jews and blacks are in powerful government positions. Their day of reckoning will soon come.

* * *

While sitting quietly and chewing gum, George watches the trailer for fifteen minutes. A dim light on the porch attempts vainly to chase shadows from a concrete stoop, but no lights are lit inside. However; a car is parked at one end. Perhaps his target is asleep.

When George checks, the time is fifteen minutes after midnight. No one is around except a dirty drunk with a ragged beard asleep atop some folded newspapers on a nearby damp bus-stop bench. The bum wears a long filthy Army coat with Private First Class Stripes on one sleeve and torn threads on the other where the matching insignia is missing.

The drunk's right arm and hand hugs a half-full bottle of cheap wine, while his left is curled under his body. As he sleeps, he snores through his nose. The sole of one shoe is loose and hangs over the heel, flapping in a light breeze like a cat's tongue lapping milk from a bowl.

George climbs from his vehicle carrying a pry bar under his left arm and walks to the bench, where he nudges the drunk. The boozer smells like yesterday's vomit and fresh urine mixed together. He snorts, and his hand slips from the bottle, but he doesn't awaken.

George leans close, and odor of an unwashed body wafts up to attack his nostrils. The bum's breath is rancid, with a strong scent of liquor. George shakes his head in disgust. *Where do they come from, and why do we allow them to live?* If this were any other time, George would enjoy beating hell out of the degenerate, but tonight he must accomplish other chores. If the idiot is there when George finishes, he will kick his ass.

Taking his time and watching where he steps, George creeps toward the trailer and up the stairs to the stoop. There, he removes a rag from a pocket, wraps it around the small bulb in the light fixture above the doorway, and turns his hand until the light is extinguished, but leaves the bulb in place.

When he tries the door, it is locked. Placing the pry bar between door and frame, he pushes with steady pressure until the door pops open. With gun drawn, George moves hastily into the darkness within and stands with his back against a wall. The air inside the trailer reeks of stale cigarette smoke.

Although outside the weather is chilly, George feels sweat from his fear run down his spine. This is something new; he has never killed before. The metallic taste of terror causes a desire to spit in the worst way, but the dry lump of phlegm sticks in his throat.

The dim light from a far-off street lamp allows him to see no one is in the living room or kitchen. In case someone in another room heard him enter, he pauses for a few moments. There are no sounds, so George creeps quietly to the bedroom. Worn linoleum squeaks, and he stops in place. The silence remains unbroken, so he continues walking slowly to where the bedroom door is open, and peeks around the frame. In the dimness, he sees a mussed bed and full ashtray of cigarette butts, but no sign of Mohammed.

After checking the remaining rooms, he curses when viewing the evidence of Mohammed's recent occupancy; empty candy bar wrappers and a bent soda can. As he stepped on one of many scurrying across the linoleum in darkness and ended its life, a roach cracked under George's heel. Silently, he asks, *Where are you, fool?*

George turns on the lights and double-checks everywhere, but finds nothing. Suddenly a thought occurs. *Mohammed's car is still here. Perhaps he took a stroll; but at this late hour?* George has his doubts. On the way here, he didn't see any fast-food places or a convenience store in the neighborhood.

More nervous than he will admit, George turns off the lights and walks outside. He attempts to close the door, but the lock is broken. Finally, he gives in and allows the door hang free. Then, as if mocking him, the door swings back and forth in the breeze. Foolish in his anger, George kicks his offender, which strikes the frame with a noise like a gunshot and rebounds to hit his leg.

While rubbing his sore knee, he silently curses his stupidity. *Damn, that wasn't very smart.*

After screwing the bulb into its socket, George glances around the outside area. To his surprise, the drunk moved on. Except for crumpled newspapers and empty bottle, the bench is vacant. *I must have disturbed his sleep, and he went looking for more rotgut. He was lucky. In the mood I am, I would have beaten him half to death,* George thinks, then asks the solitude, "Damn you anyway, Mohammed; where are you?"

Suspecting his quarry may be asleep there, George walks slowly and deliberately toward the car with gun drawn, only to discover the vehicle unlocked and interior empty. As he turns toward the trailer for a second inspection, scuff marks in the sandy driveway draw his attention there. *Something or someone was dragged for a short distance. A fresh set of tire tracks does not match others. Am I too late? Hushan isn't going to like this.*

He lopes toward his truck and climbs in. As he drives away, the tires squeal, and he doesn't see the supposed drunk hiding behind another trailer. A smile is on his dirty hairy face and a Glock fifteen-shot automatic pistol warm in his hand – similar to one issued to FBI agents in the field.

* * *

Joe waits two days for Mister Jones' call. When he does and Joe answers, he can tell his caller is in a good mood. But his cheerfulness doesn't last long. "Good morning, Sergeant. How are you?"

"Not so well, Mister Jones. You lied to us."

"What do you mean?" Claude asks and sits up on the couch where he has been slouched watching the morning news on TV.

"The bombs weren't where you said."

"My God, Joe, I was sure Mo told the truth."

"I doubt Mo knew they were missing. Hushan probably heard of Mo's latest killings and moved them. You must admit he was a liability."

Claude smiles when Joe uses his nickname for Mohammed. "Yeah, but this leaves us both in a bad situation. Not much time remains before the Cotton Bowl celebration and football game."

"We know," Joe says. "Do you have an idea or someone to torture until he provides more info?" Claude chuckles, and it sounds evil. "No, I believe gentle persuasion will be better for all concerned."

Since Claude heard the news of the disappearing bombs, his mind has been racing, and he is already formulating an extensive plan. Before Joe can say or ask more, Claude adds, "I'll get back to you," and disconnects.

Once again, damn you, Joe mutters. Speaking with Mister Jones brings out the worst. Without realizing, aloud Joe says, "Son of a bitch." Kris looks up from his desk to ask, "Who was it?"

"Mister Jones again – he is still running amuck."

"What do you think he will do next, nail someone else's dick to a board?"

"No, he said something about the use of gentle persuasion. Let's wait to see. So far he is way ahead in the clue department." Kris nods in agreement. "While we wait, we have our mysterious 'George' to investigate. Our undercover agent reported a big, blond-haired perp with a crew-cut and driving a SUV did a B and E at Mo's trailer after midnight last night. Our guy got the license number, which is registered to a George Schroeder living at 1479 Mocking Bird Lane in Fort Worth."

"It must be him," Joe says. "The Fort Worth cops reviewed the employee lists for the fire department, and his name popped up. He works at the Butler Street substation."

As he throws his notebook into his briefcase and checks to ensure he has everything, Kris says. "I believe we should take a good look at George. Let's move our base of operations to Fort Worth."

CHAPTER 22

U nique DeVain "Specks" Washington is a young black man that has worn ugly black glasses with near-coke-bottle lens since he was diagnosed with a rare form of near-sightedness during his sixth year of life. When thinking of his name, which caused him to be bullied from kindergarten through ninth-grade, until he finally said, "Fuck it" and quit school, he wonders what his mother was thinking. She died of a drug overdose when he was sixteen, so he had no doubt she was on "blow" when it came time to give him those terrible first and middle names.

In a way, he is almost thankful to need glasses. Without them, he wouldn't have earned his nickname and watched his unwanted names fade into obscurity. (God how he hated to be called "Unique", but believe it or not, "DeVain" was worse.) Now, since he recently turned 21, he is celebrating his birthday a few days late, plus nearly a seven year absence of any further bullying. None of his current acquaintances or friends, (he doesn't have many close ones), are aware of his true names, and he intends to ensure they never do. Specks is fairly happy, but wishes for more money to do the things he has dreamed of so long he doubts his desires will ever come true, but continues to hope and pray when he doesn't think anyone is watching.

Speck also has learned his street smarts to a point where he earned a small smidgen of respect for his ability to write and sing rap crap. Dressing the part of a successful rapper calls for overly long, kinky black hair to be braided into tight cornrows, and wild-colored shirts open from throat to stomach. Specks also wears trousers with overly long legs that drag underfoot, while a beltless top appears ready to slide from its perilous perch on his skinny hips, while displaying a seemingly mandatory six inches of red and white striped boxer shorts above belt buckle loops.

Together with those gross glasses, (he can't afford to replace them of his own volition, and his old man just kicked him out the front door of his crib, saying, "I'm tired of supporting your deadbeat ass), Specs maintains a slim goatee in an attempt to conceal a bad case of acne.

Specs enjoys listening to hip-hop music, also. Since he occasionally sings at a Karaoke bar, he naively believes he is God's gift to the rap movement sweeping into the black community and spilling over into mainstream America. Most days he spends dreaming of how to make the big time, while doing part-time jobs no one else will accept, such as acting as a guard for an apartment in a better neighborhood than his own.

* * *

When Specs was younger, he tried a little pot and took a toke of coke another night, which made him sick instead of high, so he never touched the white powder again. Today Specs hopes to earn enough bread to pay the rent on a small one-bedroom apartment with a shared bathroom down the hall he found a couple weeks ago. Each time he uses the bathroom, shit is on the stool or someone has pissed all over the seat or on the floor. The smell is enough to make him puke, but the dump is all he can afford.

Specs could have turned to pushing dope, but is no dummy. The white powder is killing the blacks. He joined this far-out organization of old Hushan to further his people, not harm them. If Specs had his way, the dopers would have their balls cut off and served to them for lunch.

* * *

His thin lanky frame shivers in the cool afternoon air, and goose bumps flit up and down his arms. He is tired, half-starved and ready to call it quits, but can't until George turns into his driveway in his big SUV and goes inside to check his apartment.

After George gives Specs the high sign to say everything is cool, then and only then can Specs take off, but that won't happen for a couple more hours. George works the day shift and doesn't arrive home until 6:00 p.m.

As Specs attempts to keep warm, he thinks, *All this for a lousy twenty frigging dollars an hour. I wonder what George has in his crib that is so cool I have to spend my time as a guard.*

* * *

Today wasn't too bad. For part of the afternoon, he had company. Two buddies from the street that enjoy rap dropped by to chat and compose new tunes. They spent most time sitting on the curb across from George's joint attempting to outdo each other with tales of what they will do after making their first million.

Franklin, an old friend from high school, and "Twist," an older wino, took a few hits from a joint and tried to talk Specs into joining them, but he said "No," and was adamant. After a few more war stories, they departed for greener fields, leaving him alone.

* * *

Now Specks wishes he asked one of them to watch the place while he took a piss break. His bladder feels like it is on fire. If he is lucky, he might also get rid of the pizza he ate last night. *Should I take the chance? If Hushan discovers I left my post, he will have my ass, but I need to piss. To hell with it. No one has been here all day. Who will know?*

He could have gone to the poolroom a block south, but the old buzzard behind the counter doesn't want anyone but customers using his crapper. So that leaves only a burger joint, two and a half blocks the other way. Specks starts off at a run, but is out of shape. After the first block, he slows to a brisk walk. Although the day is cool, by the time he arrives, he has worked up a sweat. Then he discovers someone is in the can and has the door locked.

Finally, after a three minute wait, a young Hispanic approximately fourteen walks out with a grin on his face and a paper towel in one hand. "Sorry," he says and throws the wadded paper at a trashcan, misses and says, "Damn," but doesn't pick up his litter.

Specks hurries into the bathroom, locks the door and drops his drawers, sits down, empties his bladder and strains until he finally hears a small splash in the bowl. Then he wipes, pulls up his pants and exits the restroom.

As he walks by the counter, the smell of hamburgers and fries get to him. *What the hell, a man's got to eat - don't he?* There is no one waiting in line, so he hurries to the ordering counter and waits until a young mulatto teenybopper, a mixture of black and Hispanic heritage with a nametag reading Sally ambles over to take his order.

Sally concentrates on working her gum from one side of her mouth to the other before she says, "Welcome. How can I help y'all?"

"A cheeseburger and fries," Specks says.

"Ya want anything to drink?"

"Yeah, throw in a small coke, and can you hurry?" Nervously, Specks glances over his shoulder. The street is empty, but he can't see all the way to where he is supposed to be. The cash register hums and spits out a long white receipt. After smacking her gum, Sally says, "That'll be three dollars and twenty-seven cents." He hands her four, wrinkled one-dollar-bills and waits until the cash register tells Sally the right amount of change. He knows she can't figure it on her own, and he is correct.

Sally finally determines how much she owes him and hands him the change without counting the amount aloud. Then she walks to a window behind to find a cheeseburger and fries baking under a yellow light. Specks has no idea how long they have been toasting there, but is in a hurry. *To hell with it.*

After Sally packages them and gives him a cup for his drink, he runs to the fountain, fills the cup half-full with ice and pushes the mechanism to active the spigot. The foam takes forever to dissipate, and in his haste, Specks doesn't wait to fill the container to the top. As he hurries out the door, he attempts to suck soft froth from the edge, but several drops spill onto his new, stone-washed jeans, and he curses again.

* * *

Five minutes later, Specks returns to his post and gives a large sigh of relief. No strange cars are on the street, and George's crib looks the same, so he sits on the curb to eat his lunch. When finished, he crumples up the napkin and wrapper from the burger, puts them into the sack and takes time to walk across the street and throw his trash into a small dumpster outside George's apartment house.

* * *

From a block away Claude spots the guy watching George's apartment. The black kid is leaning against a lamppost and looking bored. But every other minute he stares across the street at the apartment building where George lives. *Unless he is peddling dope or paid to be there, a young black wouldn't be out alone on the street in the cool air - not in this part of town,* Claude reasons. This guy isn't doing the bop most dealers do or paying attention to traffic on the street. *No, he isn't a dealer. He's a guard.*

Instead of continuing down the street, Claude pulls up the collar of his jacket, turns the corner and circles the block, where he discovers a poolroom with a coffee shop and bar to one side that overlooks his targeted street. He walks in and sits on a stool at the counter where he can look out the window. The black kid is still there, stomping his feet to keep them warm.

* * *

At a pool table near the door, an old black man plays a solitary game of eight ball, shooting bank shots and looking as if he was searching for a sucker to hustle. When he notices Claude watching his action, he asks, "Care to shoot a little pool?"

"Don't mind if I do, old timer," Claude says. "I haven't held a cue in my hand for a long while, so don't laugh if I scratch or flub a shot."

"You wouldn't try to hustle an old man out of his social security, would you?"

"Not me. Rack 'em up."

* * *

While keeping an eye on the guard, Clause shot pool for two hours, loosing more games than he won. A few minutes after they finished their first game, Claude noticed two men join the black kid. One is a young groupie and the other an older boozer holding a bottle of cheap wine in one hand and a rolled joint in the second. They hang around for another hour until the booze and hash are exhausted. Then they take off, leaving the guard alone again.

* * *

From where Claude is standing, he sees the guard shifting his feet around and crossing his legs - the sign Claude has been waiting for. He watches while the young black looks around and then takes off at a lope down the street.

Claude hands his opponent twenty dollars. "Thanks for the games."

His new friend holds the bill in his fingers and gives Claude a salute with the same hand. "Thanks yourself. You play pretty good pool for someone that hasn't held a cue in a long time." Claude shakes the old man's hand. "Yeah, but you would take me nine times out of ten. Maybe I'll see you again, and we can play some serious pool."

He walks out and moves quickly down the opposite side of the street to George's apartment building. A fast look around determines the black kid is the only lookout. After removing a small brown leather container from his pocket he selects a pick, and within a minute, is inside. After closing and locking the door, Claude does a quick search of the living room furnished with worn-out junk in the style of the fifties and a ragged carpet stinking of stale cigarettes and spilled beer.

Next is the bedroom, with a sweat-stained, unmade bed and soiled sheets knotted at the bottom. A swastika flag and picture of Hitler giving the Nazi salute hang over the bed. Several twisted gum wrappers are spread in a sloppy Swastika sign atop a bedside table also littered with well-creased propaganda pamphlets from the Aryan Brotherhood. Claude is satisfied of two things – George isn't married; but is a slob.

Hanging from a wooden peg in the bedroom closet is a loaded .45 caliber automatic in a shoulder holster, with two full clips attached to the straps in individual leather pouches. Claude takes the rig, ejects the clip and live round from the chamber, pockets both and the extra clips, and hides the holstered weapon under a sagging couch in the living room.

Then he checks the kitchen, which smells of day-old bacon grease and has dirty dishes piled in the sink. The residue of scrambled eggs clings to one plate, while another holds a tomato stain that looks like spaghetti sauce.

The only interesting item in the entire dump is a certificate issued two years ago certifying George Schroeder as a licensed jet pilot. George must be proud of his accomplishment, as the diploma is framed in dark oak with non-glare glass.

Claude moves on to the garage, where under a tarpaulin in the far left corner, he finds what he is looking for – two large black suitcases. Each supposedly holds sixteen fire extinguishers.

After Claude opens the top case, he feels the hair on his arms and the back of his neck rise. It is frightening to think that here in the middle of Fort Worth, there for the taking, is enough nerve gas to kill everyone for miles around. Claude's hands shake, and sweat runs down his spine as he carefully re-closes the case and pulls the tarp in place to where it has been to cover both. *How brazen or stupid can they be?*

He checks his watch, noting the time is five-fifteen. If Claude's information is correct, his target will be home soon. Quietly, he walks to the bedroom closet, where he pushes the clothes to one side and leans against the wall, out of sight, with the door half open, the way he found it.

A clock on a bedside table is ticking away the seconds, but he doesn't mind waiting. In fact, Claude is looking forward to meeting George – up close and personal.

CHAPTER 23

Today Sadie is being sprung from prison. Only she and the rookie cops assigned to clean up after her are happy to see her depart. When you have scooped monkey crap once, especially after too many ripe bananas, you never care to do so again. Word has passed around the station; the next guy overfeeding Sadie will find his car full of chimp do-do.

Bert had a brilliant idea to videotape Sadie's testimony for evidence at any forthcoming trial, as she signs her way into fame with the assistance of Alice and Mona. Alice has become quite proficient at signing, so Mona allows her to be a co-star of the show. But now, they are finished, and everyone has stopped by to say goodbye to the little widow chimp.

Mona told Sadie that Wilbur died. They can tell the news broke her up by the way Sadie mopes around her cage. But when Alice arrives to take her home to the research lab, Sadie perks up. "Sadie will be okay," Mona says. "When she sees the other chimps and monkeys, it will be like old home week."

Alice smiles and says, "I will visit her every chance I get." Joe nods and points toward her friend. "Sadie is free to go."

* * *

Last night he flew to Sulfur Springs to acquire some clean clothes and clear his desk before returning to Fort Worth. At least that's what he told Fad, who laughed and asked, "Who do you think you're fooling? We all knew you wouldn't miss a chance to spend time with the lovely Miss Mona." Joe grinned like Sadie. "That thought did cross my mind."

* * *

Later, Joe and Mona shared a few moments alone and made the most of them. "I'm sorry I haven't been able to see you, Mona. I've been in Fort

Worth and have to head back there tomorrow. Kris and I will be there for some time."

"I've missed you, Joe." If anything, her smile was brighter than before. Joe could sense her perfume hanging in the air. When she was this close, he had an involuntary erection. "When we finish this job, I hope you will let me take you out to eat, or dancing or something."

Mona reached over to pat his groin possessively. "Definitely something - we wouldn't want this to go to waste, would we? It's too bad you have to leave tomorrow morning."

Joe grinned knowingly. "Yeah, but we still have tonight." She returned his smile. Hers was prettier. "Do you think you could tear yourself away from the paperwork you mentioned?"

"Possibly," he said, took her arm possessively and poked his head around the doorframe to Fad's office. "I'll be out of the office until tomorrow morning. If you need me, try my cell phone."

"Okay," Fad said. *Yeah, as if you would answer - get some, Joe.*

* * *

Claude hears the garage door motor activate, followed by a high-pitched squeal like a rat with its tail caught in a trap, as the door struggles against gravity and rises reluctantly into the air. As its diesel motor pulls the heavy vehicle into the garage, George's SUV sounds like a freight train switching cars in a rail yard.

The engine noise dies, and the truck door opens and slams shut. Then Claude hears George walking through the door and into the kitchen. After taking a cursory look and being satisfied, George returns to the garage.

Claude hears him say, "See you tomorrow, Specks." Then the garage door squeaks downward again and thumps against the concrete. The motor whines for an instant longer, and silence returns. As George walks into the bedroom, he is whistling a merry tune, and has his shirt half off, when Claude pushes from the closet with gun in hand. George is startled and struggles to get his arms untangled, while asking "Who the hell are you?"

"I'm a friend of Mohammed's and Hushan's." He waves the gun, telling George to have a seat on the unmade bed. George seems puzzled but follows Claude's instructions. "I've never seen you before. What's your name?"

"Mister Jones," Claude says and notes the change in George's eyes. His irises had been narrow. Now they have widened in fear or cunning. "I've heard of you."

"I thought you may have. Just before I killed him, Mohammed said to tell you hello."

"My God," George says. His hands shake, and he clasps them together to hide the fact.

"<u>He</u> won't be much help to you," Claude says. "But don't be nervous. I'm not here to kill you. I need you to deliver a message to Hushan." George attempts to lie, but is a novice. "How would I know someone named Hushan?" Claude shakes his head at George's stupidity. "You have his merchandise stored in your garage. Why attempt to deceive me?"

"What's the message?" George asks and looks like he might be growing bolder. Claude notices. "Turn around, lie on the bed and put your hands behind your back. Don't do anything stupid, Georgie boy. Your weapon isn't where you think. Use your head. I told you that I don't want to kill you – not yet."

George looks into Claude's eyes and knows his opponent is telling the truth. He turns over and does as Claude ordered. After taking a pair of handcuffs from a pocket, Claude slips them around George's wrists, snaps them shut and lays his gun alongside George's head.

"Tell Hushan he will have his merchandise returned when I receive my four hundred thousand dollars, plus an additional two million for my trouble. I'll give him five days to gather the money. Then I'll phone his cell to let him know where the exchange will take place. You got all that?"

"Yeah, I do. You do know you're a walking dead man, don't you?"

"Not yet, Georgie Boy," Claude says and hits George in the back of the neck with his weapon. George slumps to the floor, unconscious. Claude ensures George is out of business. Then ties his legs together, pushes a rag into his mouth and tapes it shut. When he is finished, he walks into the garage to unlock the door.

Returning to the front door, Claude strides out boldly as if he owns the joint. Continuing to move briskly, but not running so as not to attract attention, he makes his way two blocks down the street and another half-block to the right, where he parked Carla's Pontiac. After firing up the engine, Claude returns to George's apartment, backs into the driveway, climbs out and raises the trunk lid, then the garage door.

* * *

Specks turns to watch the fancy, dark red Pontiac Firebird drive by. He hasn't seen anything that sweet in quite a while. With a possible exception of a drug dealer he doesn't know, the car can't belong to anyone living in this neighborhood. Pushers are the only ones able to afford something that nice.

He is seated on the stoop of Helen Sanchez's porch, near the door with his back resting against the jamb, as he tries to work up the nerve to ask her out. While looking bored, Helen is seated on the top step, concentrating on putting the final touches to her bright red fingernail polish.

Specks has heard; if you treat her right, Helen puts out. He never had the courage before to ask her for a date. She is twenty-five and probably thinks he is a kid. He points to the car and says, "Look at that." Helen uses her wrist to brush brown hair away from grey eyes so she won't spoil the new polish job, takes a quick look and says, "Neat-o."

She is wearing a yellow halter-top under a jade-green short jacket and Capri pants in a darker shade of olive. Her pert nipples are pushing against the material of her thin bra, the sight of which causes an erection that makes Specks wish he were older.

As the car drives down the block, Specks' eyes follow in envy. He is surprised when the vehicle stops and backs into George's driveway. Then a big white dude gets out, pops the trunk, raises the garage door as if he lives there, and disappears inside. In less than a minute, he comes out carrying a large black suitcase on its side, which must be heavy, as he uses both hands to support the case and struggles while placing his load into the trunk.

Forgetting Helen's presence, he says, "What the fuck is he doing?"

"Watch your dirty mouth," she says and frowns.

"Sorry," Specks says contritely, knowing his motor-mouth probably screwed up his chances with her, and points down the street. "I meant the white dude hauling stuff from George's crib. Look."

Helen turns as the white guy comes out again with another case. After loading it, he closes the trunk lid very slowly and cautiously, as if the cases contain glass or something very precious and fragile.

Specks stands and begins to walk down the stairs, but the white dude climbs into the car, starts the engine and turns his way. Specs jumps into the darkness of the doorway, where he stares at the license plate number on the front bumper.

Then he says, "They are Colorado plates, 8 4 N 6 4 5. Help me remember the number, Helen. Write it down somewhere."

"With what? I don't got no pen."

"Use your lipstick. 8 4 N 6 4 5 – did you get it?"

"Yeah," Helen says. "But repeat the numbers to be sure, and you owe me six bucks for a new tube."

"Okay. 8 4 N 6 4 5," Specks says as he checks the numbers and figures she scrawled big block style on the stoop.

"Yeah, you got them right. Stay here, I have to check on George. Something weird is going on."

* * *

Just after he and Mona completed their second round in the sack, Joe's cell phone rings. Their first coupling was frantic, and the scratches on his back will be a reminder for several days. The second was slower, more romantic. Joe thinks, *Mona is a tiger, and I have her by the tail.*

He laughs inwardly at his own joke and is reaching for her left breast to see if the nipple is as firm as it appears to be, when the jingle interrupts him. "I have to answer. Sorry."

"We have all night, Joe."

Joe thinks Fad is probably phoning to yank his chain, so snarls into the phone, "Yeah, what do you want?"

"Hello, Joe. This is Mister Jones." Joe sits up in bed and reaches for his suit coat to retrieve his pencil and notebook. "Yeah, I recognized your voice. What's up?" Mister Jones' voice sounds upbeat. "I thought you might want to do a little horse trading."

"What do you have to bargain with?"

"Thirty-two fire extinguishers," Claude says, and Joe hears him laugh. "You mean you have them?"

"Would I lie to you?"

"You did once."

"I wasn't lying, Joe. They were in the storage area. Hushan grew frightened and had George move them."

"You know George, do you?"

"Yeah," Claude says, "You might say he and I are good buddies. He thinks I'm a knockout."

Joe asks sarcastically, "What do I have to trade that you might need?"

"What about an unconditional pardon or immunity from prosecution for any and all crimes I may have committed on your turf, to include Katie and the others?"

"You have a large pair of balls, Mister Jones. What makes you believe you can get away with that?" Now his caller's voice sounds like he is grinning. "Check with your FBI buddy and his bosses. If the fire extinguishers are returned, I'll bet they won't give a damn about me. In fact, if you will listen, I have a good idea."

"Go ahead," Joe says in the same tone of voice. "What do you have to lose?"

"You should ask someone at the chemical lab if they can siphon the nerve gas from the fire extinguishers and replace it with something harmless. If so, I can trade them to Hushan for the money he owes, and he will believe his plans are still viable. In this way, Hushan and his friends will proceed with an innocuous attack, which gives you time to discover the names of all the players and capture them."

Joe wonders if innocuous means the same as ineffective. He hates people that use big words. "I don't have any idea how long it would take to do something like that. How much time do we have?"

"I gave Hushan five days to get my money together." Although Claude can't see, Joe frowns. "So, it's all about money after all."

"Not really, but a man has to live, Joe. If everything goes my way, I plan to retire and never be heard from again. If not, I'll have fun playing this game to its conclusion."

Joe asks, "What if Hushan double-crosses you and tries to take you out?"

"I have a fool-proof plan to make the switch. I will have the upper hand, and my campaign platform is the best. Trust me." Joe thinks, *There he goes again, making up puns I can't figure out.* But he says, "Okay, I'll make some calls concerning your immunity, which may take a while."

"I'll phone at 0800 hours tomorrow, but no traces, Joe. If we have a deal, I will tell you where to find the cases. You can return them to me later. Don't go back on your word. Before you receive the merchandise, I want the offer of immunity in writing."

"If I can get it, you will," Joe says. "God, I hope this works. Just knowing that stuff is out there somewhere makes me sweat. Are you sure you know how to handle the fire extinguishers?" Claude chuckles. "Like a baby, gentle and easy. I've talked too long. See you tomorrow."

When Joe swears, "Damn," Mona asks, "Who was it?" Joe checks his watch on the bedside table. "A murderer wants to make a deal. In the next ten hours, I must convince my superiors and several other important people to agree. I'm sorry to cut this session short, Baby."

"There will be others," Mona promises and kisses him. "Go save the world." As Joe begins to dress, he says, "God, I hope so."

* * *

When his leader answers, George says, "Hushan, the merchandise is missing. Your paid assassin got into my apartment and knocked me out. When Specks woke me, we discovered the cases are gone."

"You fool! Why didn't Specks see him enter? There are only two ways in; the front door and garage. He was paid to watch both." George knows he and the guard both are in trouble, but attempts to talk his way out. "Specks took a piss break and was away from his post a few minutes. Mister Jones must have been watching and got in then. He hid in my closet, and I didn't see him."

"You are both idiots!" Hushan shouts. "Now years of dedication to our cause and meticulous planning are ruined. If you weren't the only pilot we have for the emergency escape plane, I would shoot you myself."

George interrupts his rage to say, "Mister Jones left you a message."

"What is it?"

"He wants to trade the two cases for four hundred thousand dollars you owe him, plus another two million for his trouble. Was it smart of Felix and Mohammed to attempt to kill him? Now he is on our case. They should have paid him." Hushan knows George is telling the truth. "That was my fault. They did so under my orders. Did anyone see this man?"

"Yeah, the good news is Specks got his license number from a Colorado plate. He said it is 8 4 N as in Nancy, 6 4 5. A buddy of mine on the police force will trace it if I ask. Do you want me to?"

"Yes, you fool, why wouldn't I? You should have done so already. Phone when you know his address."

"Okay," George says and then asks, "Will you make the deal?"

"We will see," Hushan says, and unknowingly repeats, "We will see. Tell Specks it was a good job getting the license number. But if he ever leaves his post again, I will take personal pleasure in tearing his head from his skinny body."

"Yes Sir. I am sorry about this, Hushan, but there is some good news. Mister Jones said he had killed Mohammed after the fool gave my address. At least we won't have to worry about the police questioning him."

"Sometimes there is a rainbow behind the clouds," Hushan says. "I am pleased to hear the good news. Losing the fire extinguishers was not your fault George, but I have a favor to ask. After you tell Specs how proud I am of him, kick his ass to teach him a lesson."

CHAPTER 24

Six a.m. is early for a phone call, but Claude knows Carla doesn't sleep late and never leaves for work until seven-thirty. He dials her number, and a mental picture of her naked body dances in his mind. God, he misses her. When she answers on the second ring, he says, "Hi Babe, do you miss me?"

"Yes, when are you coming home?"

Claude departed two days ago. According to his story, he was headed to Denver to assist the cops again, but Carla worried and wondered if he was telling her everything.

"A few more days should do, Babe. There has been a new development, so I must remain in Denver to see what happens. I wish I could tell you everything, but can't. You will have to trust me."

"As long as you swear you won't kill anyone, I believe you."

"Pile up the Bibles. I really have helped the police. When this case is resolved and the bad guys incarcerated, you will hear the entire story. Then you will be proud of me."

"I am now," Carla says. "And I love you."

"I love you too, you know that."

"Yeah I do, but have to hear you say so every day or I become frightened. Oh, before I forget, the rental car agency phoned. You're off the hook. The police located the car with no damage in a mall parking lot, so everyone is happy."

"That is good news." Carla smiles at his reaction. "Okay, take as long as you need. Then come home to me. I'll be waiting."

"See you soon," Claude says. "I'll phone tomorrow at the same time."

"I'll be here."

* * *

"The car is registered to a woman, not a man," George says. "Her name is Carla Roberson, and her address is 363 Wharf Avenue in Sulfur Springs." Hushan writes down the address. "She is probably Mister Jones' girlfriend. Remember, he drove a rental car, and we took it."

"Yeah, the next morning I dropped it in a mall parking lot."

"Get your ass in gear, George. Come by and pick me up. We need to take a trip to Sulfur Springs to meet the lovely Miss Roberson."

"Give me ten minutes, and I'll be there."

* * *

After they are ushered into his office and seated in front of his desk, Kris' supervisor, Cowboy "Hoot" Henninger says, "You have been busy, Kris. You also made some important decisions on your own initiative. How positive are you this Mister Jones is legit?"

* * *

His first name truly is Cowboy. His rodeo father gave him the title a year before a renegade bull buried him under six feet of arena dirt. Cowboy received his alias when his third grade teacher saw his name and said, "That's a hoot." The nickname stuck. Now Hoot is how everyone addresses him. He doesn't give a damn about the Cowboy moniker anyway.

Hoot is dressed sharp in a tan pair of Dockers and matching shirt. Nearly 65, he has a full head of snow-white hair under his Stetson and as many wrinkles on his brow as his years. He is suntanned, skinny and looks taller than his five foot and six inch height. Kris believes the cowboy hat does that for him. Hoot is his immediate supervisor, in charge of the entire district, to include Denver and Sulfur Springs.

* * *

In answer to Hoot's question, Kris says, "So far Mister Jones has panned out and is our only lead to the nerve gas. I had to make a snap decision to allow him to join our investigation. If somehow I goofed, I'm sorry."

"No," Hoot says. "I've supported you 100 percent and will continue to. I would have made the same decisions. No apology is necessary, and I'm pleased you kept us informed."

"Thanks, Hoot."

"So, where are we now?" Hoot asks.

After referring to his notes, Kris says, "Our Mister Jones suggested a somewhat complicated plan I believe is viable. He will trade the cases with the nerve gas containers to us for full immunity. The scientists at the chemical lab will drain the fire extinguishers of nerve gas and replace it with a non-lethal fluid. Then Mister Jones takes the cases and trades them to this Hushan character for the money he has coming, since Hushan reneged on his fee when he killed Katie and the chimps and the two other victims."

Hoot frowns and asks, "Why would we agree to his proposition?"

"If the terrorists believe they still have the nerve gas, they will continue with their original plans, allowing enough time for us to either infiltrate their organization or discover other terroristic signs by tracing their movements and telephone calls. Then, just before the big game, we perform a raid and capture every member of the cell."

Hoot leans back to think for a moment. Then he says, "Mister Jones' plan is somewhat radical, but I like his idea, Kris. Can we replace the nerve gas in five days?"

"We have only four days remaining, but Mister Witte at the chemical lab says they can complete the transfer process in three. They have more equipment there, far superior to what Felix manufactured in his cabin."

Hoot turns to Joe to ask, "How do you vote, Joe?" Joe shrugs helplessly. "You have jurisdiction now. I'm just an interested bystander."

"Yeah," Kris says. "But your cell phone number is the one he dials." Joe shrugs again to acknowledge the fact. "I've established a rapport with Mister Jones and believe he is being truthful. Hell, when he trades the fire extinguishers to Hushan, he's the one taking chances. I say let him try. We know the main characters now. With any luck, we could probably capture most, but if this works, we get them all."

Hoot asks, "And you, Kris?"

"I say go for it."

Hoot smiles at their responses. "Let me speak with the director. This has to come from the top. He is the only one to make this type of decision and has the juice to have the immunity approved and drawn up in a hurry."

Joe stands and says, "I don't mean to tell you your business, Hoot. But you had better be quick."

"Take a seat in the outer office and wait," Hoot orders.

"Yes Sir," they say in unison.

* * *

After they are seated, Kris says, "That's 17 I've seen today, Joe."

"Seventeen what?"

Kris points toward a red cylinder hanging on the wall by the door. "Fire extinguishers – In the past, I've never thought much about them. They are just there, and I guess we all get used to having them around but don't actually see them. This case has changed my viewpoint. Now I count fire extinguishers whenever and wherever I notice one, and am amazed how many there are."

"You're right. I have also been noticing them a lot more."

* * *

George and Hushan are seated in his SUV, easing down a blacktopped lane toward the dock area of the same canal where Mister Jones was unsuccessfully ambushed. George points toward Carla's home. "That's the address on the left." Hushan also points, but farther down the road. "This is only two blocks from the warehouses where Felix and Mohammed first met Mister Jones." George notes, "The house looks deserted."

"Most likely she is at work, George. The time is only four-thirty. We will sit and wait. Pull under the shade of that tree so the sun won't heat up the car."

* * *

Thirty minutes later and half a pack of gum for George, a white Buick drives down the lane and stops in front of the house. Carla climbs out with a small stack of books in her arms. She shuts the door and leans in the open window to say something to the female driver. Then she watches as Sherry makes a U-turn and drives away.

She takes no notice of a vehicle at the side of the road. Someone is always parked there while fishing in the canal. Carla doesn't blame them. The day has been very warm. She wouldn't want to return from out in the sun to a hot vehicle.

Walking quickly through a white picket fence with gate hanging permanently open on one hinge, she makes her way up three steps to her door. As she reaches into her purse to find her key, she hears a sound behind and turns to see a swarthy Arab type older man and a younger white man walking up the sidewalk.

At the sight, the caution light in her brain blinks bright orange, but she asks politely, "May I help you?"

Hushan asks, "Do you own a red Pontiac Firebird convertible?" Carla drops her books and attempts to insert the key into the lock before they reach her, but in her haste, fumbles with the chain. They are on her in a heartbeat, one at each side. The same man says, "I believe the answer is yes. Here my dear, let me help with your key."

After taking the ring from Carla's hand, Hushan finds the right key on his second attempt and opens the door. George pushes her rudely into the living room and holds Carla's arms tight against her side. "She is something else." His eyes run over her body, and his hands reach up to cup under her breasts. Carla pushes against his pawing with her own and struggles to get away, but he is bigger and stronger. Then Hushan grabs George by the upper arm and squeezes until he yelps. "Control yourself, fool. We can't trade damaged goods."

He stares into Carla's eyes and asks, "Where is the elusive Mister Jones?" Carla lies, but her eyes tell the truth. "I don't know who you are talking about."

"I believe you do," Hushan says. "Sit down." When Carla doesn't immediately respond to his request, George pushes her rudely onto a straight-backed wooden chair. Hushan continues to stare at her. "Your friend has been up to no good. He has something of mine I believe he will trade for you."

George shakes his head. "I think he will want his money more than her." Hushan is amazed. "Look at her. Would you prefer money to this?"

"Hell yes," George says. "Two million dollars will buy a covey of quail like this one." Hushan chuckles and says, "You are not a romantic, but something tells me Mister Jones is." He pauses a moment to think. "Perhaps you are correct. The merchandise is the most important thing. We will go ahead with the trade as planned, but I will send our opponent a video of our guest so he will consider returning the money."

Hushan turns to Carla to ask, "What do you think, my dear? Will he trade?" She lies again. "I still don't know who or what you are talking about. You have the wrong person. Let me go." Hushan points to her eyes. "No matter how you attempt to hide a lie, the eyes always give you away. Tie and gag her, George. We have a long ride to Fort Worth. Let's see how she likes lying on the rear floorboard under a blanket."

George frowns in defiance. "Hell, put her in the trunk." This time, Hushan shakes his head. "Carbon monoxide from the muffler might kill our passenger. Do as I say, George."

"Thanks for using my name."

Hushan smirks and says, "That is the least of your worries. Mister Jones knows your name and where you live. Let's hope he hasn't shared that information with anyone else." As George thinks of the implications of Hushan's remarks, he says, "My God."

"And Allah, too, George," Hushan says. "Pray to both."

CHAPTER 25

Five minutes before Claude walks into his office, Charles "Gordo" Gordon is seriously contemplating suicide. For his young age of thirty, Gordo is fifty pounds overweight, growing balder by the year, and stone, cold broke.

* * *

Although Gordo has faithfully attempted to reduce his debt, he still owes more than thirty thousand dollars on his college student loans; another forty-two thousand and change on his run-down home on the wrong side of town, and is two months behind in the rent for his law office.

Married for a short time, Gordo supposedly fathered one child; a boy named Thomas. Then he discovered the kid wasn't his. Wanda, his bitch of an ex-wife was cheating with his best friend, Louis. Gordo was the only one in town that didn't know.

Two days ago, his car, a ten-year-old wreck finally gave up the ghost. Now Gordo has to walk fourteen blocks from his home to his office. He knows his legs, heart and mind can't stand much more. So Gordo is sitting at his beat-up desk with a plastic top cracked on one corner, in his small office in a run-down mall, debating what action to take.

Without thinking, he glances at his reflection in a mirror that is peeling silver from the back on the far wall. Gordo feels just like the mirror - old and used up, and his life reflects nothing but trouble. Born of mixed blood lines; Creole, French, Spanish and perhaps a little African black thrown in for good measure, Gordo grew up on the mean streets and alleys of New Orleans. He got his street smarts early, but by the grace of God had a good mother that made him study hard, no matter how much Gordo wanted to run with the pack and chase whores on Bourbon Street.

She kept on his ass, and Gordo graduated from high school in the top ten-percent of his class and went on to college. Then he made it through law school, where he managed to graduate by the skin of his teeth and good favors of a kindly professor that liked Jazz as much as Gordo does.

From there, Gordo was hired by a firm in Dallas that went belly-up a year later when they lost a large lawsuit against one of the partners for sexual misconduct. Gordo was out on his can when he was just getting started. Deciding not to place his fortune in the hands of others, Gordo opened his own small law office near the outskirts of Fort Worth. But things haven't worked out. Maybe eating a gun is the way to go.

* * *

His guest wears a nice blue suit, white shirt and black tie. Gordo looks up politely, smiles and asks, "What can I do for you, Sir?"

"That depends; I am looking for a good lawyer. Are you one?"

"I think I am. I try hard."

"Let me ask a few questions. Then we will see if you wish to represent me."

Gordo stands up and moves a steel and plastic chair from near the wall and sets it in front of his desk for his guest. "Have a seat and fire away." Claude sits down, leans forward and asks, "If I hire you, aren't you bound by the lawyer/client privilege? In other words, you couldn't tell anyone, including the police, what I look like, where I live, what I tell you etcetera. Am I correct?"

Gordo wonders, *Who the hell is this dude and what in hell has he done?* But he says, "Yeah, once I agree to take your case and receive a retainer, I'm your attorney for life. I can't talk of you to anyone or tell them a thing you say."

"Good," Claude says, "Let me explain my situation, and you decide whether you wish to be my attorney."

"I will listen with an open mind."

"Okay, here goes: The police would like to charge me with a crime, but are not aware of how I look. I won't say if I am guilty or not, but I have something they want so badly they are willing to grant me immunity for any and all crimes I may or may not have committed. Are you with me so far?"

"Yeah," Gordo says. "I follow you."

"What I require is a go-between."

Gordo is becoming interested, but still a little frightened. "What do I have to do?" Claude smiles to ease his fears. "I hope the police will grant the immunity, but accordingly, I cannot receive the documents in person. I need your assistance as my intermediary to receive the papers, review them for authenticity and notify me when they are approved and finalized."

"That's all?" Gordo asks. He is amazed with the simplicity of his guest's request. "Yeah, for now - if everything is copasetic, I stand to make some big bucks from this deal. As a result, I will need someone to handle my investments and keep his mouth shut. Are you in or not?"

"What sort of retainer are we speaking of?"

Claude extracts a thick stack of bills from an inside pocket and lays the money atop the desk. "What do you say to fifty thousand now and an additional one hundred and fifty when I receive my immunity?"

"Damn," Gordo says. "Did I hear you correctly, fifty thousand?" Somehow, Claude senses he has made a new friend and replies, "Yeah as I said, and with the remainder to be paid later. Now, are you my attorney?"

"You bet your ass," Gordo says. "Let me prepare a contract." He forgets any thoughts of suicide and repeats, "Damn!" Gordo is back in business, and things are <u>definitely</u> looking up.

* * *

The next morning when Claude phones Carla at six a.m., she doesn't pick up, and he is worried. Every fifteen minutes until eight a.m. he tries again. Then he dials the number of the library where she works. When an elderly lady answers, Claude asks, "Is Miss Roberson there?"

"No, Carla hasn't shown up and didn't call in."

"Could she be sick?"

"When Carla left yesterday afternoon, she was fine. Who is this?"

"If she comes in, tell her Claude called. I'll phone again later."

Something is wrong. When we spoke yesterday, Carla said she would be there. She wouldn't miss work unless there was an emergency, Claude realizes.

He decides to take a chance and dials Joe's cell phone. When Joe answers Claude says, "Joe, this is Mister Jones."

"The approval isn't in yet."

"That's not why I phoned, Joe. I need a favor."

"You do? What's in it for me?"

"You might save someone's life." Joe attempts to joke. "Are you running around with your nail gun again?"

His words fall on deaf ears. Claude isn't laughing. "No, a friend of mine may be in trouble. I want you to check on Miss Carla Roberson at 363 Wharf Avenue in Sulfur Springs."

"Is she your girl?"

"No," Claude lies. "She's just a friend. I phoned, and she doesn't answer, which is not like her. If our mutual friends learned of her, she is in trouble. Please, I'm asking you as a personal favor."

"That's the first time you've said 'please' since we met, Mister Jones. Okay, I'm in Fort Worth, but will have someone drive out to take a look. Phone me in a couple hours. I'll let you know what they discover."

"Thanks, Joe, I appreciate it."

Joe adds, "I'll have the word on your immunity by this afternoon. When you phone, we can kill two birds with one stone."

"Don't mention the word 'kill'. I'll speak with you later."

"You become a little squeamish when it is your friends, 'eh?" Joe asks, but is talking to a dead phone. He hangs up and says, "Damn Mister Jones anyway. He always gets the last word."

* * *

In the middle of an empty, rundown warehouse reeking of rotting vegetables and several winos' urine, Carla is seated on a straight-back wooden chair staring into the lens of a video camera Hushan holds in his hands. "Smile," Hushan says, but she frowns instead. George says, "He said 'smile'," and slaps Carla's face. *I don't give a damn if I'm on tape. Mister Jones knows my face, but I also know who he is. If he sees me hit his chick, maybe he will be mad enough to let me have a crack at him, man to man.*

"You bastard," Carla says. George must admit she is one tough broad. He wishes Hushan hadn't placed her body off-limits. Man, what he could teach this redhead. Perhaps later, if things pan out the way Hushan hopes.

"This is your lucky day, Mister Jones," Hushan says for the camera. "As you can see, we have your girlfriend. She is a lovely woman and wears a very nice ring. Hold up the heart-shaped diamond, George."

George grabs Carla's left hand and twists it around to display the diamond ring Claude gave her. She sobs, and tears run down her cheeks.

"Good," Hushan says. "You will notice we have treated her kindly so far. But, if you don't meet us at the old rock quarry on the west side of Fort Worth off Boulder Avenue at nine o'clock tomorrow night with our money intact, there is no telling what we may do to such a lovely girl. George would love to have her, but for now, I have placed her off-limits.

"Do I make myself clear, Mister Jones? Meet me at the rock quarry off Boulder Avenue at 9:00 p.m. the day after you receive this video. Don't be late."

Hushan turns off the camera. "That should do, George. Tie up our guest. Then go out and buy some food. We can't afford to let her starve."

* * *

"Your friend wasn't there," Joe says. "My guy said she must have departed in a hurry. The front door was ajar and a stack of books was scattered on the porch. As far as he could tell, there was no sign of forced entry or struggle." Claude hates himself. "Damn, Hushan and his men may have her. When I retrieved the nerve gas, I was driving her car. Someone may have seen and copied down the license plate number. I was stupid."

"Yeah," Joe says. "If they have her, you were. What do we do now?"

"If my immunity comes through, we go ahead with the transfer."

"We received it an hour ago," Joe says. "How do you want to handle the paperwork?"

"Take it to my lawyer, Charles Gordon at the Landmark Mall on Stewart Street, Suite number four. When he certifies the deal, I'll phone with the location of the containers. Make it fast, Joe. We don't know what Hushan will do, and I must make plans to combat them."

"Okay," Joe says. "I'm on the way."

"Stay by your phone," Claude says. "I'll phone soon."

* * *

Claude is more afraid than any other time in his life. His mind is racing almost out of control. They have Carla, which is his fault. He curses the life he has led. *How could I have been so stupid to involve Carla in my troubles? Why didn't I leave when I was healed, and let her get on with her life?*

No, he had to fall in love when he had no right. Now Carla might pay for his error with her life. If so, he can't go on living, and many people will die before he does. Claude unclenches his fists and attempts to relax. *Calm down, Claude, and get your mind straight and make plans for any eventuality. If you outthink them, these guys can't win. They aren't that smart.* He takes a deep breath, clears his mind of negativity and begins to plan.

* * *

When Gordo answers, Claude says, "This is Mister Jones. Has my immunity been approved?"

"Yes, it has, Mister Jones. I have the papers here. You are a free man."

"They will have to wait, Gordo. Later today, along with your final payment, I will send a sealed envelope to you by courier. Should anything happen to me, the sachet contains instructions I want you to follow. Will you do that?"

"Yes I will, Mister Jones. You were a lifesaver. I will do anything you ask."

"Thanks, Gordo. In case I don't see you again, it has been a pleasure knowing you."

"Thank you, Sir. Whatever you do and wherever you go, I wish you the best."

* * *

"Joe, this is Mister Jones. I received word from my lawyer. Thanks."

"You're welcome. Where are the containers?"

"They are in a storage locker at Store and Go on Winterhaven Drive, unit 13 for good luck. The key is at my lawyer's office. When you have replaced the real containers with phonies, return them to the same place. I'll have Hushan pick them up."

Joe wants more details. "How will you handle the switch?"

"I'll receive the money, and tell him where the bombs are. If they have Carla, he will let me know after the swap is made and he has his merchandise. Then we'll see."

"Phone if you need my assistance, Mister Jones. You're a free citizen now."

"Thanks, Joe, I may take you up on your offer. I'll speak with you soon. Good luck when you transfer the gas."

CHAPTER 26

"Sergeant Francone, this is Hershel Witte at the chemical laboratory on Camp Shaffer."

"Yeah Hershel, what can I do for you? How did the transfer go?"

"Fine, but that's not why I want to speak with you. How many containers did you say there were?" Joe's blood runs cold. "There were thirty-two – why? How many did you receive?"

"Only thirty-one - the second case has an empty space. At first, I thought you made a mistake in the number Felix prepared. But then, I remembered Agent Hefner said there were thirty-two. I thought I should let you know."

"Thanks, Hershel," Joe says, but doesn't mean it. Normally, Joe isn't a religious man, but now he prays, *Please, God, don't let this news be true.* Then he thinks, *Damn, I can't reach Mister Jones. He contacts me. I wonder if he knows.* As Joe gets up from his desk, he suddenly feels much older. With fear reflected in his eyes, he walks wearily to the rear of the building and into an office where Kris has taken up residence as agent in charge.

Kris is leaning back in a chair with his feet on a drawer. Apparently, the long hours finally caught up with him. Kris' chest rises and falls as he sleeps, and Joe is tempted to leave him be, but knows deep in his heart he must wake him, so says, "Kris," a little louder than normal.

* * *

"These are the times that try men's souls…

As Kris slept, that old phrase so familiar from the hundreds of times he heard it repeated by his grandfather, Hugo, who, when faced with an arduous task, or attempting to solve an unsolvable problem, would utter it aloud, turn to his only grandson and ask, "Ain't that the truth?" Then he would laugh to chase away the blues, and before much more time passed, arrive at a solution no one had considered before, and prove scholars of the past were wrong in their erroneous assumptions.

As his mind switched gears to another portion of his brain, the thought came into focus that his grandfather's favorite saying was certainly appropriate as far as the progress he and the others working this terrorist threat is concerned.

Then, as dreams are want to do, unconsciously he felt hunger, and his father, Karl a carpenter from Columbus, Ohio came to mind and into focus. He remembers the times his father reminded him hard work always paid dividends, sometimes when least expected.

"My first job was as an usher in a movie theater with a wage of 35 cents an hour, plus all the free popcorn I could eat." He laughed at the thought, and continued, "Then my grandfather found a better job for me; hoeing watermelon mounds for the same small amount, but working 12 hours a day, from 6 a.m. until 6 pm. I never want to see or eat another watermelon as long as I live."

But then, supposedly as a reward from his Maker for his dedication, (but Kris thought it was just plain dumb luck), after lying about his age of 15, adding a year to circumvent the child labor laws, and applying for work as a "gandy-dancer" with P&PU railroad, his watermelon hoeing days were quickly abandoned when to his surprise he was offered $2.50 an hour by P&PU.

"Hell, in mid-stride, I dropped that damn hoe, ran from the watermelon patch and was out of sight before the foreman could uncoil his whip," Karl said and laughed again, then smiled with a sly grin that in his youth had charmed many a bobbysoxer from her socks, and sometimes her bra and panties.

When he was a youngster of 12, Karl's mother, Nan, pointed toward such a facial expression by her mate and said the grin was what won her heart. (Young, inexperienced with sex, and too embarrassed sharing intimate details with his mother, (*after all*), Kris didn't inquire whether Nan's undies had been added to the vast and varied collection supposedly attributed to his father's winning ways.)

Now, older and wiser, and knowing his mother much better, he is sure Karl kept those trophies in a very special place, and although unknown to his conscious self, in his slumber, his father's words and that practiced sly, but wicked grin makes a similar smile appear on Kris' face, and he chuckles aloud softly.

* * *

BAM! That brain circuit becomes overloaded and a breaker trips. Instead of normal, almost slow motion interesting videos flowing through his dreams, a series of disjointed, short scenes flick through his mind like someone is fast-forwarding a slide projector as his dream is routed through another system.

Blink, and there is Bill Clinton sitting at his desk in the oval office. A fly is on his nose, a huge unlit cigar in his mouth, and his fly is unzipped as he discusses foreign policy with two advisors. At the same time, Monica is hidden under the desk, servicing him. Then the cigar drops from Bill's mouth and falls to the floor, where Monica retrieves it and… whizz – they are sucked off into a void.

And Zip, there is the guy in that movie, (name not recalled – come on brain, what is it? Oh, yeah, Peter Sellers) sitting in a room as pictures of atomic blasts are interspersed with others of children playing, Hitler giving a Nazi salute… and Whoa! There's the crazy actor riding an atomic bomb on its way to Moscow while waving his hat… Go get 'em cowboy!

A can of Campbell's tomato soup – Andy Warhol, more TV and movie reviews: Kris' hero, John Wayne – "The Cowboys" and "The Shootist", where Kris cried out, "NO, he can't die!" Eddie Albert and Eva Gabor spoofing a famous painting in "Green Acres", those three lovelies bathing in a water tower tank in "Petticoat Junction", Steve McQueen – Bullitt – car chase, explosion – enough said.

Clint Eastwood being shot in the chest while wearing his homemade metal plate – shot, falls, gets up, shot, falls, gets up, shot, staggers, keeps walking, but never loses that stupid little cigar – ridiculous; Zap, Robert Redford being shot as he raises old glory in "The Last Castle" – great movie!

Scene change - the second amendment, right to bear arms, YEA!

Zing, a bottle of Butter Pecan Ensure, Nan's favorite since Alzheimer's claimed possession of most of her mind… then suddenly; a plate of food, and…

BAM again, his hunger pangs return, and at that instant, a minute brain electrician within his skull completes needed repairs, closes the circuit breaker and pleasant memories return to replace nonsensical garbage.

* * *

Kris's computer-like brain latches onto other memories of the past, and the present.

To this day, Karl maintains a garden in a vacant lot next to their home. Kris remembers his father filled the lot with a wide variety of vegetables each year, and Kris assumed incorrectly because Karl enjoyed gardening as a hobby. The fact that the Victory Garden was necessary to put food on the table or do without didn't enter his mind.

Years later, when Kris was living alone and finally realizing the true value of each penny earned and how it was spent, only then did he focus on the true reason. Without the delicious vegetables his father grew and mother canned all summer, winter would have been a bleak season, and many nights the family table would have been bare.

For some reason the image of a baby chick comes into focus; fluffy yellow feathers, skinny legs, forked leather-like feet and tiny beak chirping merrily. Then Kris suddenly remembers why.

Another of Karl's "hobbies" was raising chickens. Each spring, when grass was returning to the brown yards of town, Karl ordered a big box of 100 tiny, peeping yellow chicks, which would soon arrive at the local feed and grain store. When the merchant phoned, he and Kris would go there, load them, (and Kris), into the rear of Karl's pickup and head home. Kris' unpaid job was watching to ensure none made their way from the box to fall from the truck and be mashed by vehicles behind.

During the following months, Karl, (plus Kris, reluctantly), nurtured the chicks into two categories, those that laid eggs, and those that didn't and were thus destined for mother's frying pan.

Another shift, another image; this one is not so pleasant, as he sees Nan standing in their backyard wringing the necks of two hens at the same time, one in each hand. With ease of practice, she makes a twisting motion with both wrists until only the heads remain clutched in her fists, while the chicken bodies fly from her hands, and blood spurts from their necks as, with hearts still beating, they flop in circles on the ground. He is glad when that ugly picture fades slowly and is erased from his mind.

Being truthful, he also rationalizes that if not for Nan's chicken-slaying prowess and culinary powers, their meals could have tasted like cow dung. *(Ugh, what a thought!)*

But then, another wonderful TV-like memory: in his dream, Kris licks his lips after taking a bite from a fried chicken leg, and...

Then Joe's voice breaks through his reverie.

* * *

Startled, Kris' feet fall from the drawer. As he comes half-awake, his body pitches forward, and automatically he asks, "Yeah Joe, what's up?"

Joe sounds like James Lovell on Apollo 13, when he says, "We have a problem. Hershel Witte phoned to say they only received thirty-one fire extinguishers. One is missing and unaccounted for." At the news, Kris blinks twice and runs his hands through his hair as he attempts to focus blurry eyes on the matter at hand. "I'll be damned."

"My sentiments exactly," Joe says. "Do you think Mister Jones knows?"

"He didn't say anything about one missing, did he?"

"Not in any of our conversations, Kris. Since the exchange, he has been quiet. I suppose he will contact us again to let us know what is going on before he and Hushan meet. I'll ask him then."

Kris looks at his hands that suddenly have begun to shake. "God, I thought we had this thing under control. If we can't locate the missing container, we will have to cancel the Cotton Bowl and evacuate both cities. Imagine the nightmare that will create."

"I don't know if we can cause that kind of panic," Joe says.

"What alternative is there?" Kris asks. Joe shakes his head. "I don't know, Kris, I just don't know."

* * *

Locked in a small room with a folding Army cot for a bed, and two thin sheets and a lumpy pillow for bedding, plus a wooden folding chair to sit on, and a chipped white chamber pot with a roll of toilet paper for her "necessities", Carla is so weary she doesn't know up from down.

A single, sixty-watt bulb hanging from a ceiling fixture on a white, plastic-coated wire remains on twenty-four hours a day. Since there are no windows, she isn't sure whether it is day or night. Time has lost all meaning, so Carla guesses at the hours and days she has spent here by the number of meals they provided.

Today no one came to empty her toilet. In the overly-warm cubbyhole where she is confined, the odor emanating from the chamber pot is almost overpowering. Carla is wearing the same outfit she wore when they kidnapped her; a brown skirt and white blouse. Neither garment has fared well. Thus far, her captors haven't had the decency to supply a change of clothes or fresh underwear.

After three days her clothing is wrinkled and stained. How much longer her jailers intend to hold her before attempting to trade her for their two million dollars is anyone's guess. Other than her love for him, the only hope Carla has to cling to is knowing Claude is working on a scheme to rescue her safely. She knows his heart must be torn because he feels he betrayed her by using her car.

Hushan offered that juicy tidbit of information the day they kidnapped her. "If your boyfriend hadn't been so cheap and rented a car, we wouldn't know who you are. The least Mister Jones could have done was change license plates. He is not as smart as he thinks."

George bragged, "Wait until I get a chance to even the score." Although George is well-built and has muscles, Carla doesn't believe he can take Claude in a fair fight. She doesn't want to discover if she is wrong or right. Instead, she prays, *Please let us get out of this in one piece.*

* * *

Then she hears footsteps outside the door, and a key rattles in the lock. Determined to display resistance for as long as she is able, she stands up with fists clenched. As Hushan walks in the door, he is trailed by his ever-present shadow, George the goon.

"Good morning, Carla," Hushan says, and George nods in her general direction. She doesn't return their greetings.

Then Hushan sniffs the foul air and points toward her chamber pot. "My God, it stinks to high heaven in here. I am sorry, Carla." He turns to George to order; "Take the pot and empty it, George. See if you can locate an antiseptic spray to cleanse the room."

As he retrieves the putrid container and walks from the room, George grumbles under his breath and "accidently" bangs the chamber pot against the doorframe, where foul fluid slops out.

"Bring a mop when you return," Hushan says sternly. When George is out of sight, Hushan says, "I believe George did that on purpose, Carla, and shall chastise him later. I apologize for such rudeness."

"Thank you," she says. Hushan waves his hand as if it is nothing. "You're welcome." Then he looks into her eyes. "For your information, we will depart very soon. Tonight we settle old debts. I pray your friend will cooperate, and we receive our goods. Tomorrow night we trade you in return for our money. I would hate to harm such a lovely woman as you, but if I must, I will. Remember my warning; do as you are told and things will go smoothly. Make waves and you will pay the consequences."

News of her impending release brings small tears of relief to Carla's eyes. "I understand and will do what you say." Hushan notices and hands her a clean handkerchief. "Thanks," she says and wipes her eyes. When she attempts to return the hanky, he says, "Keep it."

George returns with the empty pot, a damp mop and insect spray in an aerosol can, and says, "This is all I could find." He drops the empty pot near Carla's bed, and it makes a hollow ringing noise. Then with one awkward swipe, soaks up most liquid, and leans the filthy mop against a wall in the hall.

As George sprays the room, the odor reminds Carla of a repellent she once used in an outhouse at a country school where she taught years ago. She also remembers the spray never killed any wasps. To the contrary, they seemed to thrive on the supposed poison. The memory brings a smile to her face and a little joy to her heart.

"We shall return shortly and advise you of how the exchange went," Hushan says. "Before we leave tomorrow, I will give you a few minutes to freshen up in my bathroom." A battler to the end, Carla says sarcastically, "You are too kind."

* * *

Tonight is the dark of the moon. With a heavy cloud cover and possible thunderstorms forecast for the local area, anyone with a rifle but without a night scope will find it difficult to see, let alone hit their target.

* * *

The afternoon of the exchange, Claude phoned Joe. When he answered, Claude asked, "Hey, Joe, is everything ready for the big exchange?"

"I'm glad you called. We have a small problem. One of the fire extinguishers is missing." Joe hears Mister Jones' quick intake of breath. "What do you mean; one is missing? There were supposed to be thirty-two. I saw them in George's garage."

"Are you sure? Did you open both cases?"

"No, I didn't want to take a chance George might notice the tarpaulin had been moved. I looked in the one on top. There were sixteen in that case. Naturally, I assumed there were the same in the other. I guess I goofed."

Joe asks, "You have no idea where the missing one is?"

"If I did, it wouldn't be missing."

"Don't be a smartass, Mister Jones. This is serious."

"Don't you think I know? What will Hushan think?"

Joe believes Mister Jones is being truthful, and sweat breaks out on his brow, as he asks, "What is the possibility Hushan will take time to count them in the storage area?"

"Probably none, but the shortage is bound to be discovered soon after they are moved to their final destination. Hell, Joe, if he thinks he still has the real thing, what is one less to Hushan?" Joe isn't convinced. "The problem is; who has the fire extinguisher? If we can't account for all the bombs, we'll have to cancel the football game and clear both cities of millions of people. That will cause a panic the likes of which I don't even want to think of."

Claude's voice sounds sincere. "We do have a problem; and just when I thought we were in the clear. What do you want me to do?" Grasping at any straw in the wind, Joe asks, "Do you know more of Hushan's men? Can you get to one or more to see if they know anything?"

"Yeah, I do, and I'll give it the old college try. But tonight I have my hands full. The exchange should go well, but afterward my situation may be tenuous. If I am still alive after we meet, and Hushan does have Carla and wants to trade, you and I can discuss a few plans I have for that party."

"Good luck," Joe says and means it. So much hangs on the outcome of the exchange tonight. Sweat continues to run down his brow when Joe thinks of the consequences if Mister Jones doesn't pull this off.

* * *

When Claude phones, Hushan says, "I have been waiting for your call. I have your money. Are my goods safe and ready to be returned?"

"Good and yes," Claude says. "Meet me tonight at midnight at the Wheeler Street entrance in front of the Tyler Building in downtown Dallas. Come alone and bring the money in one suitcase. No tricks. You don't get the location of the merchandise until after I receive the money. I will call your cell phone before I arrive, and wear a red rose in my lapel so you will recognize me. Are my instructions clear?"

"Completely Mister Jones – I look forward to finally meeting you face to face."

"Until tonight, Hushan," Claude says and disconnects.

* * *

That evening, when Claude walks toward the cockpit of a sleek blue and white helicopter setting on an asphalt pad at a small airport on the west side of Dallas, the pilot leans out and asks, "Mister Jones?" Claude bends unnecessarily under the slowly moving blades and approaches the cockpit. "Yes, that's me."

The pilot holds out his hand. "My name is Paul – Paul Stokes. I'm the one you spoke with concerning leasing the helo." Claude shakes the outstretched hand and then hands Paul a manila envelope full of cash.

"It's nice to meet you, Paul. Here is your money as promised - ten thousand dollars in cash." Without counting the money, Paul places the envelope under his seat. Then he turns to ask, "This trip is legal, isn't it?"

"Yes; all you have to do is take me to the top of the Tyler Building in downtown Dallas and land on their helicopter pad at fifteen minutes before midnight. I am to meet a friend there for a short business transaction, which shouldn't last longer than twenty minutes. Then we will return here. I assure you; this trip is very simple and entirely legal."

Paul tilts his head to one side and grins like Wilbur. "Your request sounds peculiar, but who am I to question your motives? As long as the police don't come calling afterward, I'm fine." Claude nods and says, "On the return trip, I will have a large suitcase weighing about fifty pounds. Will that be a problem?"

"No Sir, Mister Jones. It should fit easily into the passenger compartment. You can ride in front with me if you choose so." Claude checks his watch. "Fine, the time now is eleven-fifteen. "Will we arrive on time?" Paul does a quick calculation and says, "Yes, if we depart within the next ten minutes." Claude grimaces and climbs aboard. "Then let's go."

* * *

While waiting for his phone to ring, Hushan paces the sidewalk from the curb to the entrance of the building and back again. Armed with a high-powered rifle equipped with night-vision scope, George is stationed in an office across the street that overlooks the door. Two blocks away, Specks is seated in a rental car, monitoring another cell phone. If Mister Jones runs, and George doesn't kill him, Specks will cut him off.

A strange sound seems to come from somewhere around the building, but Hushan sees nothing, so shrugs and continues pacing. As he turns toward the entrance again, his cell rings. "Yes."

Mister Jones' voice echoes in his ear. "Keep walking. When the window-washing platform arrives, place the suitcase aboard and stand back. After I am sure I have my money, I will lower the platform. The location of the merchandise will be inside." Hushan knows he has been outfoxed and frowns, "You sneaky bastard."

He glances up; the platform hangs ten feet above his head. As he watches, it drops slowly to within a foot of the sidewalk, where it bounces lightly as if made of rubber and rocks gently from side to side. In his ear, Claude's voice orders; "Put the suitcase on board."

Hushan grits his teeth and grimaces, but does as he is told. Then he watches the platform begin to rise into a dark sky. For such a large item, the platform moves quickly. When it reaches a height above the streetlights, they blind his night vision, so Hushan is unable to tell how far away the platform is.

He pulls the second phone from a pocket and speed-dials George's number. When George answers, Hushan shouts, "He's on the roof. Can you see him?"

"No, it's too high."

"Can you see the window washer's platform?"

"Just barely, it's at the top of the building. Wait, now it's on the way down."

As he waits for the platform to return, Hushan stands on the balls of his feet and curses aloud. He has been outsmarted, and feels like a kicked dog. Up above, he hears the beat of a helicopter's blades as they bite into the night air, and sees a dark shape flutter from the roof and flit away into the darkness.

Hushan curses again, "As Allah is my God, tonight was yours. But tomorrow night will be mine."

190 of M? 190

CHAPTER 27

Af

fter Paul drops Claude at his car, he considers opening the suitcase, but knows to wait until he walks into his motel room. A feeling of trepidation continues to haunt him. Hushan said nothing about Carla over the phone and made no threats while delivering the money. Hushan was too smug. Something in his voice told Claude that Hushan thought he had the upper hand.

As this late hour, traffic is light, so the return trip from the small airfield to his motel off I-45 is easy. Although Claude knows he is stupid, he still is driving Carla's Pontiac because her vehicle makes him feel closer to her. Thoughts of what she must be going through torture his mind, but he knows he must separate the memory of Carla from his conscious thoughts or he might make a mistake that will cause her death.

After pulling into a parking spot near the front of the motel, Claude shuts off the engine and sits for a moment staring at the suitcase on the front seat. Like a silent partner in a business deal gone bad, this is something you don't want to face, but know you must, sooner or later.

Claude eases from the car, reaches across the seat, pulls the brown leather case across the fabric and hooks his hand through the handle. As Claude approaches the glass doors, they slide open. The clerk on duty is a Vietnamese girl approximately twenty-years-old, with slanted eyes and long black hair. When she sees Claude, she smiles shyly but remains silent.

He walks through the entrance and makes his way to his room on the first floor. Along the way, the hallway holds both the scent of disinfectant and a lingering odor of a pepperoni pizza someone ordered for delivery not long ago. The two don't blend well.

As sounds of passionate coupling are heard through the thin wall from the room next door, Claude attempts to smile, but a picture of Carla in her bed comes to mind, so he can't. His reflection in the dresser mirror displays a weary, yet determined man staring at a suitcase as if he is almost afraid of what he will discover inside.

Cold shivers run through Claude's shoulder blades and up and down his spine as he reaches for the case and pushes the two sliders. The lid pops up, and he helps open the top the remainder of the way. The money is there all right, but so is a videotape with an envelope attached atop. The message is signed in large letters with the name "Hushan."

"Before you revel in your wealth, Mister Jones, please view the attached."

After taking the tape from its resting place, Claude inserts the cassette into a video player setting under a TV in a built-in cabinet by the dresser, turns on the TV and waits for a picture to appear before hitting the Play button.

A blank blue screen is replaced by a picture of Carla sitting on a wooden chair in the middle of a nearly empty, unkempt room. George is standing next to her, holding her down with one hand on her left shoulder. She looks frightened.

Claude hears Hushan say "Smile." But Carla frowns, and George says, "He said 'smile'," and slaps Carla's face. Claude's fingernails dig into the handles of his chair as he curses the day he allowed George to live to deliver his message.

"You bastard," Carla says, and Claude feels her courage in those two words, while he thinks, *You will pay for that, George.* Then he listens carefully to the remainder of the message and Hushan's instructions. Claude winces when George twists Carla's wrist to display the diamond ring. The action makes Claude's blood pressure rise, and he feels a pounding behind his ears - a warning to calm down and think rationally.

The screen goes blue, so he rewinds the tape and watches the entire video again. Carla's tears and the condition of her clothing make his eyes mist. Claude wipes his tears away with the back of his hand and attempts to calm his emotions. When he feels he is in control again, he stands and turns off the TV and recorder, pops out the cassette, rips the tape from the case in anger and throws the entire mess into a trashcan next to a desk. Finally, he phones Joe.

* * *

With sundown the following day, rain begins to fall. Within an hour, the storm becomes a hard, pouring torrent blocking out any stars and adding to the darkness of a moonless night.

* * *

Earlier in the day, Claude and Joe scoped out the quarry from an unmarked police helicopter and got a good feel for the layout. At 6:00 a.m. they finally meet in the parking lot outside police headquarters. Joe looks nothing like what Claude pictured in his mind. But Joe's intelligent eyes tell Claude this man is no fool. Although his clothes hang from his overweight frame like wrinkled curtains too large for a small bay window, instinctively, Claude knows Joe can take care of himself in any given situation.

As they shake hands, Joe says, "So, you are the elusive Mister Jones. Do you have a first name?"

"It's Claude. Thanks for meeting me. If I were you, I wouldn't have." Joe frowns. "I'm not too happy about Katie and the drivers of the other vehicles. You got away with murder. That goes against my grain."

"When Saint Peter and I meet, I hope my actions to save thousands of innocent people might wipe my ledger clean."

"Yeah," Joe says. "I took that into consideration when I agreed to assist you. You were more than helpful in this investigation. If not for you, we would still be clueless."

"Thanks, Joe."

Joe points toward his cruiser. "I have an unmarked helicopter standing by to check out the site. Hushan might have someone there watching to ensure our deal is not a trap, but an early flyover by an aircraft shouldn't shake him up too much. As dumb as these guys have been, he probably won't even notice."

"Thanks again," Claude says. "Let's take a look. Then we will make our plans."

* * *

That conversation was earlier. Now the downpour has changed the situation. He and Joe can't expect any assistance by air. Due to weather conditions, the helo is grounded. They also agree too many people on the scene would spook Hushan and he will call off the meeting.

* * *

Although this isn't an FBI case, they cleared their plans with Kris, who said, "You are in charge, Joe. I can't assist you in an official capacity. If you made any arrests, my being a member of the FBI might taint the charges.

"Claude believes he and I can handle this, Kris, and I agree."

Shortly after they returned from the flyover, Joe introduced Kris to their one-time foe. He could tell Kris was uncomfortable around Claude. Hell, Joe doesn't blame him. Although Kris likes Claude's looks and the way he carries himself, Claude is still a murderer. Well, perhaps an ex-murderer, pardoned and given immunity, but everything Claude stood for in the past still goes against Kris' beliefs.

The most important item now is to rescue an innocent woman from the clutches of Hushan and his cronies. Claude confessed Carla is more than a friend, something Joe knew from the beginning. Not many smarts were required to figure that. Claude was too worried when he phoned asking Joe to check on her.

* * *

The rugged worked-out, worn-out and deserted quarry looks like a graveyard for giants. Huge broken blocks of different-colored stone are lying on their sides like toppled tombstones, or standing as silent sentinels strewn about the landscape in no logical sequence.

Piles of gravel are interspersed with boulders the size of cars. Water is everywhere – in a deep pit lake created by removal of the marble, in small wide pools where large machines scooped out sand or gravel, and shallow puddles underfoot.

Jagged streaks of burning white lightning cut through the night, while thunder crashes and echoes from the high walls of the unnatural canyon quarrying created over the years. A bent and battered fence once surrounded the area, but has been trampled to the ground as thrill-seekers and teenagers discovered the place and took over the quarry for illegal and dangerous, swimming, necking, joint smoking, partying and sex in the back seats of their cars.

Shattered Styrofoam coolers, beer and soda cans, torn, stained and soaked pizza boxes, wrappers from every fast food place in town, and used condoms are afloat atop the puddles. Large rivulets of rainwater cut through the mud, moving the trash toward larger pools and the lake, where they gather atop the muddy surface like debris from toppled sailboats caught in a hurricane.

* * *

Claude pulls alongside the wide muddy entrance in Carla's car, where a badly bent double-wide, woven-wire gate hangs from two posts. The scene reminds him of the maw of a giant whale feeding on plankton, or the mouth of a great white shark on the attack. No other vehicle is in sight. Apparently, Claude is the first player to arrive. He backs the Pontiac in close to the ruined fence and shuts down the engine. For a few moments, he sits quietly, listening to rain beat on the roof while watching lightning flash against a black sky.

Finally, after pulling up his collar, Claude grabs the grip of the suitcase in his right hand and the door handle in his left and climbs out into the maelstrom. The wind tugs at his jacket, as the suitcase sways and beats against his legs.

Claude walks quickly, splashing through puddles and mud toward a group of cracked blocks of granite a hundred feet away, where he stops behind the largest, drops the case to the soggy ground, and pulls out his weapon, a Glock fifteen-shot automatic pistol. The weapon feels warm in his cold hand, like an old friend from his past.

Somewhere above him, Claude knows Joe is watching his back. He hopes Joe can see through the spray and foggy mist surrounding them. Claude's hair is stuck to his scalp and his coat already soaked through. Cold water runs down his spine, making him shiver, as he thinks, *Come on, Hushan; let's get this over, one way or another.*

Twin headlight beams cut through inky rain-blown darkness. Then they rise and fall as the driver makes his way down the rocky road to the quarry, where the car stops at the entrance gate, and the lights flick off and on. Claude doesn't know what the signal represents, but hopes the occupants aren't teenagers looking for a thrill. This isn't the time or place.

He reaches down, retrieves the suitcase and moves farther into the jumble of man-sized rocks and boulders at the rear of a U-shaped bowl of the quarry. By the light of an occasional lightning strike, Claude sees the muddy, oily and litter-laden surface of the lake behind him. Large drops of rain splatter against the surface, creating a pattern of interlocking concentric circles among the trash.

A car door opens. Claude hears muffled voices, and a shout echoes hollowly against the sodden cliffs, "Show yourself Mister Jones." Claude steps halfway from his hiding place, but remains in the shadows. "I'm here. Show me Miss Roberson."

A flashlight comes on and the beam shines on Carla standing huddled against the downpour, clothed only in the outfit she wore in the video. She is already drenched, with her thin blouse stuck tight against her breasts as wind rips at her. Carla throws her arms up to shield her eyes and face from the onslaught. Under his breath, Claude swears, "You bastards."

The light snaps off, and he is temporarily blinded. Hushan shouts, "Where is the money?" Claude holds the suitcase aloft, "Right here."

Over the noise of the wind and rain, Hushan shouts, "I'll send George for the case. When he begins to walk my way, I will send Miss Roberson on hers. No tricks. Do you understand?"

"Yes," Claude replies and watches George open his coat to display he is unarmed. *I'll believe that when cows give chocolate milk.* He keeps his gun sight held tight on George's chest, as his opponent walks slowly to where Claude is waiting. Then Claude uses the toe of his left shoe to push the suitcase away from the rock he is standing behind. He doesn't want George too close. If the opportunity arises, Claude isn't sure he can restrain himself from cold-cocking the terrorist bastard.

George approaches with his hands held high above his head, and says sarcastically, "Nice to see you again. That's a sweet piece of fluff you have. I enjoyed my time with her." Claude grits his teeth but remains silent, knowing George is only attempting to provoke him into showing himself.

There can't just be two. A third must be hiding in the rocks and waiting to pop me. Where is he? Think, Claude.

While keeping his weapon aimed at George, Claude says, "Handle the case with your right hand, Georgie Boy, and keep your left in the air. If you so much as blink, I will take great pleasure in shooting you. Don't start walking until I tell you." George smiles, doesn't reply and picks up the case as instructed. With his left hand held high, he turns his back to Claude.

"Start the woman," Claude shouts. The flashlight comes on again so he can see Carla begin to walk toward them, stepping carefully over rocks and trying not to stumble. After two steps, Hushan shouts, "Stop." Carla does, and stands there, shivering in the cold. Hushan shouts again, "Let George go."

Claude waves his weapon in the general direction of Hushan. "Go ahead, Georgie boy, but walk slowly. Keep your hands where I can see them and stay away from Carla. Walk in a circle to return to your friend. If you come within ten feet of her, I will shoot you in the back." George snarls in defiance, "And Hushan will kill your girlfriend."

"Yeah, but you will die first. Do as I said."

"Okay," George says. "Your day will come." Claude ignores George and watches as Carla matches him, step-for-step on her agonizingly slow journey.

Then she stumbles and falls headlong into the mud and water. The unexpected act startles Claude, and without thinking clearly, he steps from behind the rock. To his rear, Joe shouts, "Look out!"

In rapid succession, two shots boom out, and a bullet ricochets from the stone close to Claude's head. Several chips hit his face, but he ignores the pain. At Joe's shout, George runs toward their car. Claude fires two quick rounds in his general direction, but isn't able to achieve a good sight picture. Then he feels warm blood flowing down his cheek. Knowing he isn't severely wounded, he looks for Carla. She is still on the ground, with arms reaching out toward Claude, pleading for his help.

The rain beats down in sheets, making it difficult to see what is happening. Claude hears a single bullet impact against the rock a foot above his head and an echo from the shot in the canyon to his rear. From behind, two more quick shots come in succession, so Claude knows Joe is covering him.

Suddenly, a scream comes from the darkness, and Claude hears a thud like a body hitting a roof after a suicide jumper decides to end his life. Then, for a split second, except for pouring rain, there is silence.

Without warning, Joe opens fire with a four-shot volley. The side windows of Hushan's car shatter into a cascade of glass chips as Hushan and George hide behind the vehicle and return fire. In the confusion Carla begins crawling toward Claude. Then the impact of two bullets hit to either side of her, throwing up mud and dirt. "Stay where you are, Miss Roberson," Hushan shouts. Carla places her arms over her head and screams in fear.

Joe pumps two additional rifle shots into the car, and more glass shatters. Then, either George or Hushan stands up behind the hood with an automatic rifle and returns fire. More shots ricochet from the walls, but as far as Claude can tell, hit nothing. Behind him, Claude hears a sound of falling rocks striking the surface of the lake. *Joe must be moving to a better location.*

Suddenly Hushan shouts, "Hold your fire." With his voice whipped by the wind, Joe asks, "Do you give up?"

"No," Hushan says. "But I have a proposition."

"What?" Claude asks.

"Apparently we have a stalemate, Mister Jones. Let us go, and you can have the woman."

"No way," Joe shouts. Claude realizes Joe's mind is fogged in the heat of the battle and he doesn't remember the main reason they are here is to rescue Carla. He wants to countermand Joe's comments, but isn't quick enough. Hushan shouts, "Then we will do this the hard way."

Claude is not prepared for what happens next. Both George and Hushan stand up quickly. George sprays the rocks around and behind Claude with a full thirty-round clip, while Hushan shoots Carla in the back. The sound of the bullet smacking into Carla's body and her scream of pain will remain in Claude's memory forever afterward. He is stunned, falls to his knees and shouts, "You bastard! Now you will die."

Calmly, Hushan replies, "Perhaps, but before that happens the woman you love will bleed to death. Let us go, and you can phone for an ambulance. Keep on with the battle, and regardless of what we do to each other, she will die."

Behind him, Claude hears Joe say softly, "I'm hit, Claude. Let 'em go and take care of Carla." Claude turns to see Joe lying with his back against a boulder, with blood flowing slowly from a wound in his upper right chest area. Not wanting his opponents to know the score is now two to one, with the odds in their favor, he whispers, "Are you okay?"

"Yeah, I got the bastard behind you, but George put one in my chest. I can't help you much, so let 'em go."

"All right," Claude shouts. "Go. We will meet again." After their opponents climb into their car and begin to drive away, Hushan shouts, "I hope so."

* * *

The night before, due to lateness of the hour and fear they may have somehow been betrayed by this mysterious Mister Jones, thoroughly checking the bombs in their packing cases was not an option. Hurriedly, Hushan retrieved the location from the shoebox and George drove to the storage area, where Hushan opened the door, took a quick glance at the contents of the top case, saw the fire extinguishers nestled neatly in their foam-encircled spaces, smiled and latched the top.

Turning to Specks and George, he ordered, "Carry them to the car. Let's get the hell away from here."

George said, "Take one, Specks, and I'll get the other." As Specks grabbed the top case, he complained. "Damn, they are heavy." Hushan smacked Specks on the side of his head with his open palm. "Quit whining."

After hurrying outside, Specks struggled to load the case into the trunk, while George stood by offering no assistance. As low man on the whipping post in this funky organization, Specks is weary of the verbal and physical abuse he is expected to take. At first, working to put the "man" down and perhaps kill a bunch of honkies was fun and exciting. But the longer he continued to hang with Hushan, the more Specks grew to hate the bastard. He is still smarting from the slapping around George gave him for not watching his crib.

Hushan has decided no one else could protect the bombs better than he, plus he also learned not to trust anyone. George drives the trio to Hushan's house and then he and Specks unload the cases in his garage. While standing to one side and watching his underlings perform manual labor, Hushan thinks, *Too many members of my cell are dead. If they continue killing each other, I won't have anyone left alive.*

* * *

Afterward they walk into the kitchen for a drink, where Hushan reviews their plans for the next evening. "We'll drop you at the quarry early, Specks. Pack a lunch and bring a cooler of soft drinks. You'll have all afternoon to find a spot where you can take out Mister Jones. George and I will attempt to lure him into the open so you can nail him."

Then, reminding George of a Mafia figure, and reinforcing his contention that Hushan was less than capable of being one, and as far as he was concerned, a poor leader of men, he listened as the fool asked Specks, "Are you ready to make your bones?"

Specks isn't sure, but is unwilling to display his fear. "Yeah, Hushan, I'll get rid of him."

In the past, Hushan asked Specks to do many strange things, but never murder. If he is successful in this ambush, perhaps Specks will receive a promotion to Hushan's right-hand man, or at least be on a par with George. With Felix and Mohammed missing from the equation, Speck's feeble mind rationalizes his thoughts as reasonable that he should be next in line after the guy with the spider tattoo.

* * *

In order to be fresh for the evening's work, they sleep in the next morning. If Hushan is successful, their recovered money will go a long way toward paying for their upcoming forced vacation in Aruba - the place he decided to go after detonating the bombs.

They realize Fort Worth and Dallas will be ghost cities, contaminated and littered with dead bodies. When thinking of the end results, shivers run up Specks' arms, but he is looking forward to sandy beaches and dark-skinned natives he read of in a travel folder. Any survivors can have the cold weather in northern Texas.

* * *

At one in the afternoon Hushan and George drive Specks to the rock quarry and drop him near the front gate. His backpack contains a small cooler with six soft drinks, three sandwiches in a plastic sack and a separate package of chips. Knowing the ice is already melting, Specks hopes the food won't get soggy.

Low-hanging ugly grey and black clouds cover the sky, making the day dismal and muggy. As Specks climbs upward through a rock chimney behind the small lake, he is perspiring heavily while listening to rap music through earphones.

The sides of the steep cleft are cracked, and provide occasional hand and foot holds, but the rock is crumbly and frightens him. As he crawls slowly through the narrow slit, a rifle with a night-scope is heavy on his shoulder, and swings like a pendulum, occasionally banging into his knees

Looking down, he discovers he is more than fifty feet above the hard rock quarry floor. If he slips and falls, they will need a spatula to retrieve what little remains.

When Specks discovers a ledge jutting from the cliff, he also discovers the outcrop provides a good view of the surrounding area, including the gate, plus piles of rocks and boulders to the rear. Specks doesn't glance to his left or he would have seen Joe staring at him through a telescope attached to his rifle. Joe is on another rocky shelf seventy-five feet away, hidden behind a large flat rock extending three feet from the side of the cliff. After taking one last look, Joe ducks out of sight. A small cave is to his rear, so he climbs in and settles in for a long wait.

Specks lays his rifle atop the ledge, increases the volume of his disc player, plugs earpieces into place, and snaps his fingers in time to an old rock and roll tune from the fifties. Sometimes he tires of the rap crap and turns to Elvis or the Righteous Brothers for variety. Hungry from the climb, Specks reaches into his cooler, removes a cold diet soda, pops the top, leans his back against a rock wall, takes a large hit and waits.

* * *

Two hours later, rain begins to fall, and Specks is miserable until Joe shoots him just after he draws down on Claude. Then he screams in pain and falls from the ledge. Without his knowing, Specks lifeless body crashes hard onto the floor of the quarry, and he feels nothing.

* * *

The nasty wound is not in Carla's back. She was hit high on her left hip, and the wound is bleeding heavily. When Claude reaches her side, she is unconscious with her eyes rolled back in her head. He takes her into his arms and attempts to stem the flow of blood.

Joe is on his cell phone trying to reach his fellow officers, but the storm is interfering with the transmission lines, so he can't get a signal. He tries to stand to move around until he makes a connection, but is too weak. After sliding into to a sitting position, he asks, "How is she?"

"Hushan shot her in the hip and the wound is bleeding. I can't stop the flow. I think he hit an artery."

Joe murmurs, "They got us good. Can you apply a tourniquet?"

"I'll try," Claude says, pulls off his sodden jacket and squashes the material together to create a wet pillow to cushion Carla's head. She is still unconscious; her breath ragged with pain. Claude uses strips of cloth from his shirt to tie around her hip. With the barrel of his gun as a fulcrum, he turns the cloth as tightly as possible, but blood continues to course down her leg in red rivulets. He watches the artery spurt out more, swears, "Damn it," and says, "The tourniquet won't work, Joe."

"I still can't get a signal, Claude. You'll have to drive up the road until you can. Haul me over there, and I'll try to help her while you're gone."

Claude cries out in anger, "You know I can't leave her!"

Joe shakes his weary head. "If you want to save her life, you must."

As his anger dies, and reason prevails, Claude knows Joe is correct.

With fear in his heart as big as Texas, he kisses Carla's face, and tenderly wipes blood from her cheeks that his fingers deposited there. Then he races to Joe and pulls him to his feet. They stagger to Carla's side to find she is awake and moaning softly.

Claude takes her hand in his. "God, I'm sorry Babe."

"Go," Joe says forcefully. "Get help fast – I'm not doing so well myself."

Claude squeezes Carla's hand gently, smiles and promises, "I will return. Hang in there. I love you." She attempts to smile through her pain, but can't. Instead, she nods and lays her head down again on his coat.

Claude grabs the cell phone from Joe's hand and runs through the rain, stumbling through mud and puddles until he reaches Carla's car. He jumps in and manages to place the key in the ignition with shaking fingers, fires up the engine and stomps on the accelerator.

For some reason, the car seems to be running over huge bumps and refuses to move very far before the motor stalls. Then he notices the vehicle is leaning to one side.

Claude climbs from behind the wheel to discover the tires on the left side are slashed. Knowing the Pontiac isn't going anywhere; he turns and runs up the rocky road to the top of the hill and the highway. At this time of night, the road is deserted - no one in sight, and no headlights from either direction. He begins jogging down the road, trying the cell phone every time he is winded and pauses to catch his breath.

Nothing; no signal - the storm continues to roar around him. Hard rain pounds his skin as Claude splashes through wide, muddy streams rushing across the blacktop and crashing into a ditch. When he sees the friendly lights of a gas station up ahead, he thinks, *Thank God!*

His aching lungs and feet say he has run five miles, when in reality the distance is only three. But, determined to save his companions; he struggles on, only to discover the station closed.

Claude grabs a broken piece of a yellow concrete car-stop and throws the heavy chunk through the plate glass of the front door. Then he pushes through the splintered remains, while cutting his hand until he is able to reach the dead bolt and lock. Once inside, he searches for and finds a phone behind a littered counter, and dials 9-1-1.

When the operator answers, Claude feels like crying. He manages to choke out the story of an officer down and tell her of the second victim. He knows the report of an officer being shot will receive priority over any other call. After he gives the operator his position and location of the quarry, she says, "Remain on the line."

"How long will it be until someone gets here?" He asks. "The two victims need medical attention immediately."

Her response is, "Six minutes to your site, and three more to the quarry."

As weary and winded as he is, Claude knows he can't run all the way to the quarry in less than fifteen minutes. He decides to wait and says, "Have an officer stop here and take me to the quarry."

"On the way," the operator says and repeats again, "Remain on the line."

Claude leans against a wall and slides down until he is seated, lays his head upon his arms crossed over his folded-up knees, and as tears run down his face, prays aloud, "Please God, don't take her from me!"

CHAPTER 28

As they drive away, Hushan says, "They were on to us, George. That was too close. Mister Jones had assistants, I believe there were two." Still pumped and with adrenaline flowing through his veins like oil from a west Texas drilling rig, George asks, "What do we do now?" With an evil smirk, Hushan says, "We can't wait for the Cotton Bowl. We must strike now."

"Whoa!" George exclaims. "We aren't prepared for that, are we?"

Hushan speaks as if addressing a small child in a kindergarten class. "The original plan was to fly low over the stadium in a helicopter with the signaling device. Although now they may be on to us, we will use the same plan with a few minor variations." George is perplexed. "Like what?"

"We place the fire extinguishers throughout Fort Worth and Dallas on main streets easily located from the air. The next morning, we follow the same path in a light rental aircraft, detonating bombs one at a time or in groups. We will still kill thousands, perhaps hundreds of thousands. The only juicy target not available is the President. But we can embarrass his administration in such a way the people will rise up and call for his impeachment."

George continues to question his leader. "Your plans seem reasonable, but how do we escape? Nerve gas will travel for miles." Hushan displays his brilliance for planning for such contingencies. "After detonating the bombs, and before the gas can reach the airport, we meet there and you will fly us to Aruba as planned."

"I hope your plans works, Hushan. I would love to settle with Mister Jones for all his interference. On another subject, I'm certain they killed Specks. I heard his body hit the ground." Hushan smiles an evil grin. "We will allow the nerve gas to repay our enemy and wreak vengeance upon him. What a fitting end for the man supplying the means to our end. Don't you believe his demise will be poetic justice?"

George has to smile. "Yeah, I like the idea." Then his face turns somber, almost white with fear. "But hey, I just thought of something - I can't go home. Mister Jones knows where I live."

Hushan disagrees and points to rain pouring in through shattered windows. "You're forgetting we are riding in this shot-up wreck. We need to get off the street and out of sight. Thanks be to Allah that the rain will prevent anyone from noticing. Head for your apartment, where we will switch vehicles and leave this one hidden in your garage. If you have anything of value you care to bring with you, pack in a hurry. Then we will leave your place behind forever."

For once, George is surprised Hushan actually has some brains. "Yeah, you're right. In the rush to get away, I forgot what shape the car is in. Now I'm glad we moved the fire extinguishers."

Hushan sits back in his seat with a smile on his face. "Now you see the wisdom in storing the gas at my home. Good leadership always conquers adversity. Next stop - your apartment, George, and then, on to mine; we have work to do."

* * *

The state police patrol car bounces down the rocky road to the quarry with its lights flashing red and blue against the force of the storm that still rages. As they leave the highway, the driver, Sergeant Bill Fisher doesn't let up on the accelerator. Bill knows his passenger wants to return to the crime scene as fast as humanly possible.

Claude points toward where three blue and whites and two ambulances are setting with their light bars lashing out into the darkness. "Down there." Near the center of the muddy quarry, two vehicles are illuminating the scene with spotlights. A blue blanket covers one still form lying on the ground, and three EMS personnel are kneeling by that victim, while several other medics apparently are assisting another lying on a gurney.

Claude notes several flashlights moving among the rocks and columns of stone as police search for other possible victims. When the car slides to a halt, he crosses himself, praying again that Carla and Joe are still alive, jumps from the vehicle and runs to the gurney. When he looks down, Joe has pain on his face. But there is something else there - sorrow too.

Joe looks up at Claude, shakes his head and attempts to speak, but chokes up and covers his mouth with a knotted fist. "God, no!" Claude cries to the heavens above. Then he turns quickly to kneel by and uncover Carla's body, grab her cold, still hand and weep.

One of the medics says, "I'm sorry, but we arrived too late to help her. She bled to death. Sergeant Francone attempted to stop the bleeding, but couldn't. Whoever shot her shattered a main artery, so a tourniquet couldn't stop the flow. I'm sorry," he repeats and pats Claude's back.

Claude's shoulders shake with fury and shock. As if the clouds are joining in his grief, rain pours down on Claude's head while he continues to hold Carla's hand. The medics stand back, letting him have his private moment alone with her.

Claude strokes Carla's face tenderly. "Please forgive me." Then, as he traces her eyes and mouth with his fingers, remembers when she was alive and so full of love. A medic leans down and asks quietly, "Can we move her now? We want to get her out of the rain."

"Thanks," Claude says and stands to watch them lift Carla tenderly onto another gurney and cover her from head to toe with a clean white sheet and then roll her body to a waiting ambulance. By the time the medics and the litter arrive there, her sheet is soaked, but when they place the gurney inside the vehicle, they replace the damp fabric with another dry one.

As Claude turns to where Joe lies watching, he knows his friend asked the medics to wait until he could speak with Claude to divulge Carla's last words. Tears run down Joe's cheeks to mix with the rain.

"I'm sorry; I couldn't save her, Claude. She told me to tell you that she would wait for you in heaven. Toward the end, she wasn't in any pain. She smiled, turned her head and was gone. I thought you should know."

Claude's eyes overflow, and he allows the tears to course down his face unabated as he sobs uncontrollably. Joe reaches with his good hand, grabs Claude's and holds on. They may have once been enemies, but now share their grief like brothers.

Another medic shakes water from his poncho and says, "We must get you to the hospital, Joe."

Claude asks, "May I ride with him?"

"Sure, let us load him aboard, and then you climb into the rear. I know he will enjoy your company."

But first, Claude turns and walks to the other ambulance. "I'll say goodbye to Carla and be with you in a minute, Joe."

Carla's body is lying cold and still as a rag doll. Although Claude knows she is gone, he hopes somehow she can hear him. He kneels by her side and takes his hand in hers. "I will see you very soon, and will always love you. Goodbye for now." Then Claude steels himself, stands and walks away without looking back.

* * *

The next day Hushan and his men are busy planning where to place the bombs. After George lays out a map of both cities, they mark a likely spot for each fire extinguisher. Hushan says, "Be sure to locate parks or baseball diamonds. We will hang the bombs on posts or out in the open, and no one will notice. Fire extinguishers are something people see every day, but don't register on their subconscious."

"What about a few of the taller buildings?" Ali Zabara asks. He is a small Arab that lost his family to American bombs in Afghanistan, and vowed reprisal, although he knows the result may mean his death. After sneaking across the porous Canadian border, he joined Hushan in Fort Worth. Now he is employed as a gas station attendant. Ali is a wonderful candidate for a suicide mission, but Hushan hopes every member of his cell who is still alive will survive to fight again.

"If the bombs detonate high in the sky, the gas will be caught by the wind and spread farther."

"A wonderful idea," Hushan says. "Do so."

George walks into the room with one of the cases cradled in his huge arms. "Look at these babies."

He raises the lid, stares down at the contents and begins to count. "One, two, three..., and continues until he reaches fifteen. Then he stops abruptly. Hushan waits for George to add the sixteenth container. Instead, he turns and walks toward the garage for the other case.

"Wait, George," Hushan says. "Are you sure you counted them correctly?"

"Yeah, there are fifteen - why?"

When George shrugs as if Hushan is stupid, Hushan walks to the case and checks the fire extinguishers. There were four rows and four containers in each, except the last, where one empty space seems to glare like the mouth of a hungry mongrel. Hushan is shocked.

"There should be a total of thirty-two. Bring in the other case, George. Check to see if any others are missing."

After returning with the second case, George checks the contents. "Sixteen here, none missing."

"Heavenly Allah," Hushan cries out. "Someone has taken one. When was the last time you checked the cases, George?"

"Hell, I never opened them. Just having them nearby frightened me. I didn't want one or more exploding by accident. Perhaps Mohammed removed one."

"Why would he?" Hushan asks. "He never mentioned a thing to me about something like this. I know he wouldn't do so without my permission; they are too dangerous to handle indiscriminately. Who else do you suspect?"

George shrugs again. "Not me, but perhaps Mister Jones. Remember, they were in his possession for five days."

Hushan frowns and asks, "Why would he steal only one? Besides, there is no way to detonate a single container by remote control without the signaling device. Opening the fire extinguisher manually would mean his death. No, he is too smart."

"Then who has it?" George asks. Hushan shakes his head, but appears more relaxed. "Perhaps Felix filled only thirty-one. Apparently no one opened the cases before today. Why should one missing cause anxiety? We have plenty."

George pats the top of one case. "That's true."

* * *

As the ambulance skids on wet pavement, Claude hangs onto Joe and the gurney to keep him from sliding off. The vehicle slows, the tires regain their grip, and they continue their conversation. Joe says, "You mentioned a black kid guarding George's place. Was he skinny with cornrows and a thin goatee?"

"Yeah, was he the one you shot back there?" Joe nods and grimaces in pain. "His description matches the one of the shooter I gave to the cops. I only saw him once before, when he was setting up camp on a ledge about seventy-five feet away."

"I'm glad you took him out, Joe. Thanks, he came close." Claude wipes his face with a towel he finds on a shelf and feels his cheek. There are several small open sores that make him look like he has measles. Joe smiles through his pain. "You made them bleed again."

Claude holds the towel against his bloody cheek. "I truly believe you will survive to fight again another day, Joe. When we arrive at the hospital, I'll disappear. Thanks again for the care you gave Carla while I was away. I'm so glad she had a friend like you when she passed on."

Although Joe already knows the answer, he asks, "Do you have some unfinished business to accomplish?" Claude's black eyes become steely, and his jaw is clenched in determination. "You might say so. Be aware; from this point forward, all bets are off. Tonight death walks the streets of Fort Worth and Dallas; and his name is Claude Werner."

"So that's your real name."

Claude smiles grimly. "Yeah, you might remember it for my tombstone before the next few days are over."

Joe asks, "Are you sure you don't want my guys involved?"

"No, I don't need or want any more collateral damage. Carla was the last innocent person I killed. There won't be more. From this moment forward, only the guilty will die."

Joe nods his approval. "I can't officially sanction your efforts, but if they ask me, you never said a word - just disappeared. Go slow, but get the bastards for me, too."

"Keep your cell phone handy, Joe. If I can, I'll give you a blow-by-blow account."

CHAPTER 29

After the answering machine picks up, Claude hears George say, "Ben, this is George. We leave for Aruba tomorrow at four in the afternoon. I need you as my co-pilot. This is a matter of life and death - your life if you are not aboard. I believe you know what I mean. Meet at the airport at three to preflight the aircraft."

* * *

Ben won't be going anywhere tomorrow. His body is lying in a pool of blood next to the phone. He is one of the men Mohammed gave up and Claude kept secret from Joe and the Feds. The black hair of Ben's nearly severed skull is glistening in the lamp light, and the matching irises of his dead eyes stare at the ceiling as if he were counting flies. Laying in a row by his side are four severed fingers and a thumb.

Nearby, wearing only blood-speckled underwear, Claude is seated in a recliner. While listening to the message, he continues to wipe his bloody hands and thinks, *Hedging your bets and getting good odds always pays great dividends.*

After George disconnects, Joe address Ben's body. "I imagine knowing you're already dead and not available as his co-pilot would cause George grief. Don't worry though; I will take your place."

Then he glances at his shirt lying on the couch and notices several small bloody splatters on the collar. He hopes anyone noticing them will attribute the blood to small cuts adorning his right cheek. Before holding his question and answer session with Ben, Claude removed his clothes to avoid just such an accident. But sometimes flying blood tends to travel great distances. Apparently this was one of those instances.

* * *

Claude felt he was too soft with Mohammed. Now is the time to get down to business, and he doesn't have time to fool around with niceties.

When Ben answered the door in his pajamas, Claude hit him in the head with a large ball peen hammer, knocking him unconscious. Ben fell to the floor, while blood ran from a nasty cut to his brow.

After locking the door, Claude ties Ben's hands behind his back by wrapping his wrists with duct tape, slaps a small piece of the same over the cut on his forehead, and uses more to immobilize his bare legs. In the kitchen Claude discovers a pretty pastel towel with small embroidered hearts on the face in a drawer. After ripping the material in two, he stuffs half in Ben's mouth and stretches duct tape across his face to hold the gag in place. He leaves Ben alone to sleep for a few minutes and walks around the farmhouse, checking rooms.

The kitchen is clean and smells of roast beef. Claude discovers a plate with leftover meat stored under an aluminum tent in the refrigerator. Using a very sharp butcher knife in a wooden holder by the stove, he cuts a slice to eat while inspecting the living room. He takes the knife with him.

On the coffee table are several books and magazines. The main theme of most is aviation and aircraft. A framed certificate on one wall is very similar to the one in George's apartment. This certifies Ben Romero is qualified as a pilot of reciprocating aircraft. An overflowing ashtray is setting on the floor next to a worn recliner chair. Other than the diploma, there is nothing of interest in the room.

Claude moves on to the bedroom, where he finds a .38 caliber revolver in a holster in a drawer. A .12 gauge shotgun is leaning against one wall, with one shell in the chamber and three in the slide. After ejecting them all, Claude puts the cartridges in a pocket and leaves the empty weapon in place. He retains the handgun for possible use later in the day.

The closet contains nothing but men's clothes, so no woman lives here. Claude thinks, *Good.* He doesn't want or need anyone to stumble upon them while he is questioning Ben. In less than an hour, nothing like that will matter. He will be gone, and Ben dead.

Ben is where Claude left him, so he moves a recliner close by his victim and slaps Ben's face until he regains consciousness. While Claude is peeling his clothes until wearing only underwear, his captive stares with fear in his eyes. They seem to ask, "Who are you?"

In answer to Ben's unspoken question, Claude says, "I see by your eyes you're wondering who I am and what I want. You may have heard of me. I'm Mister Jones, here to ask you a few questions."

The name registers. Ben's eyes flicker and grow larger until they seem to bulge from their sockets. Claude continues to smile. "This is a nice farm you have here, Ben; far enough into the country to have clean air, and the noises of the city won't bother, right?"

Ben doesn't attempt an answer. His head remains still, and his eyes follow Claude's every move. Then Claude's face becomes serious. "That fact also works against you in times like these, Ben old buddy. As I speak with you, no one will hear us. Now, I am about to ask a question. You will provide an answer by a nod or shake of your head. Do you understand?"

When Ben isn't fast enough to comprehend he is supposed to nod his head, Claude does so. He grabs Ben's hair and rocks his head back and forth. "I said, 'Do you understand'?" This time, Ben nods alone.

"Good; here is question one: Do you know a man named Hushan?"

Ben shakes his head. Claude says, "Liar," reaches behind Ben, picks up a hammer and with one cruel swing, breaks the big toe on Ben's left foot. As Ben attempts to scream, he chokes. Sarcastically, Claude says, "Oh, now you are having second thoughts concerning your answer, aren't you?"

Reaching inside his coat jacket, he pulls forth a small pair of pruning shears. When Ben sees the tool, his eyes grow larger, and his head nods so quickly he appears to be a bobble doll. While opening and closing the shears with an ugly snap, Claude continues to play Jeopardy.

"Okay, once again, do you know Hushan?" Ben nods and large salty tears run down his cheeks.

"What about Georgie boy? I believe his full name is George Schroeder. Do you know him?" Another nod, and more tears. "Good, now we are getting somewhere. Do you know the location of the bombs?"

The question evokes a frightened response from Ben, but no reply. He looks as if he is close to losing control of his bladder. Claude bends down and looks deep into Ben's eyes. "I'll remove the tape now so you can answer several more questions aloud."

Ben nods, but isn't ready when Claude rips the tape from his mouth. Small chunks of facial hair and skin from Ben's bottom lip come along. A thin trail of blood runs from Ben's torn mouth and drips onto the collar of his pajamas. After spitting the towel from his mouth, Ben takes a large gulp of air as Claude asks again, "Where are the bombs?"

With the gag removed, Ben suddenly becomes belligerent and stubborn. He shouts, "Kill me if you will, but the bombs will avenge me. Allah be praised!"

Calmly, Claude reaches behind Ben with his pruning shears and snips Ben's index finger from his hand. Blood spurts, while Ben screams in agony. Claude holds the still pink finger in front of Ben's face and repeats his question. "Where are the bombs?"

Through torn lips and clenched teeth, Ben spits out, "Go to hell."

"Not quite yet," Claude says and clips Ben's middle finger.

Four fingers, a thumb and positive coercion on Claude's part are required before Ben will talk. After laying the digits on the carpet in front of Ben like tiny toy soldiers on parade, so he will view and possibly realize the result of his futile stubbornness, Claude says, "Come on, be a man, Ben, and don't be so asinine. Tell me what I want to know, and I'll phone for the cops and an ambulance. The doctors may be able to sew your fingers onto your stumps. I'm not after such small fry as you. I want the big boys. I'm also weary of snipping fingers and getting nowhere. The next item I snip by a quarter of an inch at a time will be your dick."

When Ben sees the certainty of his captor's intentions in Claude's eyes, he suddenly begins to sing like Elvis. While staring at his severed digits, and as his body shakes with pain, he shouts, "At George's home in Fort Worth."

"What is the address?"

"Fourteen seventy-nine Mockingbird Lane."

"What do they plan to do with the bombs?"

"Kill the President and many others at the Cotton Bowl," Ben says and spits in defiance. "I hope you will be there."

"No, but thanks for the invitation," Claude says while waving the pruning shears in the general direction of Ben's crotch. "How do they plan to escape?"

"Hushan owns a plane in a hangar at Harris County Airport – a small jet. George is the pilot."

"And you? What is your role in this stupidity?" Between sobs of regret and pain, Ben says, "I was to help by posing as a fireman, putting the bombs in place. Then I would be the co-pilot on the trip to Aruba."

Claude nods. "I saw your diploma – very impressive. What is the tail number?"

"F W dash 4 7 1 4."

Claude asks a few more important questions. When his captive has provided the answers, Ben pleads, "Please call the ambulance. I'm bleeding very badly."

His captor stares grimly at Ben. "You never had an opportunity to meet my fiancée, did you, Ben? Your friends Hushan and George killed her when they left her to bleed to death. Since you are a cohort of theirs, Ben, that also makes you guilty by association. What is good for one asshole is good for another."

After grabbing a surprised Ben by his hair with his left hand, Claude raises Ben's head sharply and uses Ben's own sharpened to a fine edge butcher knife to calmly slit Ben's throat. Ben's piercing scream turns into a bloody gurgle. Either the knife is sharper than Claude believed, or in his anger he exerted more pressure than necessary. Ben's head is nearly severed from his torso.

Claude possesses all the info he needs. Obviously Ben wasn't aware of the loss of the fire extinguishers. As he looks down at his handiwork, Claude thinks, *Ben must not be a member of the inner circle, but now there is one less flunky.*

He gathers several towels from the bathroom and begins to clean up. Suddenly, the phone rings. Ignoring the noise, Claude continues to wipe his hands as the shrill tone sounds four times. Then the answering machine picks up, and he hears George's message.

* * *

Winter isn't far away. Today is a typical fall day in the Dallas/Fort Worth Metroplex. High above, thin clouds resembling wispy cotton balls are racing across a light blue sky tinted grayish-green by the exhaust fumes from thousands of vehicles on untold miles of concrete highways cutting through and around the twin cities.

One vehicle holds three men dressed as firemen on a mission they hope will bring the hustling and bustling cities to a standstill for years to come. Another contains a man with bloody sores on one cheek intending to keep the cars, buses and trucks running well beyond his life span.

* * *

As Ali climbs into the SUV, he says, "That's four of them."

When George couldn't reach Ben by telephone, Ali became his replacement. He is wearing one of George's extra uniforms, which fits him poorly. Ali is slimmer and three inches shorter, but no one paid any attention to him or his sloppy attire during their last four stops. Three targets are high-rise rooftops located approximately one mile apart, where the terrorists simply laid a nerve gas container out of sight behind a chimney.

The fourth is a baseball diamond used by local softball league teams in the evenings. In the morning hours, the area is deserted, so they screwed in a hanger and installed the fire extinguisher outside an announcer's booth behind a backstop. Surrounding the field is at least an acre of open ground, and adding to Hushan's pleasure in their success thus far is a brisk breeze blowing from right field toward home plate.

Hushan sits in the front passenger's seat, puffing a filtered cigarette as he supervises placement of the devices. Apparently manual labor is beneath the dignity of the leader of the pack, but George doesn't mind. He has seen the money in the suitcase awaiting their return to Hushan's shack, and knows when the job is completed; a large portion of those unaccountable funds provided by foreign terrorists will be his.

He can't wait for a chance to get his hands on one of those dark-skinned babes in Aruba. A friend that travelled there last spring reported the young tourist chicks on Spring break are looking for love with a passion. If so, when the ships dock or aircraft arrive, George will be first in line.

* * *

The next target is another high rise two miles away. George steps on the gas pedal and speeds away. Startled, Hushan orders; "Slow down you fool, and don't attract the police. By now they may know of us, but not our recent plans. Don't give them a chance to prevent our success."

"Sorry," George says, but since Hushan knows besides his big mouth and stupid spider tattoo, speed is George's main weakness, he isn't fooled. When they reach the fourteen-story tower, George climbs from the cab.

He stretches his tired back and brags, "I'll deliver this one personally. Hand me one of those things, Ali."

Ali reaches into the case and attempts to pull a fire extinguisher from its nesting spot. The chain to the ring of the handle catches in the foam, and he pulls harder. When the container finally comes free, and as he hands it to George, the ring loosens and begins to fall to the pavement. In his haste to catch the object, Ali knocks the fire extinguisher from George's hand, which hits the concrete curb with a loud clang, the handle flies open and nerve gas escapes in a green cloud.

Hushan shouts, "You've killed us all!" and dives down in his seat, as if hiding will prevent the gas from reaching him. Ali seems transfixed in the rear, with his eyes bulging and mouth agape in fear.

Attempting frantically to escape, George dives to the sidewalk and crawls behind the truck. Then he turns his head, watching in horror as the fire extinguisher expands its contents into the air. The deadly green cloud spews out and spreads across the pavement.

* * *

A gentle wind blows the gas farther down the street, where several bystanders are looking inquisitively at the firemen, wondering what the hell they are doing. The small crowd watches the cloud slowly dissipate around them and sink to earth.

After holding his breath as long as possible, Hushan exhales loudly and then cautiously inhales a small amount of air. Then he peeks over the dash at the pedestrians to discover none were affected by the gas. The few that stopped to wonder about their actions soon move on, shaking their heads in disbelief at the stupid antics of firemen. They don't believe it appropriate for public servants to roll around in the gutter or set off fire extinguishers on a public thoroughfare.

From the back seat, Ali says in awe, "They don't work." He stares into space and unknowingly repeats, "They don't work." Transfixed by a scene that will dwell in his mind for as long as he lives, Hushan says, "I know."

Recovering from his initial shock, George stands and returns to the driver's seat. "Did you see that? The bomb went off and nothing happened."   Comprehension of the past few days finally makes its way into his mind, and Hushan says, "They switched the contents. They knew every detail and played us for fools. We must escape somehow, and soon."

CHAPTER 30

Joe's cell phone rings and the nurse hands him the hated contraption. Even with the aid of narcotics, his chest hurts like hell. Joe wonders who could be phoning so early in the morning. Then he realizes the caller can only be one person, so asks, "Yeah, is that you, Claude?"

"Hi, Joe. What do you do when bad apples appear in your crop?"

"What is this, twenty questions? Hell, I don't know."

Claude laughs. "You prune the branches that don't produce."

"What are you now, a gardener?"

"Yeah, I thought I might enjoy a change of pace."

Joe shakes his weary, sore head. "I wish I knew what the hell you mean. Come on, Claude; give me a break, my chest hurts. All this talk isn't doing my poor weak body any good."

Claude is still smiling. "One down - several more to go. Stay tuned. You will find this one on Old Potato Road in Irving, seventeen hundred block, big farm. He isn't going anywhere and might need a hand when you get there."

Joe says, "I hope you haven't gotten hitched up for more than you can plow."

"I haven't. How are you?"

"The doc says I'll live. I lost some blood, but they have been feeding me so much steak I'm worried I will grow horns and start chasing heifers."

"Mona wouldn't like that. Has she heard about your heroics?"

"Yeah, I'm a real stud muffin. She's sitting next to my bed, wondering who I'm speaking with."

"Give her my love," Claude says. "Good women are hard to come by."

Joe asks, "Is that all you called for?"

"No, I need your assistance one more time. Then I won't bother you again."

Joe laughs and asks, "Is that a promise? What can I do for you?"

"Who do you know that could lead me to a good, reliable, but shady locksmith?"

"If we were in Sulphur Springs, I know just the guy," Joe says. "But since I'm not, I'll have to ask someone I know on the Fort Worth police force. How soon do you need the info?"

"As soon as possible."

"Give me an hour and phone again, Claude. By that time I should have a name and address."

"Thanks, Joe. Tell Mona 'goodbye' for me."

"Will we see you again?"

"Probably not – I'm taking a one-way flight tomorrow. After I land, I'll phone to let you know how what I thought of the ride."

Joe is surprised. "Where are you off to?"

"The promised land. Oh, before I forget - you may rest easy concerning the missing fire extinguisher. I retrieved the sucker and intend to return it to the rightful owners. If I don't have a chance to say so to your face - thanks for everything."

"Good work," Joe says and breathes a deep sigh of relief. "Everyone will be relieved when they hear the news that you found the one we were missing. Remember what I said. Go slow and watch your back."

"Via con Dias my friend," Claude says. "I'll phone in an hour." The line goes dead, and Joe says, "You always get in the last word." At his statement, Mona reaches up to pat Joe's hand, and chuckles.

* * *

The following day, Hushan continues to act like a big shot. "Take the trunks to the airport, George. We'll meet you there at four."

They spent the remainder of yesterday and all this morning disposing of the fire extinguishers in Dumpsters along a seldom-used alley and packing items Hushan feels they must have if they are to begin anew in Aruba. George thinks Hushan is taking everything but the frigging stool in the bathroom. As he checks the pile of boxes, he shakes his head.

"By the time you get there, I'll be finished with the preflight. Don't be late or forget the money."

Hushan isn't stupid enough to allow George to haul the money suitcase to the plane. *Maybe he believes I would take off without him,* and knows, *He's right.*

Hushan stops packing for a moment to ask, "Did you get in touch with Ben?"

"I left a message. Don't worry, Ben will be there. When I phoned, I thought we would be running away from the nerve gas and told him so in a round-about way. He will know what I mean and be there on time. I hope the plane can haul all this junk."

Hushan wipes perspiration from his brow with an already stained handkerchief. "Believe me when I say everything I am taking is necessary. Get on your way, George. I'll stop by to pick up the others, but won't bother with Ben. He lives too far in the country. If he doesn't make the flight, it is his funeral."

And you wonder why no one believes you are a great leader of men, George thinks. But, he keeps his mouth shut. Hushan still holds the purse strings.

"Remember to tell the fools no more than one suitcase apiece. They can carry their luggage on board and stack them in the rear of the plane. Your junk will fill all the space underneath. Any more weight and we'll never leave the ground."

After carrying the last load to his SUV, George fires up the engine and spins the tires in gravel as he speeds away. He hates to give up this little toy, but if he can find a Hummer for sale in Aruba, he knows a vehicle like that will impress the chicks.

* * *

Hidden behind a generator and its wheels, Claude is standing across the tarmac and watching George as he finishes unpacking his truck and loading the boxes and trunks into the underbelly of the small eight-passenger jet setting several hundred feet from the nearest building. As George puts the last item in place and locks the compartment, his jacket swings open.

George is wearing the .45 rig hidden under the couch. *I am surprised. From the appearance of his apartment, I doubted George did any housework. He probably stumbled across the weapon by accident, but now I know he is armed.*
Maybe there is a God and He is helping. Just in case, Claude looks skyward and mouths, "Thank you." In the next few hours, he can use all possible help. *Perhaps our alliance isn't so ungodly after all,* he muses.

George climbs into his undersized tank and moves the vehicle to the side of a hangar. As Claude watches, he climbs from the cab for the last time, pats the hood and says something. Claude thinks sentimental Georgie boy is telling his ride goodbye, and wonders if his eyes are misty. As George strolls across the tarmac with his hands in his pockets, Claude thinks, *Dream about those Aruba girls all you want, Georgie. That's all you will do. In a little over five hours, you are in for a big surprise.*

* * *

While he waited for an hour to pass so he could phone Joe, Claude did research on his laptop computer. He also transferred half his retirement money into an offshore account under another alias.

* * *

The aircraft Hushan owns is a twin-engine Gulfstream Model #G-150, with a flight range of more than 2,900 nautical miles. The seventeen-foot-long cabin seats six to eight passengers and is equipped with leather seats, a bathroom, small refrigerator, adequate storage space for luggage, both inside the cabin and the belly of the aircraft, plus many other modern features to enhance the comfort of passengers.

From the specifications referring to speed of the aircraft, Claude is able to determine how many hours and minutes are required for the plane to reach open water in the middle of the Gulf of Mexico, far from any land. *Just what I wanted to know,* he mused.

Then he searched for information concerning how one gains entry to the plane. When he found what he needed, he copied the specifications onto a pad. *Thank God for the internet. I hope Joe has a name for me.*

* * *

An hour and forty-five minutes later, Claude pulls up in front of a rather seedy building in a rundown part of the inner city of Fort Worth. The address of 1475 West Elm Street is painted in faded black letters above a grimy front door with wrought iron bars crisscrossing a dirty glass pane.

"Now to see if Mister Beaker is in."

He approaches the doorway and is about to knock when the door opens. An older man of perhaps 60 peers out through heavy glasses perched on his nose, and asks, "You Mister Jones?"

What little hair he has around a nearly bald pate is snow white. The same colored whiskers displayed on his chin indicate he hasn't bothered to shave in some time. His teeth are tobacco-stained, and his beady eyes have brown irises.

"That I am. I take it you are Larry Beaker."

"That I am," Larry mimics Claude's reply and chuckles. "Come in. Sergeant Harris told me that I am to give you anything you want. What has him all fired up?"

"It's nothing to upset you, Larry. All I require is a master key to open the cabin door on a Gulfstream G-150 aircraft. Can you furnish such an item?"

"Does a dog have a tail? The key is going to cost you."

When Claude asks, "How much?" Larry grins, "Five hundred dollars." Claude nods in agreement. "How long will it take to make the key?"

"Depends on how soon you want it."

"I need it tonight."

"Then double the money," Larry says and spits tobacco juice into a cup he picks up from a nearby shelf.

"Do it within an hour and I'll pay you two thousand," Claude says.

"Whoa!" Larry says. "You aren't going to do anything illegal, like a terrorist attack, are you?"

"No, just the opposite."

"Then let's get started," Larry says. He leads Claude into his shop, where he adds, "Take a seat, Mister Jones, and I'll get to work."

* * *

An hour later, Larry turns away from his workbench and hands Claude a silver key. "There you go."

"You're sure this will fit any Gulfstream G-150," Claude says in more of a statement than a question.

"That's what you asked for, and that is what you got. You owe me two grand." Claude counts out the money into Larry's hand. "You do good work, Larry, but you never met me."

"Mister Jones – never heard of him," Larry says and grins as he folds the wad of one-hundred-dollar bills and puts them in a shirt pocket. Without another word, Claude pockets the key, turns and walks through the shop and out the door.

* * *

Later that evening, in a grey overall uniform, over which he wears an orange vest with reflective tape strapped across the front and back, Claude walks across the tarmac toward Hushan's private jet. Attached to the flap of his left hand pocket is a phony I.D. card, identifying him as Inspector Claude Werner from the National Aerospace Administration.

In Claude's right hand is a large briefcase. Inside is a small can of lighter fluid attached to a low-powered blasting cap, which in turn is wired to a battery taped to the side of a small electronic alarm clock. There is also a familiar red fire extinguisher lying to one side of the case.

* * *

Claude hated to lie to Joe. He had the fire extinguisher since the day Carla went missing. But, if truth were told, he said he would give it to the proper people. *Well, they will arrive shortly, so in that respect, I didn't lie.*

When he reaches the aircraft, Claude looks around to see if anyone is watching. The nearby hangars are all dark, and no one is on the tarmac.

I guess there aren't many late-night flights from this small airport.

With his fingers crossed for good luck, he removes the key from a pocket and inserts it into a panel near the door. The key fits snugly and slides all the way into the cylinder. "Here goes nothing," Claude whispers and turns the key. The panel comes open slightly, and Claude breathes a sigh of relief.

Once more, he takes time to check the area. Again, no one is around. He opens the panel all the way and pushes the button to lower the folded stairs. Waiting for the door to fold downward out of the way, and at the same time pull the stairs into their proper position seems to take forever. But the noise of the small engine controlling the steps isn't as loud as Claude would have imagined. Again, he breathes another sigh of relief when the stairs stop moving, and he is able to climb into the cabin.

Less than ten minutes later, Claude emerges from the aircraft and hurriedly pushes the retract button. While the stairs and door do their thing, he checks the area one last time. Apparently no one has noticed his action or questioned why anyone would be aboard a private jet at this hour.

After closing and locking the panel, Claude pockets the key again, looks toward Heaven and whispers, "Thank you, Lord." Then he calmly walks across the tarmac and out an unmanned gate, where he makes his way to his vehicle, opens the trunk and throws in the still heavy briefcase. With a secret smile on his face, Claude climbs into the driver's seat, starts the engine and drives to his motel.

Now for a good night's sleep. Tomorrow is going to be a very busy day.

* * *

As Claude continues to watch from his hiding place, something on the tarmac catches George's attention. He bends to retrieve a piece of tinfoil from one of his gum wrappers he must have dropped while loading Hushan's junk and luggage. He doesn't want anything being sucked into an engine.

George walks slowly around the aircraft, pulling safety pins and counting to make sure he has them all. Everything looks fine - the stabilizer moves correctly, the tires look like they contain sufficient air, and all other memorized points of the safety preflight check out satisfactorily.

Then George inserts his key, waits until the steps are in place and climbs in to check the passenger cabin, which is clean, as it should be for the price they pay the service company. Fresh white linen covers are fitted over the top of each seat, and the lap belts are laid across each cushion to form a neat X. The pattern reminds George of a game of tic-tac-toe, where only one person plays and wins every game.

Whistling a catchy tune, the title forgotten, George opens the small door to a two-man cockpit and climbs into the left-hand seat, which feels warm from the sun shining in through four small windows.

As he sits looking over the instrument panel, George revels in the mystery of flight, and his ability to control the same. The fake wood glows with a fresh coat of polish, and the dials shine like diamonds in a coalmine against an ebony finish. A faint aroma of flowers hangs in the air, probably something new the cleaning crew uses. The scent masks the smell of oil and aviation fuel, two things of which he never grows tired.

George glances through the left hand side window, but no one is in sight. If Ben is coming, he will arrive shortly, so George pulls his pre-flight checklist from its resting place and begins to mentally mark each item as okay. When he reaches to tap a dial, his shoulder holster gets in the way. He shrugs the rig from his shoulders and hangs the weapon over the back of his seat. Then George continues with his thoughts of the future.

I wonder if I will have any trouble smuggling the gun into Aruba. Probably not, the cops there allow just about anything to happen without saying a word or arresting anyone. Aruba's police force must be a joke.

CHAPTER 31

The hospital room gathering/party looks like a meeting of the entire law enforcement community. The only ones missing are the Royal Canadian Mounted Police and a Bobbie from London. The atmosphere inside resembles a wake for a fallen fellow officer, but Joe is definitely alive. Booze is flowing like, well, booze, when there are cops in attendance. Joe is holding an unauthorized-by-his-nurse half-full cup in his hand, listening to the buzz around him.

They are celebrating his recovery, but mostly reveling in the good news of retrieval of the last nerve gas container. The relief they feel is like a heady tonic that flows through the crowded room, cheering them all. Bert takes a swig and says, "I can't believe what your buddy did to the guy out in Irving. I have seen blood before, but this was more than I thought one man could hold."

Kris asks, "Do you think Claude got the info about the last bomb from Ben before cutting his throat?"

"I don't know," Earnest says. "Would you talk if he snipped four fingers and a thumb? I know I would." Joe is amazed. "Did he really do that?"

"Yeah," Sarah says. "They were aligned like soldiers on parade. I have them on ice in the morgue, together with his body. His blood tank is a little low." Joe chuckles, and it hurts. *Now I know what he meant by 'needing a hand.' Claude is something else.*

With his Stetson jutting over his face, Hoot asks, "What will he do next?" When Kris thinks about it, he can't remember ever seeing Hoot without the hat.

Joe holds his side to keep from moving too quickly. "I don't know. Claude said something about taking a one-way flight. But the way he makes puns, I don't know if he means on a plane or up some stairs."

From a chair near the door, Fad says, "I guess we will have to wait until we find the next body or bodies to discover what other tools he knows how to use. Claude is mighty handy with a nail gun, hammer, knife and pruning shears. What's next, a Roto-Rooter?"

Bert adds his two-bits worth, "Either that or a jackhammer."

Despite his efforts not to, Joe chuckles again and grimaces. "Quit you guys, or you'll make me drop a stitch."

"You're not too slow with the puns yourself," Fad says, as he lifts his drink in a salute. "Here's to Claude Werner, if that's really his name. Staple one for me buddy, right in the scrotum."

* * *

Claude watches a black Cadillac Escalade van pull alongside the plane, then it slows and the driver, Hushan, parks fifty feet away. Several suitcases are tied to the outside overhead rack. Eight people, counting Hushan, step out, and to Claude's surprise; one is a woman of oriental or Arab descent. From this distance, he can't tell which, but that really doesn't matter.

Each newcomer brought a suitcase of a different size, color and design. While struggling with the weight, they make their way to the plane and climb the stairs awkwardly. As the passengers stow their gear and buckle up, various sounds and muffled voices filter through the open door. The clink of metal on metal from seat belts is followed by the sound of someone retracting the stairs upward and locking them in place.

* * *

Inside the aircraft, knuckles rap against the door and a voice booms from the speakers overhead. Hushan is using the intercom to communicate with George. "We are all aboard and the luggage stored away. Did Ben make it?"

"No, he didn't," George replies into his microphone. "I guess he didn't get my message."

"Too bad," Hushan says, but George can tell he isn't sincere. "Get buckled in, Hushan. We're set to go."

"Next stop Aruba and sandy beaches," Hushan says, and the microphone clicks as he hangs up. After returning his mike to its holder, George starts the right-hand engine, which catches quickly, and the sound builds as he feeds more fuel. Then he repeats the sequence for the left. When both motors are running smoothly, George synchronizes their rhythm, contacts ground control through his headset, then taxies the plane toward the runway.

* * *

From across the tarmac Claude pushes down on the button of a remote control device. A light glows green, indicating the signal was received and alarm clock activated.

* * *

In a small air vent above the refrigerator at the rear of the aircraft, the clock and other articles are resting atop a large pile of crumpled paper napkins. The alarm dial on the clock's face indicates there are three hours and ten minutes remaining before the time will register as midnight or twelve O'clock noon – take your pick. With what will happen then, time makes no difference.

* * *

At the hold short, after receiving their takeoff clearance, George lets off the brakes and advances the throttles. The plane roars down the runway, and into a clear blue sky. "Wheels up," George says aloud, and pushes the correct knob to retract the struts into the fuselage. The small plane flies like a bullet, rocketing rapidly upward until reaching their assigned cruising altitude of Flight Level 240, or 24,000 feet.

A few minutes after reaching level flight, George hears a rapping at the cockpit door. Via the intercom, Hushan says, "Let me in. I want to sit up front a while. Since Ben didn't make the flight, I will fill in as your co-pilot."

Great, George thinks. Hushan doesn't know a damned thing about flying, but is the boss. George puts the autopilot in the On position, waits until it takes over, and then stands to open the door. "Have a seat," he says and points toward the empty right-hand seat. Hushan sits down, adjusts the belts around his ample body and leans back to watch the darkening sky and a few stars off in the distance. "How long will it be until we clear the coast?"

"Flight time is a little over two hours; then four more to Aruba. I can't wait to see those dark-skinned girls." Hushan nods. "Just so we get away clean."

George matches his nod, but doesn't say anything more. He busies himself with flying the aircraft, ensuring he follows the flight plan filed prior to departing. Occasional clusters of ground lights indicate when they pass over large cities or smaller towns. For the next two hours, until they fly over the outskirts of Houston and then into the blue of the Gulf of Mexico, except for the sound of George steadily chewing gum, and as far as he is concerned, ignorant questions or short sentences from or by Hushan, they remain mostly silent.

As the lights of Houston fade behind them and the darkness of the Gulf of Mexico takes over, Hushan says, "Goodbye to the U.S. of A." Then he laughs wickedly, and George joins in.

* * *

An hour and ten minutes later, the electrical alarm of the small clock indicates twelve O'clock and sends an impulse from the battery to the blasting cap. There is a loud pop and flame shoots from the vent above the refrigerator. "Fire!" a passenger shouts, and everyone reacts differently.

Most unhook their seat belts and race toward the front of the aircraft, where they beat against the cockpit door and shout, "Fire, Fire!"

Two men attempt to douse the flames by shaking bottles of water at the refrigerator, but water can't get through the small air vent slits, which does nothing to prevent the fire from spreading to the napkins, which in turn begin burning brightly. A tiny vent fan concealed behind the refrigerator fuels the fire with oxygen, and as the wood surrounding the refrigerator catches fire, darker smoke billows in to fill the cabin.

Inside the cockpit, Hushan jerks awake. Thirty minutes ago, he fell asleep. George was glad. Over the din of the passengers beating on the door, Hushan shouts, "God, what is happening?" George is excited, and fear is reflected in his voice. "They say there's a fire in the cabin." Hushan cries out in, "Where is your fire extinguisher?"

"Behind you, on the wall," George shouts, automatically puts the autopilot in the On position again and climbs excitedly from his seat. Hushan beats him there, but has trouble unhooking the fire extinguisher from the clamp holding the cylinder in place. "Here, let me do that," George says and pushes his way in front of Hushan.

Hushan stands aside to allow George to remove the red cylinder from the clamp. When it comes free, George opens the door to the cabin and pushes his way through the crowd. "Get the hell out of my way!"

Black smoke makes it difficult to see, but he notices a glow from the fire, breaks the string holding the handle in place, aims the fire extinguisher at the red flames and pulls the handle. Instead of the white foam he expects, a stream of green gas shoots from the nozzle. Almost instantaneously, his throat constricts. "My God, it's the nerve gas," he manages to say.

Hushan stares at the greenish cloud and reaches for his throat. Before he can say anything, the cloud of nerve gas passes over him, and continues to flow swiftly toward the front of the cabin. He gags once and again attempts to speak, but cannot. Then his knees buckle, and his body slips to the floor to join that of George, already lying there, writhing in pain.

Two passengers storm their way into the cockpit and attempt to close the door, naively believing they might escape. But others fight to join them, keeping the door open long enough for the green cloud to flow into the small space. In less than ten agonizing minutes, the interior of the aircraft is as silent as a lamb asleep in the hay. Nine bodies lay scattered about the cabin and cockpit, where they fell as victims to their own diabolical plans.

As far as Claude is concerned, their fate is poetic justice.

* * *

Although the dead aren't aware, flames continue to grow in intensity and eat away at the fuselage as the unmanned aircraft speeds on controlled by autopilot. Eighteen minutes later the flames reach the fuel tanks, and the aircraft explodes in a giant ball of fire. Flames from the explosion consume the remaining nerve gas. Any that might have survived falls harmlessly to the ocean surface, where trillions of gallons of cold water soon dilute the gas, rendering it harmless to fish or humans.

The flight to hell is over.

* * *

The door to Joe's hospital room opens slowly and a fat man wearing a thousand-dollar suit walks in. But to Joe, the stranger still appears to be a gypsy drifter from Louisiana. He carries a new leather briefcase in his left hand, with a suspicious round bulge at one end, as if the case holds a bottle of booze.

Joe just completed reading the story of the plane crash in the local rag. He looks up to see who his visitor is. "Sergeant Francone?" Gordo asks.

"In the flesh and bandages," Joe jokes. "What can I do for you?"

"My name is Gordo. I have a letter from Mister Jones. He asked me to deliver this to you if anything happened to him. I see you have been reading the story of his demise."

"Yeah," Joe says. "What a way to go."

* * *

When the report of the crash reached the FBI, and Kris recognized the owner of the plane as Hushan Ziare, he, Joe, Fad and Bert figured everything out, (*or at least thought they had*).

Kris knew the name Ziare from somewhere, but the fact hasn't yet registered that Hushan is the brother of another terrorist now residing in a federal prison for his part in hijacking a cruise ship. (*Another month will pass before Kris makes the connection.*)

* * *

Now perhaps this letter will close the case and ease everyone's mind. Joe asks, "What are you, a lawyer?"

"Yeah, I am, and thanks to our mutual friend, a very rich one."

"Good things come to those that sit on their fat asses and wait, even lawyers," Joe jokes. "No offense meant."

"None taken," Gordo says and laughs with him. "Anyway, here is his letter." Joe takes his time and reads the letter carefully. Then he re-reads it. The contents are fascinating. Claude's message confirms Joe's suspicion and Kris' contention their ex-murderer took the place of Ben as George's co-pilot and was somehow responsible for the destruction of the aircraft, together with all idiot members of Hushan's sleeper cell.

Fad disagrees with their concept. His desire is for Claude to continue his winning ways when it comes to ridding the world of terrorists without long drawn-out court proceedings when they are guilty as hell. Now, although he has been proven wrong, Fad still won't be happy with a signed self-certification of Claude's demise. If truth be known, neither is Joe.

I suppose I understand why Claude took his own life – he felt he couldn't live without Carla and wanted to personally settle the score on her behalf. But dying by nerve gas must have been horrible. In that respect, Claude was more of a man than I will ever hope to be.

As a tear runs down his left cheek, Joe says, "Sulfur Springs will soon have a new library. Claude gave everything in the bank account book they found in his motel to Carla for her love and to cover other provisions of his hand-written will he had notarized a few days before he died. In case Carla passed on, Claude wanted a library built in her memory."

"Two million should build one hell of a library," Gordo says.

"Damn, he had that much?" Gordo smiles, "Yeah, he did - that, and a lot more. He bequeathed two hundred thousand to me to ensure the monies remaining are properly distributed and received by his beneficiaries. Alice Grabowski receives the same amount for her college education. A half-million in sorrowful retribution and to atone for foul deeds is given anonymously to Nora Smith's twins. The same applies to Ted Branski's two children. The last half-million will go to Claire, Larry Holgram's daughter."

More tears run down both Joe's cheeks. "I suppose he told you the whole story in the letter he mentions he gave you." Gordo repeats, "Yeah, he did. It's strange. First, Mister Jones was a killer. Now, he is a hero."

Joe nods in agreement, but then shakes his head. "It's too bad he won't get credit for saving nearly a million innocent lives. They kept that part of the story from the press. If I were you, I would burn any evidence of his involvement, including his letter. Thanks for dropping by, Gordo."

"There was one other thing he wanted me to do," Gordo says.

"What's that?"

Gordo holds out a bottle of expensive French wine, and says, "For you and Mona." When Joe opens the attached envelope, there is a small card inside: "Go slow and marry the girl. Live long and prosper." It is signed simply, "Claude".

Joe shakes his head, but laughs at the same time. "I'll be damned. Claude got in the last word again."

The End

Epilogue

On a white-sand beach on the west side of the Island of Saint Marteen, a tall, black-haired man of perhaps forty, known as Karl-Heinz Kruger, according to his German passport is lying atop a flower-patterned Hawaiian beach towel with his firm chin resting on crossed muscular arms.

Karl-Heinz's coal-black eyes seem to be staring into space, but seeing nothing. The shade from a nearby, tall umbrella is covering most exposed skin. In the sunlight, his feet are partially covered by a pair of black flip-flops.

* * *

When a young Hispanic waiter named Juan Ortiz walks up and places a tall, frosted glass filled with imported German beer on a nearby folding table, he notices a fairly large, ragged circular scar on the bather's back near his right shoulder.

The pattern of the stitches appears to be very un-professional, almost as if someone did the suturing with a sewing needle. Then, when Mister Kruger turns over and reaches for his wallet, Juan sees a small, almost matching scar high on his right chest.

Juan wonders if his latest customer has been wounded in action in one of the senseless wars the United States wages periodically on someone else's behalf. As far as Juan is concerned, such conflicts only increase the terrorists' will to fight and cost more American lives.

* * *

Mister Kruger interrupts Juan's musing by handing him a ten dollar bill. "Thanks, keep the change."

"Thank <u>you</u>, Sir." Then Juan cautions, "Until you acquire a better tan, don't stay in the sun more than fifteen minutes at a time. The sun here is vicious and will burn in a very short while."

"Thanks," Mister Kruger says again. "I'll remember that." He smiles as Juan departs with a wave.

* * *

Then Claude turns and lies down again to watch small waves breaking quietly against the sandy beach, while continuing to think of Carla and how she would have loved to be here with him. *But in my heart, she is. No matter what happens in the future, she will always be with me.*

Reaching up, he takes the frosty bottle from the table and raises it high in a silent salute. *I will love you until the end of time, Babe. Keep your eyes open for me. I won't be long.*

While tears run down both cheeks, Claude drinks half the bottle in one satisfying gulp. It tastes sweet, but does nothing to relieve his sorrow. *This fight isn't over yet. I still have much to do.* With that thought in mind, he reaches into an inner compartment of his black, water-stained leather wallet and removes a piece of paper containing a list of names. Picking up his pen from the table, he marks through those of nine persons, now deceased, of the twenty given to him by Mohammed.

As Claude glances at those that remain, he thinks, *Where shall I begin?*

If you enjoyed Karl's book *Terroristic Signs*, may we suggest you try his other titles published by BluewaterPress LLC?

From China With Love is a fast paced and exciting thriller. The Chinese have decided to take over the entire North American continent and the way they have planned the attack is amazing. Most of the Americans, Canadians, and Mexicans are killed off at the exact same moment. It falls to those remaining to find a way to defeat the aggressors and start building North America all over again.

For more information, go to www.bluewaterpress.com/china.

Another fantastic story from the fertile mind of master storyteller Karl Boyd is *The Lost Priest*. Once again, in his longest novel thus far, *The Lost Priest*, Karl Boyd works his magic and paints vivid pictures with words to bring a diversified cast of characters to life. Set in Texas, Bermuda, and Brazil, this two part masterpiece, (The Lost Soul and The Lost Spirit), introduces you to:

Jocquin "Jock" Becker, who, while mourning the death of his young wife, Lori, becomes the resident drunkard of Bermuda and a lost soul.

Lorna Hayden, a nurse from Peoria, Illinois who is an angel of mercy to Jock just when he needed one the most.

www.bluewaterpress.com/priest.

www.ingramcontent.com/pod-product-compliance
Lightning Source LLC
Chambersburg PA
CBHW020400030726
47496CB00007B/2237